ABOUT THE AUTHOR

Sarah Earl lives in Queensland, Australia with her husband and three young children.

"I have always enjoyed stories which take well–known myths and legends and give them a twist. I hope you enjoy the first book of The Rise of Darkness series."

You can follow Sarah's Facebook page for the Rise of Darkness series here: @theriseofdarknessbooks.

Dedication

With love to Steven, for supporting me and my writing nights, and to my three beautiful children; Sienna–Grace, Jack and Katelyn.

Sarah Earl

THE RISE OF DARKNESS

Book One

Austin Macauley Publishers™
London • Cambridge • New York • Sharjah

A CIP catalogue record for this title is available from the British Library.

ISBN 978-1-78693-875-6 (Paperback)
ISBN 978-1-78693-876-3 (E-Book)

www.austinmacauley.com

First Published (2017)
Austin Macauley Publishers Ltd.
25 Canada Square
Canary Wharf
London
E14 5LQ

I, was the Morning Star
Bringing light to the darkness
He, was the Evening Star
Casting the world in shadow

CHAPTER 1

The Beginning of the End

Kess Grayson's breath fogged in the cool morning air as she sprinted through the dark woods, jumping over swollen tree roots, and pushing through clusters of spindly branches which sought to snag her. Her heart cavorted madly in her chest and lungs screamed for air, yet she pushed herself faster. As she broke through the edge of the woods, she scanned the clearing but there was no one about at this early hour. Without pausing, she kept her pace across the open expanse of dew soaked grass, over the wooden bridge which clattered under her feet, then put on one last burst of speed towards the blue door of the stone building in front of her.

She hit the button on her watch stopping the timer, and leant over to catch her breath. Glancing at the time, she gave a satisfied nod, faster than yesterday.

Still breathing hard, she turned away from the building and jogged down the path to a smaller structure, which although filled with state of the art gymnasium equipment, was seldom used by her fellow Chroniclers who dwelt within the Haven, but rather by their protectors, the Guardians.

That's why she came at this time of the morning. It was quiet now, but in a few hours this room would be full of toned, muscular, super fit warrior men and women, which was intimidating to say the least.

Grabbing a drink from the water fountain she sat down at the rowing machine and lost herself in the routine of her morning circuit which ended with the boxing bag. Not worrying about gloves, she began to pound at the bag.

The jangling of the chain and the thumps of flesh on canvas hid any other sounds, so she jumped when a male voice spoke behind her. 'You're getting much better. You'll have to spar me next.'

'Jeez Samael! You scared the life out of me.' She stilled the bag and turned to face the bulky, sandy haired Guardian behind her. Layered with muscle upon muscle he was a brick wall of a man. 'Spar with you, I don't think I'd make it out alive.'

The man mountain shrugged, then pressed a few buttons on the running machine and began a mile eating sprint, which she knew he could maintain long after she would have collapsed from exhaustion.

She continued striking the bag with a variation of punches, strikes and kicks, all taught to her by Samael, who after watching her attempts a few months back, had taken pity on her and given her a few tips. After a particularly forceful front kick, her watch began beeping. She looked at it and sighed. Time to go.

'See you tomorrow,' she told the Guardian who hadn't slowed his pace an inch, and received a nod in return. He was a man of few words, never talking unnecessarily.

As Kess ventured back out into the cold morning air, a familiar restlessness filled her like an itch deep within her bones.

She wandered unenthusiastically back to her room, gaze drifting around the spartan space, which even after five years, had never felt like home. Home was with her father and sister, in their cramped north London flat where the smell of coffee permeated the air from their coffee shop below.

Kess crossed to the window and watched the sun inch into the morning sky. She loved this time of day, it was always quiet, the paths empty of Chroniclers scurrying about, or Guardians on their way to training, so the large procession which passed quietly below her three floors down was unusual. Curious, she edged closer, but the warmth of her breath fogged the glass, obscuring her view.

'Watching a fella?' Kess jumped as Lisbeth's voice sounded at her shoulder. Lisbeth Yorke was tall, blonde, beautiful, and Kess's best friend. Distracted by the delegation, she hadn't even heard her enter.

'No,' she replied shortly. 'Look.'

The chill from the pane seeped through her sleeve, nipping her skin, as she wiped the condensation from the window. The flicker of movement drew the eyes of several Guardians surrounding the group, their hands flying to weapons as they assessed, but, deciding she was not an imminent threat, the warrior's attention moved on, continuing their scan of the area.

'What are Custodians from Weichen, Asile and Bandar doing here?' Kess asked, identifying the pairs of fiery orange, glacial blue and earthy brown robed figures.

The delegates walked close together, the cowls of their hooded robes turned towards each other like they were speaking quietly. Following several metres behind were the lighter coloured robes of the Head Chroniclers. Like those they were following, they wore their hoods up, obscuring their features.

Lisbeth's face had taken on a bored look which Kess ignored, caught up in her own inquisitiveness.

'What's got the four Havens stirred up enough to convene the Quaternary council?' Kess paused remembering a hushed conversation she'd heard between two Head Captols a few weeks earlier. 'There have been rumours you know, of attacks on Chroniclers on assignment. Would that be enough to convene the Council?' She mused aloud.

'Your curiosity is going to get you into trouble one day.' Lisbeth's pretty face had taken on a disapproving cast. 'We'll find out when the Consilium make an announcement.' The blonde peered at her friend's face closely. 'You won't do anything foolish, will you? Like trying to find out sooner?'

Curiosity burned within Kess but she shrugged. 'Course not. Besides trying to listen in would be problematic to say the least. Have you seen the number of Guardians they have with them?' All in all, she estimated the party to number about forty–five, with fifteen officials and double that number of guards.

Kess's gaze wandered back to the brightly coloured robed figures. Each Haven had four Custodians that made up the Consilium, the ruling council. That two of their number were here, meant something big was going on.

Lisbeth shivered, 'I don't see why we need *them,*' she enunciated the last word scornfully.

Kess sighed and turned, searching her friend's face. 'Why do you hate them so much?'

'Why do you like them so much?' Lisbeth retorted, ignoring her question.

'They protect us. Our way of life.'

'Protect us? From what? They are thugs nothing more.' Anger danced in Lisbeth's eyes.

Kess shook her head, but didn't argue; they'd had this conversation too many times before. She would never be able to shift Lisbeth's irrational dislike of the warriors, just as her friend would never be able to convert Kess to her biased way of thinking.

She turned back to the window and watched the Guardians stalk past, their dark brown leathers contouring to the muscular lines of their bodies like a second skin. The gracefulness of their movements was a living thing, a rhythm, that none but a warrior could match. So unlike their own simple formal robes, which many of the older generation still wore as everyday garb, the foreignness of their apparel and the array of weapons strapped to their bodies made them appear to be exactly what they were, deadly exotic creatures.

They were two different species. Guardians were the hammer and sword, the physical protection for Athenaeum, their veiled realm. They were tough and decisive, trained to watch and question. By contrast, Chroniclers were expected to be still and silent, as bound in their duties as the books and the knowledge they cared for.

Kess glanced out of the corner of her eye at Lisbeth, who was the perfect example of a Chronicler; intelligent, gifted and dedicated – yet she didn't envy her.

'I take it you've been running around again?' Her friend arched a perfectly shaped eyebrow, wrinkling her nose delicately as she looked in Kess's direction.

Kess sighed softly again, this was becoming a regular point of contention with her. 'And if I have?' she answered shortly. 'What's wrong with me wanting to keep fit?' She pulled her hands from the window sill, not wanting Lisbeth to see the red marks around her knuckles from the punching bag. The Angels only knew what she'd say about that.

'You are *not* a Guardian, Kess. You're a Chronicler. Not that you act like it.' Lisbeth put her hands on her hips. 'What's going on? The Choosing is soon. Have you given any thought to which Chapter you will pick? Have any approached you?' At her silence Lisbeth crossed her arms, face scrunched with unveiled annoyance. 'I didn't think so. Well I have. Head Captol MacFadden from the Linguists has invited me to join them.'

Kess's stomach twisted. The Choosing.

The day where Chroniclers picked one Order that would set the course of study for the rest of their lives. Though there was no official ceremony, it was still a big deal within the Haven, involving each Initiate approaching the head of the Chapter they wished to join, seeking admittance. The thought of it made her stomach churn and chest tighten. Closing her eyes, she leant her hands against the window sill and focused on breathing deep and slow until the feeling disappeared.

Kess opened her eyes to see Lisbeth who, far from noticing, had turned to the small mirror in the bathroom adjusting her long blonde locks.

'Captol Wessler will be meeting with us over the next few days, to talk about our decisions. You'd better have an idea by then.' Lisbeth continued completely oblivious of Kess's distress.

Kess pulled a sour face. 'Can't wait.' Captol Wessler – or the Weasel – as everyone called him behind his back for his reputation of ferreting out transgressions and reporting them, had, for some reason, taken a personal dislike to her, keeping an eye on her more than the other new initiates.

Shaking her head, sending her perfectly arranged blonde hair flying, Lisbeth left Kess to watch the Delegation as they strolled out of sight.

CHAPTER 2

Into the Fire

Kess looked at her watch again for the third time in as many minutes.

8:27 a.m.

She didn't have to be in the Archive for scribing for just over half an hour yet. She paced the six short steps of her room, reconsidering the craziness of her plan, but she could argue back and forth with herself all morning and not get anywhere, so before she could talk herself out of it again, she marched out of the room.

Kess strode towards the Guardians training area trying to look like she belonged there, ignoring the little voice that screamed at her what a crazy idea this was.

Following the closest section of the chest high fence, she scanned the faces of the battling warriors and found the woman with the dark brown ponytail she'd been searching for, standing on the far side of the yard.

Dressed in the tight–fitting clothes of her kind; Miah, Sub–Commander, second in charge of the Guardians, made an imposing figure.

Miah leant against the railing, attention focused on the practising warriors. Her stretched poise emphasised the muscular contours of her slim figure, and made her seem that much more unapproachable to Kess, who couldn't help but envy the brunette's naturally–exuded confidence.

A few metres away Kess's steps faltered, and she was on the verge of turning back when the dark–haired woman spoke.

'Can I help you with something, Chronicler, or do you just like to stand and gawk at people?' the warrior asked wryly, not bothering to shift her gaze from the battling pairs.

The dust kicked up by so many feet irritated Kess's eyes, yet she resisted the urge to rub them. 'May I speak with you?'

'About?' Miah asked shortly.

'I have a request. But I would prefer to speak in private.' Kess stumbled over the words, unsure of herself.

'Here's fine.' The warrior turned to face Kess, looking at her for the first time. She watched her with dark impenetrable eyes as she crossed her arms and leant back against the rail. The interlocking metal plates on the forearms of the warrior's elbow–high arm guards, glittered in the morning light drawing her attention.

Taking a steadying breath, she looked the warrior in the eye. 'I want you to train me.' She glanced away after a few seconds, unable to hold Miah's hard stare, which had the same intensity she imagined, as staring down an angry lioness. Her breath caught in her throat waiting for her inevitable negative response, yet, when the expected rejection didn't immediately follow she raised her eyes from the ground.

The warrior looked at her speculatively. 'Now why would a bookworm want to come and play with the birds?' Miah mocked.

'I want you to train me.' Kess repeated stubbornly. Instead of deterring her like it was intended to do, the Sub–Commander's derision only strengthened her resolve.

'Why?' The warrior stepped closer into her space, seeking to intimidate her. As much as she wanted to back up a step, Kess stood her ground and held the warriors eye, hoping this was part of a test and that she wasn't about to end up on her backside.

'I–' Kess trailed off not sure how to explain something she didn't understand fully herself. How could she describe that desperateness inside her that constantly clawed to be let free? That doubt that she was not supposed to be a Chronicler.

She shrugged. 'Every Chronicler here is contented with their work, with being shut away from the world, living in the long dead past. I'm not.'

The Sub–Commander looked at her speculatively. 'Chroniclers are born. Guardians are born. They do not, have not, ever swapped sides.' There was an inflection of finality in the warrior's words.

‘Aren’t we both on the same side?’ Kess didn’t want to beg, knew that the warrior would see it only as a sign of weakness. Glancing around desperately she tried to think of a way to convince her, then nodded her head in the direction of the battling pairs. ‘Let me try.’

‘Against one of the warriors? You’ll be thrashed in moments.’ There was little doubt in her tone about the outcome of such a match, but underlying that, Kess thought she heard curiosity.

‘It shouldn’t be a problem then,’ Kess said, ignoring the butterflies twitching frantically in her stomach.

Miah turned away, long plaited ponytail swishing about her back as she moved. ‘Halt.’

The silence was almost immediate as twelve pairs of eyes turned towards their instructor. ‘Conall. Forward.’

A young man with bright ginger hair and a cheeky look about him, sheathed his short sword and wound his way to the front of the group. Despite being involved in a vigorous training session, his breathing was calm, and his brow only lightly dotted with sweat.

He looked towards Miah expectantly, hands clasped behind his back.

Despite his youthful looks she knew better than to underestimate him. He was Guardian trained, which meant fast and deadly.

A light smile played across his face, as he looked Kess up and down.

‘The scholar here wants to spar.’ The sub–commander’s lips pulled back in a frightening smile. ‘Send her back to her books.’

Conall nodded sharply then stepped back a few paces, giving Kess room to advance. As she climbed through the wooden rails, entering the field, the remaining warriors formed a solid ring around them, effectively blocking any escape.

A Guardian stepped forwards breaking the formation, capturing her attention with his topknot hairstyle, like samurai wore in the movies.

Kess was so busy staring at his hair that she didn’t see the weapon he held out to her until he raised it higher, offering it to her in both hands.

She met his eyes and saw both curiosity and amusement twinkling within them. With a brief smile of encouragement, a mere tightening of lips, he returned to his space within the circle leaving her alone to face the Guardian whom Miah had called Conall.

She glanced around the ring, and noticed that the warriors didn't display much in the way of emotions; good or bad. Their blank stares could make a stone seem expressive.

Kess held the dulled sword in her hands, feeling its weight for a moment before raising it to mimic the position of her opponent.

Conall gave her a wink then lunged forward suddenly, bringing his sword crashing down.

She swept her blade around just in time to deflect the blow which otherwise would have struck her in the stomach. The force of the blow jarred through her arms, almost causing her to lose her grip on the unfamiliar weapon.

He retreated a few steps giving her a moment of respite before he lunged again, but this time, somehow, she managed to deflect the blow more purposefully. Kess took a chance and lunged forward pushing out her blade like a stick and jabbed him in the shoulder.

Conall looked down with wide eyes, clearly unable to believe that she'd touched him.

The only warning she had was a furrow of his ginger eyebrows, then faster than she would have thought possible, he leapt forward sweeping his sword first left then right, confusing her.

Unskilled as she was she didn't realise the first move was a feint, until he pulled the blow redirecting the blade to the right, hitting her firmly across the ribs. The breath whooshed out of her lungs but she remained upright, trying not to clutch at her side.

Kess was totally unprepared when he ran at her, sliding to the ground just before he reached her. His legs scissored out, capturing her feet as he twisted, dumping her unceremoniously onto the dirt.

Conall leapt up again, and leant over her. 'Yield?'

Taking a leaf from his unorthodox fighting style she propped herself up as if to take his outstretched arm, then, as he leant down, punched him as hard as she could, hitting the hard bone of his cheek. He rocked backwards, hand holding his face where she'd connected.

She bit back a curse. Punching a bag hadn't prepared her for the jarring pain of striking bone. Kess rubbed her knuckles with her thumb trying to relieve some of the pain.

Instead of being angry she saw a smile on his face. 'Well doon,' he said cheerily, helping her to her feet. 'Did nae see tha coomen.'

His accent was so thick it took Kess a moment to understand what he'd said.

She stood brushing off the dirt and looked to Miah who, arms crossed about her middle, did not look pleased. The fierce glare she aimed at Conall wiped the smile from his face as he hastily retreated, taking a place within the circle.

The stern–faced warrior looked around the gathered Guardians, then focused on Kess who shifted uncomfortably under her intense stare. 'No.' Miah turned, deliberately exposing her back to Kess. 'Training's over,' she barked.

As one the Guardians turned and silently walked away, exiting the training field, gathering their gear as they went.

Kess stood alone within the fenced area, unsure what she'd done wrong. The topknot warrior glanced back, but continued on with the others, disappearing in the direction of Aldoak, their compound.

Shoulders hunched, she walked slowly back towards her room, wandering gloomily down the hall, until a lanky youth intercepted her.

'Chronicler Grayson?' At her nod, he spoke again. 'Please come with me.'

'Where are we going?' She recognised him as a message runner for the Custodians. She looked at her watch and grimaced – 9.03 – 'I'm already late for scribing in the Archive.'

With a disinterested shrug, he set a fast pace towards the council offices ignoring her completely.

As she traipsed after him Kess realised that dust and little bits of crushed leaf clung to her clothes. Keeping an eye on the youth, she tried to brush them off inconspicuously, removing all evidence of the extracurricular activity she'd just engaged in.

The youth remained silent for the journey, and paused only to open a door, before gesturing her though.

She stared at him seeking some clue to the summons, but his downcast eyes refused to meet hers. She was obviously not going to get any information out of the lad so she strode through, entering the reception room for the offices beyond.

Instead of following her through, he closed the door firmly behind her.

She looked around the room, expecting to be met by the secretary who was permanently seated at the small wooden desk, however her small, uncomfortable looking chair was empty.

'Chronicler Grayson, come through.' The door to an office had opened and a tall, moustached man stood in the doorway. The creased lines of his brow, the downturn of his mouth, were clear indications of his displeased mood.

She'd had very little to do with the Custodians since her arrival and all she could recall of this one was that he sat on the Quaternary Council representing Athenaeum, their Haven. Being in a position of such power, where he could make her life a misery should he choose, he was definitely not someone she wanted to annoy.

Kess sat in the chair that he indicated repressing the urge to shift nervously on the hard surface. She waited until he had seated himself behind the crescent shaped desk before asking, 'May I ask why you called for me, Custodian Drazen?'

'I'm surprised you can't figure that out. I have been told by Captol Wessler that you are an intelligent woman.'

Kess stared at him in silence, astonished that he knew who she was.

At her reticence he shook his head, and pressed his hands together forming a point with his fingers. 'Very well then. This morning you approached the Guardians. Why?'

Taken aback, she took a moment to gather her thoughts. 'Am I not allowed to associate with our protectors?'

He ignored her question. 'Why?' he repeated.

'I wanted to train with them.' She didn't see any reason to deny the purpose of her visit.

Drazen's eyebrows climbed so high on his forehead she thought they might merge with his somewhat receding hairline. 'Chroniclers are not warriors. They do *not* train with Guardians.'

'That's what they said,' Kess replied.

'At least *they* know their place. Chroniclers are Keepers of the knowledge, by birthright of the blood of our ancestors. The Guardians are our protectors. They have their place. Just as we have ours.' He made a motion with his hand indicating their conversation was over.

Kess stood slowly, bewildered by his interest in her activities.

'I trust that I am understood,' he said firmly just before she was out of earshot.

She didn't answer, knowing he wasn't expecting a response.

She walked quickly back towards the living quarters, not wanting to run into anyone.

Obviously, someone had seen her, and informed Drazen. But why? What was so forbidden about her actions that would warrant an immediate summons before a Custodian?

As she strode into her small room to collect her scribing tools, Kess's foot crunched on a folded sheet of paper which had been thrust under her door. She unfolded the note and saw two words scrawled within.

Aldoak 2200

A grin spread across her face, was this an acceptance from the Guardians?

CHAPTER 3

Forbidden Liaisons

'We are ever striving after what is forbidden,
and coveting what is denied us.'

Ovid

Kess waited until fifteen minutes prior to the meeting time before slipping quietly out of her room.

At this time of night, the corridors were empty, but after today's meeting with the Custodian she wasn't taking any chances. She checked each junction before moving on, determined not to be seen.

Trying her best to remain inconspicuous she only just made it to Aldoak before the stipulated time. Yet she was alone, waiting outside the barred doors, trying to ignore the cool wind which blew straight through the thin material of her jacket.

Kess pulled the crinkled sheet of paper from her pocket, worried she'd read it wrong, but it definitely said 2200. She checked her watch, and saw the hands ticking away past the hour.

She tucked the note back inside her pants pocket and glanced around, tensing at a flicker of movement behind a stone column a few metres to her left. A tall dark–haired warrior stepped out of the darkness, making as little noise as a spectre would.

'I thought you said no.' Kess couldn't believe the note was written by the woman who'd dismissed her so quickly earlier that afternoon.

'Where were you called after you left the training grounds?' Miah asked, a knowing look on her face. Without waiting for a response, she pushed against one of the large panelled doors easing it open, and padded softly down the hall.

Kess followed the warrior into a building she had never entered before – the Guardian complex – and tried not to gape at the high columned corridor or the simplistic decor, which, while spartan, suited the space and its non–materialistic inhabitants.

The woman led her unerringly along several corridors until she stopped at a wide, open doorway.

For the first time, she glanced back as if making sure Kess was still there, then passed through the arch leading her into a huge training area filled with boxing bags, mats, climbing ropes and a variety of other training apparatus. Three tiered shelves lined the walls crammed with kick pads, hand mitts, and what looked to be blunted training weapons.

She was so preoccupied by the room that she didn't hear the doors close behind her. She also failed to notice the two other people in the room until one of the men spoke.

'You showed up then?'

Kess turned sharply, and saw two familiar faces. 'Who could resist a mysterious note under a door?' she remarked to the samurai, drawn again by his different hairstyle.

'Oh, I like her,' he said to Miah before turning back towards her. 'Are you sure you're a Chronicler? They are usually so–' he paused, tilting his head trying to find the right word.

'Boring,' she supplied for him.

His laughter echoed through the room. 'I'm Kisho.'

'Kess,' she said nodding, then looked at his so far silent companion. She saw bruising around his eye and winced. 'Sorry about your eye.' Somehow, during their fight earlier, she had failed to notice the double black bars piercing his left eyebrow, which now sat at an odd angle with the swelling on his face.

'Wa 'is? Ee've ad wuurs befur.'

She was still trying to decipher his drawled words, when Miah spoke up.

'Cut the crap, Conall.'

The redhead grinned at her. 'Sorry couldn't help myself.'

'You will have to ignore him, he's Irish – weird sense of humour.' Kisho laughed as he danced out of the way of Conall's punch.

'Ahh, may your pipe never smoke, may your teapot be broke,' he countered, in what Kess assumed was some sort of Gaelic insult.

'Right, Chronicler,' Miah's voice sounded from behind her.

'Kess.'

The leather clad woman stared at her, holding her eyes unblinking before she continued speaking, not acknowledging the interruption. 'You want to train with us. That's not a request we've ever had from your kind. But,' she cocked her head to the side, peering at her like an eagle would a rabbit – her being the rabbit, 'you don't seem like the rest of them. We will train you. But we have conditions.

'Firstly, you are to tell no one about these sessions. Chroniclers are not good with change or things out of the ordinary, so keep this to yourself.' Miah watched her until she had nodded her understanding before continuing.

'Secondly, make sure you're careful coming and going. We don't want anyone to see you sneaking about suspiciously, and follow you here.' Kess nodded again though the woman wasn't watching her this time.

'Third, we three,' she indicated the two men, 'are the only ones who know about your training so do *not* discuss your sessions with any other Guardians.

'Lastly. You have to follow *all* of our directions and commands.' She eyed Kess. 'Whether you understand them or not.'

Kess considered the stipulations which were nothing beyond what she thought were reasonable requests and precautions. Not questioning their directions would be difficult but as long as they didn't put anyone in danger she couldn't see a problem. 'On my lineage as a Chronicler, I agree to abide by all of your conditions.'

The warrior's dark eyes sharpened as she considered Kess's oath, then nodded her acceptance.

Kisho stepped forward, taking over. 'We need to assess your abilities, strengths, weaknesses and general fitness to figure out how we can best train you. We'll start with these.' He led her to a table which held an array of weapons including knives and of all things, a bow.

She picked up one of the smaller throwing knives and headed towards a line painted on the ground in front of two very battle–scarred mannequins.

She had never held a weapon before, so took a moment to get a feel for the knife before raising her arm, taking aim. Holding the hilt, she made sure of her target, then let the blade fly.

To her amazement it hit the mannequin in front of her squarely in the chest, sinking in almost up to the hilt.

She looked to Kisho and saw his eyebrows quirk.

'Keep going,' he smiled, throwing her a black bundle of material.

Unrolling it Kess found six knives laid out in separate pockets. She ran her hand over the top of them, feeling the chill of the metal against her palm. They were beautiful. Not that she knew anything about knives but they seemed to be of good quality. She pulled one carefully from its sleeve, surprised at the weight. It was heavy but not overtly so, balancing well in her hand.

She took aim and hit the mannequin again, right next to the first blade.

The murmur of voices echoed across the room, from where Miah and Conall spoke quietly. Both were looking directly at her so there was no doubt as to what they were talking about.

'Am I doing something wrong?' Kess asked Kisho who had moved beside her to watch her throwing technique.

'Nothing at all. That's what's surprising. You've never trained with weapons before?' He picked up a larger blade from the table and let it fly. The blade struck with a deep thunk, quivering in the dead centre of the small red circle. Barely glancing at the target, he looked at her, waiting for her answer.

She shook her head. 'No, never.'

The warrior kept watching her, his eyes full of curious speculation. Unsure what else she could say she turned back and kept throwing until she was out of knives. All seven landed within the red target painted on the chest of the dummy, yet because of the warriors' reactions, trepidation fluttered in her chest overwhelming the elation she'd felt earlier.

'Try the bow.'

She picked up the bow and a black feathered arrow which lay next to it. She looked to Kisho not even sure how to hold it, but he watched her patiently, hands resting behind his back. Not receiving any instruction, she held the arrow as best as she could, guiding it with the fingers that held the curve of the bow.

Just as she was taking aim, the arrow slipped away from the bow. Mortified, she pulled it back in against the wood, and looked down the shaft, before releasing it quickly. To her dismay the feathers brushed her fingers as they flew past, sending it spinning wide of the target. The arrow bounced harmlessly off a boxing bag to her left before falling to the ground.

'Pathetic.' Kess spun at the unfamiliar male voice, and caught Miah's flinch at the newcomer's word. A blonde–haired man lounged in the frame of the door behind them, a contemptuous look plastered across his face.

'Thrain.' Miah's voice emerged cool and calm however, yet there was a tenseness to her poise which hadn't been there moments before.

'What's this?' He aimed his statement at the dark–haired woman not even bothering to look in Kess's direction.

'She shows promise,' Miah justified to the man who was obviously her superior.

Conall and Kisho remained quiet watching the exchange.

'We were discrete,' Miah said brusquely.

'You thought you could bring a Chronicler here without me finding out?' Thrain all but spat her title, twisting the word contemptuously.

'No. I just knew you'd stop me if I told you what I was going to do.'

'You're damned right I would have. *They–'* he jabbed his finger in Kess's direction, 'are not like us. She should *not* be here.' Thrain turned a cold disdainful look in her direction and with a raise of his eyebrow took his time to look her up and down.

Kess felt her cheeks flame at his scrutiny, yet forced herself to remain still, meeting his penetrating steely gaze with all the determination she could muster.

Anger spiked fierce and hot through her, but she kept silent, knowing she couldn't influence this conversation in any positive way. She settled for crossing her arms about her chest, and fixing Thrain with a level stare, silently telling him he was an arrogant git.

Like Kisho he too sported an unusual hairstyle, shaved at the back and sides, yet grown long on top and tied back in place, like a ponytail only covering the top third of his head. His face was lean and hard, and his slate grey eyes glittered angrily.

He turned back towards Miah and even from this distance she could see a vein bulging in his clenched jaw. 'You *will* be held accountable when this goes bad.'

'If,' Miah countered.

'When.' He ended the conversation by walking out of the room without a backward glance.

Conall let out a huge whoosh of air. 'Well that was uncomfortable.' He walked back to the middle of the room and stood on the edge of a large padded mat.

Kess let out the breath she hadn't realised she had been holding. 'Who was that?' She asked the question of no one in particular, but it was Miah who answered.

'Thrain, the Last Defender, Commander of the Guardians.'

'Oh.' What else could she say. The leader of the warriors didn't agree with her being trained and made no attempt to conceal his dislike of Chroniclers. But, he hadn't tried to stop them as she'd feared he might.

Kisho moved to the centre of the mat gesturing her closer as he strapped a long pad to one arm. 'Punch.'

She jabbed her left fist out striking the pad with a thump, then followed with her right falling into the rhythm of her morning workouts.

'Who taught you to punch?' the samurai asked startling her out of her concentration.

She hesitated, not wanting to get Samael into trouble.

'Don't worry, your secret, or should we say the giant man's secret is safe with us,' he said with a wide smile.

'He told you?' Kess was unable to hide her surprise.

He shook his head. 'Miah figured it out. Why do you think she agreed to train you?'

'How?' Considering the time of morning and the fact that she'd never seen any other Guardians, Kess had no idea how Miah knew.

'We Guardian have our ways,' Kisho said, giving her a mysterious smile. At her sceptically raised eyebrows he sighed. 'You're no fun. Our patrols saw you running through the woods and anything "unusual" gets reported to Miah, or Thrain if it's serious enough.' He shrugged. 'She was curious about a Chronicler doing non–Chronicler things, so she went out and watched you, and saw you talking to Samael in the gym. If you hadn't approached her, she would have sought you out.'

'What's wrong with me running?' Kess queried, thinking how this was starting to sound like her conversations with Lisbeth.

'Nothing's wrong with it, it's just unusual. It's our job to look into things out of the ordinary.'

'If Miah was going to approach me anyway why mock me the way she did?'

Kisho looked at her for a moment, eyebrows coming together as his forehead wrinkled. 'For a number of reasons. What would it have looked like, if she, Sub–Commander of the Guardians greeted you amicably in front of the other warriors?'

'She was afraid of what people would think?' Kess didn't think Miah was the type to worry about the acceptance of her peers. 'And the other reason?'

'She was testing you.'

'Why?'

'To see if you had any mettle about you. To train as a Guardian you learn how to be not only proficient with weapons, but resilient against the other forms of battle which include ridicule and scorn, trying even in the face of adversity and overwhelming odds, even when you believe you have no chance of success. If you didn't stand up to her, the challenge, she would have deemed you incapable of completing your training.' He moved the pad in front of his chest signalling the end of their conversation. 'Right, let's see how much you have learnt. Front kick.'

Kess kicked her right leg out striking with enough force to push Kisho back slightly. The half metre length of hair flowing from under his topknot swung around his shoulder wildly as he leant to regain his centre of gravity.

'Good. When you kick you need to hold the upper half of your body firm but not stiff. Now roundhouse kicks, alternating legs.'

Kess aimed her kicks at the rapidly moving pads, praying to the Angels she wouldn't miss and strike him instead.

'Enough.' Miah's voice came from the edge of the mat. Kess had been so focused on what she'd been doing that she'd forgotten all about Conall and the sub–commander watching.

'Assess.' She looked to Kisho who moved to stand beside the warrior woman.

'Your knife throwing technique is excellent. Don't pick up a bow again, without a hell of a lot of training.' He joked, but Miah's cool look had him continuing quickly. 'Hand combat you have good technique and we can work with that.' He looked to Miah who stood beside him arms crossed.

'We will continue your training,' she said making Kess realise this had been a trial to see whether they believed she was competent enough. 'Same time tomorrow night,' Miah said before stalking out of the room.

'Don't worry she thaws out when you get to know her,' Kisho said watching the direction of her gaze.

'Really?' Kess didn't think there was much to defrost with the woman; that Miah was as hard as she looked.

'No. Not really,' Conall piped in, giving her a grin and a wink before leaving the room as well.

‘Come on, I’ll walk you to the door,’ Kisho said leading her back into the hallway along the maze of identical looking corridors. He saw her looking around the areas they passed with interest. ‘All the corridors are the same, that way if an enemy enters they will have trouble negotiating the layout, giving us time to dispatch them.’

She shivered at his calm mention of “dispatching” intruders, but at the same time her curiosity flared. How would anyone breach the Obiex and gain entry to Athenaeum?

‘We will leave you a message in the same way if we need to contact you,’ he said, before he shut the doors quietly but firmly behind her.

Though the air nipped at her cheeks, turning them red, she barely noticed.

She had done it! She was being trained by the Guardians!

CHAPTER 4

Chance Encounters

Kess woke with a start into pitch blackness, hopelessly tangled in her sheets.

She didn't bother looking at the clock, knew that it would be some ungodly hour, flung from sleep by dreams she could never remember. With a sigh, she grabbed the top of the sheet and flapped it up and down trying to free it from its snarl around her.

As she lay back down, the restless sensation which always appeared after the dream, coursed through her legs. It felt like burning ants were running up and down the veins of her calves and thighs. Sometimes rubbing the affected muscles helped relieve the sensation, yet tonight, unsated by her ministrations, the unrest twitched through her limbs demanding movement.

Throwing back the covers she paced the five short steps of her room – back and forward, back and forward – moving definitely helped, yet the moment she stopped pacing, the itching restlessness returned worse than ever.

Tonight her mind was as agitated as her legs, and refused to stop whirring while her heart strummed, ignoring her attempts to steady its rapid beat.

She needed to get out of the claustrophobically small room.

Rummaging through her drawers she threw on the first clothes she could find; jeans and a black long–sleeved hoodie and slid her sneakers on, not worrying about socks.

She eased her door open, freezing at the creak which sounded infinitely loud in the dark silence and padded quickly down the hallway and out into the night towards the bridge, where she found herself going most nights when she couldn't sleep.

The night sky was black with clouds, allowing only sparse light from the moon to filter through. Usually she strolled along, but tonight uneasiness found its home within her and she found herself peering to either side of the path, into the wooded darkness, thinking herself a fool for doing so, but unable to stop each glance.

She reached the crossing with its rickety wooden slats and eased herself down, putting her legs through the railing. She trailed them above the water, watching the moon's reflection on the surface as it tried to battle through the thick cloud cover.

The restlessness which had consumed her, ebbed away, as if drawn from her by the river and washed downstream with its sluggish current.

Relieved, Kess leant her forehead against the cool metal of the rail and watched the inky blackness flow past her.

'At this hour, this may not be a safe place to idle the time.' A melodic male voice spoke from the edge of the bridge.

Kess jumped startled by the stranger's silent approach, banging her forehead against the rail before scrambling to her feet, rubbing her head with her fingers.

Several paces away was a man she'd never seen before. Taller than most Chroniclers, and of similar muscular build to a Guardian he stood confidently, watching her, as she assessed him. Even in the dim night his hair seemed to glow with a golden light of its own. But it was his eyes which held her attention, the blue of evening twilight; bright and intently focused on her.

She tried to shift her gaze, blink even, but was unable. Like a deer mesmerised by the headlights of a car, she was inextricably caught, totally incapable of moving. After what seemed like an age, just as a strange sensation began to rise up within her – pulling at her, he tore his gaze from hers looking out into the darkness.

She should have felt uneasy at being approached by a stranger, at night and whilst alone, but the emotion wouldn't come. 'Why wouldn't it be safe?'

His statement though delivered in all seriousness should have been laughable. They were within a Haven. By definition it was one of the few "safe" places in the whole world. 'The Obiex stone protects us,' she continued, hoping to elicit a response from the stranger.

'Nothing in life is infallible, least of all those things we take for granted as being so.' As if to reinforce his caution, he glanced over his shoulder, into the deepest dark of the forest behind them. 'You are safest indoors.' He took a step towards her, arms extended like she was livestock to be herded, ushering her off the bridge and back along the path towards the buildings.

She wanted to argue with him about the absurdity of his claim, but something made her stop. His worry about lurking dangers appeared genuine. This man was a stranger to her, but if he was part of the recently arrived Delegation, as his accent suggested, he must be someone she could, if not trust, then not entirely distrust.

As they distanced themselves from the bridge, a prickling sensation at the back of her neck got the better of her. Kess shrugged her shoulders, trying to rid herself of the feeling that something was watching them. She tried to dismiss it as fancy, a creation of the minds susceptibility to the power of suggestion, but the itch didn't disappear. She *could* feel eyes upon her.

He walked her to the front of Cantonment without her direction. She didn't wonder how he knew where to take her, these days, with declining Initiate numbers, this was the only building open to house them prior to their Choosing.

'Take care wandering about in the dark,' the blue–eyed man said.

Pulling her eyes from the dark brick building she caught him watching her intently like she was a puzzle he couldn't solve. Seeing her eyes upon him he carefully schooled his features to blankness before he walked away not offering any farewell.

As she neared her room she padded quietly along the carpet not wanting to wake any of her neighbours, considering the early hour.

As soon as her door closed behind her she flicked on the light, then looked around the small space at a loss for what to do. It was too late to try to go back to sleep now, and she didn't think she'd be able to even if she tried.

Kess saw the book she'd thrown onto the desk the afternoon before and with a sigh flicked through the pages until she reached the damaged section she had been tasked to replace and set to work.

~

A loud thump awakened her.

Bleary eyed Kess looked around her daylight filled room disorientated. She was sitting at her desk, work unfinished beneath her arm, still gripping a quill in her hand. She stood stretching her stiff limbs and rotated her neck around loosening the tight muscles.

'Angel feathers,' she cursed as she caught sight of the clock on her bedside table, which announced it was six minutes to nine.

The knock at the door sounded again. Short and impatient.

'Come in, Lisbeth,' she said, knowing exactly who it would be. Lisbeth, her sole friend in the Haven, was the only person who ever came to her door. She had never understood why the other Initiates all gave her a wide berth, but for years now they had.

Lisbeth, looking fresh and beautiful as always, halted with a concerned look as she took in Kess's dishevelled appearance. 'You haven't been sleeping again.'

Seeing no point in denying it Kess shook her head.

Lisbeth pressed further, 'Are you alright, you seem,' she faltered, searching for the right word, '–preoccupied of late.'

Kess didn't think she had been acting any differently than usual, other than falling asleep a few times when she should have been working. 'I'm fine.' It came out a bit more sharply than she intended and not wanting to offend her friend she added, 'I just haven't been sleeping the best. But I'm fine, really.'

'Your dreams again?'

Kess knew the question was well intentioned, but she regretted telling Lisbeth about the intangible dream which plagued her nights. She didn't want to try to explain to her once again why something she couldn't remember disturbed her so much. How could she when she didn't understand herself?

'Have you remembered anything more?' Lisbeth pushed.

'No,' she said shortly, hoping her friend would get the hint and move on.

'Okay. But you know you can talk to me if it gets worse.' Seeing she wasn't going to get an answer, Lisbeth tutted. 'So where did you vanish off to last night?' She watched Kess's face, searching for a response.

'When?'

'I knocked on your door last night but there was no answer. Don't tell me a fella caught your eye?' she asked coyly.

'By the Angels, no.'

'Oh.' Lisbeth seemed dismayed by her denial of a romantic interest. 'I thought I saw you headed towards the warrior's area, so I thought you must been meeting someone.' Contemptuous disgust oozed from her at the thought of a Chronicler doing anything inappropriate with a Guardian.

Kess felt the blood drain from her face but forced a smile. 'I needed some fresh air so I went for a walk. I took the path around the grounds,' she said, explaining – she hoped – her reason for being seen near Aldoak at that time of night. If the Guardians found out she'd already been spotted heading in their direction they may revoke their agreement to train her.

She glanced again at the clock, three minutes past nine. 'I'm sorry, Lisbeth, but I need to go.'

Annoyance pinched the corners of the blonde's mouth as she finished her inspection of her flawlessly manicured nails.

Trying to thwart another argument Kess spoke quickly, 'I'm going to see Mum.'

The displeasure vanished as Lisbeth's face softened with sympathy, which was even worse. Forestalling her again, Kess grabbed her jacket from the back of the chair and ushered Lisbeth out the door and strode quickly away.

~

Kess stopped at the gate, halted by the Guardian who had materialised seemingly from nowhere. The warrior's stern countenance moulded into a small smile as he saw her. 'Chronicler Grayson.'

'Morning, Samael.' No matter how many times she asked, he never called her by anything other than a title she hadn't even earned yet. She'd given up trying to convince him otherwise.

'Going out?'

She nodded.

'Got your pass?'

Kess handed over the sheet of paper signed by a H.C. and countersigned by a member of the Consilium, allowing her to leave Athenaeum. Had her mother not been a former Chronicler she doubted she would have been permitted to leave; as it was, the Custodians were not entirely convinced about the necessity of her monthly visits.

'Where's your Guardian?'

Kess looked around. Her escort for the day was usually waiting for her when she arrived. 'I'm not–' she cut off as she spied a familiar red–headed warrior approaching.

'Not late am I?' Conall asked with a grin, as he gave her a wink so exaggerated it pulled the corners of his mouth.

'Desperate for a guard today are they?' Samael waved them past shaking his head briefly before his attention returned to the area surrounding the only access point into or out of Athenaeum.

She braced herself as she took a step forwards. Even though she knew what was coming, the icy sensation of passing through the barrier always came as a shock. She didn't think it was something she would ever get used to. She likened it to jumping into an icy river, in the dead of winter, during a blizzard, naked, but that probably didn't even come close.

She turned around after passing through and couldn't help but marvel that even so close all of Athenaeum was gone, hidden behind the barrier. Her eyes, tricked by the illusion, saw only forest. She could sense something there, a tingling, and a faint pull in that direction, like her body recognised the place where it would be safe, but that was it. Nothing else to reveal what lay behind the sensory illusion.

She reached out, uncaring that Conall and Samael could see her. The protective boundary felt soft, indenting under the pressure of her hand. Yet no matter the tension put against it, the protective border would not part and allow access to Athenaeum without a Guardian by your side.

She'd read once that people with no lineage ties to a Haven couldn't even feel that, they were just guided around the area without even knowing they'd been diverted.

'Ready, Kess?'

Removing her hand, she fell in beside Conall as he started up the dirt path, which wound through the forest emerging near Saint Anne's Hospital.

She glanced at Conall out of the corner of her eye, wondering what he had been told about today. She loved her mother, and wasn't embarrassed by her or the fact that she wasn't well, but dreaded people's reactions when they found out; which ranged from pity – which she didn't want – to an involuntary step backwards and suspicious sideways glances at her like madness may somehow be catchy.

Far too quickly for her liking, they stood at the edge of the path, looking across at a small building. The white columned stone facades with red brick backing, looked like an old–fashioned manor house, camouflaging its true purpose; an institution.

CHAPTER 5

Something Wicked This Way Comes

'You'll believe in more than that by the time I'm finished with you.'

Wicked Witch of the West, *Wizard of Oz*

Kess climbed the steps and pushed open the door heading to the right, towards B wing, where her mother and the other "less stable" patients were roomed.

Her footsteps echoed ahead of her, as she strode down the long, empty corridor. She automatically modified her breathing to shallow breaths, hating the overpoweringly sterile smell of this place.

Her mother's room was at the end of the wing, last door on the right yet curiously the halls were empty of residents this morning, making the place seem deserted.

She turned towards her Guardian hesitating, as she saw the door to her mother's room was shut.

'I'll wait out here.' Conall gave her a nod of encouragement.

She shot him a small smile then pushed the lever down, slowly opening it, not sure what she would find in the room beyond.

As regular as her visits were, she had begun to dread them.

Her mother's mind was like a broken clockwork toy, some days working better than others, but lately she had changed, more prone to erratic, and sometimes aggressive behaviour. Yet she couldn't not come, couldn't leave her mother here alone day after day, that wouldn't be right.

Kess hadn't had the heart to tell her father yet hoping she would get better. But she knew he was planning a visit soon, so if it kept up, she would have to warn him.

The curtains were drawn and the overhead lights off, making the room dark for such a sunny day. She walked to the windows and drew the curtains halfway letting enough light in without it becoming overly bright.

Kess turned and stared down at the woman sleeping on the bed, who was a stranger to her.

This was not her mother.

Her mother, Anna, had been vibrant, so full of life it seemed to explode out of her.

The woman on the bed was pitiful, flesh so wasted that her bones jutted unnaturally, skin so pale it looked like wax. Her once lustrous hair now lay lankly about her head in a dishevelled tangled mess.

This was *not* her mother.

Kess opened the top drawer of the little cabinet beside the bed and pulled out the orange handled brush, one of the few possessions Anna was allowed to keep, and set about trying to right the tangled mess.

Gently, so as not to pull on her mother's scalp and wake her, she brushed and brushed until the red gold hair, darker than her own, regained some of its shine.

With one final sweep, she returned the brush, catching a glimpse as she did of a tattered rectangle of paper pushed to the back of the drawer.

Curious she pulled it out.

It was a photo of her family, before her mother's breakdown. It was battered around the edges with small tears and creases, but was obviously important to Anna and had been handled a lot.

She placed the photo back where it had been and shut the drawer with a thud, swallowing back the lump which had formed in her throat.

Despite her repeated requests, the nursing staff still hadn't gotten around to swapping the chair, so with a sigh she dragged the heavy uncomfortable seat closer, slumping down in it.

Sometimes she spoke to her mother, sometimes, like today, she just sat in silence.

~

Kess felt something rub against her cheek. Dragging her eyes open she realised she must have dozed off, head propped on the palm of her hand.

She jolted backwards as she saw her mother's face inches from hers. 'Mum? You scared me! Are you alright?'

'Yes, ohhh yes. But your mother, *she* is surrounded by the darkness.'

'Do you want me to turn on the light?' Kess asked, disorientated with sleep.

'You have the stink of Angels on you.'

'Wh – What?' Kess stuttered, taken aback.

'You reek of burnt sunshine.' The words drawled out of Anna's mouth as she breathed deeply through her nose smelling the air around Kess.

'Mum, are you feeling alright? Have the nurses given you something?'

'Don't get smart with me, girl.' The voice that came from the bed was not a woman's voice. It sounded like the scrabbling of insect legs on a wooden floor. The alienness of it made the hairs on the back of her neck stand up.

'Mum?'

'Mummy. Muummmy,' her mother taunted.

Kess's chair scraped backwards, crashing to the ground as she tried to get away from the bed.

'Where is He?' Anna demanded.

'He? Dad's not here, he's back in London. You're in a hospital outside of Athenaeum. Do you remember?' Kess replied, trying to jog her mother's befuddled mind.

'Tell me! Tell me where *He* is and I won't flay the skin from your bones!'

'By the Angels!' Kess blanched, dumbstruck by the words spewing from her mother's mouth.

'They're not listening. Not liiistttening. Tell me! Tell me!!' Anna roared as she leapt from the bed bearing Kess to the ground as she pounced.

The air whooshed from her lungs as her mother's weight settled on her chest. She thrashed, trying to roll her mother off but her arms were pinned against her sides by Anna's knees.

Kess's stomach twisted as she looked at her mother and found her eyes completely devoid of any trace of rationality.

'Mum,' she pleaded. 'It's me, Kess.'

Anna's face twisted to the side, assessing. A low growl rumbled in her throat menacingly, sounding totally inhuman. 'Keesssssss,' she hissed. 'Ohhh, I have someone who will want to meet you.'

The protruding bones in her mother's hand crunched against Kess's cheek as she struck her.

'Mum, please,' she gasped, struggling.

Her mother's scrawny frame seemed inordinately heavy, and she was beginning to have trouble breathing under the weight.

She tried to shrink back as Anna lowered her face inches away from hers, but her head pressed firmly against the floor, allowing no movement.

Dots danced before Kess's eyes, as she gasped trying to bring oxygen into her lungs which were starting to burn.

She glanced around trying to find something to shift her mother's weight and froze, horrified, as the veins in Anna's neck bulged and distended grotesquely. Blackness oozed upwards through bloated veins spidering up her neck, moving across her jawline, cheeks and forehead. Tiny black lines entered her eyes, flickering about like little worms.

Kess bit back a scream and bucked her hips trying to displace her mother.

Anna's lips curled upwards, baring her teeth.

Frantically, Kess managed to pull one arm free and shielded her face, terrified her mother was about to bite her.

Before she could launch forwards, two arms encircled Anna's chest pulling her backwards.

As she sucked in a lungful of air, she saw a flash of bright red hair struggling to hold onto Anna.

The muscles in Conall's arms bulged as her mother flung herself around wildly in his arms. 'Guards!' He yelled towards the door.

Within moments two well–muscled men ran into the room and grabbed Anna's flailing arms, helping to subdue her. Together they managed to manoeuvre her onto the bed just as a dark–skinned nurse rushed in.

Taking in the scene she approached Kess, who was still sprawled on the ground in shock. Her almond brown eyes scrunched with concern as she reached down and helped Kess to her feet. 'Are you okay, dear?'

'I'm alright. I think they could use a hand though,' Kess said pointing out the trio who were battling to strap restraints onto Anna's still thrashing arms and legs.

Kess backed away, wrapping her shaking hands around her chest trying to steady them. She risked a glance at her mother, but saw only unblemished cream skin on her face and neck.

Had she imagined the blackness?

As she reached the doorway Anna stopped thrashing and focused intently on her. 'We will find you, Kesssssss. I will make you beg for death. Soon.' The dry voice began to chuckle, a low sinister sound which raised goose bumps along Kess's skin.

Kess fled from the room, bashing into the door frame, bruising her shoulder in her haste to get away. She rounded the bend of the corridor and didn't slow until she stood on the concrete footpath outside the suddenly claustrophobic building.

The sun broke through the clouds shining down on her brightly. She stood in its warmth trying to drink it in and alleviate the numbed shock which had frozen within her.

The fear–fuelled adrenaline which had filled her faded, leaving her cold and empty.

Now that she had stopped her knees began to shake and refused to hold her any longer. She let herself go and sank to the cool concrete.

‘Kess, is she – are you alright?’

She jumped at the sound of Conall’s voice, having forgotten about him in her need to flee. Taking a deep breath, she levered herself to standing and turned to face him. ‘Yes.’

She expected questions yet when he remained quiet she looked up and was surprised to find him fiddling with his hands in a very un–Guardian like pose.

‘Conall?’

‘Kess, I’m so sorry. I should have been there but I thought I heard something down the hall and went to look. Then I heard the commotion in the room and well–’ His rush of words slowed as his gaze flicked to her stinging cheek before meeting her eyes. ‘I failed to protect you.’

‘By the Angels, Conall, you have nothing to apologise for. If you hadn’t been there–’ she cut off. She’d been close to passing out. *If Conall hadn’t come in when he did, what would her mother have done to her?* ‘When you grabbed her, did you see anything?’

‘Apart from her trying to strangle you?’

Worry filled her at his words. Conall had been right there, if he hadn’t seen anything then perhaps it hadn’t been real.

Was madness hereditary?

‘Is she always like that?’ he asked softly.

Kess shuddered. ‘No. She hasn’t been herself, especially recently, but she’s never been that bad before. You won’t say anything will you? If the Custodians find out about this, they’ll stop me from visiting.’ She hated to put him in this position but couldn’t risk them revoking her visitations.

Conall looked troubled. ‘If that’s what you want.’ A stern look crossed his face as she smiled in relief. ‘But if it happens again you will have to tell someone.’

At her nod, he inclined his head back towards Athenaeum and kept pace beside her.

She didn’t look back, glad to be heading away.

~

Within moments of reaching the carefully concealed entrance, Samael strode towards her seeming to appear out of thin air. He took one look at her face then scanned the surrounding woods, ushering her behind him. 'You alright?' he asked once he had satisfied himself that no imminent danger was about to come charging the barrier he guarded.

She nodded, fighting the urge to pat down her dishevelled hair.

'What happened here?' He pointed to the cheek her mother had struck.

'Fell over.' She knew how lame it sounded but couldn't think of how else to explain the obviously visible mark.

Samael raised an eyebrow sceptically, and cast a pointed glance at Conall who returned what she was sure he thought was an innocent look, but thankfully the concerned warrior led them through the barrier, and let them leave without asking any more questions.

Kess followed her Guardian as he led them along the quieter, lesser used path that ran towards the stream rather than the main buildings.

She hadn't realised she'd stopped walking until Conall called her name.

'Kess? Are you alright? Are you sure you don't want to tell someone?'

'No!' She cut him off a bit more forcefully than she intended. 'No,' she repeated, moderating her tone.

He pursed his lips at her stubbornness. 'Do you have to be anywhere this afternoon?'

She shook her head. She had been excused from Chronicler duties for the rest of the day as visits with her mother usually lasted into the afternoon.

'Come on.' Kess let the Guardian lead the way, and was surprised when he headed towards Aldoak.

'I'm not supposed–'

'Don't worry.' Conall cut her off, giving her a cheeky grin which reminded her too much of a small boy about to make trouble.

She climbed the stairs, following him to the heavy wooden doors and almost bumped into him when he stopped suddenly and poked his head into the hall beyond.

'All clear,' he whispered exaggeratedly.

He walked quickly, keeping her right by his side, so close to the columns lining the edges of the hall that she had to curl her shoulder to avoid hitting them as they passed. She had just navigated a particularly large lintel when a voice called out behind them, echoing down the corridor.

'What are you up to now, Conall? You're not exactly being inconspicuous, sneaking around like that.'

Recognising the Guardians voice Kess stepped out from behind the column where Conall had pushed her.

Raising an eyebrow at her, Kisho looked at the red–headed warrior and folded his arms about his chest waiting for an explanation.

The heavy tread of approaching footsteps echoed along the corridor, breaking the warriors' stand–off. Both of their heads whipped around towards the sound yet Kisho was the first to move. Grabbing her arm, he half led, half dragged her into the training room and shut the doors firmly behind them.

'What's going on? You can't just turn up here out of the blue. Miah told you there were conditions to us training you. What would've happened if another Guardian had found you and Conall sneaking about? Caddar for instance?'

Kess hadn't met anyone called Caddar but guessed his reputation when she saw the grin slide off Conall's suddenly pale face.

'It's my fault, Kisho, not Conall's,' she said trying to deflect the blame. 'Sorry. I'll go.'

As she turned the warrior saw the side of her face and grabbed her arm, halting her. 'What happened?'

'Nothing,' she said briskly, trying to free her arm from his grip, wanting nothing more now than to get out of there.

Kisho released her, crossing his arms about his chest again as he stepped in front of the door blocking her escape. He didn't say a word, just looked at her.

She felt her cheeks flame at the thought of having to explain to him that her mother was in a hospital for the mentally disturbed. Aside from her father – who not being of Chronicler blood lived outside of Athenaeum – Kess didn't talk about Anna with anyone.

'Who hurt you?' Concern had replaced his irritation.

She looked to Conall who stayed silent, letting her decide what she was going to reveal.

Though the warrior's face was carefully blank, devoid of any emotion, his eyes showed what his face didn't.

Worry. For her.

His concern loosened her tongue inducing her to say what she normally wouldn't.

'My mother.'

'What?!' The question exploded out of him, sounding harsh.

'She's – not well.' The words came haltingly from her mouth.

His sharp glare swung to Conall. 'You were on guard today?'

The redhead nodded, but didn't add anything else.

Wanting to stick up for him Kess added, 'He saved me.'

Kisho nodded but didn't ask any more, sensing her reluctance. 'Want to train?'

'Please.' Anything to clear the image of her mother's vacant eyes from her head for a while.

~

Kess swept the hair from her face and stared at the man facing her.

Kisho's angular face held a look of disinterest which belied the poised readiness of his body. His hand flashed out aimed at her head.

She blocked his strike with her forearm, biting back a curse at the force of his attack. Then retaliated with a roundhouse kick aimed at his ribs which he dodged easily, and turned it into a spinning kick which caught him in the side of the head.

'Much better.' A female voice sounded from the sidelines. Kess flinched at the voice, unaware of Miah's entrance. Arms folded across her chest, the brunette's mouth pursed in thought as she watched them sparring. 'This is not a scheduled training session though,' she chided.

'Thought I needed the extra practice,' Kess said, hoping that was sufficient to stop the questioning. She didn't risk a glance at Kisho, afraid of giving her half–truth away.

Miah's eyes narrowed, but she didn't pursue the matter any further. 'Keep to the scheduled times in future.'

'Sorry.' Kess turned back to Kisho who launched as soon as she looked in his direction.

'Oompff.' The grunt exploded from her chest as his unexpected kick knocked the wind from her. She hit the mat hard, gasping like a fish out of water, as she tried to coax the air back into her lungs.

When her chest muscles loosened and she was able to breathe again, Kisho leant over offering her a hand. She gripped it in the manner she had observed other Guardians use, forearm to forearm and was rewarded with an approving nod.

Their short intense bout had left sweat trickling down her face and she gratefully accepted the bottle of water he handed her.

'Can I ask you something?' Kess gulped a sip of water, as she considered how to phrase her question. 'I understand the secrecy around the Chroniclers. But why so hush hush with the other Guardians?'

Kisho looked silently at her, making her wonder if she'd asked something wrong.

'Because there are those among our number who wouldn't condone our actions in training you.' Miah's voice carried a contempt she didn't bother to disguise.

'Like Thrain?' Kess asked curiously.

‘He is more adaptable than most,’ Miah said evasively, but didn’t deny her statement. ‘It’s time for you to leave,’ the brunette said abruptly. She looked to Kisho who nodded and began to usher her from the room.

‘Is she always like that?’ Kess asked unable to keep the frustration from her voice.

‘Miah has taken a big risk in agreeing to train a non–Guardian. She must see something special in you. Remember that before you judge her too quickly.’

Kisho’s words sent guilt coursing through her. She had never considered the risk Miah had taken, even after Thrain’s hostile interruption during their first training session.

As they reached the door, Kisho placed a heavy weight in her hands. Kess looked down and saw the metallic gleam. A knife.

‘A warrior should always have a weapon,’ he said, handing her a leather sheath as well before turning and walking away.

With a heavy guilty heart, she left the compound and stepped out into the darkness of well–settled night.

CHAPTER 6

Murder and Mayhem, Chaos and Death

'Every great change is preceded by chaos.'

Deepak Chopra

Kess peered around her, trying to see into the darkness surrounding the path. There should have been a nearly full moon lighting the sky yet not a trace of it could be seen through the thick clouds. Its absence made the night seemed more condensed than usual – thicker somehow.

The crunch of the loose stone beneath her feet, sounded unnaturally loud in the tense silence. She hastened her pace, not sure why she should be afraid tonight, but there was something, a wrongness in the air which caused the hair on the back of her neck to stand.

She continued walking, eager to make it back to her building when a stench of death and corruption engulfed her. Her stomach convulsed, wanting to wretch the foulness from her system. She leant over, hands on knees, waiting for it to pass and was almost pulled from her feet as a hand gripped her arm, trying to drag her off the path, into the night. She gasped at the heat of the skin holding hers, as scalding as a boiled kettle.

Kess wrenched her arm back, breaking the tight grip and back–peddled, trying to put space between herself and whatever had grabbed her. Panic stabbed through her as a figure emerged from the blackness, coming after her.

'Mum?' Confused, she stopped and stared at the woman who had birthed her, but was now looking at her like a stranger. 'How did you get in here?'

Alarm prickled the edges of her mind, demanding attention but she ignored it.

This was her mother. She took a step forward.

The prickling grew stronger.

'What are you doing here?'

Something was wrong.

'How did you get out of the hospital?' Fear clenched deep within her stomach as she again felt her mother's hand strike her, felt her weight crushing the air from her lungs.

She looked again and noticed, this time, the fluidness of her mother's movements and saw, to her horror, that the distended veins had reappeared covering Anna's neck and face, making her skin appear more black than cream.

Like a contagious rash, the dark pallor had extended to her hands as well, the only other part of her visible beneath her tan hospital pant–shirt outfit.

There was no answer from Anna, just the crunch of dead leaves under her feet as she continued to flow forwards.

The darkness shifted, flowing towards her mother, swirling around her until she vanished from sight.

Kess cringed at a horrible squelching sound which came from the darkness nearby, like a foot stepping on an overripe tomato.

Lightning zigzagged through the sky above her illuminating the area like a huge spotlight, revealing a figure crouched on the ground.

As she watched, it rose, shaking like a dog ridding itself of water. Head down, it appeared disorientated.

All that she saw, in the few seconds of light.

Then darkness.

Kess peered around wildly, unable to see anything, even her hand extended in front of her.

She started to back away again, faster this time.

A strong wind whipped up out of nowhere, tearing at her hair, whipping it about her face. The thick cover of cloud shifted in the gale, revealing the moon and a creature more hideous than anything her worst nightmares could have conjured.

Its hairless body was similar to a human's, yet more elongated as if stretched out another foot, making it anorexically thin. The creatures skin was darker than the deepest night, covered in grotesque misshapen lumps visible even in this light.

Bile rose in Kess's throat, disgusted even as panic threatened to freeze her limbs in place. Somehow despite all of this, a small part of her mind remained calmly detached, assessing the situation.

With a terrifying roar the creature charged, closing the gap between them. It moved similar to a monkey, using long spindly arms to propel itself forwards in great jumps. Several feet from her it started to run extending its fingers, revealing razor sharp talons, reminding her of a raptor from Jurassic Park.

The blade Kisho had given her found its way into her hands, sheath discarded somewhere to her right, and before she thought, she lunged, scoring the abomination across the middle.

It was like hitting a slab of rock with a stick.

Her breath hissed between her teeth as the impact jarred her wrist. Kess frantically tightened her grip on the hilt as the weapon shifted in her hand against the boulder–like resistance.

Unhurt it hissed with laughter, apparently amused by her ineffectual attempt to wound it. 'Foolish human.' It rasped struggling to form the words through its piranha–like mouth. The stench of its foetid, decaying breath oozed into the air sickening her.

'Demon,' she spat.

Kess had read ancient accounts about these creatures, but had never once thought they were actually real, or that she would meet one in the flesh. Anger warred within her, winning supremacy over her fear.

'What did you do to my mother?' The bones in her hand crunched as she danced forward, slamming the knife down where the creature's collarbone should be, hoping to find a vulnerable spot.

She darted back as the blade hit the hard bone–like skin, doing no visible damage.

It hissed again, laughing at her. 'She is goooone.' It drew the word out, delighting as disbelief, then sorrow contorted her face.

Kess clenched a hand to her heart which felt like it had been torn from her chest.

Gone.

She wanted to fall to her knees, beat her fists against the ground and scream her grief into the night. Her mother had been taken from her years ago, taken, but still there. Now she was really gone.

She looked at the abomination in front of her clearly delighting in her pain. Her grief solidified to rage. A rage which she flamed, to use against this hells spawn.

The slits on its face quivered as it sniffed the air. Its head clicked to the side, peering at her in confusion. 'You no longer sssmmell of sssunsshine. Not you. Not you.' It hissed angrily.

She didn't have a clue what it was talking about, so dismissed it, stepping to the side, trying to find a weak spot she could attack.

The demon ignored her movements. 'Where isss He?' It hissed before she kicked it squarely in the chest, knocking it back a few feet.

Her body was fighting on an instinct she didn't know she possessed, reacting before she had a chance to think about what she was doing.

'He who?' she responded, voice low with contained anger.

'Tracked him here. Where. Is. He?!' The hellion roared biting her blade as it slashed past its face. Its piranha–like teeth closed over the metal, snapping it as easily as she would a twig. Angered by her attempts, the creature lunged slashing talons towards her.

Kess screamed as its claws raked long scratches down the arm she'd hastily raised to protect her face.

'Chronicler!' A voice yelled behind her.

She turned in time to see the flash of a short sword as it slid to a halt at her feet.

Ignoring the burning agony racing up her arm she bent quickly, retrieving the weapon.

Kess gripped the hilt tightly as she took two quick steps and twisted, sweeping the blade in an arc, cleaving the head from the spindly abomination.

The body collapsed, thudding lifelessly as it hit the ground. She watched in horrified fascination as the corpse erupted in a geyser of iridescent orange flame.

In the light of the demon fuelled inferno Kess saw the golden–haired man, standing several feet away.

As the demon was consumed, darkness again claimed the area, leaving white dots dancing around, blinding her vision.

'Thank you,' she walked towards him as her eyes readjusted, offering his blade back to him, hilt first.

He stared at her, eyebrows raised as if surprised by what he'd seen. 'Keep it.' His fingers closed her hand around the weapon. 'I told you the night wasn't safe.'

Kess flinched back as a shock jolted through her, like static electricity. 'What–'

She lifted her eyes meeting his fathomless blue gaze, and in that instant the world around her ceased to exist.

A whirlwind swept through her so violently it seemed it would tear her apart with its ferocity.

Her hands reached out, trying to find something to anchor herself against. Imbalanced she closed her eyes tightly, and saw the golden–haired man – *Kai* – his name echoed in her mind – standing in a calm centre of the assaulting maelstrom.

Kai looked at the raging storm surrounding him, confusion clear on his face. His eyes locked with hers and again she felt sucked into them, the same way she had the night they'd met. He held out his arm, trying to reach her through the whirlwind separating them. As their fingers touched a shockwave jolted through her bringing Kess back to herself.

As she regained awareness of her body she opened her eyes and found that what she'd anchored herself to was the man himself, clenching both of his forearms like a Guardian.

She released her grip hastily, retreating a few paces, putting a safe distance between them.

'You are *not* a Chronicler. *What* are you?' Kai's voice was strained.

Kess heard his question in stereo.

It reverberated within her mind as well as in her ears.

She clapped her hands over her head trying to drown out the sensation, yet the deprivation of sound made her aware of something else lurking within her mind. As she concentrated on the bubble–like presence it swelled, resonating a strong male presence.

Kai.

Bewilderment and worry flooded through her yet she didn't think they were entirely her own emotions.

'What are you?' he repeated.

She ignored his question, unsure of what he meant. 'What was that?' she asked, taking another step back, trying to increase the distance between them, yet despite the gap, the bubble within her mind remained large and undeniable.

The skin between his brows creased yet before he could answer another sound intruded. The tread of multiple pairs of feet coming fast.

Glancing back over her shoulder she saw Guardians running in their direction.

Kess looked back to Kai, ready to joke about the cavalry turning up after the battle was done, but found herself standing alone in the darkness.

~

She faced the approaching warriors, sliding the short sword Kai had given her through her belt at the small of her back. As they halted several

Guardians broke away scouting the area, as the rest of the group fanned out in front of her.

She saw the glint of metal in the hands of some of the warriors yet the wicked looking axe of the stern blonde–haired Guardian at the front of the pack remained sheathed. 'What happened here, Chronicler?' Kess recognised him from her first training session – Thrain.

'Demon.'

The exclamations which erupted through the group were quickly silenced as he glared at them.

'Oh yes? Where is it?' His eyebrows rose mockingly.

'I killed it,' Kess said carefully, realising she was starting to feel light headed.

'You?' he scoffed, eyes narrowing with scorn.

'I cut that foul creature's head from its shoulders.' She pointed in the direction of the singed patch of grass behind her, as proof of her claim, almost losing her balance as she spun.

She blinked trying to clear her eyes as the night suddenly darkened.

Thrain glanced to a familiar brown–haired Guardian who strode forward.

Dropping to one knee, Miah examined the grass. 'Hells fire,' she confirmed, causing another stir through the group of warriors.

'You killed a demon!' Conall exclaimed stepping forward, a broad grin painting his face.

She shrugged, wincing as the movement pulled at the cuts on her arm. 'It attacked me first.' At least that was what she meant to say, however her words slurred, emerging as an unintelligible *'Ith takd m furss.'*

Kess saw Miah's face whip up in alarm before her head did a sickening swirl and her legs crumpled beneath her. She found herself looking up at the pitch black starless sky and realised belatedly that she had fallen.

The warrior appeared over her, blocking the night sky. 'Kess. Did the demon bite or scratch you?' Miah asked in a slow firm voice.

Kess tried to answer but couldn't seem to make her mouth move. Unable to fight the urge, her eyes started to close.

'Kess! Open your eyes! Kess!'

She tried to obey but her eyes stayed firmly shut, refusing to open. Something slapped her cheek, hard enough to rouse her. Her eyes flew open to see Miah's hand raised for another strike.

She dropped her arm. 'Where?' The Guardians voice was urgent. 'Kess! Where?!'

With a huge effort, she lifted her right arm up onto her stomach where Miah could see it, hissing through her teeth at the fiery pain.

'This is going to hurt.' Miah muttered as she knelt at Kess's side and pulled out a knife.

She nodded to someone Kess couldn't see.

Panic flooded her fogged mind as hands grabbed her shoulders and images of the warrior cutting off her arm filled her thoughts. She fought against the weight pinning her down, but the hands didn't budge.

She continued fighting, thrashing her head around wildly until she saw Miah cutting the torn fabric away from her wounded arm, rather than the limb itself. She was glad she was lying down, as she saw white bone glistening between the red chunks of torn flesh.

Kisho knelt opposite Miah and held out a small brown packet which the warrior ripped open with her teeth before sprinkling its contents onto the wound.

Kess clamped her jaw shut grinding her teeth together against the pain. She craned her neck forward as much as she could with the weight on her shoulders and stared at the glowing white powder covering the deep scratches. Her wonder turned to horror as it began bubbling and an inky blackness started to seep out.

A hand reached past her, offering Miah a bandage which she promptly unwound covering the wound.

The combination of the powder and sharpness of the pain, helped clear Kess's head a little.

She glanced around finding herself surrounded by a ring of Guardians. Kisho nodded his head in approval as their gaze met. Conall, standing next to him, was grinning like he'd never had so much fun, and not one to miss an opportunity, winked at her.

She shook her head, then groaned as it kept revolving making her feel sick. 'What was that?' Her voice was rough but at least she was making sense now.

'It will help flush the demon's toxins from your wound,' Miah said distractedly as she finished dressing the wound.

'Can you stand?' Thrain questioned, not bothering to look in her direction as he scanned the surrounding area.

She nodded, shifting her feet under her unsteady legs.

Kisho moved behind her and placed his hands under her arms helping her to stand.

'Thank you.'

'My pleasure, Chronicler,' the smile on his face faltered. 'Are you alright, Kess?' he whispered softly, pitched so only she could hear.

She nodded not sure how else to respond. She was definitely not alright but she wasn't going to melt down anywhere near the warriors, especially their stone–faced commander.

Standing this close to Thrain she saw what she hadn't the other day – that he was the epitome of a Guardian, a man who radiated danger and menace like a caged lion. He looked ready to take on an army of the demon she'd just fought single–handedly, and dispatch them without raising a sweat.

'Thrain–' Miah cut off as he glared at her.

'Move,' he ordered in a tone which brokered no argument.

The Guardian pack fanned out with Kess at its centre. Then as one, the group moved forward, with Miah and Kisho standing on either side of her.

The initial benefits of the powder wore off quickly and Kess found herself starting to lag as her head grew lighter and her legs became increasingly heavy.

Hands grabbed her elbows helping steady her and keep her moving, for which she was grateful.

It was not far to Aldoak yet sweat already dampened her brow.

CHAPTER 7

A Rock and a Hard Place

The Guardian pack came to an abrupt halt several feet away from the base of their stairs.

Kess peered past the leather clad bodies frowning as she saw the reason the warriors paused.

Waiting at the top was Custodian Drazen, looking at them with contemptuous disdain like they were the ones barricading his doorstep, rather than the other way around. He was flanked by Captol Wessler and a short dumpy pasty–skinned man she didn't recognise.

'What has occurred here?' Drazen's voice was sharp.

'A demon has attacked within the grounds.' Thrain's eyes raked the Custodian with such loathing and aversion, Kess was surprised he was still standing.

'Impossible!' the moustached Custodian scoffed.

Kess had been watching the weasel–like Captol Wessler, and saw his eyes dart to the Custodian in alarm at his obvious dismissal.

'Improbable yes, but apparently not impossible,' Thrain countered, not at all ruffled by being confronted by an angry member of the Consilium.

'What does the Chronicler have to do with this?' Wessler asked, spying her amongst the pack. His gaze remained firmly on Kess, paying no attention to the Guardians surrounding her.

If she didn't know better she would have thought he looked worried.

'That is yet to be determined,' Thrain answered evasively.

Miah looked at him sharply, but didn't contradict him.

'She will return with us.' Drazen pointed to the spot in front of him, like Kess was a dog expected to heel.

'This Chronicler has information vital to determining what happened here tonight – like how a demon was able to breach the Obiex and enter Athenaeum undetected. Defence is the jurisdiction of the Guardians. She stays here.' Thrain crossed his arms, and though he made no further move, Kess felt the warriors tense about her.

Realising he was unable to exert his will over the Commander, Drazen addressed her instead. 'You will see me when you leave here.' Without looking back, he twitched angrily away towards the Chronicler buildings, with the unknown man in tow.

A deep crease marred the centre of Wessler's brow as he remained on the stairs watching her, rather than following the departing Custodian.

'I think he likes you, Kess.' Conall mocked, causing the Captol to turn a very unattractive shade of red before scurrying away.

Kess heard a few chuckles around her before the pack moved forwards entering the compound.

With an ominous boom, the large wooden doors shut behind them, initiating the groups dispersal – with a wink in her direction, Conall disappeared leaving only Thrain, Kisho and Miah as her escort.

She was ushered through unfamiliar corridors into a small room which contained only a few chairs positioned around a plain wooden table.

She sank gratefully into a chair, which was as uncomfortable as it looked and concentrated on stilling her shaking limbs.

Miah placed a glass of water on the table in front of her, then sat to her left as Kess gulped down the liquid, not realising how thirsty she'd been until she placed an empty glass back down.

She repositioned her bandaged arm laying it carefully across her lap. Though the pain had lessened she could still feel the cuts throbbing fiery hot in time with her heart.

As she looked around the sparse room a flood of anxiety washed through her. It was so overwhelming she almost rose from her seat and ran from the room.

She raised her uninjured hand to her head, realising, as she made contact with her temple that was where the torrent of emotion was coming from – the bubble she'd sensed in her mind earlier.

But that was impossible!

Had she been hit in the head during the fight? Was she was now imagining things which couldn't possibly be there?

Kess didn't realise she had been staring across the room at Thrain until he spoke, bringing her attention to where her gaze had been drawn to a beaten copper ring, sitting on the middle finger of his left hand.

'So, Chronicler, care to tell us what really happened?'

'Kess,' she said flatly.

'What?' Thrain demanded.

'My name is Kess, not Chronicler.' Normally she would have ignored his overt disdain, but she was exhausted and in more than a little pain, and his dismissive, arrogant tone irritated her.

He didn't respond, just folded his arms across his chest and continued to stare at her in that uncompromising way of his.

She shook her head slightly. She was no match for the commander's stubbornness, especially feeling the way she was. She hesitated though, unsure if he knew that Miah was still training her. 'I couldn't sleep so I went out for a walk. I was heading back to my room when I smelt something horrible and then someone grabbed me and tried to pull me off the path. It was my mother.'

She stopped at Miah's sharp intake of breath.

'I don't know what happened then. It got darker, Mum vanished, and then a creature appeared.'

'Can you describe it?' Kisho asked.

She didn't hesitate, the image was burnt into her memory. No doubt it would be featuring in her dreams for the foreseeable future. 'Long arms, pointy teeth, sharp claws, skin as black as charcoal.'

'Rask,' Thrain said disbelievingly.

'Couldn't be! What would a tracker be doing here?' Miah's voice held a question that neither Guardian answered.

'It asked me where "He" was.'

The intentness of the stares from the three warriors as they gave her their undivided attention was unnerving. She wasn't sure she wouldn't rather face the demon again.

'It spoke to you?' Disbelief was heavy in his tone, along with something that in anyone else she would have called worry.

She nodded. 'Not very well, but yes. It kept asking me where "He" was.'

'He?' Thrain demanded, clearly wanting a name.

'It didn't elaborate,' she said, knowing that answer wouldn't satisfy him.

'Where did it come from?' Thrain asked.

'The woods.'

'Did you kill it?'

'Yes.'

'How?'

'How what?' she asked shortly.

'How,' he replied just as testily, 'did you kill it?'

'With a blade.'

'Where did *you* get a blade from?' he asked scornfully.

Kess hesitated, fighting the urge to look at Kisho. Thrain clearly didn't like her – the Angels only knew what he'd do if he realised Kisho had given her a weapon.

She folded her arms about her chest instead, ignoring her galloping heartbeat, as she levelled him with a flat stare of her own. She kept her eyes firmly on his grey gaze repressing the growing urge to look at the samurai.

'I gave it to her,' Kisho said, breaking their stare off.

The hard, grey gaze immediately broke from hers as the commander turned the force of his formidable stare upon the samurai. 'You armed a Chronicler?'

'Yes,' Kisho said simply.

Kess looked to Miah who with a slight upturn of her brows, as if to say – *This is none of my business* – remained silent.

'If he didn't I would be dead,' she said heatedly. 'I know how much that would distress you.'

With one final hard look at Kisho, Thrain turned back to Kess ignoring her sarcasm. 'How did you kill it?'

'I beheaded it,' she said flatly.

'How did you know to do that?' Kisho asked.

She craned her neck around to where he stood behind her, leaning against the wall. 'I tried to stab it but couldn't pierce its skin,' she shrugged, 'I took a chance.' Kess looked at Miah's face and saw her eyes narrow.

'Did someone help you?' Thrain demanded.

The image of the blade sliding towards her flashed through her mind, reminding her of the moments that followed; the whirlwind, and the sense of him – *Kai* – in her head. 'I killed it,' she said carefully knowing the commander was watching her closely.

'Have you ever associated with demons?' he asked, continuing his barrage of questioning.

'Associated?' The very thought of working with a demon turned Kess's stomach, yet the look on his face demanded a firm answer. 'No. I haven't,' she said through gritted teeth.

'Studied them?' Thrain persisted.

She gave that question some thought. 'Hells spawn have been mentioned in a few texts I've copied but none had much detail. Certainly not how to kill them, or that there were different types. I thought they were just tales, like dragons, or the Loch Ness Monster,' she gasped. 'My mother! When the demon first arrived, it looked like my mother.'

She saw a look pass between Miah and Thrain, and felt a cold weight settle in the pit of her stomach.

Miah broke the silence first. 'Has your mother seemed herself lately?'

Kess's hand rose to her face touching her bruised cheek. 'Earlier today she attacked me. She had – well – I thought I imagined it.' Even after everything that had happened tonight, she still couldn't believe what she'd seen was real.

'Imagined what?' Miah leant across the table towards her, an intent look on her face.

'The black veins bulging up her neck and across her face into her eyes. Nobody else saw them so I thought–' she cut off shrugging.

Miah flinched backwards, hitting the rear of her seat. 'Gid–dim!'

The word meant nothing to Kess. She looked from Miah to Thrain seeking an explanation.

'The word gid–dim comes from ancient Sumerian, it means one possessed by demons,' Thrain said slowly as if not wanting to reveal too much.

Kess remained silent not understanding what it all meant.

Miah continued reluctantly. 'It means the demon was taking over your mother's body, possessing her.'

'Where is she?' Something cold, dark and panic filled nestled deep within her chest filling her with an irrepressible dread. 'What did it do to her?' She rose from her chair only to be halted by Miah placing a hand on her uninjured left arm.

'Kess.' Miah spoke softly, gently, which was infinitely more alarming than her usual sternness.

She allowed the warrior to guide her back to her seat. She was suddenly, absolutely sure that she didn't want to hear what the warrior was going to say. 'I have to find my mother. She's out there somewhere.'

'No, she isn't.' Thrain took the seat opposite Kess and held her gaze so she couldn't look away. 'Your mother is gone. The demon consumed her life force to gain entry to this world.'

She stared at him, unable to process what he was saying.

'Kess, she's gone,' he said again softly reinforcing what he'd said the first time.

He'd used her name, she thought distantly, not Chronicler.

Gone.

The word echoed in her mind yet she pushed it away unable to face what it meant. They had to be wrong.

'I'm so sorry,' Miah spoke softly, looking at her with undisguised sympathy. The break in Miah's tough facade was enough to shatter the denial Kess had built around herself, and then her world began to crumble.

Gone.

Her mother was gone.

The pain of her arm was forgotten as an avalanche engulfed her.

Kess wrenched her arm free from Miah's grip and fled into the night, trying to outrun the pain.

~

The night had turned horrid while they'd been inside, yet Kess stood in the pouring rain, uncaring as the torrent soaked through her layers, saturating every inch of her.

Her mother was dead.

Nothing would ever be right again.

She had run unthinking to the wooden bridge where she stood now, gripping the rail so tightly that the veins on the back of her hands stood out. She clung to it like it was the only thing holding her up.

Her great gulping sobs had subsided leaving a deep raw chasm within her chest which threatened to open up and swallow her.

Surprisingly the one part of her that felt better was her arm. The rain had soaked through the bandage cooling her skin, relieving the fiery pain.

The bridge vibrated under her feet with approaching footsteps. 'I'm sorry I ran away I just needed some time.' She didn't turn as she spoke so the male voice that responded threw her off guard. She'd expected Miah.

‘Kess–’ Thrain cut off as she turned, her red eyes meeting his steady gaze.

Though her tears had stopped, the rain flowing down her cheeks gave the appearance that she still wept.

She watched as he walked closer, taking a place beside her at the rail. His shoulder brushed hers and his closeness radiated warmth towards her, making her aware how cold she was. A shiver tremored its way through her body, chattering her teeth with its ferocity.

‘I’m sorry about your mother,’ Thrain said softly, in a voice lacking his characteristic harshness. ‘Losing someone you love is an unbearable pain. One which feels at the time that you can’t possibly survive. But you are strong, Kess. Miah would not have chosen to train you were you not.’

She raised her head, and looked at his face wanting desperately to cling to the thin hope his words offered.

‘Remember them as they were. It will help,’ he uttered softly.

Kess raised a hand to her mouth trying to stifle a sob. He’d clearly lost someone he had cared about and despite his attitude towards her previously, was trying to help.

She flinched, unable to hide her shock, as he haltingly patted her shoulder a few times. He was clearly uncomfortable with the situation and at odds with having to comfort someone.

Kess turned and somehow found herself in his warm embrace. Thrain stiffened, taken aback by her contact. His arms twitched as though to hold her, then stilled, remaining stiffly at his side. Yet he didn’t move away.

Her hands rested against the solidness of his chest. The steady thump of his heart helped calm her.

‘You need to come back to the Compound.’ His breath was warm against her sodden head, before he stepped back, removing himself from her reach. ‘The others are waiting and there are things we need to discuss.’ Stone–faced Thrain, Commander of the Guardians, Last Defender of Athenaeum was back, making her doubt the softening in his facade had ever happened.

‘How did you know that something was wrong tonight?’ Kess asked trying to delay the moment she had to return.

‘Guardians can sense the presence of hells spawn when they are close.’

‘Oh.’

Their walk back was silent, but not uncomfortably so as they strolled back side by side.

As they entered the room, Kisho and Miah, who had been talking softly, fell silent, looking at her carefully.

Miah shot her a small smile then inclined her head towards the empty chair.

‘Raining, is it?’ Kisho asked straight faced, as he took in her sodden appearance.

‘No, I just felt like a swim fully clothed,’ she retorted as she ran her fingers through her hair pulling it back from her face. She knew she must look a mess but didn’t make more than a cursory effort. Her grief raged molten hot inside her, contained below a fragile barrier she’d managed to erect. Thin though it was, it helped pull herself together.

Thrain handed her a folded towel as he took the seat to her left.

‘Thanks.’ She looked up at him trying to see the man she’d glimpsed earlier, not the warrior who was before her now, yet when his grey eyes met hers, they were as cold and as expressionless as ever.

He didn’t answer, just nodded once in her direction as he addressed everyone. ‘Kisho, send a team to search the area, find out where the demon entered.’

‘Already arranged,’ the samurai replied.

Thrain gave the warrior an approving nod.

‘You said the demon was a–’ Kess paused not quite remembering the name they’d used.

‘Rask,’ Miah supplied.

‘How many types of demons are there?’ She wanted to focus on something, anything that didn’t allow her mind to wander.

‘No one is sure really. There have been over two hundred documented species but who knows how many more have never crossed over.’

‘Crossed over,’ she paused thinking, ‘from the demon realm to ours?’ None of the books she’d read had gone into great detail about demon kind save to say they were very dangerous, hated humans and their dimension was, thankfully, separate from our own. But all had been written in a fictional sense – like the tales of Perseus killing the Gorgon Medusa. She’d never, even for a moment, believed they were real.

‘What I don’t understand is how the demon was able to breach the wards and possess someone.’ Miah pushed herself out of the chair and began to pace the room. ‘It shouldn’t be possible!’ she exclaimed, showing a rare display of frustration. ‘And did it come upon our young Chronicler–’

‘How the demon got in is indeed troubling,’ Thrain interrupted, shooting Miah a hard look.

Her lips quirked at Miah’s mention of “our young Chronicler”. It seems she’d been accepted, by Miah at least. Thrain, however, had made his views on her quite clear the first time they’d met.

As their talk went around in hypostulative circles, Kess could barely keep her eyes open, yet their discussions continued. She didn’t bother trying to stifle a yawn as she covered her mouth with the back of her fingers.

‘–to figure out–’ Thrain cut off mid–sentence. ‘Kisho find Conall.’

Taking one look at Kess, Kisho left the room, returning minutes later with the red–headed Guardian in tow. Conall looked around the room expectantly, gaze falling on her with a wink, before looking to his leader.

‘Take Kess back to her room,’ the commander said.

Far from looking disappointed, excitement lit his face, no doubt thinking he may meet another demon out there. She started to say that she would be fine walking the short distance by herself, then stopped. She hadn’t been fine earlier walking that same path.

As she stood, Miah spoke. ‘We’ll be in contact to let you know what’s going on.’

The culmination of pain, fatigue and her sodden chilled state muddled her mind making it difficult to think coherently. ‘What do you mean?’

Miah, who looked as fresh now as she had earlier in the evening explained patiently. 'The Custodian will want to question you.'

At Kess's look of alarm she held out her hand. 'Don't worry, Thrain and I will be there.'

'When?'

'Get some sleep. We'll let you know.' Miah gave her a small reassuring smile, but the furrow in her brow showed she was not as sanguine about the night's events as she seemed.

The brunette warrior turned back to Thrain but after a short murmured conversation they stood, falling in behind her. They followed as far as the path outside, yet as she and her exuberant guide turned right, they disappeared in the opposite direction.

Her walk with Conall back to Cantonment was quick and thankfully uneventful.

Though she tried to ignore it, her eyes strayed to the patch of scorched grass, right beside the path. It was still visible but thankfully the deluge of rain had washed away the charred, smoky stench.

At her door Conall waited beside her while she fished a key from her pocket, but as she slid the metal into the lock was unable to contain himself any longer. 'What you did tonight was–'

'Shh,' she hissed, finger to her lips as she scanned the corridor. That was all she needed. Someone in the dorms finding out what had happened and go running to the Custodians with wild tales.

He quirked his mouth sheepishly, as he checked the hall belatedly. 'Whoops.' He gave her a wink, then sauntered off down the hallway.

Before the warrior was out of sight, he turned and caught her watching him.

Kess rolled her eyes as he did a ridiculous looking mime of shutting and locking a door, but did as he suggested, bolting the slide lock firmly in place.

She stood in front of the closed door looking around her room, unsure what to do.

Kess pulled off her damp clothes, throwing them to the corner and changed into a polo shirt and a light blue pair of jeans.

She was exhausted, her eyes burned with fatigue yet despite the hour she hesitated to sleep, scared of what waited in her dreams.

Instead she opened the desk drawer and stared at the album inside before removing it with shaking hands. Settling on the bed she lay the book on her lap looking at the navy leather cover. Ignoring the sudden thickness in her throat she turned the page, wincing as the movement pulled at the wound on her arm.

There was a single photograph on the page; her Dad, Mum, younger sister Jinnah and her eight–year–old self sat smiling at the camera. She remembered the day well, they'd been having a picnic at Primrose Hill and moments after this photo had been taken, the heavens had opened up soaking them all.

A soft splat, followed quickly by another brought her back to herself. The tears blurring her eyes had run down her cheeks onto the page. The chasm of pain opened again fresh and raw, leaving her sobbing uncontrollably.

Her heart fought against what she'd been told. Surely if she went to the hospital her mother would be there, lying in her bed.

She couldn't accept that her mother was just gone, consumed by the demon. She curled in a ball hugging the open album tightly to her and let her pain engulf her.

CHAPTER 8

Earning a Guardian's Respect

'He makes no friends, who has never made a foe.'

Alfred Lord Tennyson

A loud pounding on the door roused her but she rolled over not caring who it was, or what they wanted.

'Kess open up.' She sighed at the familiar voice knowing she wouldn't be able to ignore Miah. Anyone else yes, but the formidable sub–commander, no.

Dragging herself up she made it to the door just as a fresh round of knocking started.

'You look like crap,' Miah said as she strode past her uninvited, into her room.

'Thanks.' She saw Miah's sharp gaze take in the photo album on the bed and cut her off before she could say anything. 'What's going on?'

'The Custodian wants to talk to you.' Standing in the middle of the room, hands on hips, she looked the picture of a warrior, ready to brook no nonsense.

Kess was infinitely glad that Miah was on her side; she wasn't sure how well she'd fare under that hard stare if it were directed at her instead.

'Now?! What do they want me for?'

'They want to question you about what happened. Drazen apparently doesn't entirely believe our account,' Miah said wryly, perching on the edge of Kess's bed, elbows balanced on her knees. She fixed Kess with an intent look.

'Why? What did you tell them?'

'A version of the truth,' the warrior replied shrugging her shoulders.

'Why would they believe me, over you?'

'Because you are one of their own. Your word will carry more weight than ours.'

Kess sensed there was more than what Miah was saying, but didn't press the issue, for now. She had never understood the friction that existed between the two groups, and not one of her teachers had ever explained it to her when she'd asked. 'What do you suggest I tell them?' She was under no illusion about telling the truth.

'That you were taking a walk, that you smelt something foul and the creature came out of the woods. It attacked you and was then dispatched.'

'By the Guardians.'

'Of course,' she paused looking intently at Kess. 'How's your arm?'

'Hurts like hell.'

Without asking Miah grabbed her arm and began to unwind the bandage poking and prodding the inflamed skin.

Bile rose in her throat as the last layer was unwrapped revealing the black stained material. Kess smelt the corruption wafting towards her, making her want to retch the contents of her stomach just like it had the night before.

'Ahhh! Can you not do that!' Kess tried to yank her arm away from the warrior.

Ignoring her protestations, Miah focused on the wound not looking up. 'I'm checking to make sure none of the demon's toxins have spread and infected your body. But if you'd rather leave it–' The warrior pulled her hands away, giving a nonchalant shrug.

'No,' Kess grumbled, holding out her arm. She clenched her jaw and squeezed her knee with her free hand as Miah started prodding the wound again.

The Guardian unzipped one of the pockets in her pants and pulled out a small packet like the one she'd used earlier. Tearing it open with her teeth, she sprinkled the white powder onto the oozing gashes.

Kess gritted her jaw against the pain and sucked in a breath through clenched teeth but managed to keep still as Miah finished her examination and wrapped the wound in a fresh bandage which she pulled from yet another pocket.

'Don't suppose you have Revels in any of those pockets?'

She was rewarded with a small smile from the dark–haired warrior. 'No, sorry.'

Miah walked to the door and pulled a towel from the hook, dampening it with a bottle of water from the desk. 'Here.'

Kess wiped her face and tidied her hair. Running her hands over her clothes she thought she looked slightly less dishevelled than before.

The Guardian looked her over, then, with a small nod, opened the door and strode out into the hall. Kess followed, surprised to see Thrain take up the rear, making their configuration seem like bodyguards sent to escort her.

The creak of the warriors' leathers and the steady tread of their heavily booted feet, so unlike the soft tread of the Chroniclers, had doors cracking open up the corridor. Though she knew she would be the subject of much speculation, Kess couldn't bring herself to care what the other Chroniclers thought.

They walked in silence to the Custodian offices. Miah looked back and gave her a small nod before opening the door and continuing through, marching straight up to the timid secretary who stared at them wide eyed.

'Chronicler Grayson to see the Custodian. She is expected.' Miah's voice rang through the room.

The mousy secretary gaped at the tall confident warrior in front of her, making no move to inform anyone of their presence.

'*She* is expected. *You* are not.' Custodian Drazen's voice was cool, not attempting to disguise his annoyance at their presence with feigned pleasantries. His eyes flicked to Kess's face, noting her red eyes, then glanced lower, at the bandage on her arm.

‘After the attack earlier, with the alarming revelation that we are not as safe within our Haven as we assumed, I asked them to escort me here.’

Both Guardians had flanked her upon Drazen’s arrival in the room. As she glanced at Thrain she caught the slightest raise of his eyebrow at her defiance, which was akin to a gasp from anyone else.

Drazen smiled at her thinly. ‘Despite the occurrence yesterday, I can assure you, that yourself, and every other denizen of our Haven remain safe.’ He glanced at the timid secretary who looked on the verge of meltdown at the mention of the attack. ‘But I believe this is a matter best discussed within the confines of my office, so as not to cause undue and unnecessary alarm to our people.’ He stepped back, gesturing Kess into his office. ‘Your escort can wait out here.’

‘If it’s all the same to you, Custodian, I would prefer them to remain with me.’

Drazen looked even more annoyed than before – eyebrows pinched together he looked on the verge of refusing.

Kess returned his gaze, refusing to back down.

‘Very well,’ he sighed, as if the matter was of no import to him.

Thrain went through the doorway first, passing by the Custodian without a glance. After a moment, she felt Miah prod her in the back to start walking. Thrain stood on the far side of Drazen’s office, where he watched them enter.

She stood behind one of the chairs not willing to push the Custodian too far by sitting before being invited. A glance behind showed Miah to her left where she was clearly guarding the doorway. The sentry positions within the room suggested they expected trouble, even here. Or maybe especially here.

The Custodian was clearly out of sorts but with a demon entry into the Haven, something that wasn’t even supposed to be possible, she guessed he had a right to be unsettled.

It was lucky she, and not one of the other Chroniclers had come upon it. She shuddered to think how many the hells spawn would have killed if it had made it to one of the common areas or dormitories before the Guardians had located and dispatched it.

Drazen glanced at the warriors but spoke instead to Kess who seated herself, at his inclined hand, in the all too familiar chair opposite his. His fingers ran down the length of his moustache meeting at the point of his chin abstractedly. 'I have asked you here to find out what happened last night.'

'Have you not been briefed by the Guardians?' she asked innocently. Normally she wouldn't be so insolent with her superiors but his attitude towards Miah and Thrain annoyed her.

'They have told me a version of events, that is true. But I wish to hear from you what happened.' His tone seemed perfectly relaxed, but his eyes kept returning to the warriors, betraying his unease.

She launched into a highly modified version as per Miah's instructions. 'So as you can see, Custodian,' she summed up, 'it was only due to the diligence of the Guardians that the demon was extirpated, and I escaped with only minor injuries.' She raised her bandaged arm to emphasise her point.

Drazen had remained silent throughout her narration bridging his fingers together in front of him as he listened. He continued to stare at her, even after she had finished, as if trying to sift truth from fabrication. 'That is a similar account to the Guardians. Very similar.'

Once upon a time, that stare would have had her willing to confess to anything, yet compared to Thrain's everyday withering countenance, the Custodian's lowered brow and pursed thin lips, made him look like a pouting child. A small smile passed her lips before she smoothed it.

'Is something amusing, Chronicler?'

Kess shook her head. 'Our versions are similar because that's what happened.'

'Of course.' His tone clearly conveyed his doubt.

A timid knock sounded at the door. 'Yes?' Annoyance laced Drazen's voice.

The mousy secretary entered, looking as if it were the last thing she wanted to do. Heading straight for the desk, her eyes flitted nervously towards Miah whom she gave a wide birth.

The Guardian sneered which caused the mouse to walk even faster, and as soon as she handed a folded note to the Custodian she fled.

Drazen unfolded the paper leisurely, ignoring them completely.

Kess watched his eyes scan back and forward reading the short note. Before he was halfway through his eyes widened, with surprise or alarm, she wasn't sure, but whatever it was, he reread the note before folding it again and placing it on his desk in front of him.

'Your mother is Anna Grayson?' His dark beady eyes watched her intently.

She tried to school her features carefully blank even though tears threatened and her heart felt like it was about to pound out of her chest. 'Yes.'

Miah had spoken to her about this on their way here and regardless of whatever he said, she was to respond with ignorance.

'Is she alright?' She concentrated on Drazen's face, on the deep frown lines forming around his mouth, and tried to ignore the prickling in her eyes.

'I have just had a note from one of the administrators within Saint Anne's Hospital.' His fingers touched the note pushing it idly back and forward. 'It appears that your mother has disappeared.'

'What do you mean disappeared? She is in a secure ward.' She made her voice cold, proud that it only trembled slightly.

'The staff have been unable to locate her during their nightly rounds.' He leant forwards putting his weight on his elbows. 'When did you see her last?'

'Yesterday,' she replied stiffly, glancing at her watch noting the early hour.

'Ah yes, how was she during your visit?'

'Agitated.' She kept her answers as short and as close to the truth as possible, so she didn't confuse herself with fabrications.

'The staff are searching the hospital and its grounds,' Drazen turned to Thrain. 'Guardian, even though it's unlikely she has entered the Haven, inform your patrols to search for the missing woman. Chronicler Grayson can provide her description. Advise them she may be *agitated*,' he said mimicking her choice of words, though it came across as mocking.

'Custodian, I request that I be kept informed of what you find.' Even though the Guardians had told her that her mother had been killed – consumed by the demon – Kess couldn't suppress the glimmer of hope, deep within her, that she may still be found.

'Should she be located we will of course let you know,' Drazen replied smoothly. 'Now,' he said, clearly changing the subject, 'we do not want word of what happened here to spread. It would cause undue panic to those not only of Athenaeum but the other Havens as well. It is unfortunate that this happened now when the Quaternary Council is meeting, but I can not undo what has been done. I can however control it. You will not mention this incident to anyone.'

'I won't tell anyone.' Annoyance crept into her voice. 'But what about the others who already know?' Kess couldn't imagine the Weasel keeping quiet about something like this.

Drazen waved his hand dismissively. 'They have agreed that silence is the best option.'

'What have the Delegation been told?' Thrain questioned.

'Nothing at this stage,' the Custodian replied without looking at the warrior.

'I trust that you and your fellow Guardians can be trusted to keep silent?'

Thrain levelled the Custodian with a hard glare. 'Of course.'

Kess didn't bother to hide the yawn which had her eyes watering. 'If that's all the questions you have for me, Custodian, I request your leave. It's been a long night, and I haven't yet slept.' Not waiting for his response she stood, taking care not to move her injured arm too much.

Just before she reached the door, it flew open and a stern–faced woman stormed into the office. Everything about her screamed structure and order, from the straight impeccably groomed bob haircut, and the defined angles of her face which stored no extra flesh, to the navy–blue pant suit which even at this time of morning was neat and wrinkle–free.

Giving the Guardians and herself no more than a cursory glance she strode up to Drazen's desk standing in the place Kess had just vacated and thumped her fists onto the solid timber surface. 'You thought you could conceal a demon attack from the Consilium?'

Annoyance flashed in Drazen's eyes at the woman's words, before he carefully concealed it. 'You are excused Initiate.'

Kess followed Miah out the door but not before she heard his reply. 'Considering the hour, Seren, I decided to gather the information first so that I was well briefed when I informed the Council at a more reasonable hour.'

'*More reasonable* hour!' she hissed. 'A demon enters our haven. A demon! And you dither about!'

Drazen's reply was lost as they passed by the secretary, but Kess couldn't help but wonder why the Custodian was obviously trying to hide the incident from the other Council members.

She caught Miah's look of disdain as they passed by the meek woman, who kept her nose buried in the papers on her desk, avoiding looking in their direction at all. Kess didn't wonder at her reaction; the timid mousy Chronicler was the very antithesis of everything the brunette warrior stood for.

Thrain exited the doorway first, clearing the way.

'Why would Drazen not inform the other three members of the Consilium?' she asked as soon as they were outside the office.

'That is a very good question,' Thrain sounded troubled. He turned and looked at her speculatively, like he was seeing her for the first time. 'Chroniclers don't usually have any gumption about them. Maybe we are rubbing off on you.' A twitch of a smile ghosted his lips before it was gone, back to his stony countenance.

Kess blinked, stunned. By the Angels! Was that a compliment from Thrain?

Miah stopped outside her door while Thrain continued to the exit. She peered into Kess's eyes. 'Get some sleep, you'll need it.'

Kess nodded, then looked sharply at the woman. 'What do you mean?'

'Don't think the matter with the Custodian is finished.'

She opened her mouth, determined to get some answers, however Miah forestalled her with a raised hand. 'We will talk more tomorrow. Right now, you need sleep more than answers.'

Another yawn brought tears to her stinging fatigued eyes. 'Perhaps you're right.'

'Of course I am,' Miah said straight–faced. 'Someone will meet you here tomorrow to bring you to Aldoak. No wandering about by yourself,' the Guardian emphasised, ensuring Kess couldn't misunderstand.

'Do you think there will be more demons?' She lowered her voice so her words wouldn't carry along the hallway.

'Just a precaution,' Miah said carefully. 'But make sure you always have that knife of yours handy, just in case.'

Despite her fatigue, curiosity burned as always within Kess and unable to help herself she opened her mouth to ask what the "just in case" could refer to.

The warrior cut her off again with a held–up hand. 'Off you go and lock the door behind you.'

Only after she had slid the bolt home in the lock, did she hear the tread of Miah's footsteps disappearing after Thrain.

Exhausted, she collapsed on her bed and fell straight asleep.

CHAPTER 9

The Death of Hope

Awareness returned to Kess, slowly.

She was lying on her stomach, with one arm dangling over the side of the bed, and a terrible crick in her neck. She peered about her room through slitted eyes, which burnt with the dry sting that came from lack of sleep, and would happily have remained in bed, until her gaze fell on the open photo album on the ground.

She flung back the covers, and scrambled over to the book, pulling it onto her lap. Kess stared at the auburn–haired woman – her mother – and closed her eyes against the barrage of memories which flooded back.

The darkness of the night. The stench of something foul. Her mother disappearing in a cloud of black.

She raised a hand to wipe the tears from her cheeks and hissed, the movement pulling on the wound she'd forgotten all about.

'Kess, are you alright?' The voice was a man's, but muffled through the door she couldn't tell who it was.

Combing her hands through her hair she opened the door and found a grinning red–haired Guardian lounging in her doorway. 'Conall! What are you doing here?'

'Miah sent me,' he said simply, as if that explained it all. It probably did. If she told him to do something he would, no questions asked.

'Give me a moment?' Without waiting for a reply she shut the door and ripped off the wrinkled clothes she'd slept in, exchanging them for fresh ones. Walking to her small ensuite, she tied her hair back, and splashed some water on her face. Then with a hurried brush of her teeth, she rejoined her Guardian, who immediately led her out of the building.

At Aldoak they were met at the door by Kisho who led them to the room she'd been taken to the night before. With a one–eyed wink Conall continued walking down the hall, leaving the two of them to enter alone.

'How are you?' The warrior scanned her from head to toe with his sharp gaze.

'Alright.' His sceptical look made her continue, 'Tired. Sore,' she said lifting her arm.

His gaze lingered on the bandage as he nodded. 'We are to wait here.' He waited for her to sit before dragging one of the chairs back, tilting the chair back as he eased his long legs onto the table.

'Kisho–' The words died on her lips as he glanced at her, losing her nerve to ask about the demon they said killed her mother. 'Where's your WC?' she finished lamely.

'Down the hall on your right.'

Kess had only taken a few steps out of the room when she realised there was more than one door on the right. 'By the Angels,' she muttered.

Which one should she try? She could imagine the reception she'd receive if she barged into a room full of Guardians.

She walked to the first door and gingerly tried the knob, locked. She glanced around, looking back towards where she'd come from.

Keep looking or go back?

The second door, only a few metres away looked slightly ajar so she padded towards it.

'Do you think she's telling us the truth?' Thrain's distinctive voice was hard, as uncompromising as he was.

She froze, fingertips millimetres from the door knob. Taking a careful step back, she was about to walk on – not wanting to be caught eavesdropping – when a very familiar voice spoke.

'We have no reason to doubt her,' Miah said. 'Besides, a demon was killed, if she didn't do that, then who did?'

No doubt as to who they were speaking about. Kess hesitated knowing she shouldn't listen, but, unable to help herself, leaned closer.

'Exactly.' The commanders tone was troubled.

'I believe her. She has such an aptitude with training that did I not know better, I would think her warrior born. I think her capable of killing that creature.'

'She does show too much spirit to be one of those tedious Chroniclers,' he conceded. 'So was she the target, or did she just happen upon the Rask?'

'The use of her mother suggests she was the target.' Worry laced Miah's voice.

'What could the Chronicler possibly know that's important enough to risk sending a demon here?' Thrain's harsh tone left little doubt that he believed she could know anything of any importance.

'What makes you think she knows something?'

'It spoke to her, Miah. A Rask! You know as well as I, they are mindless trackers. Lower dominion demons don't speak. That an upper dominion was sent here is worrying.'

Kess knew that if stone cold Thrain was worried, she should be terrified.

Why would a demon be after her?

'No more worrying than how that demon came to be within Athenaeum in the first place, or, of even more concern, was it assisted?'

'Anna Grayson's life force granted it access to our plane, but still wouldn't have given it leave to enter the Haven originally,' Miah said thoughtfully. 'We have to assume that someone within Athenaeum helped the demon to get in. Have you checked the Obiex?'

'I looked upon the stone this morning and it seems fine but I'm no expert.' Thrain's voice became tight with annoyance. 'I spoke with the Chroniclers in charge of its upkeep and they admitted there were fluctuations earlier in the evening, but when it settled they thought no more of it. They didn't even bother to tell anyone about it.' Frustration tinged his voice. 'That is if they're telling us the truth. For all we know it could have been one of them that sabotaged the Obiex long enough for the hells spawn to enter.'

Kess had heard enough. *They believed someone within Athenaeum was assisting demons? Who could do such a thing? And why?* She crept away from the doorway retracing her footsteps and ran into Kisho.

'Ah I was just coming to look for you, thought you may have gotten lost.'

She gave him a tight–lipped smile, unable to summon more. *If the demon truly had been after her it had failed, but would there be more?*

Kisho led her back to the small room. 'Miah and Thrain will be along shortly.' He lounged in one of the chairs, giving the appearance of nonchalance – only his frequent glances towards the door gave lie to his charade.

Kess nodded and took a seat opposite him, glad she had walked away when she did. If Thrain had caught her listening he would likely have ordered her thrown out of Aldoak and told never to come back, regardless of the possibility of further demon attack.

Though this was her second time in the room she hadn't taken much notice last night, she looked around now not feeling like making idle chit chat. The room was small with only the chairs and the table they sat at for furnishings, so it didn't occupy her mind for long. She glanced at her companion, who even with his eyes closed, still looked ready to leap to action.

Warrior born. Miah had said. *Was that how warriors were chosen, through lineage lines?* Kisho, with his topknot hair style could have walked out of an old samurai movie. *Was he descended from those ancient warriors? Had they been Guardians as well?*

Kisho's eyes slitted open feeling her stare, but after reassuring himself she was fine, closed them again.

Uncomfortable at being caught staring and with nothing else to look at, her gaze fell to her hands folded across her lap. But after several yawns which left her blinking away watery eyes she slouched back in the chair and closed her eyes.

Kess let her thoughts drift unfocused, until she realised what she could feel – a bubble – the best word she could think of to describe it – in her head, sitting just above her left ear. Her fingers probed the area feeling skin and hair but nothing else. The “bubble” was inside her mind.

But that was impossible.

Maybe she had hit her head and was concussed, or she had a tumour causing her to hallucinate things. Or maybe it was all in her head, and she was going crazy, just like her Mother.

‘Kess?’

She opened her eyes to find the dark–haired warrior looking at her with concern. She raised her eyebrows questioningly.

‘Are you alright?’ Kisho asked.

‘Just tired I guess.’

‘As long as it’s just that.’ His dark eyes strayed to the table for a moment before looking back at her. ‘I know you don’t know me very well, but you can trust me enough to talk to, if there ever is anything.’

‘I thought we were more than strangers now. Or am I still just another Chronicler to you?’ she asked with a smile, knowing how much of an insult that was amongst the Guardians – even though the cause of the enmity between the groups was still a mystery to her.

There was the obvious contempt from Chroniclers in authority like Drazen, and cautious worry, or even fear from those in the lower ranks.

The Guardians however, no matter their rank, showed only cool disdain. Yet she also knew that if a Chronicler was in trouble a warrior would not hesitate to defend them, with their life in need be.

Strange didn’t begin to cover it.

Kisho opened his mouth to respond when Miah strode into the room, with a serious look in her eyes making her way straight towards Kess who jumped to her feet.

‘A patrol found something that we believe to be your mother’s.’ She pulled a piece of fabric from one of the pockets in her pants.

Kess’s wonder of how she fit anything into those pockets was forgotten as she realised what it was the warrior held.

A shredded bit of tan cloth.

The same material as her mother's hospital outfit.

The scrap was in her hand before she realised she'd taken it. She held it up in front of her, peering at it closely, as if somehow the bit of material could give her some clue, confirmation that her mother was still out there somewhere. Looking at it this close Kess saw a discolouration she hadn't noticed before, visible now in the light.

It was flecked with hundreds of tiny red dots.

She dropped the fabric as if were a deadly adder.

Blood.

It was covered in thousands of minuscule droplets of her mother's blood.

She clenched her jaw, choking off the sob rising in the back of her throat. Even though she had seen it with her own eyes, she had still hoped that somehow her mother would be found.

Pain rose within her until she felt like she was drowning in it.

Miah stepped forward and placed a hand on her arm, squeezing it gently. It was a small gesture but gave Kess the platform she needed to compose herself.

'I know you told me she was gone, but I hoped–'

'I understand, Kess.'

'Where did you find this?' She already knew the answer to her question but needed to know for sure.

'It was found near where you killed the Rask,' Thrain said as he stepped into the room, folding his muscled arms about his chest. The gesture made him appear even more imposing than usual. 'When the Custodian informs you of this, you must act surprised.' His eyes tightened in frustration when he saw she wasn't following. 'No one knows of your – association with us. If they realise we have already told you, it would seem unusual and you could be watched.'

Though he did not say it Kess knew he was talking about Drazen and felt like a fool for not realising sooner. Well it wouldn't be too hard to act distraught. She nodded her agreement, not surprised when she didn't get a response from the commander.

‘There is something else we have to ask you about.’ Miah took a seat opposite her and leant forward across the table, watching her intently. ‘You said that the demon asked where “He” was, and that you had no idea who it meant.’ She paused as Kess nodded. ‘What males have you had contact with over the last week?’

The question came as a surprise, she hesitated, thinking. ‘Well, there are you two,’ she nodded to Kisho and Thrain. ‘Conall. Samael was at the gate yesterday when I left. Captol Wessler who oversaw my work this week. Custodian Drazen. I think that’s it.’ She paused, reviewing the last few days. ‘There was also a boy who took me to the Custodian’s office. I don’t know his name though.’

‘No one else?’ Miah pressed.

Kess hesitated. ‘There was one other man.’ The reluctance in her voice, focused the Guardians attention, like hounds with the scent of their quarry. ‘I couldn’t sleep the other night so I went for a walk to the bridge. I had only been there a few minutes when a man appeared, telling me that it wasn’t safe to be outside. He walked me back to my building.’

‘Who was he?’ Kisho asked.

At the same time Thrain said, ‘What did he mean it wasn’t safe?’

‘I don’t know.’ She shrugged her shoulders, answering Thrain first, then looked at Kisho. ‘I’ve never seen him before, I assumed he must be part of the delegation.’

‘The others are easy enough to find. We will need a description of your mystery man,’ Miah said raising her eyebrows.

As an image of him appeared in her mind, the bubble in her head seemed to pulse in response to her thoughts. She gave her description then looked up as movement near the doorway caught her eye.

A young Guardian she hadn’t met before stood waiting for Miah to notice him. ‘What is it, Lucan?’ she asked, eyes never leaving Kess.

His gaze shifted from his superior, to her, then back again. ‘There are Chroniclers at the door. They said Chronicler Grayson,’ again a glance in her direction with slight uplifting of his brow, ‘is summoned to the Custodian’s office.’

‘How do they know I’m here?’

'You were followed.' Miah looked at Thrain, gaze hard. 'Conall!' she growled, all but grinding her teeth.

'What do I say if the Custodian asks why I was here?'

'We were questioning you again about the nights events.' Thrain spoke slowly like he was addressing a simpleton. Maybe he was. She hadn't portrayed herself as having a particularly keen intellect around him.

She nodded, then said softly. 'And so it begins again.'

'Indeed it does, Chronicler,' Thrain answered, sounding as if he was talking about more than just the meeting with the Custodian.

~

Kess entered the Custodian's chamber flanked by the two Guardians.

Drazen's mouth pulled into a tight line when he saw them but he didn't argue this time. He focused his gaze on her instead, as if by the sheer will of ignoring the warriors they would cease to exist. 'Chronicler Grayson, we have more information about your mother's disappearance.'

Kess gripped the back of the chair tightly, indenting the soft leather with crescent shapes from her nails, as she fought to blink back the tears which blurred her vision.

'As you know your mother disappeared from her room last night. We have questioned the nurses on call however none saw her leave. There was something in her room however.' Drazen sounded uncharacteristically hesitant. 'Blood was found in her bed and there were scratches gouged into the wood near her window. It appears as though your mother was a casualty of the demon just like yourself.' Drazen continued unmindful of the effect of his words. 'We will send word to your father of course.'

'What? You'll phone him to tell him my mother, his wife, is dead.' Kess's throat constricted but she forged on. 'I will tell him.'

'Of course. I will give you some time.' Drazen stood, pushing a black phone from his desk in her direction.

Kess stared at the phone uncomprehending for a moment. 'I'm not telling him like that.' Her voice rose with building anger. 'I will tell him in person.'

'Young Chroniclers rarely leave the Haven,' Drazen replied. Standing behind his desk he placed both hands on its dark polished surface, leaning towards her as he spoke.

'I have been given permission to visit the hospital.'

'That was different,' Drazen spoke carefully, enunciating each word.

A voice spoke from behind her. 'I think an exemption can be made in this case,' Thrain said.

'Do you, warrior? Need I remind you whose duty it is to keep Athenaeum, and all those who dwell within it safe?'

Thrain stepped forward, level now with Kess. Though his voice remained stony calm, Drazen flinched away from him. 'We are charged to protect Athenaeum, with our lives if need be. We do not take that responsibility lightly. The Haven's defences are not easily breached, especially from outside. Inside however–' his statement hung between them like a bared blade.

Kess watched as a wave of red rose up the Custodian's throat settling high in his cheeks. A strangled sound emerged from his open mouth before he composed himself. 'Do you suggest an occupant of Athenaeum is responsible?' Drazen's voice whipped around the room.

Thrain's expression remained unchanged at the Custodians anger. 'Merely stating fact,' he responded calmly.

Kess spoke drawing their attention before the tension in the room grew worse. 'I am requesting permission to travel to London to see my father.' She petitioned, chagrined about the need to ask so submissively.

As she had hoped Drazen's attention focused on her, forgetting Thrain for the moment. His dark blue eyes watched her, calculating, then with a slight shake of his head he spoke. 'I'm sorry–'

'Forgive my interruption, Custodian,' Miah interjected. 'I will accompany Chronicler Grayson on her journey. The presence of a warrior would surely allay any fears you have for her safety.'

‘That is an unusual request but it is a big world out there with many dangers. I fear one Guardian, however competent,’ he added when he saw Miah bristle, ‘would not be enough.’

‘Then she will be sent with more,’ Thrain stated.

‘Surely your energies would be better served protecting the Haven.’ Drazen, clearly losing ground was unwilling to give in so easily.

‘We will be protecting one of Athenaeum.’

Drazen looked from Thrain’s stoic calm; to Miah, who met his glance challengingly, and sighed as his gaze returned to Kess. ‘You may go.’ He turned to Thrain. ‘I trust you will ensure both the Chronicler, and our Haven are adequately protected during this time.’

‘Of course,’ Thrain replied in a voice hard enough to chip ice.

Drazen nodded then turned his attention to a stack of papers on his desk, ending their audience.

As soon as they were out into the hallway Thrain turned to Kess. ‘It’s too late to leave today. We will meet you outside your building at sunrise. Pack light.’

CHAPTER 10

A Long Drop

Kess jolted awake and saw not the familiar walls of her room, but the clear star filled night sky. Her hair cavorted madly about her, stinging her eyes and the soft skin of her cheeks. Confused she looked around trying to figure out where she was, for she was surely not in her bed where she had gone to sleep.

She let out a cry as she realised she was standing on the roof of the tower, one foot raised ready to step out into the air. The wind gusted around her whipping her clothes forward.

Kess wobbled, arms whirling frantically as she tried to right herself as the wind blew up again, and a strong gust tried to tear her from the ledge. She fought to balance herself against the wind which seemed bent on tumbling her over.

The breeze died briefly allowing her the seconds she needed to right herself, but came back with such a vengeance that she was almost blown straight off again. Her heart stuttered, as she realised the next gust would likely tip her over.

Then just as her balance failed and she looked set to tumble that long, long way down, Kess felt herself pulled backwards away from the four–storey drop.

The air whooshed from her lungs as she thudded against the ground.

When she tried to move she found herself restrained by a set of arms holding her firmly around the waist. Kess twisted her head around trying to see her rescuer and saw a mop of bright red hair. 'Conall?'

At the sound of her voice he relaxed his grip, letting her crawl off him. She sat by his feet not wanting to test her legs further just yet, for they felt as wobbly as jelly.

'Are you alright, Kess?' He sat up mimicking her pose, his light blue eyes usually so full of mischief now held only concern. 'I know things have been rough lately but that–' he indicated the drop, 'is not the answer.'

'What?' It took her a moment to catch up, but when she finally did, she wasn't sure whether to be angry or embarrassed. 'Satan's breath! I didn't try to kill myself,' she cursed, almost laughing at the look of surprise on his face. 'I woke up on the edge about to walk off!' She paused as the reality of the situation hit her.

What if she did it again?

Kess didn't realise she had spoken aloud until Conall answered her.

'I'm sure it won't happen again. It's probably because of everything that's happened in the last few days.' He looked at her closely. 'You really didn't know what was going on, did you?'

She shook her head, embarrassed by the tears which had sprung into her eyes. 'How did you get to me in time?'

'I didn't know if I would,' he said softly. 'By the Angels, Kess, you certainly know how to liven up a boring night patrol!'

She smiled briefly knowing he was trying to make light of the situation regardless of the unanswered questions which filled his eyes.

'How did you know to look up?'

'Guardians watch everything. From whence you least expect danger, from thence it comes.' He spoke sarcastically, yet the words held a roteness to them, like a lesson learnt over and over again.

'Thanks, Thrain,' she mocked dryly, earning a small chuckle from the warrior.

'Saving a fair damsel in distress – all part of a night's work,' he said, adding his trademark wink. Looking around the rooftop, his levity faded. 'Seriously though, has this ever happened before?'

‘Waking up just about to take a swan dive off a four–storey tower? Yeah all the time.’ She regretted her sarcasm as she saw his obvious concern. ‘No, never. I’ll be afraid to go to sleep now,’ she said softly.

‘We should tell Miah or Thrain. They might know something.’

‘There’s nothing to know, Conall. Just sleepwalking,’

His ginger eyebrows rose, and a frown formed, looking out of place on his usually jovial face.

‘Of the extreme kind,’ she conceded. ‘Please don’t tell anyone. I don’t want them to change their minds about London.’ She tried to give him her most sincere smile, which wilted under his intense look.

‘I don’t like it Kess. But I will keep silent. If it happens again though, you have to tell them. Or I will,’ he added, obviously seeing something rebellious in her face.

She nodded, praying to the Angels that it never would. She may not be lucky enough to have a Guardian there next time. As her breathing returned to normal, the adrenaline fuelled heat which had warmed her body faded, allowing the cold night air to seep into her bones. Kess shivered rubbing her arms where goose bumps had risen.

‘Right. Time to get you back safely indoors, we’ll be leaving soon.’ Standing he extended his hand helping Kess to her feet.

Kess’s rubbery limbs had firmed allowing her to stand, and although she felt a bit wobbly still, they headed for the stairs. ‘You’re coming?’ She hadn’t put much thought into who would come, but she had assumed it would be just Miah and Thrain.

At his nod Kess asked the next most obvious question. ‘Won’t you be tired after being up all night?’

‘I only started shift a few hours ago, so I’ll be fine,’ Conall’s gaze lingered on her thoughtfully.

‘What is it?’

‘You are not like other Chroniclers. They wouldn’t care about a Guardian. Most try not to notice us.’

‘I’ll take that as a compliment.’

‘It is,’ Conall said softly.

‘What is it between Guardians and Chroniclers? Shouldn’t we all try to work together?’

‘Long ago, we did.’ His tone was wistful, and for a moment his voice sounded like it belonged to someone else; like an elderly person pining for the grand old days when everything cost a pittance.

Kess looked into Conall’s eyes and saw an agelessness there, which she recognised from other Guardians gazes, but had failed to connect. It was the look of someone who had seen too much for their years.

Curiosity burned within Kess. Nothing like that had ever been mentioned in her training, nor in any of the books she’d read. She knew her best chance of getting answers would be from Conall who was happy to chat with her, yet as she was about to ask they reached the main door to the living quarters, and realised her questions would have to wait. This was not a conversation to have where other ears could listen in.

They walked the short distance to her room in silence. When they got to her door, Kess paused. ‘Thank you, Conall,’ she leant in and gave him a quick kiss on the cheek.

Much to her surprise, his cheeks flamed with colour making his freckles stand out even more than usual. He muttered goodnight, and took off down the hall, nearly running in his haste to get away.

Before Kess shut her door, she saw Conall touch his cheek where she’d kissed him.

Smiling softly to herself, she closed the door bolting it firmly behind her. She looked at the easy to remove latch. Perhaps she needed a deadbolt to lock herself in each night, in case she wandered about in her sleep again. That request though would raise a few eyebrows.

Life, was not simple any more, if it ever had been.

CHAPTER 11

Departure

Their departure from Athenaeum was made quietly, lacking any fanfare, and without the knowledge of any, except the Guardian at the gate who let the five through without question. Thrain nodded to Samael, who returned the gesture immediately.

As they rounded the bend, he disappeared from sight, leaving only the memory of the concern she saw in his gaze. Not for her surely. But the fact that the commander and sub–commander were leaving the Haven together which, she gathered, was a rare occurrence.

Considering the commanders dislike for her she had been surprised when he had shown up with the other Guardians this morning. *Why had he decided to accompany them? Was it just because of how much it would annoy Custodian Drazen? Or was it something else?*

Though the days were cooling with the coming winter Kess soon broke out in a sweat at the fast pace Thrain set. She shifted the pack which had started to dig into her shoulders, and wiped the moisture from her forehead with her arm, wincing at the pressure to both the bruising under her eye – which had turned a lovely mottled purple – and her arm, which was still puffy and sore. She tried to concentrate on the pack in front of her, rather than the niggling aches in her body.

Each of the Guardians had a black pack strapped to their backs and carried a matching duffel bag in one hand, which she assumed held their larger weapons; which were conspicuously missing, though she was sure they still had an arsenal concealed about their bodies.

They came out along the same road as Saint Anne's hospital, but thankfully turned right heading away from it. Sticking to the main road, they reached Merrowley, a small town nearby within minutes. Though not encouraged, young Chroniclers were allowed to visit their families on occasion. However due to the secret nature of Athenaeum, and the other Havens, they had pick up points, like in this town, from where they could be collected.

The group headed towards the train station where Kisho lined up and bought tickets. Kess couldn't quite get used to seeing the Guardians in ordinary clothes, doing ordinary things. She had never seen them in anything other than their leathers and had assumed they didn't own any other clothes, especially not the trendy, skin tight jeans, knee high boots and v–neck top Miah had turned up in.

Yet no matter how they dressed, nothing could hide the air of readiness they held around them, nor their dangerous feline grace.

Within minutes of Kisho handing out the tickets a sleek bodied train ground to a halt with a whoosh of air. Conall broke away from the warriors who upon their arrival at the station had formed a ring about her, centring her safely in the middle, and set off down the platform passing several carriages before he stopped and waved them down.

Miah grabbed hold of the back of Kess's elbow, guiding her forwards, and didn't let go until they were in the centre of the empty carriage, gesturing Kess into one of the more spacious seats where the rows faced each other. She sat down opposite Kess, no doubt to give her the room to move should she need it.

Thrain sat lengthways across a seat, at the far end of the carriage, within easy access of the rear door. Although resting his back against the window, she had no doubt that he could be on his feet and engaging a potential enemy, before she even realised there was a threat.

Kisho positioned himself similarly at the other end, leaving Conall to sit opposite the side door they'd entered, where he could watch anyone getting on.

Each kept the backpack they were wearing strapped to their shoulders, despite the discomfort they must have felt.

A small smile found its way to her lips. If she got onto this carriage, and saw the four of them, she'd back straight out again. Despite their apparent ease, there was an obvious danger to the tetrad.

‘So the train?’ Kess queried Miah, as they lurched forwards and the station fell behind them.

‘The Custodian, in his omniscience, deemed this not important enough to warrant the use of one of Athenaeum’s vehicles.’ The thick disapproval in the warrior’s voice wasn’t hard to miss.

‘Don’t Guardians have their own vehicles?’ Kess asked, taken aback by Drazen’s bizarre refusal.

‘Several of our smaller transports wouldn’t mysteriously start last night.’ Miah gave her a measured look. ‘Apparently someone didn’t want you leaving the Haven, and went to some trouble to try to stop you.’

‘Why would anyone do that?’ Kess asked bewildered.

‘*That* is a very good question.’ The warrior settled back and looked out the window, ending their conversation.

Though she fought it, the rocking motion of the train, and the lack of sleep caught up on Kess, and unable to keep her eyes open, she dozed, and dreamt.

The wind whistled past her ears numbing her face with its icy fingers. Enveloped in white, she was unable to see anything through the thick cloud as it swirled around her.

Pain flared between her shoulder blades, as intensely as if her back was on fire.

A torrent of biting sadness choked her, strangulating her heart with its intensity. If she were able, she would have screamed until hoarse from its lurid torment.

Her face was dry, the tears she shed, ripped away before they could moisten her cheeks.

She fell, for what seemed time immeasurable. Then the clouds parted, giving her the first glimpse of the land below.

She closed her eyes, and opened her arms, ready to embrace the Earth.

Kess woke with a start, flinching with the expected impact, as Miah's hand touched her shoulder.

'We're here,' the warrior murmured softly.

Disorientated, Kess sat up from where she had curled up on the seat and looked around. The vividness of the dream clung to her, and the shakiness that coursed through her limbs was very familiar.

She'd had this dream many times before, over the past few months, but this was the first time she had actually remembered it.

As Kess stood, trying to rid herself of the feeling of falling, the train pulled to a lurching halt into a white tiled station. She flung out her hands, gripping the seat in front of her to stop herself stumbling.

The warriors rose silently around her, and as she entered the narrow walkway, Miah pushed her gently into their midst, so once again she was protected on all sides.

A loud recorded voice boomed 'Mind the gap' beside her, as the quartet of Guardians moved towards the exit, as the doors whooshed open.

As Kess stepped down onto the platform she saw the iconic London tube logo, the red circle, black rectangle, and bold white writing declaring the station name – 'Camden Town'.

She was home.

~

Kess stood on the street outside of the coffee shop, ignoring the press of people around her. Miah, who had volunteered to stay with her while the other warriors patrolled, gave a snort of amusement.

'What?'

'Your father has a sense of humour,' Miah said, a small smile gracing her lips.

Kess looked at her quizzically.

'The name of the shop, 'Hermitage', it means Haven,' Miah explained.

Kess had always thought it a strange title for a coffee shop. Trust her father to name his business after the one place where his wife and daughter were the safest.

'Go on,' Miah urged, giving her a gentle prod in the middle of the back. 'You can't stand out here all afternoon.'

'I'm not – not going in. I'm just–'

'Stalling.'

With a roll of her eyes, that she was careful not to let the warrior see, Kess opened the door, sending a little bell jingling.

The room was just as she remembered from her visit last year, cosy arm chairs dotted the room interspersed with more traditional cafe chairs, whilst scattered lamps provided a warm light. A delicious smell of roasted coffee beans permeated the air welcoming you as soon as you stepped foot inside.

The young blonde–haired woman behind the counter looked up as the portly bald man she'd finished serving moved away, coffee mug in hand, paper tucked under his arm.

The smile on her face faltered.

'Kess,' the girl said stiffly, a hint of question in the word. Anything else she may have said was forestalled as her attention was drawn over Kess's shoulder.

She didn't bother to turn, knowing who had drawn her sister's attention. 'Jinnah this is Miah. Miah meet my little sister.'

'Greetings Jinnah, sister of Kess,' Miah stated formally.

'Well do I get a hug?' Kess asked, drawing Jinnah's stare from the warrior. Though not dressed in her leathers, Miah had an air about her that her little sister obviously found imposing.

Kess met the petite blonde at the end of the counter, and drew her sister into her arms. 'Haircut looks good,' she said, ruffling her short blonde style.

'Hey.' Jinnah's green eyes, much lighter than her own, flashed angrily as she pulled her head back out of touching distance.

‘Sorry,’ Kess said, puzzled, as she noticed the tightness around Jinnah’s pursed lips, the stiff way she held herself.

‘Are you al–’ Kess was interrupted from quizzing her sister, when she heard the clomping of footsteps down the stairs and saw her father’s silhouette in the bright doorway.

‘Kess?’ Surprised delight filled his voice.

Kess rounded the counter and flew into his arms. ‘Dad!’

As he encircled her his warm, lovingly tight embrace she smiled, feeling like a little girl again. Though grey was starting to tinge his hair, he was the same, that steady constant force that had always been there for her.

He loosened his grip and pulled back slightly, looking his daughter over.

‘What happened to you?’ He looked at her eye with concern. ‘Are you alright? You don’t usually visit at this time of year.’ His gaze flicked to Miah and she felt his muscles tighten, ‘and with a – friend,’ he finished stiffly.

She ignored the question about her eye for the moment not wanting to start that conversation here in the middle of the coffee shop. ‘Dad – Miah, Miah – Robert.’

The warrior had placed herself against the wall, no doubt so she could keep an eye on the whole room without anyone sneaking up behind her. ‘Greetings Robert, father of Kess.’

Robert nodded offhandedly as he turned back to her. ‘What is *she* doing here? Are you in some kind of trouble?’ A crease formed between his brows as he searched her face for an answer. He obviously knew who Miah was, just not what her role was in accompanying Kess – Protector or Jailer.

She felt her eyes sting but schooled herself with a deep breath before continuing. ‘I’m not here for a visit. I need to talk to you about something, but–’ she added, as her father started to turn away towards the back stairs which led to his overhead flat, ‘after you close today. Jinnah needs to be there too.’

The worried crease stayed on her father’s face as he nodded silently.

'Would you like a coffee?' Robert asked, accepting she wouldn't say anything more for now.

Kess looked to Miah, who returned her look levelly, but didn't respond one way or another. 'No, we should get back to the others.'

'Others? Kess, what is–'

'When the shop closes, Dad. It's only a few hours,' she said trying to calm the rising worry in her father's voice.

'We are here to protect your daughter should the need arise. Nothing more,' Miah said, as she padded quietly over, coming to stand at Kess's shoulder.

She knew that Miah was trying to help, but she could see from the deepening crease on her father's face, that the warrior had compounded his worry, not alleviated it. She could almost hear the questions compiling in his mind. *What kind of trouble was she in that she would need to be accompanied by Guardians? What couldn't she tell him now?*

'We'll come back later this afternoon, after you close,' Kess reassured him.

Her father gripped her in a hug again which he seemed reluctant to release her from. With one final squeeze, he stepped back. 'This afternoon?' he confirmed, touching the coloured skin at the side of her eye lightly.

She nodded then returned to Miah's side. 'See you, Jin.'

Instead of answering, the blonde turned to the coffee machine and banged the used coffee grounds from the portafilter.

Robert glanced at his youngest daughter, eyebrows lowered, looking ready to reprimand her, but stopped as he saw Kess shake her head.

As soon as they stepped out the coffee shop, the trio of Guardians materialised, as if by magic.

'Kess is to return later,' Miah told Thrain.

'What do we do now?' she asked.

'Now you follow us,' Miah said, striding away up the street.

The paths were crowded, yet they strode through unhindered as people moved out of the way of the warriors instinctively, seeing something in the group they wanted to avoid.

They walked a few blocks away from the busier, touristy end of Camden, towards Mornington Crescent. Not slowing her quick pace, the brunette warrior led them to the left as the street forked away from the tube station.

They had just passed Costa's, with its outdoor seating area full of people huddling over their coffees, when Miah stopped in front of what looked like a tall, dark brown fence.

On closer inspection Kess realised that it wasn't a fence but two giant double doors which she gathered could be opened from the inside. On each of the large doors there was a green 'emergency exit keep clear' sign.

Miah approached a tall narrow door, set within one of the larger double doors.

As Kess stepped closer, protected by a wall of Guardian males at her back, she saw that it wasn't a key that Miah was inserting, but a code, which she was pressing into a small keypad.

With a barely audible click the door opened and the warrior ushered them through.

The brunette warrior led them to the back of a brown brick building to another door with an identical electronic lock. Although the muddy brown timber door looked like it hadn't been used in years, it opened smoothly offering the warrior no resistance. Miah strode through hardly breaking pace, it was only moments before Kess heard her call out, 'All clear'.

Hesitantly she crossed the threshold into the dark interior and looked around the narrow corridor spying a familiar red brown brick. 'Was this a tube station?'

'It still is. We are in a section of Mornington Crescent tube that has been closed since the twenties.'

'Why was it shut?'

'A surveyor's report conducted after the end of world war two advised that the rock bed suffered substantial fractural instabilities during the Blitz bombings and as such the tunnels were deemed likely to collapse.' Miah informed her as they caught up to where she waited along the corridor.

'Looks like they were wrong,' Kess said glancing around the walls which looked as structurally sound as any tube station she had ever entered. 'Why weren't further reports done?'

'Several have been conducted over the years, and all have provided the same findings.'

'How is that possible?' Kess asked as they descended a short set of stairs, entering the familiar semi–circular shaped corridors, which many of the older stations still had.

Instead of the usual odour of the tube – *Eau de Commuter* – the tunnels smelt musty and somehow, abandoned.

'Oh.' Kess looked at a steel mesh door off to her right. 'Tell me that's not the way down!' She peered through the criss–crossed wire into the darkness of an old lift shaft.

'No, there are stairs, but you're welcome to try it if you like,' Kisho teased.

They continued along the domed corridor descending a stone staircase. Although many of the fixtures had been removed when the station had closed, the metal handrails, though aged, were still in place.

The stone beneath her feet had been worn smooth almost to the point of slipperiness from use over the years, and with the only illumination from a dim light at the base of the stairs, she trod carefully.

At the base of the stairs the corridor continued, though this section looked much older and darker, as if it had been disused for longer. Their footsteps bounced around the emptiness, multiplying the sound, making it seem like there was a crowd traipsing along the tunnel, instead of just the five of them.

Miah led her towards an open door a short distance away, and again entered without hesitation.

Kess paused, looking around in wonder at the cavernous space before her, which extended for about sixty yards in both directions. The circular roof reached high above her, with the arched corridor they'd just walked through visible nearly directly above her to the left.

Though the stairs remained, the area where the platform and lines once ran was now a flat open floor. Boxing bags and speed balls hung from frames close by, all worn from use.

'What is this place?'

'This is one of our refuges.' At her astonished look, Miah continued, 'We have hundreds of them, spread out over most of the continents.'

'But it's an abandoned tube line. Doesn't anyone ever come down here?' She could just imagine a railway inspectors shock expecting to find an abandoned tunnel and finding instead a wooden floored training room complete with residents.

'No,' Thrain said, in his usual brusque manner, not giving anything away.

'So this is where we're staying?'

'Cosy hey!' Conall laughed.

Kisho came to stand beside her. 'Don't listen to him, there's a kitchen, bathroom and rooms at the far end.'

'So what now?'

'Now we train,' Thrain gruffed. 'Let's see how much you remember.'

Kisho fitted pads to his hands, tightening the Velcro straps with his teeth. 'Left strike.' She punched the pad as forcefully as she could. 'Good. Right strike.' Again, she struck the pad. 'Left kick,' he swivelled the pad around to his right waist, then rotated it around to his left waiting for her next strike. He continued to rotate the pads around his body, expecting her to hit them quickly and accurately.

'Great.' He removed the pads and dropped them to the ground, kicking them out of his way.

Kess brought her hands to her hips, sucking in deeper breaths than earlier.

'Now you can move onto more advanced stuff,' he grinned, a devilish glint in his eyes. 'Turn around.'

Kisho grabbed her around the torso pinning her arms against her sides, pulling her up so only the tips of her toes touched the ground. 'What do you do now?' he asked, his breath ruffling the wisps of hair around her ear.

She wriggled but could barely breathe in his grasp, let alone move. 'Head–butt you.'

'Excellent! Should you ever be in this situation make sure you try to crack them in the nose. It will hurt like hell, blur their vision, and hopefully loosen their grip on you.'

Kess couldn't see when she would need to head–butt someone, but promised to remember.

'I think you're ready to progress sparring. Don't worry we'll take it slow,' Kisho said seeing her concerned look. 'Punches and blocks first.'

The samurai punched. Perhaps for him it was slow, but Kess was hard pushed trying to raise her arm in time to deflect the strike. Again and again she blocked, not having any opportunity to punch out herself, pressed as she was by his constant attack.

Her forearms ached by the time Kisho called a halt though she had noticed he had pulled his punches on her injured arm.

'Take a break,' he inclined his head, indicating something happening behind her. 'You might find this interesting.'

Miah and Thrain faced each other on another practise mat a few paces away. Even as Kess turned they exploded into movement.

She wouldn't have thought it possible to describe a fight as being beautiful to watch, yet it was. They wound back and forwards countering each other's strikes and kicks with well–practised ease.

Miah as graceful as a dancer, flitted back and forward on steady feet.

Thrain was all strength and contained power.

'You will be as good as her one day,' Kisho said from behind her. 'If you keep practising that is.' Taking that as her cue to start up again she turned, and met Kisho's attack as he launched at her.

They continued to spar until Miah approached them. 'It's almost time. I'll show you where to freshen up.'

Kess looked around in amazement at the extent of the facilities in the living area Miah led her through. She had expected a few walls with tiny rooms and not much else, but the area was like a fully–furnished four–bedroom flat.

Not delaying long enough for a shower, she settled for a wet flannel and a fresh change of clothes.

As she moved to turn off the tap, she froze as silver shimmered, reflecting in the overhead light. What she thought had been an irritation on her right palm last night, had become more visible.

A symbol.

She traced the silver pattern with her finger. Unlike ink, each line was raised like something had been inserted under her skin. A spiral whorled before her eyes, hypnotising her.

Even as she watched the mark faded, vanishing so completely she could almost believe she'd imagined it.

CHAPTER 12

A Heavy Burden Shared

For the second time that day Kess stood out the front of Hermitage, hesitant to enter.

This time though, the lights were out and the sign on the door had been switched to closed. Not giving herself any time to think about the dread which had settled like lead in the pit of her stomach, she walked down the small laneway which led to the back of the building.

'I will walk you back when you're ready.' Thrain stepped away leaving her alone on the doorstep.

Kess didn't answer, focusing already on the task to come. She held up her hand to knock, yet hesitated. Once she told her father, it would become real, her mother would really be gone. She looked back towards Thrain, who met her gaze with a nod, then knocked before she could change her mind.

Yet as the steps creaked under her father's tread, she wished for time to stop.

Robert opened the door, a bright smile lighting his features. When he saw the strained look on her face and Thrain standing a few steps behind her, it vanished completely. 'You'd better come in.'

Kess just nodded, mind already preoccupied with what was to come. She stepped through the doorway, turning at the last moment catching a glimpse of Thrain.

He schooled his features to blankness but not before she had seen a rare display of his emotions – pity – and wished she hadn't.

Tears sprung into her eyes blurring her vision as she tried to fight them back.

She followed her father up the stairs into the lounge room, which always looked the same, no matter how many years passed. The worn brown sofa sat in the same place along the wall with a small coffee table beside it, stained with years of mug rings. Sitting atop the mantle, in its usual place was the picture of her parents smiling happily at each other.

Her father sat on the double sofa lounge leaving enough space for her, yet she couldn't sit.

'Are you alright?' Robert asked, sensing her agitation. He stood, reaching for her arm.

'Dad,' she paused, as the lump in her throat choked off her words. She didn't know how to tell him. He had been devastated by Mum's illness years before. This would destroy him. 'Dad,' she started again. 'A demon got Mum.'

The colour drained from Robert's face, leaving it the pallid whiteness of a sheet of paper. He felt around behind him for the chair and collapsed into it.

Kess knelt in front of her father, hands on his knees.

'Are you alright?' he asked, voice husky with pent up emotion. He looked at her tear stained face. 'No, of course you aren't,' he pulled her into his arms. The racking sobs of his grief shook her as they clung to each other.

Minutes passed before he broke away. 'I need a cuppa, want one?'

She nodded not really feeling like one but knowing he needed time to compose himself.

Kess stood, flexing her knees which had started to stiffen, and walked down the hall to the bathroom to freshen up. She turned on the tap and cupped her hands letting the water fill them, splashing the cold liquid on her face. It took three repetitions before she felt settled enough to return to the lounge.

She found her father back on the couch, a composed look on his face. He patted the cushion beside him, pointing to her cup on the table as she sat. 'Tell me what happened.'

Starting with the trip to the hospital, Kess launched into the events of the last few days. Her father blanched at her description of the visit, but stayed silent letting her speak. As she got to the demon attack he grabbed her arm, pulling up the sleeve to reveal the bandage.

'Miah cleaned it up for me. She put something on it which stung to begora.'

Robert unwound the wrap revealing the puffy red wound beneath. 'Your mother had something–' He trailed off as he stood abruptly and walked out of the room, returning with a wooden container the size of a shoe box in his hands. 'This was your mother's. It was where she kept her Chronicler things.'

Reverently her father lifted the lid, searching for a moment before he removed a small round tub. As he unscrewed the lid, a pungent smell wafted out making her eyes water.

'Your mother used to swear by this salve, said it could heal anything.' His voice was rough as he plunged his index finger into the small container revealing a brown gooey substance which he spread over the scratches.

Within moments the heat began to ebb, and by the time her father had finished the wound felt wonderfully numb.

'What's in that stuff?' Kess asked amazed.

'I'm not sure. Though Anna probably wrote the recipe down in one of these books.'

'What else is in there?' She peered into the container curious about this piece of her mother's history.

Robert shut the lid and held his hand on top of the box, memorising it. 'Anna would have wanted you to have it.'

She looked at the box sitting in his outstretched hands. 'Are you sure?'

Any hesitancy left his face. 'Yes.' He placed the box in her lap then gently re–wrapped the bandage around her arm.

Kess looked around, only now noticing that her sister wasn't here. 'Where's Jinnah?'

Robert's lips pressed together, looking displeased. 'She said she had to go out.'

'Is she alright? She doesn't seem all that happy to see me.'

'Of course she is.' He had hesitated for only a moment, yet that pause spoke volumes. Clearly he was uncomfortable though, so she didn't press him further.

'Dad, how much do you know about what Mum was.'

'A Chronicler?' At her nod, Robert continued, 'Quite a bit, I travelled with her when she was on assignment for a number of years.'

'I don't understand how the demon possessed Mum.' It was something which had been bothering her. If hells spawn could possess anyone why weren't her Guardians more concerned.

'Your Guardians didn't explain that? No, I don't suppose they would,' he said as she shook her head. 'They always were a tight–lipped bunch. But as it happens I do know a bit about that. It was one of the things your mother had been researching before–' He trailed off staring across the room.

Kess laid her hand over his and gave it a light squeeze. Robert's eyes sharpened as he focused on her, he took a moment, clearing his throat before continuing. 'When someone is severely injured, mentally infirm or near death, they're more susceptible to demonic possession.'

'You make it sound like an infection.'

'In a way it is.' His tone had taken on a lecturing aspect, momentarily overshadowing his grief. 'When a demon enters its host, it takes over the body completely. Who the person was, their personality, memories, thoughts; everything that made them who they were, is overrun and destroyed.' He lapsed into silence again, lost in his own thoughts.

'Am I the only one who thought demons were mythological?' Kess asked, incredulous that her father not only believed in the creatures, but knew more about them than her.

'What?' Robert looked bewildered. 'No. Most people believe they're fictitious. Your mother certainly needed some convincing before she believed they were real.' His gaze fell to her arm again. 'I'm so sorry, Kess. I married Anna knowing who she was, aware of the almost certainty that her first–born would inherit her legacy. We tried to protect you by not revealing any of this until you started showing the signs. I guess I naively hoped you would be spared.'

She pulled the sleeve of her jumper down hiding the bandage. 'The only danger I usually face is death by boredom.' Looking away she voiced the doubt which had taken root deep inside her. 'I don't know that I'm meant to be a Chronicler.' She stopped as he looked up sharply, then continued, not realising the depth of her feelings until now. 'The Choosing is soon. The others know what faction they want to join, what they want to study, but I don't. They're all content, focused on their branches of study, sitting, and reading all day, but I can't find that same contentment,' she shrugged, lips pulling into a tight smile. 'Maybe I'm not supposed to be there.'

'Kess, it's not as simple as that. What happened to Anna was–' Tears glistened in his eyes as he changed what he had been going to say, 'but it *is* part of who you are. Who your mother was. And that's not something you should reject lightly. I'm not sure you could even if you wanted to.'

'What happened to Mum,' she paused gathering her courage to ask the question that had plagued her for years, 'could that happen to me too?'

'I don't know. I wasn't with your mother when she had her – breakdown. I was here, looking after you and Jinnah.'

His tone made Kess see for the first time something she'd been stupid not to realise before. 'Dad, what happened to Mum wasn't your fault.'

The fragile hope on his face made her eyes tear again, yet she could almost see the weight lift from his shoulders.

'So the demon attack is the reason for the Guardian escort? Not something else?' Robert asked cryptically.

'I think that's enough, don't you?'

'Just look after yourself and as much as I hate to say it, listen to your Guardians, it's their job to keep you safe.' He reached out and patted her leg.

'I will.' Kess meant it too, she didn't want any more run ins with demons. 'Why don't you like them?'

Pain crossed Robert's face, and his eyes glistened with tears. 'Fair or not I've always blamed the Guardians for what happened to your mother. Because they failed to save her.' He reached out and touched her hand. 'I will try to make an effort with your companions.'

'Thank you. They're good people,' she said unsure why he would blame the warriors when her mother had a breakdown. As distraught as he was now though, she didn't want to ask for the sake of her own curiosity.

'Even that one outside?' he asked sceptically.

'Thrain's – complicated.'

Her father barked a laugh. 'I'm sure that's an understatement.'

'How are we going to explain Mum's disappearance?'

'It's up to the hospital to do that. They let her escape, then neglected to inform us.'

'Won't the police come around and question us?' Kess asked worried, not sure how she would fare under questioning.

'The hospital will have their own investigation. We may have to answer a few questions, but just stick to the facts. You visited her, she attacked you, and then that's all we knew about it until the hospital called us. They should contact us soon, when they can't find her.'

'Do you want me to arrange a funeral?' As much as Kess didn't want to, she couldn't leave the arrangements for her father to face alone.

'Officially Anna will only be missing. We can't have a proper service but maybe we could have a memorial, just the three of us.'

Though her father had gotten over his initial shock, she saw the strain on his face, the shaking in his hands, and knew that he was trying to keep himself together while she was there.

It didn't seem right that they couldn't mourn her loss publicly. But it was not like they could explain that her mother had been possessed by a demon, whom she'd then had to kill.

'It's been a long day and I'm sure you need some time with all this. Besides you'll need to tell Jinnah when she gets back.' She put her arms around her father, pulling him into a tight hug. 'I love you, Dad.'

‘Love you too.’ As they reached the door he asked, ‘You’ll be here for a few days?’ At her nod, Robert continued, ‘Will you come to dinner on Thursday?’

‘I’d love to,’ she said with a smile. ‘Do you mind if I stop by Hermitage tomorrow, and help out.’

Robert’s face softened and he gave her a small smile in return. ‘That’d be nice, Kess. Thanks.’

Kess emerged from her father’s back door, and peered into the darkness, momentarily night blinded as she searched for her Guardian. When Thrain materialised a foot in front of her she jumped, and for a split second, was ready to flee back inside.

‘Jeez!’ she exclaimed, gripping her mother’s Chronicler box tightly to her chest. ‘I thought you’d have left by now.’

‘I told you I would walk you back.’ Every inch of Thrain radiated intense control, from his economical movements, to his straight–forward–to–the–point speech.

‘I know but I was ages. Sorry.’

‘It is right that you spend time with your father. Especially after what happened,’ Thrain looked up at the lit window. ‘How is he?’

‘Coping better than I thought he would.’

‘He is much like his daughter I would imagine. Resilient.’

Kess smiled briefly at the unexpected compliment.

Thrain pursed his lips, as if he’d said too much, then without another word took the lead up the narrow walkway, scanning the street before he let her follow.

Their shadows merged together in the harsh light of the street lamps above.

Late as it was, the street was almost empty, free from the congestion of pedestrians the morning hours would bring. She was glad for the freedom to walk without having to jostle her way through the crowds.

Thrain glanced at what she was carrying yet didn’t ask for explanations, returning his watchful gaze to the streets around him.

‘It was my mother’s,’ Kess volunteered. ‘Her box of Chronicler things.’

The warrior glanced at her, a slight raise of his eyebrows the only indication of his surprise at her volunteering this information. ‘Then it is a valuable gift your father has given you.’

Kess hugged the box tightly to her chest, grateful to have something tangible of her mother’s that she could keep.

‘Do you still have that knife?’ Thrain queried.

She removed the blade from where it sat uncomfortably in the waistband of her jeans, and handed it to the warrior, hilt first.

As soon as his hands touched the blade his attention focused on it. ‘This is not the blade Kisho gave you. Where did you get this weapon?’ His voice held concern, but also something else, a tenseness she couldn’t figure out.

‘Why? What’s wrong with it?’

‘Where, Kess?’ Thrain asked again, urgently.

A flash of silver in the dark night, sliding to her feet. The roar of the demon as her hands grasped its hilt. The way the sword cut through the demon’s neck decapitating it.

‘From the golden–haired man. He slid it to me after the demon snapped Kisho’s blade.’

Thrain stared, as if seeing something new in her, showing as much emotion as she’d ever seen from him. ‘This is a blessed blade.’

She had never heard the term before. ‘What like by a priest?’

‘By Angels.’ There was such reverence in his voice, as he caressed the metal. ‘I have seen only one before, many years ago. With this you can kill any infernal creature – or Angel for that matter, as easily as, well you know how easily.’

Like a hot knife slicing through butter. She thought, remembering how cleanly the blade had cut. ‘Why would he give me something that valuable? Where would he have even gotten it from if they’re so rare?’

‘Exactly,’ Thrain’s intense gaze pierced her, as if he could fathom the answer by sheer will alone.

Worry flooded through her. Gifts were rarely given freely. What would be this one's cost?

'Here,' Thrain handed her something made from heavily stitched leather. Tucking her mother's box under one arm, she turned it over in her spare hand looking up at him.

'It's a sheath for the blade. You strap it around your waist like a belt, with the holder at the back.'

'Where did you get it?'

'I called Conall. It's left handed so you can draw it easier.' He pointed out the slope of the sheath which when put around her, would allow her to draw the blade from the small of her back with her left hand.

'How did you–' She stopped as he raised an eyebrow.

Thrain saw everything.

She placed the box on the pavement in front of her, and held up her jacket wrapping the leather thong around her waist. She looked to Thrain before tightening the straps. 'Is this right?'

'Not quite.' He closed the space between them, hands moving to her hips as he adjusted the straps until he was happy with the configuration. When it was firmly in place, he reached around her and slid the blade home. She felt the weight settle comfortably at the base of her spine.

'Thank you,' she murmured.

'You should always have a weapon to defend yourself.'

'I thought that's what you did.' With him standing so close Kess had to crane her neck to look up at him, realising as she did that he was not as old as she'd assumed; probably only in his late twenties, though his stern countenance made him appear older.

Thrain looked down at her, sensing her scrutiny, and raised an eyebrow. 'We will protect you with our lives,' he said with total seriousness, stepping back a few paces.

'I don't want any of you to get hurt because of me.' Although she hadn't known the Guardians long, she couldn't stand the thought of anything happening to any of them because of her.

'That's our job, Kess,' his tone was firm, brokering no argument.

They kept a brisk pace all the way to the refuge where Thrain motioned her through the gate first, checking the street behind them before entering himself.

Miah was pacing the length of the lounge as Kess entered. 'Are you alright?' she asked brusquely, looking Kess over as if to reassure herself that her charge was unharmed. Though what harm could have come to her with Thrain watching over her, Kess didn't know.

'Yes.' And she realised that she was. Talking to her father had released the tight bands of sorrow and anxiety that had been constricting her chest since the attack.

'Your father?'

'As well as can be expected.'

Miah nodded then turned to Thrain.

Kess took the opportunity to take a seat, feeling exhausted all of a sudden, and closed her eyes as she took a few deep breaths.

She realised Miah had been talking to her when the brunette gripped her shoulder, shaking it. 'Are you sure you're okay?' Her eyebrows furrowed as she peered into Kess's face.

'Just tired.'

Miah immediately stood, and shepherded her down the hall to the room she'd been assigned. 'Off to bed.' The warrior ordered as soon as they were through the door.

'Don't you want to check my room first?' Kess joked.

'I already did, just before you got back,' Miah replied straight faced. 'Get some sleep, you look like crap.' She softened her words with a smile.

Kess sat on the narrow hard bed, staring at the box of her mother's Chronicler things which sat, unopened, on her lap.

Too tired to search through it tonight, she curled up around the box and fell asleep.

CHAPTER 13

Revelations

'There are no secrets that time does not reveal.'

Jean Racine

Kess pushed herself up to sitting, and winced as the wound on her arm twinged. Grabbing the small pot of cream from her night stand, she wandered into the bathroom, splashing water on her face, washing away the last remnants of sleep.

She looked at the bandage covering her arm hesitant to unwind it, unsure what she would find, yet was amazed to see the puffy redness had vanished, and while still sore, the wound had dramatically improved overnight. Gingerly she rubbed more of the salve into the cuts, sighing as the cooling sensation spread across her arm.

Rummaging around in her bag she found a clean bandage she'd had the foresight to pack, and was about to re–wrap it when Miah strolled into the bathroom.

'By the Angels! You could have knocked!' Kess exclaimed.

The warrior smiled, ignoring her indignant protestations. 'Here let me do that,' Miah turned her arm over, looking at the scratches. 'That looks a lot better. What did you rub into it?'

'This,' she threw the small tub of cream at the warrior.

Miah caught it deftly in the air, as Kess knew she would. The warrior looked curious as she unscrewed the lid and sniffed the contents. 'Where did you get this?' Miah asked sharply.

'Dad gave it to me last night. It was Mum's.'

Miah relaxed visibly as she took the bandage from Kess's hands and wrapped her arm again.

'I want to help out at Hermitage today, so Dad doesn't have to come in. Is that alright?' Kess asked cautiously, not sure whether her Guardian would agree.

Miah finished tying off the bandage, with a quick swirl of practised movements. 'I will speak with Thrain but that should be fine. It's almost seven, you should get ready.' With that Miah walked out of the room presumably to find the commander.

~

'You don't have to stand behind the counter with me, there are seats over there.'

Miah, dressed in a tight fitting black outfit, stood with her hands on her hips, looking at her charge. 'It's easier to protect you from here.'

'I'm sure you'd manage from over there,' Kess said sarcastically, shaking her head when Miah leant back against the sink and looked past her into the shop. 'Honestly what do you expect could happen here?'

'You were attacked in a Haven, Kess. A Haven! No place is safe anymore,' Miah said sharply, eyes scanning the room.

'Alright, alright,' she conceded, 'just don't scare the customers.' She grinned at Miah's sour look.

Jinnah rounded the counter, hands full of crockery. 'Does *she* have to be behind here?'

Kess sighed, tired by her sister's animosity. '*She* has a name, it's Miah. And if you can make her move, then good luck to you.' Kess shared a smirk with the warrior. If she couldn't budge Miah, there wasn't a chance in Hades her sister could.

Jinnah's eyes narrowed looking at the two of them, then huffed, pointedly ignoring the warrior. 'I don't understand why you're here.'

‘To tell you both about Mum,’ Kess said softly, saddened by her sisters continued hostility.

‘I know that. But why are you *here*, in the shop?’ Jinnah snapped.

‘To help Dad, to give him some time.’

‘Whatever.’ Removing her serving apron Jinnah headed towards the door. ‘I’m going to the bakery to put in tomorrow’s order.’

‘She’s a piece of work,’ Miah growled. ‘Are you sure you’re siblings?’

‘Don’t be too hard on her, it couldn’t have been easy. Mum going away. Me leaving. Dad and her left here to pick up the pieces.’ She did understand, but she wished her sister would see that her departure hadn’t been by choice, and had been hard on her as well.

‘Want to make yourself useful?’ Kess asked, indicating the sink full of dishes.

Miah raised an eyebrow, but without complaint turned on the taps, filling the sink as she pulled up her sleeves.

Kess felt the bubble in her mind flare, but she pushed it away refusing to acknowledge something which couldn’t possibly exist.

The door jingled, signalling another customer. She looked up ready to serve and stared in astonishment at who stood before her. ‘Hi–’ she cut off as something grabbed her shirt, ripping her backwards. Stitching stretched and popped in her collar as it dug into her throat.

Kai’s eyes narrowed as he focused on Miah, who now stood between Kess and the counter.

Miah looked calm and collected, but there was tension in the way she held herself, poised on the balls of her feet. She looked like a cat cornered in an alley; back arched, fur bristled.

‘What are you doing here, Angaros?’ The Guardian addressed Kai in a cool voice. She looked back, desperation in her eyes. Every inch of her screamed at Kess – *Run!*

‘I could ask the same of you, Wahtāri,’ he said, pronouncing the word *‘Vaataaree’*.

‘*You* are *not* welcome here.’ Miah’s voice cooled further, becoming as frigid as an ice storm.

‘I came to see Kess.’ His gaze moved to where she stood behind Miah in bewildered silence.

‘Kess?’ The Guardian kept her eyes on Kai, waiting for her response.

Kess ignored the question. ‘What’s going on here?’ she asked knowing something more was going on here – hating that she didn’t understand what.

Two sets of eyes looked at her. Kai – cool and calm, and Miah – radiating an agitated desperation, not for herself of course, but for her charge.

‘Kess please,’ Miah’s words were strained, ‘go to Thrain.’

‘What – No!’

Miah made a small almost imperceptible movement of hand to pocket. ‘You don’t understand!’ she hissed, urgency raising her voice.

‘You’re sodding right I don’t. What’s going on?’ Kess demanded, voice starting to rise. ‘Kai?’ No answer. ‘Miah?’ The silence was absolute. She moved forward, sidling to the Guardians right as Miah sought to block her.

The bell jingled as two shapes appeared, blocking the doorway.

Kai glanced back, an amused smile crossing his face when he saw Thrain and Conall.

‘I guess I’ll be going. See you later, Kess,’ Kai said, earning a glare from Miah. He turned from the counter, unafraid to show his back to her Guardian.

As Kai reached Thrain he paused, giving the warrior a long searching look. ‘Protect her.’ His joviality was replaced with deadly seriousness.

‘We will.’ Thrain’s tone was stiff, like the rest of him, which looked as tense as a snake ready to strike.

Nodding, Kai strolled away up the street without a backward glance. As he disappeared from sight she realised he hadn’t been surprised to see her.

Had he followed them?

She wouldn't have thought it possible for anyone to watch them without being spotted by her vigilant guards.

Conall gave Kess a cheeky grin then followed Thrain out, heading in the same direction.

Miah turned, looking Kess over, reassuring herself that her charge was unharmed.

She opened her mouth but Miah held up a hand, eyes moving behind her. The door jingled again, and Jinnah came through the door. 'This is *not* the kind of conversation we want anyone to overhear,' she said softly.

Kess waited until her sister came behind the counter. 'I know it's a few hours until closing but is it alright if we go?'

The blonde looked relieved, then without a word of goodbye left to clear tables.

Ignoring her sister's rudeness Kess turned to Miah. 'Where?'

The warrior glanced around the room. 'Somewhere we can talk uninterrupted.'

'The Hill,' Kess said immediately.

Miah tilted her head, questioningly.

'Primrose Hill. It's not far.'

Miah nodded and let Kess take the lead out onto the street.

'Shouldn't you let the others know where we're going, so they don't freak out and tear the place apart?'

'Guardians do not *freak out*,' Miah said stiffly, but with a glance at Kess, she sighed. 'But you are right.' She pulled a small phone from her pocket, dialled a number, and began speaking softly into the phone.

She felt the lump in her own pocket, given to her by Thrain, when they'd arrived. *Just in case*, he had said. In case of what she didn't know. It wasn't like the Guardians would let her wander around without them as escort.

The streets were packed with people, tourists for the most part, heading in droves back towards the tube after a day out at the markets.

Wanting to get to the hill quickly they left the press of bodies and ducked up a side street.

Having lived in Camden for years before moving to Athenaeum, she easily traversed the maze of back streets and walkways, passing the tiny lane barely wide enough for one person.

She led Miah across a road bridge, and descended a narrow set of stairs, overgrown with grass, before turning right onto the winding path which followed the Lock canal. Kess breathed through her mouth, ignoring the unfortunate odour of urine which grew particularly pungent under the bridges which spanned the water course.

The warrior remained silent beside her even as Kess indicated the steeply sloped concrete path which led to a large expanse of green; Primrose Hill.

They climbed the rise, walking up its grassy slope to the circular concrete top with the trio of worn timber bench seats, which to her had always seemed too low to the ground for comfort.

They sat on one of the benches, overlooking the area. For once, there was no one else up here.

Kess turned to Miah. 'So, what's going on?'

'You know that *man*?' she asked, turning the word 'man' into more of a question than a word.

'I've met him before,' Kess said evasively, unsure why the Guardian had reacted so violently to Kai.

Miah sighed, as if dreading that answer. 'Where?'

'The Haven.' The words had barely left her mouth when Miah's head whipped up, and if she hadn't known better, she would have said her eyes contained fear.

'You have to stay away from him. He's dangerous.'

'What? Why? The demon would have killed me if it wasn't for him,' Kess said defensively.

'I know his kind,' Miah's responded, eyes hard.

'His kind? What does that mean?' She paused thinking, 'You called him something, Ang–' Kess stopped not quite remembering the word she used.

Miah pursed her lips reluctant to answer. 'I called him Angaros.' The words dragged out of her.

'Is that a kind of Guardian?'

'Certainly not!' Miah words were clipped, disgruntled.

'Then what is he?'

Miah remained silent looking out over the green of the park, her eyes hard with repressed emotion. 'He is an Angel,' she said grudgingly.

Kess looked at her speechless, shocked to silence.

'He's dangerous,' Miah repeated, emphasising the word. 'Stay away from him.'

She reached out and touched the bubble within her mind. He didn't feel dangerous. Kess knew she should tell the warrior about it, and the mark which had branded her palm before disappearing, yet something held her tongue.

'I don't understand.'

'Short version – there was a war in Heaven and a whole bunch of Angels fell. About a third of all that were up there. After the Angels descended, a number of them lived amongst humans. Some produced offspring with human women.'

'Weren't they supposed to be giants?'

'There's a lot in the bible which is based on fact, but a great deal has been altered over the course of time. The offspring – the Grigor – were not giants but half breeds, carrying the genetic make–up of both Angels and mortals. Their mixed blood gave them special abilities mentally and physically. They were the first Chroniclers. Your ancestors,' she paused to see how Kess was taking the information.

Interested Kess nodded for her to continue.

'As time passed, and the world modernised some of their descendants forgot their heritage. Other families however remained aware of their lineage passed down from parent to eldest child, who were then sent to the Havens to study.'

'Why don't I know any of this? I've never been taught anything like that about our history.'

'Once being a Chronicler meant something far different, it was a great honour, they gathered knowledge and even fought to protect it.' She saw Kess's disbelieving look but continued. 'But over the millennia Chronicler blood has become severely diluted and now little remains of who they once were, now they are little more than librarians.' Scorn laced her voice.

'You keep saying *they*, like I am not one of them.'

'You are different, Kess. I see in you a Chronicler of old, a warrior scholar. No. I don't class you among them for that would be to look down on you, which I do not.'

She sat silently digesting it all. 'You said Chroniclers were the descendants of Angels. If he is a member of the Host, why would he be a danger to me?' Kess asked, for Miah's narration had not explained the warrior's hatred of Angels.

'Not all Angels are good. Some have become corrupted, evil creatures that would kill you as easily and remorselessly as you would swat a bug.'

'He's not evil,' Kess said shortly.

'Are you willing to bet your life on that?'

'Yes,' Kess didn't hesitate.

'Well I'm not. Stay away from him,' Miah's voice was hard, uncompromising. 'You have to be careful, Kess. Whatever you think, you don't know him at all. Angels are capricious creatures.'

'Can I have some time, to think about all this?' Kess asked, needing to stop the conversation before the Guardian made her swear an oath she may not be able to keep.

Miah nodded, remaining where she was.

'Alone?'

'No,' her Guardian said flatly. 'It's too dangerous,'

'We don't know that. I just want to sit here for a while. Please.'

Miah did not look at all pleased but she stood and walked down the slope. Whilst keeping her word and giving her some space, she was sure Miah was watching from afar.

But for now, she was alone.

CHAPTER 14

Knowledge is Power

'So, you're an Angel,' Kess asked not bothering to turn around.

She had felt Kai behind her, moments after Miah had departed, watching silently, as if not sure he should approach.

'Your Guardians told you then.'

Turning from her view of the city she saw him several paces away, a cautious look on his face. She patted the seat next to her inviting him closer. 'She also told me to stay away from you. That you're dangerous. That you might want to kill me.'

While she was sure she knew the answer already Kess wanted to watch his reaction, and was rewarded as astonishment flitted across his face as he sat next to her.

'Kill you? Why would I want to do that? What are you?' he asked quizzically, looking at her as if she was an unsolved puzzle.

'*What* am I? I'm a girl. A Chronicler.' Indignation raised her voice a few octaves.

He looked at her in a considering manner, arching an eyebrow.

W*asn't she?* She remembered what Miah had said about the ancient Grigor being half breeds. 'What do you think I am?' she asked, suddenly unsure of what she had assumed was a fundamental truth.

'Honestly, I am not sure.'

'Why do you sound so worried?'

‘I am worried. I don’t know how much your Guardians told you but over the centuries there have been many events specifically engineered to kill Chroniclers.’

‘Events?’ Kess wasn’t sure she wanted to hear his response.

‘Well to start it all off there was the great flood,’ Kai said, looking at her seriously.

Kess couldn’t help but interrupt. ‘That would be the one involving Noah, and a great big boat?’ she quipped sarcastically, not quite believing all of this.

‘Your history actually got that bit right. Noah built a large vessel but not to fill it with animals as your bible suggests. He built it to save as many Chroniclers as he could.’

‘Noah was a Chronicler?’

Kai nodded. ‘A great many of your world’s historical figures were. Though for the most part their notoriety drew attention to them, and led to their premature deaths.’

Not sure what to say to that revelation, Kess stayed silent for a few moments processing. ‘What else?’

‘In the 1600s countless family lines were erased, tens of thousands of lives lost, across the United Kingdom, Europe and America during the witch burning era.’

‘That was started to kill Chroniclers?’

‘Germany’s World War, volcanic eruptions in Bali and Iceland, tsunamis in Thailand and New Orleans, earthquakes in Tibet, the destruction of whole civilisations; the Mayans and Atlantis.’ Urgency filled his voice, begging her to grasp the importance of what he was saying.

All the random bits of information were like a puzzle that her mind seemed unable to fit together. She couldn’t see beyond the reality that tens of thousands of lives, hundreds of thousands, had been lost because of someone’s crusade to kill people like her.

‘Kess, don’t you understand? Angels. They are the ones behind the attacks,’ he paused letting the information sink in. ‘They are the only ones who have the power to alter the world’s weather patterns to such an extent as to cause floods, earthquakes and tsunamis. The ones who are able to instigate mass religious hysterias and world wars.'

Numbness began to settle through her, making her body seem leaden. *What chance did she have if Angels wanted to kill her?*

'Havens were built to keep Angels out. It is why your guards forbade you seeing me. Because of who you are. Because of what I am. Because they can't be sure which side I am on.'

'I trust you.'

'You don't know me,' he said in exasperation, sounding exactly like Miah.

'I do though,' she said softly.

He looked at her quizzically. 'You are an oddity, Kess. You have just been told the ancient line of people you belong to have been systematically wiped from existence by an Angelic force. And yet here you sit alone with an Angel you only met a few days ago.'

'She's not alone, Angaros.' A masculine voice sounded from behind them. 'You were told to stay away from this creature, Kess.'

She turned to find a very angry looking Thrain behind her. 'Thrain, this is Kai. Kai, Thrain. Don't be prejudiced.'

Astonishment lit her guard's face briefly before it quickly turned to stone again. 'I am assigned to protect you. You do not know what side this crea–' he stopped as she glared at him, '*he* is on.'

'You have no reason to believe me, Wahtāri, but I mean your charge no harm.'

'You're right. I don't have *any* reason to believe you, and every reason not to,' he replied stiffly.

'What is it with you both?' Kess said exasperated, clearly this bigotry towards each other was extremely deep seeded. Wanting to change the subject she turned to Thrain. 'Miah called you?'

He nodded.

'Where's the rest of the Scooby gang? Hiding behind the bushes as well?' she asked, making a point of looking around.

Whilst Kai chuckled softly, Thrain stared at her blankly, clearly not understanding the reference, or not finding it in the least bit amusing if he did.

'I will walk you back,' his voice was firm.

'Can I have a minute?' He looked about to protest, so she kept talking. 'You can wait where you can see me but just give me a moment, please?'

He glanced at Kai, then back to her and nodded, walking far enough away to be out of earshot but close enough that he could reach her quickly.

She turned back towards Kai who wore a questioning expression. Knowing she didn't have much time, she jumped straight in. 'What happened the other day? When I looked at you – it felt like I was being torn apart.'

He looked back towards Thrain, making sure the warrior wasn't close enough to hear him. Thrain saw the movement and stared at him suspiciously.

'Do you *feel* anything?' Her hesitation provided him with confirmation. 'You can sense me.'

'It's like you're a bundle in my head.' She fingered the skin over her left ear where she felt the bubble within her mind.

He ran his hand roughly through his hair. 'It is the forbandt.'

'Forbandt?'

Kai stared out across the green expanse, yet his eyes had a glazed faraway look. 'Thousands of years ago when Chroniclers were created, it was found that some had the ability to bond with Angels. The bond is a recognition of the kinship that exists between us. The bundle in your head that you sense is called a blære, and is the centre of our connection.'

'Is that what this is?' She held her right hand out, palm up, where the mark had appeared yesterday.

Kai looked at her, waiting her nod, before he touched her outstretched hand.

The moment his fingertips brushed her palm the symbol appeared, flaring brightly. It burned this time as if branding itself to her skin. The

Angel inhaled sharply, then looked at his own palm, at the identical symbol that had appeared there as well.

'The bond is complete,' he said.

'That's what this means?' she asked, rubbing the mark which now was visibly etched into her skin.

'The mark of the forbandt is unique to each pairing. When we are near each other, it will flare in recognition.'

She smiled as she saw him run his fingers over the mark again, mirroring her.

'This blære–' she stumbled over the word, 'it can form because Chroniclers were part Angel?' Her comment earned a nod from Kai.

'It forms a link between the two. If they are apart, and if one of their emotions are strong enough, the other will sense it. If they are hurt, the other will feel it.'

'So it's not common?'

'It was rare then. Now it's unheard of. The potency of Chroniclers has ebbed and with it their ability to form bonds. You are a rare individual.' His face took on a grim expression. 'Your Wahtāri are not going to be pleased when they figure it out.'

'Why do you call them that?'

'It is what they are; Wahtāri, Bâohù rén, Praeses. Guardians have had many names, in many cultures, over the millennia,' his gaze upon her sharpened. 'With the blære you will now be more attuned to Angelic beings, an ability your kind hasn't possessed for centuries.'

'Isn't that a good thing?'

He shook his head sharply as a stab of his frustration filled her mind. 'No. It isn't. Some Angels hate mankind. They were repulsed by the manner in which the Chroniclers were created. So to have a human capable of sensing them, recognising them for what they are, is more than enough justification for them to kill.'

'Why–'

Kai cut her off. 'I can't tell you everything, we haven't enough time and some knowledge is not yours to know. What you have to understand is that there are two main factions – those that protect mankind, and those that want to eradicate them from the Earth. I am of the former.' He glanced past her, attention focused over her shoulder. 'I think your Guardian has decided that you have had enough time.'

Kess twisted around and saw Thrain striding purposefully towards them. The stern look on his face harboured no doubts that he would deny any requests for further time.

'I guess I'm going now. Will you be here again?'

Kai didn't answer, just watched Thrain who stood, arms folded against his chest waiting for her to join him. 'You'd better go before he decides to carry you home on his shoulder.'

Kess laughed, but seeing the look on her Guardians face, started to edge towards him not sure that he wouldn't do just that, if she didn't hurry up.

Angling her in front of him Thrain started down the slope, managing to herd her in the direction he wanted without touching her.

Kai spoke softly behind them. 'She is special, Guardian. They will come for her again. Make sure you're ready.'

'You could tell your *friends* to stay away.' He watched the Angel closely, searching for a reaction.

'They are no friends of mine.' Kai looked towards her, but his eyes were cloudy, his thoughts far away. 'I dare not reveal myself, for fear of making the situation worse,' he added cryptically.

Thrain snorted sceptically before he started to move again, swivelling Kess around by the shoulders when she tried to hold her ground. She tried to look back up the hill but Thrain's muscular form blocked her view.

He shepherded her to the park's entrance before she rounded on him, having had enough. 'Is that really necessary? Why don't you walk beside me?'

'It's easier to protect you if I am behind.'

'Don't you think it will look strange, you walking so close behind me? People might think you're following me and call the police.' She goaded, knowing the Guardians desire for anonymity.

Begrudgingly Thrain increased his pace, walking alongside her as they strode along the emptying Camden streets in silence. When they got back to their underground bunker, Miah, Conall and Kisho sat waiting.

'An Angel, Kess? That's bad ass!' The red–headed Guardian grinned. 'What?' He looked to Kisho who'd elbowed him in the ribs trying to silence him.

'You think this amusing, Conall? An Angel has entered the Haven. An act which should be impossible with the Obiex guarding it. Around the same time a demon attacks within the grounds, another impossibility. One occurrence is implausible, two stretches coincidence.'

'Are you suggesting Kai was involved in the demon attack?' Kess asked coldly, focusing her anger on Thrain.

His stone cold grey eyes glared at her, jaw working as he struggled to contain his anger. 'Your judgement towards him is compromised.'

'Your prejudice blinds you! He is not the one you should be seeking to blame,' she returned angrily before storming away.

~

She paced the five steps of the room, backwards and forwards trying to calm herself down.

She felt irrationally angry that Thrain could even consider Kai had been involved in the demon attack. She *knew* he hadn't been, but couldn't tell her Guardians why she was so sure. Even Kai had warned her of the trouble it would cause if she told them she had bonded an Angel.

Kess.

She heard a voice whisper her name.

She looked around the empty room searching for its source.

Kess. This time there was impatience in the inflection of the tone.

'Where–' she started to ask aloud.

Just think what you want to say.

This time she recognised the voice. *Kai*?

Are you alright?

How are we talking like this?

The forbandt is a bonding of the mind, it allows also for communication over distances. What's wrong?

Frustration flooded back through her. *Thrain,* she sensed his concern, and was calmed by it.

He believes I had something to do with the demon attack.

I didn't say that. Alarm flitted through Kess that he could sense her thoughts through their bond.

I can't read your mind. You're projecting your thoughts.

Can you hear everything I think?

No. Just strong thoughts. You will learn to contain them but it takes practice. Just imagine them blanketed, or wrapped in cotton wool and that will help suppress it. He was quiet for a moment. *I did not let the demon enter Athenaeum, Kess.*

I never thought you did.

Amazement and relief flooded through the blære.

I trust you, she thought to him, projecting it as strongly as she could.

Thank you.

CHAPTER 15

Death and New Beginnings

'Everywhere we shine death and life burn into something new.'

Aberhjani

After her conversation with Kai, Kess felt calm enough to talk to her Guardians again. She set off to search for the warriors but paused outside the door of the lounge room, when she heard voices, hesitant to interrupt.

'What is it about her that irks you so much?' Miah asked, exasperated.

'Can we trust her?' Thrain growled. 'He gave her an Angel sword, Miah! What if she has already been corrupted?'

Miah murmured a reply that she couldn't hear.

Thrain answered in a voice loud with anger. 'She willingly consorts with Angels! You didn't see them on the hill. That one will not leave her alone now. And while you and the other two may act otherwise, she is *not* one of us. She is a Chronicler. What were you thinking when you agreed to train her like a Guardian?'

Thrain's words crashed into her like a physical force. *Why did he hate her so much?*

'She has a warrior's spirit. Surely you have seen that.' Miah's response was clipped, angered by the hostility in the commander's voice.

Kess ignored Conall's calls as she fled through the training area, heading for the surface. She needed fresh air.

She threw the door back not caring about the loud crash as it rebounded against the brick wall behind it. Walking a few metres away she sank to the ground and pulled her knees to her chest, wrapping her arms around them.

She knew what the commander's attitude towards her brethren was, but thought after the events of the last few days, he may have softened a bit towards her. But obviously there was no changing his mind. Naming her as a Chronicler showed his continued contempt and though she tried not to care, his antipathy burned a hole within her.

Head in her arms, Kess didn't look up as someone settled beside her, close enough that she could feel their warmth radiating through the thin layer of her long–sleeved shirt. She hadn't thought to grab her jacket in her haste to get away, and the temperature had dropped significantly since earlier.

She felt a weight settle over her shoulders and looked up to see her red–headed Guardian settling her coat over her. 'Thought you might need this,' Conall said quietly.

'Thank you.'

'Going to tell me why you ran through the training room like the gates of hell had just opened behind you?'

She looked up from the ground, searching the redhead's face. Conall was friendly with her, but at the end of the day he was still a Guardian.

He must have seen something in her face, because he said, 'Don't keep your tongue under your belt.'

She couldn't help the smile which somehow, despite the way she felt, found its way to her lips.

'Say what you want to say, Kess.'

'I will always be something less to him, won't I? Just a stupid, useless Chronicler.'

'Who–' One look at her face, and he answered his own question. 'Thrain,' he said flatly. 'Did he say that?' Anger touched Conall's tone. 'We don't all think that, Kess. He's just–' he shook his head, 'Thrain.' He finished, like that one word alone explained it all. Knowing the Guardian commander, she guessed it did. 'Come on, let's take a walk.'

‘I thought I wasn’t supposed to go anywhere.’

‘I’ll keep you safe.’ Conall gave her a grin as he stood, extending his hand down to her.

~

Not wanting to have to navigate the heavy press of people that always seemed to fill Camden’s High Street, they wandered along the empty back streets.

Thick cloud cover muted the afternoon light, making the hour appear later than it actually was. The filtered gloom gave the buildings around them a sinister appearance, darkening their facades and making them appear to loom ominously.

It was too early yet for the street lamps which left them traipsing through the dimming light.

Kess checked over her shoulder more than once as they walked along a narrow street.

‘What’s wrong?’ Conall, sensing her edginess, glanced around warily.

‘I don’t know. Probably nothing.’ The prickle between her shoulder blades increased, making her want to scratch it. ‘Can you feel that?’

Conall shook his head briefly, not taking his eyes from their surrounds.

The sky above them darkened, like something had obscured the sun, yet it was moving too fast to be a cloud. She pushed the thought away, not wanting to give into worry.

They had only walked a few paces further when she was pushed to the ground, as a huge weight crashed on top of her.

‘Conall!’ She screamed as she peered to the side, through the tangle of hair obscuring her vision, and saw a scaled talon beside her head. *Demon!*

The hells spawn shifted its immense weight, flattening her against the ground.

She screamed as claws pierced through the material of her jacket digging deep into the skin on her back. With a flap of wings, a gust of air buffeted around her, and she was yanked into the air.

'Damnaigh!' Conall cursed in his native tongue as he lunged grabbing her calves and pulled, trying to wrench her out of the demon's grip.

The creature tightened its claws, its sharp talons digging deeper into the skin and muscles around her spine. She stopped struggling knowing the creature would have no compunction about injuring her further.

'Kess?!' Conall yelled, as he heard her cry of pain.

The thump of wings overhead increased as the demon tried to remain aloft with the Guardians additional weight. Then with an enraged shriek it released her, dropping them into a sprawled heap on the road.

She landed across Conall's chest pinning his arm under her.

'Are you alright?' He shifted, trying to free his weapons arm. 'Can you stand? We need to get out of here.'

'What was that thing?' Demons she'd become used to but flying demons, that was something else entirely.

'A dragkheir. I think anyway, they were supposed to be extinct. No one has seen one in hundreds of years.'

'I think you can take them off the endangered demon's list.'

He gave her a strange look, a mix of incredulity and pride. 'You sensed it, didn't you?'

'I felt a wrongness.'

'The dragkheir were demonic assassins. They have the ability to cloak themselves so not even a warrior can sense them.' He looked at her quizzically, wanting to ask more but noticed the stiff way she was holding herself. 'You're hurt.'

'I'm alright. Let's get out of here.'

'You'd give Thrain a run for being the most stubborn git ever to walk the Earth,' he muttered under his breath.

She stood, gritting her teeth as the movement pulled at the wounds on her back. She clamped her jaw tighter not wanting her Guardian to know how much pain she was in. They had to get out of here before the hells spawn returned.

She thanked the Angels her jacket was made of dark material and hid the blood she could feel trickling down her back, knowing Conall's worry for her would distract him.

He grabbed her elbow and led her back towards the way they'd come. Each step jolted through the punctures on her back.

Conall kept craning his head skyward, and as the shadow passed overhead again, he increased their pace.

Then, with a great thud, the dragon landed blocking their path.

Or something that in any sense of the word constituted a dragon. It was either that or a hideously mutated creature from Chernobyl.

Its large wings were covered in taut membrane–like skin and reminded her of a bat, though much larger. The rest of its body resembled some sort of huge carnivorous lizard with giant serrated teeth and small beady eyes at the top of its head. It stood like a Tyrannosaurus with large muscled thighs but unlike the Cretaceous predator, had longer forearms with thick claws on each of its four multi–jointed fingers.

'Ssssttand asssthide human.' It hissed, extending a thin forked tongue as it spoke.

Kess looked at Conall, whose gaze flitted to her before tightening his grip on her arm. Eyes not leaving the approaching creature they walked back towards where they'd come from.

The hells spawn hopped forwards, wings partially extended, looking like a bird chasing after an insect.

Conall kept them backing up several more feet until the dragkheir growled threateningly. Its deep booming cough reminded her of a David Attenborough documentary she'd watched where a lion barked its warning before attacking a Jeep containing a camera crew.

Something in its tone alerted her Guardian who stopped their retreat. Clearly it wasn't going to let them escape. He raised his mace as he stepped closer to the creature, pushing Kess behind him protectively.

'Ssssooo be it.' The creature crooned.

‘Run!’ Conall shouted as he risked a glance behind him. Then with a burst of speed he charged the creature, swinging the steel weapon like a club landing a blow that would have crushed a human’s shoulder to splintered shards of bone.

The weapon bounced off harmlessly, looking as though it hurt the warrior’s wrist more than the dragkheir.

The creature slashed a clawed hand at Conall, as he danced back out of its reach.

A knife found its way into Kess’s hand and she threw it seeking to distract the beast, and hopefully provide an opening for her Guardian. Yet the blade clattered harmlessly to the road bouncing off the deceptively thick hide.

‘I told you to run!’ Conall screamed at her.

The knife lay about ten yards to her left.

With the creature distracted by the warrior, Kess dashed forward picking up the weapon. From here the angle was much better. She aimed carefully before letting the blade fly.

To her total amazement it hit its intended target, sinking deep into the creature’s eye. The dragon flung back its reptilian head, roaring in pain.

Taking advantage of the distraction Conall sprung forward.

Kess watched the scene unfold in almost slow motion as she pulled the Angel blade free, and leapt forward herself.

Yet she was too late.

The dragkheir whipped its long tail around using it like a spear, halting Conall’s momentum as it impaled him. The pointed tip of the creature’s tail pierced straight through his body, visible between his shoulder blades.

‘No!’ She cried out in horror as his legs collapsed beneath him, and he was held aloft only by the demon.

Spurred by rage, she raced past her Guardian flipping her blade around, severing the tail of the creature.

Conall’s knees buckled as he fell limply to the ground yet she didn’t slow.

The dragkheir roared in agony, its attention focused on the shortened length of its tail.

Kess didn't hesitate as she closed the gap and slammed the Angel blade up to its hilt into the dragon's chest. With a twist of the sword she held the weapon firmly in its chest until she saw, with grim satisfaction, the dragkheir's very human emotion of disbelief before the light fled from its eyes.

She waited until the demon's body erupted in hells fire before pulling her blade free and turned her back on the inferno. She ignored the knife which had been embedded in the dragon's eye, as it clattered to the cobbles as the creature was consumed, and rushed to her Guardians side.

'Conall?' she whispered as she threw herself down beside him.

The bright red of his hair made his face an even paler shade of deathly white. He was so pale she was sure the Angels had already come for him. She choked back a sob.

'Kess?' He breathed weakly voice barely above a whisper. 'You – right?'

'Shh. I'm fine.' He tried to struggle to his feet but she held him firmly. 'The demon's dead.'

Conall smiled at her. 'Warrior.' He whispered before his lips twisted into a grimace of pain. His breath rattled painfully in his torn chest, as his exertion took what little strength he had left.

The wound was horrific, made worse where the tip of the dragkheir's tail had exploded in hells fire burning his flesh black, yet despite cauterising the edges of the wound bright red blood still pumped from the gaping hole in Conall's chest with every beat of his heart.

Fear buzzed at the fringes of Kess's mind but she forced it back. She knew enough about first aid to know that she had to slow the bleeding. She pulled her jumper over her head and wadded it into a ball, pressing it against the horrible wound.

'Sorry,' she apologised as he sucked in a breath between his teeth. 'Just a scratch. You'll be right as rain in no time,' she said trying to reassure him. Yet they both knew the truth.

As if to reinforce her lie a trickle of blood ran from the corner of his mouth. She was so focused on the scarlet stream that it took her a moment to realise that he was trying to tell her something.

She watched his lips mouth the word soundlessly again. 'Run.'

She shook her head. 'I'm not leaving you.' Crushing despair for her Guardian rose within Kess but she clamped it down forcefully. 'Do you have any of that powder?'

Conall watched her wordlessly, face tight with pain.

Holding her jacket firmly in place with one hand, she shifted so she could reach into his jeans, trying to quell her embarrassment as she searched his pockets. Just as she thought she'd have to move around and search the other side her fingertips grazed a packet which she pulled free.

Ripping it open with her teeth Kess held it ready over his chest before she pulled away her jacket. The material was heavy, sodden with his blood. She sprinkled the powder realising how little good it could do against an injury like this, then pushed the blood–soaked jacket back over his chest.

Conall shifted, making Kess realise she'd been staring at her bloodied fingers gripping the jacket.

Yet he wasn't looking at her. His head was craned, peering up the street where they'd run from.

Kess followed his gaze and saw two fully transformed demons emerge, about two hundred yards away. Though the light was becoming dimmer by the minute, their shapes gave them away, for they were clearly not human.

'Satan's breath. We have to move.'

Conall gave her a sad smile and shook his head, that movement alone clearly an effort. 'Run,' he whispered.

'No! I'm not leaving you,' Kess argued, as she tried to work her arm under his back carefully.

Even as his life's blood flowed onto the rough cobbles, as his heart slowed with not enough liquid to pump around, his only thought was for her to get away.

A shudder ran through his body, and then the rattling of his breaths stopped. Conall's hair ruffled in the wind, the only part of him still moving.

'No!' She screamed, thumping his chest, hysterically. 'Get up!' She shook him roughly, knowing she couldn't help him, couldn't bring him back, but was unwilling to leave him lying like a piece of rubbish in the street.

His eyes stared blankly, his soul already having fled. His words echoed in her mind. *Run. Run. Run.*

The hells spawn were closer now, about a hundred yards away. Close enough for her to see them in every grotesque detail. One looked like a human octopus hybrid with a multitude of tentacles waving agitatedly around its torso, whereas the other more resembled the horrible creature in aliens, than anything terrestrial.

She lowered Conall to the ground and gently closed his turquoise eyes.

Tears blurred her eyes as she rose to her feet.

This was all her fault.

She wiped her shaking hands against her pants, unwilling to have her Guardians blood coating her fingers, and felt a hard rectangle in her pocket.

'I'm sorry,' she whispered, before she followed the warrior's dying wish and ran.

As she passed the scorched pavement where the dragon had returned to hell, she scooped up her knife, fitting it into her belt sheath as she ran.

Careful not to drop the phone as she pulled it from her pocket, she held it up so she could see the screen as she ran, and hit the only number programmed into it. It only rang once before someone answered. But instead of one of her Guardians all she heard was crackly static – the reception must be bad in the tunnels.

She didn't waste words, unsure how long the connection would last. 'Demon attack. Miller Street.'

The phone beeped as the connection was lost.

'Angel feathers!' she cursed as she jammed it back into her jeans. She hoped they'd been able to hear her.

A glance over her shoulder showed the two demons still pursuing her had started to close the gap.

Forty feet.

She put on a burst of adrenaline fuelled speed.

Taking note of her surrounds, she tried to remember the quickest way back to populated streets, hoping her demon pursuers wouldn't follow her into a crowded area, full of human witnesses.

Kess sprinted up the road and rounded the corner ducking into a narrow street; the same one Miah and herself had passed earlier that day. Her jacket grated along the brickwork as she raced up the cramped alleyway as fast as she could, knowing safety lay ahead.

So close now.

The scrabble of claws on stone announced the demon's entry into the alley behind her, but she didn't dare look back, only pushed herself even faster, glad now for all those mornings spent running around Athenaeum's woods.

Just as hope started to bloom inside her, and she was within reach of the exit, a tall figure stepped into the alley.

One look at his eyes, as blue as arctic ice and just as cold, and she knew that he was not there to help her.

Running too fast to stop Kess barrelled into him, rebounding several feet. Her tail bone ached from the force of the fall, and her palms were bloody, yet she scrabbled backwards putting distance between her and the arctic stranger, before getting quickly to her feet.

She knew the demons were at her back but she couldn't take her gaze from the blue–eyed stranger who seemed more of a threat than the hells spawn. Her hands twitched towards her weapons but she didn't bother removing either of them. She was hopelessly outnumbered, and would have no chance against two demons and that man.

The stranger's cold blue eyes watched her impassively as he stepped further into the alley forcing her back. His next step brought a crunch, as his foot firmly planted on something.

Kess tapped her pocket and found it empty. My *phone*. She thought helplessly.

He moved closer, footsteps echoing along the alley, reverberating off the tall buildings to either side.

With each forced step backwards, the light from the lamps in the main street dimmed. She glanced around searching for a window; for any sign of life, yet there were only bare brick walls. The alley was narrow and while it hampered her movements, being as large as he was, it should have restricted the stranger even more, yet even as her jumper snagged on the bricks, he seemed to pass by unencumbered.

Her foot slid on the slick cobbled surface, momentarily unbalancing her.

He nodded at the hells spawn behind her. 'Where is her companion?'

The alien demon clicked a response, sounding like an insect.

While she had no idea what it had said, the arctic stranger apparently understood. 'Really? Is her companion dead too?' he asked, a cruel smirk lighting his handsome face.

'Yyeestt.' The octopus demon distorted the word almost to incomprehension.

'Good. This one is to be taken. She may know where *He* is.'

'You can go to hell. I'm not telling you anything,' Kess spat, reviled by this man was willingly working with demons.

The alien creature hissed.

She spun expecting an attack, but realised it was laughing at her.

Kess glanced back toward the man in time to see his clenched fist rocketing towards her face. The force of the punch knocked her backwards, cracking her head against the cobbled stone as she landed amongst the scattered rubbish.

Her vision narrowed to a pinpoint.

Then the world went black.

CHAPTER 16

The Arctic Angel

Consciousness seeped slowly back into Kess, and with it pain and cold.

She was lying on her side, on a rough timber surface sprawled as if hurled there and left. The muscles in her neck had tightened painfully from where her head had lain at an unnatural angle.

Where am I?

The room was dark and it took several minutes for her eyes to adjust to the dimness. From where she lay all she could see was timber, covering the walls and lining the floor in front of her. With each breath, white mist formed in the air around her mouth.

She strained, trying to hear anything that might give her a clue as to where she was but there was nothing, nothing except the occasional creak of timber. The air was still, and smelt stale, with a hint of something else, something familiar. It took her a moment to recognise the smell from a trip to the coast she had taken with her father years earlier; rotting seaweed.

She was near the water.

Kess twisted her head trying to see the rest of the room, and groaned as a sharp strike of pain ripped through her skull, momentarily blinding her. Bile rose in her throat but she swallowed hard forcing it back down, almost gagging again at the bitter acrid taste.

This isn't right.

Fear threaded its way through her, causing her already tender head to throb, making it hard to concentrate.

What happened?

Kess tried to think back, figure out what happened; how she got here, but her thoughts were slow, and trying to remember felt like wading through a room stuffed full of cotton wool.

Sparkling white dots appeared at the edges of her vision. She blinked trying to clear them, but they grew into a snowstorm blanketing the room.

The last thought she had before she sank back into insensibility was of a pale faced Conall telling her to run.

Tears leaked from her closed eyes, pooling on the hard, wooden floor.

~

Kess found herself suddenly awake and blinked her eyes slowly trying to clear them.

She was on her back, looking at a timber ceiling. Pale light filtered into the room from a tiny window far above her. The narrow beam providing just enough brightness to see her surrounds.

The air was still cold but not as bad as the last time she had woken, though she still shivered in her long–sleeved shirt. She worked her tongue around her mouth, trying to create some moisture, and soothe her dry, burning throat.

She was a mass of aches, pains and bruised flesh. Tentatively Kess reached up and touched the warm, swollen flesh of the left side of her jaw. Even the light touch of her fingertips was uncomfortable.

The movement sent pain zigzagging across her temple, right around to the back of her skull. Gingerly she pressed a hand to her head, and found her hair matted into a congealed mess. She probed further until wetness met her fingertips.

Even in the dim light she could see its scarlet hue.

Congealed blood.

Ignoring the protests of her aching body Kess pulled herself up slowly into a sitting position, resting heavily on her arms to keep from falling again.

She looked down trying to focus through eyes which wanted to blur and saw a dark stain marking the wooden floor where her head had lain.

A rectangle of light flooded the room, silhouetting her shadow onto the ground in front of her. Kess turned, and saw a door she hadn't noticed before, was now open. A figure stood in its frame; features obscured by the brightness behind.

The figure stepped into the room, closing the door with a firm clank.

His features became visible as her eyes reacclimatised to the dimness of the room. Arctic blue eyes stared at her.

The memories came crashing back.

A flying demon.

Conall dying.

This man.

Her breath quickened as he closed the distance between them. Kess scrambled to her feet, ignoring the vertigo which sent her head spinning.

'What do you want?' her voice wavered.

The man circled her, assessing.

She was struck by his likeness to Kai, yet he was a winter blizzard compared to her forbandt's summer breeze.

He completed his circuit stopping inches in front of her.

Kess flinched as his hand rose towards her face, expecting him to strike her again.

His eyes tightened in anger at the movement. 'You are all the same. Pathetically fragile creatures. Violent, primitive animals who aren't fit to share our universe,' he spat.

'Angaros.' The word whispered from her lips before she thought to stop it.

His head whipped around, 'So you *have* met our kind before. Perhaps you will be of use after all. I am seeking one of the fallen. You *will* tell me where *He* is.'

'I don't know what you're talking about.'

His eyes narrowed with her denial.

Kai, where are you? She reached out to the blære and found it silent.

The arctic angel stepped back continuing to circle her, a step out of reach.

Kess's eyes flitted to the door which stood unguarded before her. *Could she make the distance?*

He stepped behind her, out of sight.

She tensed, intending to run towards the door when one of his arms snaked around her neck. The other gripped her torso, pulling her tightly against his body. The wounds on her back from the dragkheir's claws barked in protest at the pressure.

Instinct took over and a lesson from Kisho's training flashed into her head. Before she had time to consider the wisdom of the action, she threw back her head and heard the satisfying crunch of bone meeting bone. His grip loosened and she thrashed, trying to pull away, but his hold remained firmly around her, too tight for her to break free.

The Angel flexed his biceps around Kess's neck cutting off her breath.

Her hands scrabbled trying to find purchase against the rock–hard muscle of his arm, panicked at her inability to draw breath, yet he was immovable.

She was on the verge of passing out when he loosened his grip enough for her to suck in a lungful of much needed oxygen. As she gasped in another breath, she twisted, frantically trying to get away.

'Keep moving ape and I *will* kill you.' The cold flatness of his voice, left no doubt he would do exactly as he threatened.

Forcing her body to compliance, she hung meekly in his tight grip. It felt like being encased in concrete.

Kess closed her eyes, trying to put everything else from her mind, and concentrate on getting her breathing under control, but was unable to stop the flinch which jolted through her when a soft rasp of metal sounded behind her.

Was this how he was going to get information out of her? How long could she resist telling him whatever he wanted to know if he was torturing her with a knife?

He shifted behind her repositioning himself, bringing the slim dagger up within her vision as he moved. The dim light reflected along the length of the metal blade, sending another trill of fear through her.

The muscles pulled painfully tight down the length of her backbone as she craned her neck down clamping her mouth over the arm he held across her chest, biting down as hard as she could.

Pain flared in the side of her tongue and she tasted her own coppery blood milliseconds before her eye teeth sliced through the Angels skin. She swallowed reflexively, gagging as his warm blood slid down the back of her throat. Despite her disgust she kept hold, terrified to let go.

The Angel grabbed a handful of her hair, wrenching her head backwards. He seemed uncaring of the damage to his flesh as she tightened her grip; yet she couldn't ignore the sharp pain that felt like her scalp was being ripped off.

As she screamed through a mouthful of flesh, Kess felt her grip loosen.

The Angel must have felt her hold loosen because he tightened his grip, digging the hilt of the dagger painfully into her skull, before wrenching her head to the side away from him.

Kess thought he would let her go, until she saw his fist coming towards her face. Unable to protect herself she shut her eyes, crying out as he hit the bruised flesh of her jaw.

When he did release her, she was too dazed to run. The arctic Angel moved in front of her and hit her again.

The world around Kess spun and a wave of nausea flooded through her, accompanying the pain. Blood dribbled down her chin from the tear in her lip, splattering the front of her shirt red.

'How do you know about Angelic beings?' His voice lowered into a menacing growl.

She stared at him silently, watching his eyes grow even icier at her refusal to answer.

'Where is *He*?'

'He who?' Kess put as much sarcastic disdain as she could into the words, hiding the flash of concern that this Angel was asking the same questions of her as the Rask demon.

He hit her again, tearing the split in her lip further, staining her teeth red.

The icy blue flared in his eyes, making them appear luminescent. He levelled her with a look of such hatred she felt like she should be shrivelled on the spot.

As fast as she could, she snapped the heel of her palm forwards, and felt the crack of gristle shudder through her hand as the cartilage within his nose collapsed. She had only made it one step towards the door before the arctic Angel lashed out, the force of his punch rocketing her backwards across the room.

Kess's head thudded painfully against the wooden wall behind her. She gasped as the claw wounds, crusted to the fabric of her shirt, tore free trickling fresh blood down her back.

Despite the pain she sent a silent blessing to the Angels as she felt the comforting weight of the sword still contained in the sheath at the small of her back.

Using the wall as a balance, she clambered back onto her feet and faced him unsteadily.

Kess felt like a mass of bruises and scrapes, from her aching hip to the stinging tears on her palms; whereas even though she had struck him, the Angel didn't bear a mark. She pulled out the weapon, holding it in front of her.

The sneer on the arctic Angel's face faltered as he saw the short sword she'd pulled from its sheath. 'Where did you get that?'

A smile curled her lips. 'From a friend.'

Blood dripped from her chin, hitting the floor with a steady drip, drip, drip. 'You should have searched me for weapons.' She silently thanked

Thrain for providing the hidden belt sheath, which had been overlooked by the Angel.

Her blue–eyed captor watched her uncertainly. He took one step towards her then stopped, as a crash reverberated from outside.

The door flung open and a crustacean–like demon hurtled through, landing on the ground between them, with a sickening crunch, unmoving.

Taking advantage of her captor's momentary distraction, she charged, startling him and the golden–haired Guardian who leapt through the door.

Kess felt her captor's astonishment flood through her mind, and was so shocked she skidded to a halt, colliding with him.

Unconsciously he reached out to steady her, then recoiled as he realised what he'd done. A look of horror filled the icy–eyed Angel as he examined the hand that had touched her.

'What have you done to me?' he demanded. His roaring anger and growing disbelief filled her as he shoved her away from him, throwing her across the room.

Kess's head bounced against the wall again. Her vision blurred before starting to narrow like an old television tube, blackening around the edges.

Pain flared in her palm, but she pushed it away, ignoring it along with the rest of her injuries.

'Kess!' Thrain threw himself forward, placing his body between her and her Angelic captor.

She clasped the hand he held behind him gratefully letting the warrior haul her to her feet. She was glad when he didn't immediately pull away his grip – she wasn't entirely sure she could manage to stand unaided just yet without falling on her face. Warily he edged her sideways towards the only exit, carefully keeping the demon sprawled on the ground between them and the Angel.

'Guardian,' he sneered, eyes narrowing. 'That would make you what – a Chronicler?' He started towards them, unperturbed by the presence of the warrior.

Thrain crossed his arms about his hips, removing an axe with a flared edge and a heavy looking sword. Though focused on the Angel he kept edging Kess slowly towards the exit.

Two long thin blades materialised in the arctic Angel's hands as he launched himself at Thrain, who was barely able to raise his steel in time to meet the attack. Their weapons crashed together with an ear–splitting squeal which sent a shower of sparks across the room.

Behind the battling pair, Miah and Kisho leapt into the room, weapons drawn. Kisho darted forward hamstringing the Angel, who roared in fury, yet remained standing, the wounded flesh knitting back together even as Kess watched.

Miah headed straight for Kess, and without a word grabbed her arm and began dragging her towards the door.

Kess had only taken one step when she sensed something through her bond and stopped.

The Angel froze ignoring the advancing Guardians, staring at the figure who had materialised beside Kess.

Kai ignored everyone as he turned to her. 'Are you alright?' he asked, gently wiping the blood from her chin.

She nodded not taking her eyes from her former captor – *Azrin* – his name whispered in the air about her.

The arctic Angel watched their exchange closely, eyes lingering on her before returning to Kai. 'You are helping *them*, brother?'

'You are no brother of mine,' Kai spat as his gaze returned to Kess's beaten face.

'You would side with these–' he paused, gaze flitting to Kess before continuing, 'apes rather than stand with me.' His focus settled on her again.

She looked to Kai, and saw him watching Azrin, eyebrows furrowed in consideration, and followed the thread of thought that leaked from him.

Azrin's head whipped towards Kess, as fear gushed through her like a storm swollen river.

Kai could sense where she was through the blære. If she really had bonded this Angel as Kai believed, he could find her any time and finish what he had started. She took an involuntary step back, breath quickening.

The hostile Angel started to walk towards her before he caught himself, alerted to his movement only as the trio of Guardians closed around her, anticipating attack. She felt worry coming from Azrin in reaction to her fear, then a torrent of anger, at caring.

He looked at the Guardians, then Kess, touching his head. 'This is impossible! What is she?' he demanded from Kai, eyes wide with alarm.

Kai looked from Azrin to Kess before answering. 'Your saviour,' he answered solemnly, holding the other Angel's gaze.

Azrin glanced from Kai to Kess, who stood at his shoulder. His face twisted in anguish before he vanished, leaving behind three armed Guardians, a bonded Angel, a beaten–up Chronicler, and a soon to be dead demon.

CHAPTER 17

The Aftermath

'You will have to explain to me sometime what that was about, Angel,' Thrain said, looking first at him, then Kess. 'But for now, let's get off this boat.'

'I can get her out of here quicker than you can,' Kai urged.

Kess watched Thrain's internal struggle for the safety of his charge, versus his instinctual distrust of Angels.

'No. We go together.' He concluded shaking his head.

Without asking her opinion, Kess was bundled out of the room between Miah and Thrain. Kisho scouted the way leaving Kai to guard their rear. It was a tight squeeze through the narrow corridor, but the pair managed to hustle her through without losing their grip on her elbows.

Salty air stung her nose as they emerged onto the deck. Kess squinted against the dim afternoon light which was bright after the darkness of the cabin. When her vision adjusted she was surprised to see they were on a boat in the middle of a wide body of water.

'How are we getting to shore?' she queried, not particularly feeling like a dip.

'There's a dinghy tied to the port side bow,' Thrain advised as he continued to scan the area. Neither he nor Miah had let go of her yet, as if afraid she would disappear again.

'Tied where?' she asked, utterly unfamiliar with the nautical terms he was using.

‘Front left,’ Thrain clarified, nodding in the direction as he led them towards it.

Glancing over the side Kess saw a rope ladder descending to a very small, potentially unseaworthy boat, which to her trepidation had water pooling in the bottom.

‘Is that even going to make it to shore?’ she asked seriously, not at all sure she should get into the boat.

‘We made it here,’ Kisho told her helpfully, as he climbed over the side, and descended the ladder in moments, as easily as a chimpanzee.

‘Clear.’ She heard him yell before she was guided to the side.

‘Over you go,’ Miah told her briskly, trying to hurry her along.

Kess clambered over the side, gripping the ladder tightly with both hands. The rope was coarse under her fingers but thankfully not slippery. Though the water was relatively calm, in this precarious position over the side, she felt liable to be thrown into the icy looking water with any slight movement of the boat.

As her feet touched the safety of the deck she muttered her thanks to the Angels.

Kai appeared in the leaking dinghy beside her. ‘How did you–’ She saw his grin and knew that she wasn’t going to get any answers here. ‘Didn’t fancy the rope ladder?’ She grumbled, thinking he could have transported her down, saving her a lot of trouble.

He smiled, but didn’t answer, as he, like her Guardians, scanned the area.

As soon as Thrain descended, he untied the rope securing them to the larger vessel, then with a nod to Miah who had taken the wheel, they were speeding towards the shore.

Kisho leapt from the still moving boat, rope in hand and secured them to a sturdy looking tree stump. As the side clunked against the shore, he leant down offering Kess a hand, helping her climb onto the grassy bank.

Once safely back on dry land, Kess looked back at the ordinary looking wooden boat where she’d been taken. ‘How did you find me?’

‘Your Angel led us to you. Though he wouldn’t say how,’ Thrain muttered reluctantly, not wanting to validate Kai’s continued presence.

The Guardians led Kess to a beat up dark blue sedan, parked half up on the gutter. ‘Whose is this?’

‘We, ahh, borrowed it,’ Kisho shrugged.

‘Does the owner know that you “borrowed” it?’ she asked unable to believe the Guardians, particularly Thrain, would steal a car.

Kisho answered her with a grin.

‘I hope you’re going to return it,’ Kess chided.

‘Of course!’ Thrain gruffed, sounding affronted at the accusation.

Miah just smirked.

Kess was pushed into the middle of the back seat with Miah on one side and Thrain on the other.

As she sat back against the padded seat, the puncture wounds on her back from the dragkheir flared in protest. She eased herself forward gingerly, trying not to alert the Guardians to her discomfort.

A sharp glance from Miah told her she’d failed to be subtle enough in her movements. But thankfully, for now, the warrior remained silent.

Kisho started the car with a roar, taking off at a pace which sent grass flying out behind them as the back tyres spun madly.

Kai, turned around in the passenger seat. ‘Are you alright?’

Knowing she must look as battered and bruised as she felt, Kess tried to reassure him. ‘I’m fine.’

He gave her a sceptical look and tapped his head, reminding her that he could feel what she did.

She gave him a small smile, trying not to move her aching face too much.

Finally freed from the clutches of a psychotic Angel she closed her eyes, needing a moment, yet, as soon as she did, Conall’s lifeless blue eyes floated into her vision. She gasped causing everyone in the car to look at her in alarm. ‘Conall?’

Silence answered her.

She looked to Thrain but he only shook his head. 'There was nothing we could do but remove his body before it was seen.'

'We only just managed to get out of there before the plod showed up, sirens blaring. You must have caused quite a ruckus to have so many cars fly in. Don't know how we would have explained carrying away a body,' Kisho told her as he sped down the dirt lane, weaving the bends and turns expertly.

'Any Guardian who can be caught by a law enforcement agency doesn't deserve the title.' Thrain's tone was heated, indignant about the insinuation that a Guardian could be caught by mere mortal police.

'Why did you leave the refuge?' Miah demanded angrily.

'Because, I heard you both talking.' Pointedly not looking at Thrain, Kess continued, 'I heard what Thrain said about me never belonging with you. I ran outside and Conall followed me. He suggested taking a walk,' Kess said softly, taken aback by Miah's anger. 'We were attacked by a dragkheir.' Kess felt their attention focus at the mention of the believed–extinct hells spawn but continued, 'I think that's what Conall called it. We tried to get away but it followed us. We fought the dragon. It im – impaled him.' She forced back the lump in her throat, forging on.

'After it–' The lump in Kess's throat got bigger. She changed what she had been going to say. 'I stabbed it with Kai's blade, and killed it.'

Kess forced herself to look at the brunette warrior to her right, seeking Miah's understanding. 'I tried to help Conall – but there was so much blood–' The image swum before her eyes of the gaping bloody hole in his chest. She kept talking to distract herself.

'He told me to run but I didn't want to leave him,' Kess heard the rattle of his breath again, as clearly as if he were in front of her again. Her chest tightened, leaving her struggling for breath.

'Leave her alone, she's been through enough. Look at her!' Kai shouted angrily at Miah. 'That bastard kidnapped her, beat her, and now you are–'

'Trying to find out what happened so that we don't fail in our duties again,' Thrain said, interrupting Kai's tirade.

Though his voice sounded calm, Kess saw the muscle in Thrain's jaw bulge as he clenched it. She also noticed the way his hands kept moving to his side, where his weapons were.

'I'm alright, Kai. They need to know. Conall is dead because of me.'

'Not because of you, Kess,' Kai responded fiercely, glaring at Thrain. 'They say I'm a danger to you. But they–'

'Kai,' Kess said quietly. *Please.* She thought at him.

Kai nodded, but the tightened lines of his mouth conveyed his disapproval.

'Your Angel is right.' The words dragged from Miah painfully. 'This is not your fault, Kess. We failed you.' She reached out gripping Kess's hand tightly. 'You're like ice!' she exclaimed.

Thrain was immediately in motion, struggling to remove his jacket in the confines of the moving car, wrapping it around Kess's shoulders as soon as he got it free.

Still warm from his body heat, it immediately took some of the chill from her. The leather was smooth and supple from wear, and smelled of Thrain; a scent which reminded her of metal, and the smell in the training yards; wood and churned earth.

She looked out the window at the unfamiliar buildings flashing by as Kisho zigzagged his way through the streets. Before long they were back in Camden, pulling up outside the entrance to the refuge.

Thrain got out, scanning the street before signalling to Miah, who pulled Kess out quickly. Kisho sped off, presumably to return the car from where they had taken it from – hopefully before the owner noticed it was missing.

With a muttered comment from Thrain, Kai followed them down into the refuge.

Miah led her into the lounge, where she sank gratefully onto the comfortable couch cushions.

The dark–haired Guardian left her side, returning moments later with a first aid kit, and a bowl of warm water. Ignoring Kess's protests, the warrior held her chin to keep her still, though as careful as Miah was, the cuts and bruises covering her face stung as the cloth passed over them. Kess kept as still as she could but couldn't help a few involuntary flinches.

The water in the bowl turned pink, as Miah rinsed the cloth clean before continuing dabbing.

Though her jaw was stiff it was the cut on her lip which stung the most, as it stretched and pulled whenever she moved her mouth.

Thrain bought over a fresh bowl of water, and Miah changed cloths moving to the cut on her head. She cleaned the cut before spreading an antiseptic salve over it. 'There is a lot of blood in your hair, but you will have to wash that out. Anything else?'

Hesitantly, Kess scooted forward on the chair, angling her knees away from her Guardian. She carefully shrugged out of Thrain's jacket and placed it on the sofa beside her, before pulling the hem of her shirt up exposing her back.

'What did this?' Thrain's voice over her shoulder was tense.

'The dragon. It tried to carry me off, but Conall grabbed my legs, kept it from flying away.'

The silence in the room was thick.

'That bad, hey?' she asked trying to keep her voice steady.

'Where is that cream of yours?'

'In the backpack in my room.'

Miah stood quickly, and strode away, returning within moments with the small container.

As before when Kess had used the salve, it numbed the wound the moment it was rubbed in, making her realise how much pain she'd actually been in.

'Done,' Miah announced, as she finished bandaging, looking at her worriedly.

'I'm sure it looks worse than it is,' Kess said trying to console her, knowing it must look bad for the warrior to show so much concern.

Kai sat down beside her and handed her a cup of cool water which she gulped down gratefully.

When Kisho jogged through the door, they all sat down in the surrounding chairs, looking at her expectantly.

As much as she didn't want to talk about it, she knew her Guardians needed to know what had happened. She picked up the story from where she had left off. 'I tried to help Conall but,' she gulped again, 'then more demons came. He told me to run. Those were his last–' She cut off again as her voice seized. 'I ran up an alley but the blue–eyed Angel was at the other end. He spoke to the demons, told them that he wanted me alive. He hit me and I fell. Then I woke up in that room. You know the rest,' she finished, looking up to find she had the undivided attention of all four of them.

'What happened when you woke up?' Kisho asked.

'I'm not sure. I hit my head when I fell, so it's a little fuzzy.' She felt the back of her head which was still tender.

'That may also have been from toxins on the dragkheir's claws,' Miah suggested.

'Not long after I woke up the second time the Angel came into the room, and started asking me questions.'

All four straightened in an almost synchronised motion.

'What did he want to know?' Kai asked deadly serious.

'The Angel kept asking where "*He*" is,' she said, not able to think of her captor as Azrin yet, despite their bond. 'I said I didn't know what he was talking about. That's when he did this,' she said gesturing to her face.

Guilt flooded through the bond, strong and thick.

It's not your fault, Kess told her bonded Angel.

Kai's emotions tempered so quickly she knew he had walled them away from her, rather than was comforted by her words, for his twilight blue eyes blazed with the same emotion.

She didn't miss Miah and Thrain's glance either – their realisation that the Angel asked Kess the same questions as the Rask.

'What happened after I called? I assume you understood my message before it cut out.'

'We found the street, and Conall,' Thrain said.

‘Where is he?’ Kess asked.

‘We brought him back here.’ When she started to stand, he added, ‘He was cremated and taken back to Athenaeum yesterday.’

‘Cremated,’ she repeated dully.

‘Havens have connections everywhere,’ Thrain explained. ‘We used some of those contacts to make arrangements for Conall’s body. Guardians arrived yesterday to take him home.’

Kisho fished something out of his pocket and handed it to her. ‘Here’s your phone by the way.’

The screen was splintered with cracks rendering the phone useless, yet she held it tightly in her hands.

‘Thank you,’ she said softly, glancing up at him.

Everything had happened so fast at the boat, that she hadn’t really had time to do more than just react, but now, she saw the dark rings under Kisho’s bloodshot eyes. She looked at the other two warriors and saw the same fatigue lines around their eyes as well, suggesting they’d had little or no sleep while she had been captured.

Thrain leant forwards resting his arms on his knees as he continued. ‘There was nothing else in the street apart from the demon stains on the ground. No clue to suggest where you may have been taken. We were still there looking when your Angel turned up.’

‘Why do you all keep calling him “my Angel”?’ Kess asked embarrassed.

She glanced at Kai and saw his amused look. He looked at her pink cheeks and the grin widened further revealing a flawless white smile. *They’re trying to make me uncomfortable, not you.* He thought to her as he put his hand on her shoulder.

She nodded, and turned back to the group.

Thrain’s sharp glance had caught their exchange, but the crinkle between his eyebrows reassured her that he didn’t know about their silent conversation.

‘Because wherever you are, he eventually turns up.’ Miah levelled a dark eyed stare at the Angel who ignored her completely, focusing instead on Kess. 'He claimed that he sensed the demons and came to see what was going on.' Miah's tone conveyed her dubiousness about his explanation.

'Believe me or not Guardian, that is your choice. Angels can sense demons when they are close by and contrary to popular belief I didn't want them lurking in the area with Kess here.'

'How long was I there for?' Kess asked, interrupting their argument.

'Nearly two days,' Thrain replied seriously.

Kess was shocked. 'What took so long to find me?' she asked Kai, knowing it was him and not the others, who was responsible for locating her.

'You were on a boat. The water makes it harder to pinpoint locations. It's like trying to find your way in a dense fog, it slows everything down. Your being poisoned by the hells spawn and unconscious for so long didn't help either,' he said out loud, silently he apologised. *Sorry it took so long. I couldn't pinpoint your location exactly until you called for me through the bond. Azrin was smart to hide you on the water, it made you difficult to track, even after you called.*

You found me, she replied. *That's all that matters.*

Kess saw Thrain watching her closely again frowning, and realised she had been looking at Kai as they had been silently communicating. She looked away, cheeks reddening again as she realised he probably thought she was infatuated with the Angel. Better that, she supposed, than he finds out what was really going on.

The blonde warrior spoke bringing her attention back to him. 'You aren't safe here anymore. That Angel knows you're in the area now. It won't take much for him to send more demons to find you. Pack your belongings, we leave in ten minutes.'

'I'm not going anywhere,' she said firmly.

'Demon attacks aren't very common. For there to be two attacks on you in such a short space of time is troubling. We are your Guardians, Kess. Our job is to protect you. The best way we can do that now is to move somewhere that Angel doesn't know about,' Miah explained.

Thrain stood, with Miah following in his wake. They both looked at her expectantly as she remained seated.

'I'm not going anywhere,' she repeated. 'Moving around won't make any difference. If he wants to find me he will,' she said, deliberately not looking at Kai who alone, knew the truth about just how easily Azrin could find her if he wanted to.

'Chronicler,' Thrain said firmly.

'No, Commander. If you go, you go without me,' she crossed her arms about her chest and gave them her most defiant stare.

'Odin's beard! You are the most–' Thrain paused, lost for words; she had never seen him this frustrated before.

'Endearing Chronicler you have ever had the pleasure of guarding?'

Thrain shook his head clearly irritated, but unless he wanted to physically drag her away, he didn't have any other option but to humour her. 'Of all the stubborn Chroniclers to get stuck with,' he muttered.

'So what do we do now?' Kess asked her Guardians.

'*We* inform the Consilium.' Thrain strode from the room, phone in hand.

'In the meantime, you need to go and rest. You look awful,' Miah told her.

'I will take her,' Kai said, reaching out his hand to help Kess up.

Miah didn't look happy, but didn't disagree. 'I suppose she's safe with you,' she admitted grudgingly. 'Look after her, Angel,' she warned Kai.

'With my life,' he replied seriously before vanishing with Kess.

One moment they were in the lounge, the next she was standing in her room, both hands grasping Kai's arms.

'That was – different,' her head spun, making it hard to think.

'Sorry I should have warned you that it can be disorientating until you get used to it, but I didn't want to linger in case your Guardians changed their minds and kicked me out.'

Kess released her grip on his arms and sat on the edge of her bed, throwing her broken phone onto the night stand. 'Thank you for finding me.'

As she scooted back to lean against the wall, the blade holster at her back caught uncomfortably on the bed. She fiddled with the buckle and pulled it free of her waist, holding it in her hands a moment, before throwing it onto the bed near her feet.

Kai noticed her attention on the blade and guessed her thoughts. 'He wouldn't have thought it a threat. Mortal weapons cannot do any lasting damage to Angels.'

'But it's not a mortal weapon, is it?'

He looked at her for a moment before answering. 'No, it isn't. Who told you?'

'Thrain.'

'It's always him,' he muttered.

'Why would you give *me* a weapon like that?' She asked the question she had wanted to know since Thrain had told her about the blade.

'You are special, Kess. I realised it the first time I saw you sitting on that bridge.' Kai moved the chair from the corner of the room, setting it in front of her. 'What happened? You *bonded* that Angel,' he whispered the last words, in disbelief.

'I know.' She clasped her hands in her lap, looking at them as she spoke. 'I realised when Thrain came into the room. I felt Azrin's shock. I can still feel him there in my head.' She touched the temple where his blære nestled within her mind.

'Azrin, is that his name?' He looked at her, worry shining in his eyes. 'A forbandt with more than one Angel is unheard of. It isn't supposed to be possible.' He shook his head slightly, then peered at her like she was a bug under a microscope. 'Maybe you are something new.'

Not liking the way he was looking at her, she changed the topic back to something she could deal with. 'I don't understand how a bond could have happened. It wasn't like the whirlwind when our forbandt formed.' Kess leant back on her hands, considering. 'The only thing I can think of is, well, I bit him.'

'You what?' Kai half yelled.

'He was choking me, I bit him to try to get him to let go. I – his blood – well I swallowed some.' She felt the side of her tongue, remembered the sharp sting. 'I cut my tongue, and my blood was in my mouth when I bit him. Could that create a bond?'

'I have never heard of it before. Usually for a forbandt there has to be willingness by both parties.' He cocked his head to the side deliberating, 'But yes, I guess that by mingling your blood, if it entered you both, could form a blood bond which could possibly override the lack of willingness on his part.' Worry etched the sculptured lines of his face. 'Kess, you have to be careful. The bond may not be complete. You can't trust him.'

'Like Miah said I couldn't trust you?'

'This is different!' He slammed his hands against his knees agitatedly. 'He can find you now.'

'I know. When you figured out what had happened, I sensed it through the blære. I panicked when I realised that he could track me. You saw him. He felt my fear and started to walk towards me.'

'I also saw him fight it. He is confused and angry, Kess. That makes him even more dangerous,' he looked around the room. 'Perhaps I should–'

'No way!' Kess said, cutting him off. 'I already have a permanent warrior guard. This is my room, not a lodging house.'

'I am not a waif, nor am I a stray.' Indignation filled his voice making her laugh. 'Don't lose your distrust of him, Kess.' He begged reaching out to touch her hand.

'I trust I'm not interrupting anything,' Miah asked sarcastically from her position in the doorway, eyebrows raised at their proximity to each other.

Kess jumped, pulling her hand out from under Kai's. 'Just being warned about the dangers of strange Angels.'

Approval lit Miah's face. 'About time you listened to that advice. You ignored me before, now this one is like a stray puppy who won't go home.'

Kai shot Miah an icy look, but otherwise ignored her comment.

'What's the news with the Consilium?' Kess asked, constantly having to intervene between Kai and whatever Guardian was in the room.

'We have requested another Guardian be sent.'

'Conall is being replaced just like that?' Kess demanded, incensed that Miah and everyone else was disregarding his death so easily.

'You have to be guarded. Four Guardians are better than three. They will let us know when they make a decision.'

'Three Guardians and an Angel,' Kai amended.

Miah stared at him in a way which would have had Kess retracting her statement. Kai however just watched her impassively. She searched his face, then nodded, accepting his offer of help.

Kess let out the breath she'd been holding. Finally, a step in the right direction, maybe the Guardian–Angel bigotry wasn't so intransigent after all.

'Why does the Consilium have a say over where a Guardian goes? Isn't that Thrain's decision, as the Commander?' Kess asked, becoming aware of how little she actually knew about the finer points of law within the Haven.

'Normally yes. But as you are an Initiate Chronicler out of the Haven, the Custodians have the final say in this instance.' Miah peered at her. 'You need rest.'

Kess didn't object, her eyes were burning and becoming hard to keep open. She felt just like she knew she looked – tired, battered and sore.

Kai stood, replacing his chair in the corner. 'Remember what I said.'

Kess nodded, stifling a yawn. The movement split her lip again, and blood began to dribble down her chin.

Kai disappeared into the bathroom across the hall returning with a tissue. 'Get some sleep.'

'Where will you be?' Despite her protestations of having him guard her here, Kess felt suddenly nervous about being in her room alone.

'Close by,' he reassured her, before vanishing.

Unable to summons the energy for a shower tonight, she settled for changing her dirty, bloodied clothes instead. Miah made sure Kess was getting into bed before she left the room closing the door behind her.

Despite being exhausted, sleep evaded her. She touched Kai's blære and felt that he was nearby. He must have sensed her contact because a wave of reassurance flowed through their bond.

Tentatively she reached out to the other presence in her mind. She sat just away from the surface, and considered it.

Unlike Kai, she sensed hostility radiating from it, jumbled with disbelief and anxiety. Kess reached toward the blære, lightly touching it.

She flinched as a voice boomed in her head.

You! What have you done to me?

Panic flooded through the bond before she could control it.

Are you afraid, girl? You should be. Undo what you have done, and I will leave you be.

I can't remove it. She risked thinking back to him.

Kess felt a surge of anger and pushed the blære away, cutting off his presence in her mind.

She closed her eyes, eventually drifting off into an uneasy sleep.

CHAPTER 18

A Thaw in the Ice

'Dreams are often most profound when they seem the most crazy.'

Sigmund Freud, *The Interpretation of Dreams*

She ran back to the town, desperation increasing her speed until she felt like she was flying.

Dust filled the air, and an acrid cloud of smoke burnt her lungs making her gasp for every breath. To her horror all she saw was complete and utter destruction.

So much had changed in such a short space of time. This morning there had been streets winding through the neat rows of houses; people milling about chatting with their neighbours.

Now all was in ruins. Not a single building remained intact as far as she could see.

Rubble covered the streets. Babylonians lay where they had been struck, crushed by debris.

Crouching next to the body of an old man she felt a surge of guilty relief that his features were unfamiliar.

This whole city, all its inhabitants had met this fate because of her.

They had come.

White hot rage began to build inside her, cauterising, at least for the moment, the despair and grief.

She kept walking through the destruction, searching.

Kess jolted from sleep, struggling to free her arms from the blankets wrapped tightly around her. Her breath came in short gasps, and tears streamed down her face unchecked. She pushed herself up to sitting, wiping her face dry.

Her eyes stung with the remnants of sleep yet she kept them open, fearing what she would see if she shut them again.

She looked about the room, pitch black apart from a small dim rectangle of light at ground level, which came from a light down the hall. She blinked a few times trying to acclimatise them to the darkness.

Either the lack of sleep, or the unfamiliarity of the room had her imagining figures in the dark. She could almost see an outline in the corner of the room, a spot darker than the area around it – tall and person shaped.

Kess peered at the corner harder, sure she could actually see something. She pressed her eyes tightly shut, then opened them again, yet the shape remained.

There was no lamp near her bed. She would have to pass near the area to turn on the main bedroom light. She opened her mouth to call out to her Guardians, yet hesitated. If it turned out to be a shadow figure – the thing that come morning turned out to be a lamp with a jacket slung over it, she'd never live it down.

Steeling herself, she tensed, ready to make a dash for the light, when the shadow figure shifted.

Kess flinched, her hand hitting her phone which she'd slung on the bedside table earlier in the evening. Not taking her eyes off the figure which was definitely getting closer, she pressed the buttons praying they would work. A dim light emanated from the cracked screen, providing just enough light to show a tall figure as it moved near her bed.

She was about to yell for Miah, when she saw his features in the muted light.

Azrin stood so close she had to crane her neck up to look at him. His bright blue eyes watched her silently.

She sought their bond, and found it strangely quiet.

He reached out and lightly brushed the spot on her jaw where he had struck her. His touch was feather light, whispering against her skin.

Abruptly his chiselled face twisted in anger and he whipped his hand back. The movement was sharp, as if she had slapped it away. His features twisted with a confliction of emotions, like some internal struggle raged within him.

With a soft growl, he vanished.

Her gaze lingered on the empty space where he had stood. She felt strangely calm, despite his reaction to her. So much could change in such a short space of time. Yesterday she had been imprisoned by him, yet today, in a way he was a captive of hers.

Kess, are you alright? Kai's voice was strong in her head.

She considered telling him about her visitor, but knew what his reaction would be. *Bad dream,* she responded, and felt his anxiety immediately quell.

Try and get some more sleep, Kai suggested, before fading away.

She lay back amongst her pillows.

Azrin had found her.

She knew she should be raising the alarm, letting everyone know he had been in her room, but she didn't.

Despite what Kai thought, Kess didn't think he would harm her. A dangerous assumption perhaps, but despite his conflict she believed he had come here tonight, not to harm her, but because of her reaction to the dream she'd had.

She lay back settling herself amongst the covers, and closed her eyes.

Her last thoughts before sleep claimed her were of arctic blue eyes.

~

Kess woke feeling more refreshed than she had in a while, despite the nocturnal disturbance. She reached out to both Kai and Azrin, comforted by their presence.

She had just thrown back the covers when the door burst open.

'Morning,' Miah said brightly as she strode through the door carrying a tray of food. Even though she'd undoubtedly had less sleep than Kess, she looked lively and refreshed.

'Where did you get all this?'

'Thrain.' She lay the tray in Kess's lap, and took a seat on the edge of the bed.

She undid the scrunched top of the white bakery bag suspiciously. 'Thrain's not the type to go out for hot chocolate and blueberry muffins. What's up?'

'He is–'

'–stern, cranky, uncompromising?' Kess said listing a few adjectives that came to mind.

Miah shot a hard look at her then sighed. 'He's all those things, but he feels bad knowing you overheard him and ran out because of that, and then well, all the rest,' she added as an afterthought.

'He feels bad because I heard him, not because of what he said,' Kess said testily. 'I *am* just a Chronicler after all.' She didn't try to keep the bitterness from her voice.

Anger flashed across Miah's face. 'You don't know him, Kess. You see the Guardian. The hard leader he needs to be, but he is also a man underneath all of that. A person, who, like you and I, makes mistakes, and says things we don't mean at times, out of frustration, anger – or a million other reasons. Don't let one stupid comment cloud your judgement of him.' She took a deep breath. 'Look, I didn't come to argue. I wanted to let you know that we've had contact from the Consilium.'

Kess's hand froze halfway to her mouth. 'Well?' she asked, popping the piece of muffin in.

'We had to report the demon attack.' Miah cut off as Kess inhaled sharply, which led to a coughing fit as a piece of muffin got sucked into her windpipe. After a vigorous few taps on her back, the warrior continued. 'Don't worry, nothing else was mentioned. The Consilium tried to recall us immediately, stating it was too dangerous for you to remain in an unprotected area, but,' she added quickly, seeing Kess's mouth open to interrupt, 'Thrain talked them out of it saying that you needed a few more days with your father. Drazen denied our request for another Guardian.'

Kess shrugged. 'He didn't want us coming in the first place. It's not surprising that he wouldn't want to send anyone else.'

Miah smiled slyly. 'Your new Guardian will be arriving this afternoon.' The warrior watched her closely trying to gauge her reaction.

'Who is he?'

'Her,' Miah emphasised, 'name is Zuri. She's a bit unorthodox but that should suit you,' she said with a small smile and an arch of her eyebrow. 'She's from Bandar, the Asian Haven.'

'Why would she be sent over someone from Athenaeum?'

'The Quaternary Council is still sitting, and *somehow* word of the attack leaked. Zuri volunteered herself, and being from another Haven, Drazen couldn't refuse,' Miah smiled victoriously.

'I don't suppose one of you had anything to do with this *leak* of information?'

Miah's face became blank. 'Are you suggesting one of your Guardians divulged something they shouldn't?'

'No, of course not,' Kess replied just as sarcastically.

'Didn't think so,' the warrior said straight–faced, eyes twinkling.

'Do you trust her?'

'She is a Guardian,' Miah stated simply, as if that was reason enough.

Kess sipped her hot chocolate, then dropped the paper cup sending a fountain of liquid shooting up out of the little hole in the lid. 'Angel feathers!' she cursed, receiving a raised eyebrow from her Guardian. 'Does Dad know about any of this?'

Miah looked at her calmly. 'Robert hasn't been told anything. We thought he might become agitated if we said that you'd been kidnapped, and we didn't know how to find you.'

Kess thought that "*agitated*" was an understatement. As sanguine as her father generally was, he would have been beside himself with worry, especially after the news of her mother.

‘What am I going to do? This,’ she indicated the bruising on her face, ‘is not exactly inconspicuous.’

‘It’s Thursday. You agreed to see him tonight. He’ll think something is wrong if you don’t go.’

‘I can’t miss our dinner,’ Kess agreed, knowing he would already be worried about her lack of contact over the last few days. All she had to do now was figure out how to explain the marks on her face without him freaking out. ‘Maybe I’ll just edit what happened a bit.’

‘To what, that you slipped in the shower?’ Miah asked sarcastically. She stood, hands on hips. ‘Time to get up, things to do.’

‘Don’t Guardians ever need to sleep?’ She shook her head at Miah’s grin. ‘Alright if I clean up a bit first?’

Miah nodded. ‘If you’re quick. Training starts in five.’

Kess jumped out of bed, grabbed a change of clothes and headed across the hall to the bathroom for a speedy shower.

As she dressed again, taking care with the wounds on her back, she pulled off the sodden bandage covering the demon scratches on her arm. With everything else that had been going on, it seemed like a lifetime ago since she had gotten them. As the last layer of gauze was removed, she froze, not quite believing what she was seeing. The wound had completely scabbed over, with some bits flaking off, revealing tender, healthy pink skin underneath.

She put the tub of her mother’s salve back on the sink unopened, wondering what it was made from, that could heal a wound so quickly.

Needing to see how bad the damage was to her face, she wiped the mirror with her towel, clearing the beaded droplets, and sucked in a breath. Mottled bruising covered the left side of her face, all the way to her jaw, which was visibly swollen. The cut on her lip was tender and still pulled when she moved her mouth, but didn’t keep splitting open as it had last night. All in all, it was bad enough that she would have a hard time coming up with a plausible reason as to why she was so battered and bruised.

She cursed herself for not having enough wits about her last night to rub some of that cream into her face. If she had her face might have nearly been healed.

Not wanting to dwell on something she couldn't change, she left and found Miah pacing in the lounge. 'How would you have found me if it wasn't for Kai?'

Miah put her hand on her hips, a deep furrow lined her brow. '*We* are Guardians, and have been protecting our charges for – years.' She hesitated, changing what she had been going to say. 'We've done just fine until now without your Angel around.'

'Can you stop calling him that. His name is Kai. K. A. I.' Kess spelled it out, hoping the warrior would stop being so Guardian–like in her distrust of him. She noted that Miah had failed to answer her question, but didn't press the point, not wanting to antagonise the Guardians dislike of the Angel further.

Kess had just perched on the arm of one of the sofas when Kisho walked in looking around hopefully. 'Did you save me any breakfast?'

Kess shook her head laughing.

'How am I supposed to protect you if I'm weak with hunger?' He rubbed his stomach which chose that moment to let out a growl, much to her amusement. 'See! Starving,' he said, sorrowfully.

'Get a move on.' Thrain's voice came from the doorway behind them. His gruffness had the others moving quickly, but she stood slowly, watching him. His grey eyes were flat today, and there was a tiredness to his face that hadn't been there before the events of the last few days.

His haggard appearance softened the enmity she harboured, and she decided to take Miah's advice, and try to forgive what he'd said.

Nodding, she tried to let him know they were alright, from her end anyway. She received a nod in return. And maybe it was her imagination but his eyes didn't look as dull as they had moments before.

'In a good mood today then, Thrain?'

'You too, Chronicler. Inside,' he growled, but she saw a small twitch of his lips.

'Yes, Commander,' Kess mocked, following behind the others.

'Knife practice,' Thrain announced as he entered, sending the two warriors scuttling off.

Not sure what to help with, she remained beside him while the others dragged out two heavy looking mannequins, both pitted with holes.

'Do you still have your knife?' Thrain asked her.

She pulled the small blade out of her side sheath, offering it to him hilt first.

He nodded his head towards the dummies.

Kess held the knife briefly before letting it fly. The knife came to a quivering halt embedded up to the hilt, just left of the centre of the red target.

Thrain moved up beside her, his axe in hand. 'Try this.'

'Are you serious?'

He held the weapon out to Kess, offering it to her in both hands.

Her hand closed around the handle of the axe, gripping the wood worn smooth with use. The blade was long and thin, with a wicked looking point at one end. Though heavier than the knives, it sat comfortably in her grip.

She stepped away from him, and swung the weapon to and fro, getting used to its weight. She aimed the same way she had previously, and let it fly. The sharpened edge struck the circle and collided with the embedded knife, sending it clattering to the ground.

Seized by impulse, she darted forwards retrieved the knife from the ground, and flung it at the next target, hitting the mannequin in the forehead.

Realising what she'd done, Kess looked around embarrassed, but instead of teasing she was met by Thrain's approving glance.

'Good.' Was all he said, before walking away towards where Miah was climbing a rope attached to the roof.

Satisfaction flowed through her. A compliment – no matter how sparing – was hard to earn from Thrain.

Kess looked around, waiting for a smart comment from Conall, then caught herself. She'd miss his weird sayings and the winks he gave her whenever she came into a room. Feeling the catch in her throat and not wanting to become upset in front of the Guardians, she focused on Miah as she scurried up the rope reaching the top in moments, then descended just as easily.

'You need to build your core strength.' Thrain moved beside her and reached out, encircling her upper arm easily with his fingers. 'You have no hope of defeating anything in close combat, as weak as you are.'

Kess's cheeks heated with a flush of embarrassment and a touch of anger. *Tell that to the Rask and the Dragon,* she thought tartly, biting back the urge to voice her opinion. At least he was including her, training her as he would a Guardian. 'You want me to climb that?'

'I want you to try,' he taunted, hurling the end of the rope in her direction.

She stood at the base looking up. It was a long way to the top.

Not wanting to give Thrain the satisfaction of giving up before she'd even tried, she copied what Miah had done moments before. She reached up as far as she could, gripping the rope with both hands, then let the rope fall beside one leg. Standing on the rope with that foot Kess then slid the other foot under the braid anchoring herself in place.

Pushing her weight against her feet, hoping her grip held, she extended her arms again and repeated the process. Concentrating on the small set of movements – extend, grip, push – she kept climbing until her fingers met the cold metal of the roof.

Kess looked around in amazement at the room from her aerial view. She glanced down and saw Thrain and Miah standing near the base of the rope, both looking up at her. Miah's hand gestures appeared agitated, even from this height. Kisho headed in their direction and joined them, also peering up at her.

Looking down, she realised that although she'd made it to the top, she had no idea how to get down again. She released the grip of her hands and feet slightly and was rewarded with a slow but steady descent back to the ground.

Thrain and Kisho had moved away by the time her feet hit the floor. Miah met her with a smile, but Kess saw uncertainty dancing in her eyes.

'What's wrong?'

'Nothing.' The brunette warrior's reply came too quickly.

Kess crossed her arms and stared silently at the Guardian until Miah shrugged, and answered grudgingly, 'You're very good at all of this.'

'Is that bad?' Confusion furrowed her brow.

'No. It's not,' Miah said in a tone which didn't agree with her statement.

'Then what is it?' Kess pressed.

'You're too good for a first timer. You have never thrown a knife before a few days ago, but you keep hitting the central zone of the targets,' she continued as she saw Kess's eyebrows rise. 'You just climbed a fifty–foot rope without being shown how.'

Kess's brow furrowed yet she remained silent, unsure how to respond. She thought they would have been happy she wasn't totally useless at all this physical stuff.

'Look, just forget I said anything. You're doing really well,' Miah said, as she walked away towards the training mat. 'Care to spar?'

'Against you? I wouldn't last five seconds.'

The warrior grinned, squaring herself within the centre of the mat.

Kess shrugged. 'Guess a few more bruises wouldn't hurt,' she said jokingly, and regretted it instantly as Miah's face clouded over.

She lunged forwards, trying to distract the warrior, with a right–handed jab which the brunette blocked as easily as an adult would a child's punch, then had to scramble backwards as a barrage of strikes came her way.

As Kess's heel reached the edge of the mat, she knew she'd have to strike now, she dived to the side, rolled and came up in a crouch.

Her Guardian reacted lightning quick, and was already turning when Kess struck out with her foot seeking to unbalance her.

Miah once again anticipated the move, and reacted accordingly, dodging to the side and kicking out as Kess was rising, catching her in the stomach.

Miah stepped back waiting for Kess to right herself, which took some effort.

She moved to the side, balancing on the balls of her feet, watching the Guardian for any movement.

The attack came with a single strike which Kess managed to block, feeling pleased with herself, then before she realised what had happened, she was on the ground with her arm twisted behind her back and her face pressed against the mat.

'Ohhh,' she groaned. 'What was that?'

'A judo throw,' Miah said, breathing level and even despite their sparring. 'You're doing well, beginning to assess and anticipate your opponent's actions.'

'When does "doing well" equate to me not ending up flat on my face?' Kess asked from her prone position.

'Miah, wrap it up, we've got company.' Thrain looked down at her, craning his head sideways as if trying to figure out why she was lying on the mat. 'Tired, Chronicler?' he asked straight–faced.

CHAPTER 19

The Amazon

Kess stood nervously next to Miah, not sure what to expect of her new Guardian. But the well dressed, dark–skinned woman who waltzed into the room behind Kisho was not what she had envisaged.

The short–styled Mohawk running down the middle of her head, streaked with blue and shaved at each side, gave her the look of an Amazonian warrior woman, especially with the curled tattoo running up her neck. The most striking feature about her however was her blue eyes, so pale against her the colour of her skin they appeared almost bleached.

Zuri walked straight over to her, and looked her over, before speaking. 'I am sorry about the loss of your Guardian.'

She was wiry, yet exuded strength and confidence, like Miah, but unlike the brunette she had a ready smile that put you at ease. Kess found herself immediately liking the woman.

Thrain as always, didn't mince words, and was straight to the point. 'You can have the night off Zuri, start tomorrow.'

'I'm fine to take watch tonight. I'm sure none of you have slept much in the last few days.'

Thrain gave her an approving look, then nodded. 'You're done for the day,' he said dismissing Kess.

'Come on, I'll show you where your room is while our charge freshens up.' Miah stepped forward leading the new Guardian away.

Kess trailed behind the pair, before veering off at her room to change.

Zuri turned from her conversation with Miah, watching her intently. As she shut her door, she heard the new Guardian ask, 'She really killed a Rask?'

Kess shook her head – Guardians really were the same the world over.

Listening for Miah's response she heard her say, 'The latest attack was a dragkheir.'

'And she survived?' Zuri asked in stunned surprise.

'She killed it.'

Kess heard pride in Miah's voice and smiled, at least she was endearing herself to one of the head Guardian.

Knowing there was no rush, she took her time to freshen up, trying to conceal the damage done to her face, but after fifteen minutes, conceded defeat. There was no hiding the mass of bruises and swollen flesh. Heading out into the lounge she found the others talking with their newest member.

'I hear we have a dinner date tonight,' Zuri said, looking at her watch. She was still dressed in the same clothes as earlier and appeared unarmed, but after spending so much time around Guardians recently, Kess noted a flash of silver concealed within her sleeve as she checked the time; the leather sash crossing her chest which undoubtedly held a long blade diagonally across her back, and she also would have been willingly to bet that her knee–high boots contained a few other hidden weapons.

'Zuri was just about to tell us the news from Athenaeum,' Miah said, explaining their gathering.

'The Quaternary Council is still sitting however they did make an announcement before I left. A ferrety–faced fellow–'

Kess couldn't suppress her laugh at Zuri's description of who was sure to be Captol Wessler.

After a quizzical look at her, Zuri continued, '–stated that the Council were discussing a number of issues including the declining number of Chronicler initiates and some other nonsense. But I did happen to glean a bit of information I thought you would find interesting. Something on their agenda they neglected to mention is the recent spate of attacks on Chroniclers whilst on assignment.

‘I had a chat with a Guardian I know from Weichen who happened to be at one of the attacks. He said that it was definitely a demon attack and that they unquestionably targeted the Chronicler, withdrawing after he was killed.’ She paused, letting them digest the information.

‘I also found out there have been seventeen more attacks, not including yours, all targeting Chroniclers. Nine have been killed, six badly injured and two escaped unharmed because of some quick thinking from their Guardians. No one is admitting any link between the Chroniclers or what they could have been researching that would warrant such blatant demonic attacks.’

None of the other warriors had any more information about the attacks, which Kess found alarming. *Why were they being covered up?* At least that explained now why the Consilium had wanted their group to return to Athenaeum after learning about the assault.

She sat back in her chair, in troubled silence until her new Guardian told her that it was time to go.

After saying goodbye to the others, she walked through the network of tunnels and out into the street with her Amazonian Guardian. Zuri waited until they had shut the door behind them before saying, ‘Thrain’s a bit of a hard arse, isn’t he?’

‘He’s had a rough week.’ Kess defended her Guardian, even though she thought calling Thrain “a bit of a hard arse” was like saying steel was kinda hard to bend.

Zuri looked at her. ‘True,’ she conceded, then cast her gaze up and down the street. ‘Which way are we going?’

Kess pointed to the left and started walking the short distance back to Hermitage. ‘How did you get assigned to me?’

‘I volunteered.’ Zuri met her gaze with eerily pale eyes, which seemed to stare right though Kess, making her feel that the Guardian was looking into her soul.

‘Why?’

‘I’ve known Miah for a long time. She called and told me what was happening. You sounded like an interesting person to be around.’

Miah had called her?

‘Two people I know have been murdered in front of me in the last few days. One of them my mother. *Interesting* is not the word I would use.’ Anger thrummed through Kess, heating her words.

The dark–skinned woman grabbed her arm, pulling her to a stop. ‘I’m sorry. I know you’ve been through a lot. I only meant that you seem to be a very special person. One worth protecting.’

The fire in Kess’s chest spluttered. ‘I don’t want anyone else dying because of me.’

Zuri’s eyes softened in understanding. She let go of Kess and started walking again, changing the subject. ‘So, dinner at your Dad’s? How are you going to explain all of that?’ she asked pointing to Kess’s face.

‘Training?’ At Zuri’s sceptical look she sighed. ‘I don’t know. He’s going to worry no matter what I tell him.’

Not wanting to think about that just yet, Kess took the opportunity to find out more about her new Guardian. ‘What’s your weapon of choice?’ She may not know a lot about the warriors but she did know they all had their own particular weapon that they favoured, and carried with them at all times.

Thrain had his axe and sword; which she had learnt was called a gladius, Miah had her throwing daggers and a sword – a spatha – and Kisho carried twin tantou swords, which she had read were definitely Japanese in origin.

Zuri’s eyes lit up. ‘I use a short sword.’ She stroked the weapon at her side fondly. ‘But the haladie is my favourite.’ She pulled out a strange weapon from a scabbard on her back, that looked like two curved daggers joined together at the hilt.

Kess’s head whipped around, frantically scanning the street waiting for passers–by to start freaking out; but the few people around barely gave them a second look. ‘Put that thing away before you get us arrested!’ She hissed at her unconcerned companion.

The dark–skinned woman flashed a white–toothed grin at her before she began twirling the weapon around in hand. Cocking her head to the side she studied Kess. ‘Have your Guardians not explained it to you?’

Her brow furrowed, as she wondered what the warrior meant.

Zuri's lip curled as she shook her head – in either surprise or disgust – Kess didn't know her well enough to be able to tell yet.

'When we become Guardians, we are given gifts of sorts. One of those is anonymity. We are able to blend in with our surroundings allowing us to go unnoticed by people.'

'You can become invisible?' Kess asked sceptically.

'Not invisible but people cease to notice us, or if they do they forget us just as quickly. The same goes for our weapons, allowing us to be armed in public.'

'Why the normal clothes then? Why not just wear your Guardians outfit?'

Zuri shrugged. 'Most of the time we do. In this case, I suspect it was to make you feel more comfortable with your Guardians outside of your Haven. Though it can also help to increase the sense of normalcy of anyone that sees us. Though there is the rare person who can see past the concealments, for the most part we could run through the streets naked waving our swords about, if we chose, and not cause a stir.'

Kess couldn't help but grin at the thought of Thrain streaking through the streets of London, but her mirth vanished as they stepped into the small alley beside Hermitage, which led to her father's flat.

Standing at the back door Kess was still unsure what she was going to say to him. What plausible explanation could she come up with for why she looked like she'd been smacked in the face with a building.

His face as he opened the door, confirmed her worry about his reaction. 'Bloody hell!' Her father must have been shocked because he never swore. 'Kess, are you alright? Come in,' he ushered her through the doorway and was about to close the door when he looked outside. 'Your Guardian might as well come in.'

'Zuri?' she asked leaving the choice up to her.

The warrior sauntered over, eyeing her father in a speculative manner. 'Greetings, Mr Grayson.'

'Guardian,' Robert replied. His eyes darted to Kess, as she folded her arms about her chest. 'Call me Robert.'

They followed her father up the stairs and into the lounge. Zuri immediately took place beside the door leaning back against the wall, while Kess took a seat next to her father and was about to start trying to explain the last few days, when a burning smell wafted from the kitchen.

'Dad, what are you cooking?'

Robert leapt up and raced into the kitchen. They heard banging and clattering coming from the small room and she couldn't help but laugh when he emerged with a downcast look on his face. 'Feel like pizza for dinner?'

'Sure,' she said hiding her smile.

He returned to the kitchen and she heard the muffled sound of his voice as he ordered their dinner. When he returned he sat beside her on the couch, as she settled back, pulling one leg up under the other.

'What attacked you? And why do you have a new Guardian?'

She looked at him in surprise. 'How do you know she's new?' Kess asked, choosing the lesser of the two questions.

'What happened?' Robert repeated, not going to be put off.

'Demon attack.'

'Where were your Guardians?'

'Conall was with me, Dad.' Her throat closed up, so she paused and took a breath before continuing, with a rather edited version of events that did not include nearly two days of captivity, Azrin, or the attack by the dragon.

Even so, worry lines etched Robert's face like deep chasms. 'Kess, demon attacks are–'

'Rare,' she finished for him. 'So I keep getting told.'

'To have two this close together – and one of your Guardians slain–' he trailed off and looked at Zuri. 'What does the Consilium think?'

Kess stared at her dad. It was easy to forget how much he knew about Chroniclers, and everything that life entailed. Whenever she came home to visit, they steered away from anything to do with Athenaeum, because she knew it was painful for him because of her mother.

Zuri took his knowledge in stride, answering his question without hesitation. 'I have no idea. I'm not privy to what the Quaternary are meeting about, but they seem agitated about something.'

Robert sat back in his chair looking shocked. 'There is a meeting of the Council?' At Zuri's nod he raised a hand to forehead thinking. 'Big things are happening if they're convening. They wouldn't stir without serious provocation.' Fear filled his eyes as he looked at her. 'Your Guardians are going to want to move you somewhere safe.' Conflicting emotions played out on his face; the desire for her safety, versus his wish to have her close by.

'They've already mentioned it, and I told them I'm not going anywhere.'

A small smile played on his face. 'Stubborn, just like your mother.' He grabbed both of her hands then, looking very serious. 'You have to go, Kess. It's not safe here anymore. If they have found you once they'll do it again. If they believe you have something they want, they won't stop, until they have whatever it is, or until – until you're dead.'

She shook her head. 'I'm not leaving you and Jinnah here unprotected. Where is she this time?'

Robert exhaled. 'In her room. Apparently, she's too tired for dinner tonight.'

She was saved from answering when the doorbell rang, and their attention was diverted, at least for the moment, by the pizza.

During the meal, she caught her father watching her with troubled eyes more than once.

~

'We're being followed.' Zuri spoke quietly. 'They've been on us since we left your father's. Keep heading towards the refuge.' The warrior's hands flitted to her weapons as she spoke.

'Where are you going?' Kess whispered back, fighting the urge to look over her shoulder.

‘To see who’s behind us.’

As they passed the next street Zuri casually turned down it, leaving Kess to continue alone. She crossed the street and made it past several shop fronts before she heard a muffled cry, and the thump of someone being thrown against a brick wall.

She knew she should continue on like she’d been told, but she had never been very good at obeying orders, so she turned, curious to see who her Guardian had caught. Kess shaded her eyes as she passed back under the street light, not wanting to night blind her eyes.

As she crossed the road she saw two figures standing close to each other, in the shadow of the street corner.

A passer–by might assume it to be a courting couple, and would instinctively avert their eyes, but she recognised Zuri’s tan leather jacket, and similarly coloured knee–high boots.

‘Wait,’ Kess yelled when she saw the familiar trendy styled blonde hair. ‘That’s my sister.’

Zuri held Jinnah up against the brick wall. ‘I told you to keep walking. What if there was more than just her following us?’

‘Then they could have got me while I was walking all alone up the road then, couldn’t they,’ she retorted.

Zuri shook her head, muttering something uncomplimentary under her breath.

The smile at her Guardians displeasure slid from her face as she turned to her sister. ‘What are you doing, Jinnah? You don’t come out for dinner, but you’re, what – worried about me getting home?’

The shock on the blonde’s face at her capture was ebbing, replaced with anger instead. ‘Why would I be worried about you when you have them,’ Jinnah spat, nodding in Zuri’s direction.

‘What’s your problem?’ Kess hissed as her frustration got the better of her. ‘You’ve been nothing but rude since my – friends and I arrived.’

‘Friends!’ She laughed. ‘What would a freak like you know about friends?’

Kess took a step back, stunned by her sister’s venomous words.

‘We were doing fine without you. But then you had to come back, and now Dad can’t stop talking about you.’

‘You’re jealous?’ Kess was stunned, her life was nothing to wish for. ‘Why?’

‘Jealous!’ Jinnah screeched. ‘You’re a freak. Why would I want to be like you?’ She started thrashing in Zuri’s tight grip, trying to get away. ‘Let me go,’ she screamed.

Her Guardian looked at Kess, waiting for her judgement.

Sick to her stomach from her sister’s hatred, Kess just shook her head. ‘Let her go,’ she said softly, watching her sister run away into the night without a backward glance.

‘You can’t choose your family,’ Zuri said monitoring her charge’s face. ‘Come on, let’s get you back.’

CHAPTER 20

Breach of the Refuge

As they traipsed through the refuge, Kess and Zuri found the others in the lounge.

Relief was clear on Miah's face as she got the all clear nod from Zuri. 'Any problems?'

'Only a minor disturbance on the way back,' Zuri said.

Miah's eyes widened. 'Demons?'

'Worse.' The dark–skinned warrior said with a straight face. 'The sister.'

'Jinnah decided to follow us.' Kess explained as she took a seat next to Kisho.

'Did she see you come here?' Thrain put aside his book, looking intently at them, as he leant forward, arms across his knees.

'No. We were no more than half way here. She scurried back home after I had a little chat with her.'

The warriors tone was confident, but Kess saw a flicker of doubt in her pale blue eyes.

Thrain nodded, apparently satisfied with her report, and leant back reaching for his book again.

Kisho collected the discarded cards on the table and shuffled. 'Care for a game? I could use some help against her.' He nodded towards Miah whose face had taken on a very satisfied look.

'What are we playing?' Zuri asked.

'Nine–card brag.' Kisho dealt out their cards and was starting to explain the rules to Kess when a loud crash brought the Guardians to their feet.

For a split second, they looked to Thrain who jerked his chin sending Miah and Kisho racing from the room. Zuri positioned herself a few metres from the doorway and Thrain centred himself in front of her, shielding Kess with his body.

'I can help,' she protested.

'You can help by listening to your Guardians for once.' He turned his head. 'Please.' There was a roughness to his voice, which she hadn't heard before, unnerving her. He waited for her nod before turning back around.

Silence.

Then another crash. This one louder.

The walls seemed to shake with the concussion of the impact. The lights flickered dangerously, threatening to send them into darkness.

Zuri turned, a grim look settling on her face as she looked from Thrain to her newly acquired charge. 'I think we're about to have company.'

'Regretting volunteering yet?' Kess asked.

The Amazonian's broad grin answered her question.

'Guardians,' Kess muttered, 'you're all crazy.' She saw Thrain's head shake, hearing her comment.

Miah skidded to a halt in front of the doorway so fast Zuri had her weapons raised before she realised who it was.

'Report,' Thrain barked.

'Kisho's out in the tunnels, says there is a lot of movement out there. Something's trying to break through the western wall. The brick is holding so far, but fractures are starting to appear.'

'Time?' Thrain's voice was calm.

'Minutes, if we're lucky,' Miah replied just as sanguine.

Heart pounding in her ears, Kess didn't know how they could be so blasé about an imminent attack on their secret hideout, by unknown person or persons.

As if to punctuate the brunette's statement, another loud thud echoed through the room. This time a shower of fine dust and tiny fragments of debris rained down around them. Kess looked at the roof, suddenly worried that it was about to collapse on their heads.

'Can we get her out?' Thrain asked, looking to his second.

Miah shook her head. 'Demons are blocking the entrance.'

'Confirmed?'

'Yes.' The brunette warrior gave a short nod of her head.

'Are you sure Kess's sister didn't follow you? Lead them here?' Thrain demanded of their newest member.

Zuri looked back at Kess, hesitating. 'I didn't think she did.'

'She wouldn't consort with the demons!' Kess protested.

'Are you sure?' Thrain asked.

There was something in his voice which made her question the surety of her feelings. She thought about the way her sister had been acting since she'd come back. The hostility she'd displayed tonight, and reluctantly shook her head. 'No, I'm not.'

Thrain nodded, lips pressed tightly together before turning his attention back to the others. 'Right, this room is the best place to defend with the narrow doorway to bottleneck them. Move the furniture to the walls to give us more space to move. Where's–'

Kisho skidded through the doorway cutting off whatever Thrain had been going to say. 'We've got–'

A tremendous roar came from the direction of the training room, silencing them all. It sounded like the whole room had collapsed, the crashing and clattering of falling debris lasted what seemed like minutes to Kess, but was probably only seconds.

Then came a different kind of roar.

Demons.

Unlike her, the Guardians had not remained idle during the pandemonium of noise, quickly pushing the chairs, tables and anything else that was a potential tripping hazard to the side of the room, creating a clear space.

Miah returned from a cupboard at the corner of the room with an armful of what looked like chest armour, handing one out to each of them.

Raising it over her head Kess let the leather weight settle heavily on her chest. Her hands shook as she tried to tighten the buckles.

Thrain pulled the strap from her hand and threaded it through the buckle. He of course already had his on.

She looked down at the thick leather plate protecting her torso and felt the one on her back pull up with her movement.

'It's simple, but it will help protect you.' He moved to the other side and fixed the straps. 'Nervousness before battle is normal,' he said softly, holding her eyes. 'Even the most hardened warriors experience it before a fight, yet as soon as battle begins, everything but the moment, your next move, vanishes.'

'You don't look nervous.'

Thrain didn't answer just continued buckling her into her body armour. 'Remember this will stop most things but some species of demon have razor sharp talons which could pierce it. Don't take any unnecessary risks.'

'You too,' she said softly, unable to contemplate losing another Guardian, when Conall's death was so fresh in her mind.

Kisho and Zuri drew their weapons, and took position guarding each side of the doorway. With his twin tantou swords, and his period hairstyle Kisho looked like he could have stepped from the set of a samurai movie, except the glint reflecting from his blade appeared far more deadly than anything Hollywood could conjure.

Zuri unsheathed her haladie and twirled it about her slowly checking the distance from the warrior beside her.

Miah centred herself a few feet behind them, a throwing knife in each hand, whilst Thrain who'd finished tightening her chest plate, resumed his place in front of her; gripping his short axe in his left hand and sword in his right.

She drew her own weapons, becoming familiar with the weight of them in her hands, and waited for the mayhem to start.

They didn't have to wait long until the first demon charged into the room.

She saw only a semi–human looking shape before Zuri cut it down with her haladie, striking the first cut across its chest then reversing the swing, and slashing its throat with the back swing.

A second demon followed, attacking Kisho, before the first hit the ground in a geyser of flame. With the barest flick of his wrists the creature was felled, impaled by his swords and disappeared in an inferno of light.

The next demon foolish enough to enter this room of death was so strange looking that Kess stopped paying attention to anything but how it looked. Long black spines covered the creature like a lion's mane from its chest all the way up to its cruel hooked beak which opened in a snarl to reveal a mouthful of carnivorous teeth. Instead of skin, the creature was covered in dark feathers which looked to be coated with a tar–like substance. Small geysers of steam rose from holes burnt into the carpet wherever the dark liquid splattered.

A flash of silver spun through the air and the demon staggered with Miah's knife hilt protruding from its right eye. It wavered for a moment before exploding in a flash of sulphurous orange light.

Zuri and Kisho weaved silver webs of death slaughtering any demon who ventured too close. Metal flashed between them like hand flung bullets as Miah felled any hells spawn they missed.

Yet the demons spawn still fought and clawed past each other to get into the room in such numbers that they started to slip past Zuri and Kisho, meeting their deaths on Miah's spatha which she had drawn, having exhausted her supply of throwing knives.

As quickly as Miah slashed and stabbed, she too was soon hard pressed, as two demons replaced every one which was felled.

Kess pulled her knife holding it in her right hand whilst her left gripped the hilt of the Angel blade. Even with her untrained eye she realised they would soon be overrun. Although her grip on the weapons was slick with nervous sweat, she took a step forward, determined to help.

'Fall back,' Thrain called suddenly, sensing her movement.

Her other forbandt bubble quivered as Kai appeared in a rush of wind to her right. Striped with black demon blood, he had his long sword unsheathed already.

'Sorry I'm late.' He gave her a wild grin. 'Azrin,' he stated cordially, as if he was greeting an acquaintance at a dinner party, rather than a former foe in the midst of a battle, surrounded by a horde of angry demons trying to kill them. 'Glad to see you've joined us,' he said, clearly sensing the difference in the Angel.

'You are lucky I did or she would be dead,' the arctic angel replied coolly.

Kai looked sharply at Kess, and saw the injured arm which she held about her middle protectively.

The two Angels exchanged a glance, and plunged forwards annihilating everything in their paths. Their weapons became a blur of movement, and although she couldn't see the individual strokes she could judge where they landed from the carnage caused amongst the demons.

The hells spawn fought on, unrelenting, until the last one died growling beneath Kai's sword.

Putting his foot on the demon's carcass Kai wrenched his blade free before the hells spawn descended, and turned locating her instantly where she stood beside Azrin.

Breathing heavily Kess glanced around, and saw much to her relief, hat although covered with ichor, all of her Guardians were very much live.

The four turned, converging on Kess, shielding her behind their bodies. Veapons drawn they faced the two Angels who sheathed their own blades, nd for all intents and purposes ignored the warriors, focusing their ttention on her instead.

The tension between the two groups grew, becoming an almost lpable, physical presence.

Kess struggled against Zuri who grabbed her uninjured arm as she ied to step forward. 'Lucifer's breath! Will you listen to me!' The hemence of her yelled curse stopped the Guardians advance. 'They lped us. Without them I would be dead. We all would be!' She looked at ch of the warriors until they met her eyes. 'Neither of them are a threat

Killing the creatures they were battling, all three warriors fell back instantly, forming a circle in the middle of the room with Kess as its nucleus.

'Hell no,' she said, moving between Kisho and Zuri.

'Kess, centre,' Thrain commanded.

'I'm good here,' she replied, and risked a quick glance at him.

The muscle in his jaw tightened, but he met her eyes, and nodded.

The cacophony of howls, hisses, and clicks was jarring, inhibiting Kess. The distraction of noise was something she hadn't anticipated and hadn't yet been trained to deal with.

Firmly she sought her centre, focusing on the weight of the sword in her hand, ignoring everything else.

They stood in a ring, shoulder to shoulder, whilst the demons surrounded them, displaying a viscous array of fangs, talons and claws.

Strangely enough the hells spawn didn't immediately attack giving Kess a chance to look around their wide circle. Determination shone on the faces of the Guardians, but she knew despite their abilities they would be overwhelmed at some point.

'Fine time for your Angel not to turn up,' Miah joked.

Kess cursed herself for not thinking to contact him sooner. *Kai.* She thought. *Where are you?*

A creature that looked like a mutated prairie dog snarled sending the demons surging forwards, engulfing them in seconds. Knife in one hand and short sword in the other, Kess hacked and slashed at anything that came near her.

She heard the clash of weapons on either side but couldn't risk looking at her Guardians, needing all her focus to deal with the ugly hell ferret in front of her.

It's clawed hand swiped, missing Kess by centimetres as she pulled back fractionally at the last second. She whipped her sword around, and met resistance before wrenching the blade free. Hot liquid gushed down her arm, splattering her face. She spat the acidic taste from her mouth, bringing her weapons back around as she did, ready for the next attack.

Within seconds a reptilian demon surged forward, stepping on the smouldering ashes which was all that remained of the demon who had just fallen under her blade. Its forked tongue hissed as it licked its lipless mouth, scenting the air as it focused on her.

Fighting her revulsion, she lunged forward and rammed the blade of her knife up under its plated head, skewering through the soft skin under its jaw.

She chanced a glance around, and saw the others were as hard pressed as she was. They'd been fighting for no more than a few minutes yet already her arms already with fatigue and the demons showed no sign of thinning; if anything, their numbers were increasing.

A high–pitched growl brought her attention back to the fight. She spun towards the sound, and saw a fanged mouth launching for her throat. Kess instinctively moved her arm to protect her face, then felt the burning sharpness as the hells spawn's teeth sunk into the flesh of her forearm, scraping against the bone.

Clenching her teeth against the fiery pain she plunged her dagger deep into the creature's chest. It howled, but didn't let go, only tightened its grip on her arm instead, before shaking its hyena–like head. She screamed as the demon's razor–sharp teeth tore through the flesh of her arm.

The sword fell from her hand as the muscles in her damaged left arm went limp unable to keep their grip on the hilt. Kess plunged her knife into the eye of the canid–like creature, killing it instantly. It fell lifelessly pulling the blade out of her hands, leaving her unarmed. She watched in horror as another demon surged forwards, jaws open, talons outstretched.

Weaponless, she knew she had no chance, but she braced herself to strike, unable to just give up and die without a fight. Just before the hellion reached her, a figure materialised behind it, grabbing it by the head and wrenching its long neck backwards, snapping it with a loud crack.

She saw his ice blue eyes, and froze in amazement.

Are you alright? Azrin asked through their blære. His eyes, normally cold and contemptuous, looked her over with concern.

Thanks to you. Kess replied, scooping her knife from the ground. The blade was warm, heated by the descent flames of the extirpated demon.

She jammed it back into its holster then retrieved her Angelic bla
holding it awkwardly in her non–dominant hand.

She held her injured left arm against her middle, not wanting
Guardians to see the blood running down her hand coating her fingerti

Azrin stood beside her guarding her injured side against the onco
demons.

'Kess move!' Kisho yelled frantically from her right.

She spun to see the warrior moving towards her, weapons out. I
looking at Azrin who, upon seeing the approaching Guardian, snar
made no move to defend himself, trusting Kess to deal with the si
leaving his back exposed, whilst he dispatched the attacking demor

'Kisho! No!' she yelled, placing herself in front of her G
weapons.

'Move!' He dodged to the side trying to get past her.

'He just saved me from a demon.'

'It's a trick. He took you. Beat you. Why are you defend
Confusion filled Kisho's face.

'We have enough enemies to fight. Trust me please. I will ex
later.'

Deep lines furrowed the skin above his eyebrows; a clear in
his bewilderment about the situation, yet with an intent glanc
nodded and turned back to face the demons, taking his frustr
them, ripping and slashing any creature which came within hi

Kess turned back around and found Azrin watching her. S
a small, tight lipped smile, reaching out to grip his arm as sh
his bright blue eyes.

The world about them ceased to exist as she felt herself
whirlwind, identical to the one she'd felt when she had b
their forbandt was sealed she felt her palm tingle and k
Angel would be marked with the same symbol.

Kess came back to herself, hearing the sounds of ba
them. She looked to Azrin, and as one they moved forwa
by side against the demons that seemed without end.

to you. Or to me,' she wrenched her arm free and pushed past the four, standing beside Kai and Azrin, to prove her point.

'How can you trust him after what he did to you?' Miah questioned disbelievingly.

She looked to Kai.

'You have to tell them, Kess. They won't understand until you do.'

'Understand what?' Miah's voice was brittle, matching the anger on her face. If the warrior's expression was anything to go on, Kess wasn't sure about the wisdom of telling her Guardians anything.

She looked to Azrin, seeking consensus.

Whilst his bond was quiet, she sensed the jumble of thoughts and emotions swirling within him. After a long moment, he nodded.

'We are forbandt.' The words dragged out of Kess's mouth.

Miah looked at her blankly clearly not understanding the word.

Zuri and Kisho had the same look of bewilderment.

She looked to Thrain, and saw understanding flash in his eyes before it was engulfed by shock.

'That is not possible,' he said flatly. 'No Chronicler has had the ability to bond with an Angel in nearly a thousand years. Bonding with two,' he shook his head violently, 'has never happened.'

'Possible or not, we are her forbandt.' Azrin's tone was only slightly aggressive towards her Guardians. 'Were we not, I would not be here,' he added with a wry smile, which seemed aimed at himself rather than any of the warriors.

'I don't trust him,' Miah said, indicating Azrin.

'I do,' Kess responded. 'With my life, which he just saved.'

Zuri spoke for the first time. 'Kess was unarmed with a demon bearing down on her. Instead of trying to get away from the hells spawn like a normal person,' she said wryly, shaking her head, 'she stood her ground while it charged. I couldn't get to her in time but he appeared,' she nodded in Azrin's direction, 'behind the demon and killed it, just before it got to her.' She was peering at them, like she was trying to see the bond; like it was a visible link.

'We need to leave,' Thrain said, cutting off the argument. She heard the strain in his voice, and saw that his face was not flushed with exertion from battle, but deathly pale.

'Are you–' She cut off as he looked at her sharply. 'When do we go?' Kess asked, knowing that after this attack, she couldn't fight him anymore. They needed to leave. Demons would keep coming, and next time they might not be as lucky.

'Now.' Thrain walked a few paces towards the door, before he crumpled bonelessly to the ground.

'Thrain!' Kess yelled as she skidded to the ground at his side, beating everyone else to him. Rolling the commander over gently, her heart dropped as she saw the ground stained crimson beneath him.

Kess struggled with the clips of his armour which had been dented, squashing the buckles making them impossible to undo. She pulled her knife from its sheath and sawed at the straps until they parted. Miah sliced through the straps closest to her, and together they lifted the damaged plate from his chest.

The blood drained from her face as she saw the extent of the horrible wound which the commander had tried to keep hidden. The flesh on Thrain's chest had been shredded rather than sliced, causing a much nastier wound than she'd ever seen before.

Kess glanced away needing a moment to compose herself, and saw Kisho, Zuri and Azrin had formed a protective circle about them. Each faced outward into the room and had their weapons drawn.

Sensing her gaze, Kisho looked over his shoulder, glancing grimly at his leader before looking at her with troubled eyes.

Swallowing back her nausea, she peeled the ruined material free from the wound, and froze, horrified as she could see the white of his rib bones through his torn flesh. How could he survive such a wound?

'I need to get to my room,' she looked to Miah kneeling across from her, who nodded in understanding.

'What? No!' Kisho argued. 'Thrain said we leave now.'

‘I have a salve which can help with the demon wounds.’

‘Our powder–’

‘No.’ Miah countered. ‘This stuff nearly healed Kess’s arm overnight. We can’t have Thrain out of action.’ Her gaze moved to the floor which had once been beige carpet, but was now blackened with scorch marks and splattered with demon ichor, looking more like a war zone than the lounge it had been that morning. ‘We may need him,’ she said grimly.

Kess’s initial shock had settled, making way for a worried panic, which sent her heart racing. She sought Kai, and felt his hand settle on her shoulder.

Worry marked his face.

He may not like her Guardians, but he knew how important they were to her. ‘Azrin, guard them while we are gone.’

Without consulting her agitated Guardians, Kai disappeared taking Kess with him.

She moved towards the night–stand as soon as they materialised in her room, scooping up the container before grabbing her backpack from the cupboard. Stuffing a few clothes into it, as well as her mother’s Chronicler box, she turned back to her bonded Angel. ‘Right, let’s go.’

Within moments they were back with the others. As Kess crouched down at Thrain’s side he opened his eyes and gave her a weak smile. ‘A Chronicler protecting her Guardian. What is the world coming to?’

She heard Miah’s chuckle as she dug her fingers into the tub.

‘This may hurt a bit.’ Kess said as she ran her fingertips over his torn flesh. As gentle as she was she still heard the pained hiss of his breath.

Can you hold him upright while I wrap this around him? Kess thought to Kai, as she removed a bandage from the first aid kit she’d put together after she’d been injured at Athenaeum, and luckily thought to pack.

Kai moved to Thrain’s head and gently levered him upright. As quickly as she could, Kess wrapped the bandage around his torso, then signalled for Kai to lay him back again.

'Your turn now.' Kai pulled the salve tin from her grip and gently lifted her injured arm, which she had completely forgotten about when she saw Thrain collapse.

Kess gritted her teeth as he cut away the fabric below her elbow. As his fingers rubbed paste into the torn chunks of her arm, she closed her eyes fighting the surge of nausea which left her cheeks pale, and palms clammy.

'Can't you get through an attack without sticking one of your arms into a demon's mouth?' Kisho joked.

She opened her eyes, and saw the concern in his gaze. 'Can't let you have all the fun, now can I?' She grimaced at the pressure on her wound as Kai wrapped a bandage around her arm.

Thanks.

He nodded in return, and although he shielded his emotions well, she could still sense concern.

'Are any of you hurt?' Kess looked around and saw blood on all of them, yet they remained silent. She stood, about to tend them when Miah spoke.

'We are well enough until we reach somewhere safer,' the warrior said in a voice which brooked no argument.

'Where are we going now?' Zuri aimed her question at Miah, who was in charge with Thrain temporarily out of action.

'The Haven?' Kess asked.

'No,' Miah shook her head. 'The Guardians will want to charge to war if they see the commander injured like this. Besides–'

'Besides what?' Kess asked, as the warrior trailed off.

'Nothing. It's not important at the moment.'

Frustrated at being kept in the dark about something which was obviously important, she let the matter drop reluctantly, but resolved to ask the warrior what she meant when they were all far from here, and safe.

'There is a refuge secluded in the Shropshire Hills forest, about six miles west of a small market town called Bishop's Castle. As far as I know, no one has used it in years,' Kisho said thoughtfully.

‘Can you transport us?’ Kess asked Kai, who nodded without hesitation.

‘As long as you can tell me exactly where this refuge is,’ he told Kisho.

She glanced at Azrin, who looked unhappy.

Please, Azrin, we need to get him somewhere safe. She pleaded, looking up at him from where she crouched at Thrain’s side.

Grudgingly he nodded.

Miah watched the exchange between the two of them. ‘You can talk to each other through your bond, can’t you?’

Kess nodded, attention already focused back on the prone Guardian. Kai knelt beside her, and put a protective arm around Kess, before vanishing.

The last glimpse Kess had was of a reluctant Azrin reaching out his hand towards a similarly hesitant looking Miah and Kisho.

Zuri, grin on her face, held his other arm already.

CHAPTER 21

Two Becomes Three

They had been crammed in the secluded forest cabin for the past two days.

While quite a large space, four Guardians, one Chronicler and two Angels, who popped in and out, made it seemed rather cramped. Particularly when one of the Guardians was recovering from an injury which, even with Kess's miracle salve, was slow to heal, and required him to rest; a word not in his vocabulary. The enforced bed rest was making Thrain even more short tempered, and grumpier than usual.

The other Guardians had taken it upon themselves to increase their patrols; however, she doubted the escalation in their vigilance had as much to do with the likelihood of attack, as their avoidance of a certain commander. Which as a result, left Kess to tend to Thrain.

'You're on babysitting duty again today, are you?' he questioned as she opened the door, tray in hand.

'Don't be petulant.' She tried to smother her grin as Thrain looked at her incredulously. The colour was starting to return to his face, and she took his increasing restlessness as a good sign of recovery. Even resting there was nothing soft about him, he was all hard planes of sinew and muscle.

'Are you the only one game enough to come in here?' he asked, peering out the open door.

'Pretty much. You're not a very good patient.'

He lowered his brows glaring at her darkly. 'That's because I'm not an invalid, I am perfectly fine now.' Although he made this claim, Thrain made no attempt to get out of bed.

'You are much better.' Kess agreed. 'But please just humour me. You scared me when I saw all that blood,' she finished softly, knowing the commander's dislike of any sort of emotion, especially directed towards him.

He was not a man of excessive unwarranted movements, including his facial expressions, but she was beginning to be able to read him better. A small twitch of his mouth when amused at something, the slight furrow of his brow when he was concerned; the latter of which he had now.

'What's wrong?'

He turned to her, assessing.

'You've got your furrowed brow look, which means you're worried about something,' Kess said.

He met her eyes, and for a moment she thought the hardness in them softened, before the armour returned. He shook his head slightly, and remained silent, twisting a beaten copper ring about his middle finger.

'Can I ask you something then?' She waited for his nod before continuing. 'Why are you and Miah so concerned about my training?'

'Who said we are?'

'I'm not blind. I see you both watching me. Miah said I was too proficient for just having started. But what I don't understand is why that's a bad thing.'

Thrain's grey eyes pierced hers intently. She was about to look away, when he spoke. 'Guardians are born warriors. They are naturally skilled with any weapon, and more adept at martial arts. Chroniclers however, have essentially become historians, more intellectual than physical. You are a Chronicler, yet show all the hallmarks of being a Guardian.'

'What does that mean?'

'I don't know,' his hands swept through his hair in frustration. 'There is much about you that doesn't make sense.'

'Thanks.' She put as much sarcasm as she could into the word.

'You are a conundrum, Kess.' He stopped abruptly, and looked down at his hands.

She knew he'd been going to say more, but when he continued to look at his hands, she placed the tray she'd been holding onto the table beside his bed. 'Time to check your wound.'

'Miah usually does that,' Thrain said stiffly.

'Well she's not here. Come on, Guardian, I won't bite,' Kess smiled reassuringly at him, yet there was something that shone in his eyes that she didn't understand.

Thrain inched forward on the bed, his knees brushing against her thighs as he settled in front of her. He removed his shirt hesitantly, not meeting her eyes. His wound made movement difficult, yet he was clearly uncomfortable with exposing himself.

Kess tried not to stare at his lean toned body, but was unable to help it as her eyes flitted over the white scars dotting his torso from countless old wounds.

Her attention caught on the intricate tattoo, which covered the commander's left shoulder, running from his neck to just above his elbow. The interlocking plates of armour looked so real her fingers itched to touch them.

The design continued over his pectoral muscle, where the segmented plates gave way to what she imagined was where a knight's heraldry would have been proudly worn back in the middle ages. Emblazoned in the skewed square, was the Guardians symbol; three parallel descending lines in bold black ink. The same mark, though smaller, was also visible on one of the upper arm plates.

The base of the tattoo reached to the top of his ribs, which was now covered in gauze, marred by his injury.

She drew her gaze reluctantly from the striking tattoo and unwound the bandage, focusing on the jagged gash which started near Thrain's sternum, and extended over his ribs and down his side, which had borne the deepest of the cuts.

'May I?' Kess asked, before touching him.

He grunted a response, then looked past her out the window.

Gently Kess probed the wound, which looked so much better than it had a few days ago. Already the flesh over his stomach was knitting back together, leaving raised dark scabs, in lieu of what had been shredded skin. She touched the skin around his wound lightly, checking for signs of infection.

He shifted under her fingers.

'Does that hurt?' Kess asked concerned.

'No,' he gruffed. 'Your hands are cold.'

She pulled them back, crossing them about her chest self–consciously. 'Sorry.'

The gashes across his side, while still open, were no longer as deep as they had been. Unscrewing the lid from the salve, she grabbed a sterilised swab from the tray, and dabbed it into the ointment before carefully wiping it over his wound.

'It's healing nicely and there doesn't seem to be any sign of infection. It shouldn't be too much longer until you are up and about again.' Discarding the old bandage and gauze in a bag, she re–wrapped his torso, taking care not to touch his skin again, with her apparently cold hands.

'All done,' she said as she gathered up everything, and stepped away from him towards the door.

'Kess,' his use of her name and not '*Chronicler*' stopped her. 'I know I have no right to ask, but you and Kai–' he hesitated, as if unsure how to pose his question. 'You are close.'

She thought about Kai, and the blære bond enlarged, bringing a sense of him swirling about her mind.

At her nod, Thrain looked at his hands again.

'Thrain–'

He looked up at her sharply. 'I think I know what you are going to say,' he said in a quiet voice. 'That is one of the reasons why we wanted you to stay away from him.' Thrain's voice twisted on the last word. 'Angels have a way about them, which mortals find hard to resist. Most come to love the ones they have prolonged contact with. But it always ends in heartache for them. Loving an immortal is not an easy road,' he finished bitterly.

'Loving?' Kess was stunned into silence. 'Kai and me? Thrain, that wasn't what I was going to say.'

'It wasn't?'

'No. We are forbandt.' To her that summed it all up, but she saw that wasn't enough of an explanation for him to understand what she meant. 'When a bond is formed, a blære forms in mind of both people. It's like a bubble which contains that person. That's how Kai tracked me when I was taken. He sensed me through our blære when I called out for him.'

'You called out for *him*?' Thrain's voice dulled.

'I couldn't sense him, but hoped that he could find me. If I could have called out for you – or the others, and thought you would find me, I would have.' She saw the look on his face, and regretted saying anything. She didn't need anything else to widen the already substantial rift between her forbandt and Guardians.

Thrain made a noise which in any other person she would have called a snort. 'Don't think we have finished discussing that other Angel of yours. I know you believe you can trust him now, but I – we,' he amended, 'find it hard to believe, that after centuries of being who he was, he has changed so irrevocably, just like that.'

'This, makes it different.' She held up her palm towards him, so he could see the symbol branded on her skin. 'It is the mark of our bond. Azrin would no more hurt me than he would himself.'

She moved closer as he reached out and rubbed his calloused thumb over the ridged lines, tracing the pattern.

'I still can't believe–' Clearing his throat, he dropped her hand. 'After so long, the old ways are coming back. Guardian numbers are increasing. I have spoken with the other Commanders, and they confirmed new recruits are flooding into their Havens in numbers such as we've never seen.'

'What does it mean?'

'Nothing good,' he said grimly. 'War is coming.' He forestalled her next question. 'You called your father?'

'I checked with Miah beforehand to make sure it was alright,' she said defensively, before realising he was just trying to change the subject, not rouse on her. 'I just wanted to let him know we had left. He would have worried.'

She thought back to her conversation with him. 'He said the tunnel collapse was heard on the street and freaked out everyone in the tube. The train service was disrupted, but luckily no one was injured. Apparently, there are now whispers of the tunnel collapse being a terrorist attack.'

'Over the millennia, we have learnt the benefits of having people in strategic places within society to help blur over anything which attracts too much attention.' He looked at the covered tray on the bedside table. 'What's for lunch?' he asked, blatantly changing the subject yet again.

Taking his not–so–subtle change of subject yet again, Kess handed him the tray, and left Thrain to eat his meal in peace.

As the others were still out on patrols, she returned to her room thinking about her conversation with the grumpy Guardian.

Across from her room, she passed an open door, and saw Kisho sitting on the edge of his bed, a mace across his knees.

The last time she had seen that weapon, it was being used against the dragkheir – by Conall.

Her breath caught in her throat.

When he looked up, she saw for the first time since they'd come to the cabin, how haggard he looked. He had lost weight, leaving his cheekbones jutting angularly from his already slim face. His eyes were rimmed with red, and dark smudges circled his eyes.

'Are you okay?' she asked hesitantly.

Kisho's eyes darkened with pain, but he nodded. 'I am a Guardian.'

To some that statement would have sounded egotistical or conceited, but Kess was beginning to learn that those four words were a shield, a mantra for the warriors to hold themselves together when they were ready to fall apart.

She realised how selfish she had been, concerned only for how she felt by Conall's death, forgetting there were others who had known him for so much longer.

'I miss him too,' she breathed trying to speak through the sudden swelling in her throat.

Kisho patted the bed beside him.

'What happened is my fault. I'm so sorry,' her voice cracked, and she looked away not wanting him to see the tears which had sprung into her eyes.

'It is *not* your fault,' his tone was final, allowing no doubt that he spoke the absolute truth. 'Conall did what he was trained to do. Protect you,' he stopped, clearly considering telling her something else. 'He was fond of you, you know. He would have done anything to protect you.'

'He did, more than once.' She remembered the night on the roof so vividly, she could almost feel the wind chilling her skin, feel the rocks digging into her knees as she knelt in front of the red–haired Guardian, who had just pulled her back from stepping into oblivion.

Kisho put his arm across her shoulder, and she leant her head against him, taking solace in their shared grief. Tears leaked from her eyes, soaking into his shirt.

'I miss him,' Kisho admitted. 'He was my brother.'

A brother in arms; training, living and fighting alongside one another for years. The deep dark hole within her, from losing her mother, gave her an understanding of the depth of the grief he must feel.

They sat together like this, until, with a sigh Kisho pulled his arm away. 'It's my turn for woods patrol.'

Wiping her eyes, she stood and made her way to the door.

'Thank you, Kess,' the warrior said softly.

'For what?'

'For caring,' he said simply, before strolling out of the room, Conall's mace hanging at his side.

~

She had just shut the door when Kai appeared, making her jump. 'Stop doing that!' she reproached, unable to contain the smile on her face.

'Sorry. I wasn't thinking.' He seemed pent up, with repressed excitement which dampened when he saw her face. 'What's wrong?'

Kess scrubbed at her cheeks with the sleeve of her shirt. 'Nothing. What's going on? Are you alright? Is Azrin?' She reached out towards Azrin's bond and sensed his concentration and focus, but nothing to indicate any danger.

'I have brought someone who wants to meet you.'

'What?!' Kess screeched, before clamping a hand over her mouth hoping her Guardians hadn't heard the noise. 'How could you bring someone here to our secret hideout?' She loved using that word, particularly around Thrain who took exception to it.

'She's a friend.'

'Friend or not you're taking a risk.' She couldn't believe he would be so reckless.

'Which is why I'm here talking to you, not your guard dogs.'

'Be nice,' Kess reproached. 'Why does she want to meet me?'

Instead of responding he called out quietly, 'Lumiel.'

An Angel materialised in the empty space in front of Kess.

Everything about her was pale; from her long white hair to her skin which had the hue of fine porcelain china. It was like the colour had been leached from her, but instead of looking washed out, she seemed to shine luminously; like a full moon on a clear, cloudless night.

Before Kess could react any further, the pale Angel stepped towards her reaching for her arm. As the ethereal hand touched Kess's own, she made the mistake of looking into the vibrant purple eyes before her.

Once again, the whirlwind claimed her, sweeping her away into a maelstrom. Lumiel stood in the centre of the eye, looking around her in awe.

Sighing, Kess held out her hand to the pale Angel.

When she came back to herself, she rounded on Kai. 'You could have warned me, or given me a choice in the matter. My head's beginning to feel like a sardine tin.'

Her forbandt didn't answer, he was looking instead at Lumiel, who was staring at Kess.

'I can feel you.' Her voice sounded like chords strummed on a harp.

She could feel Lumiel's wonder seeping through their newly formed blære. Her shock was mirrored in her widened eyes, as she saw the brand on her hand.

Kess's nonchalance to her newest forbandt disappeared, and guilt filled its place.

The smile on the beautiful Angel's face faltered. 'Is something wrong?'

'Not with you,' Kess reached out touching Lumiel's slim shoulder. 'I just forgot for a moment how amazing this is.'

Lumiel's amethyst eyes hazed for a second as she concentrated on something. 'You're hurt,' she said, looking to Kess's arm.

'Just a scratch,' she said, ignoring the choking sound Kai made. 'See.' She pulled up her sleeve and held out her arm. 'It's healing now.' A thick scab now covered where the bite mark and torn flesh had been only a few days earlier. She didn't reveal the claw marks on her back from the dragkheir, which were still slowly healing, or the scars from the Rask on her other arm.

Concern still shone from her through the bond, but muted now.

Miah chose that moment to stride into the room, halting in shock for all of a nanosecond before deducing what was going on. Looking from Kess to the pale Angel she shook her head. 'Another one? What are you building your own private army?'

A sliver of thought came from Kai.

Kess spun around facing him. 'Don't you dare!'

He held up both hands in a submissive gesture. 'What?' he asked innocently.

‘I mean it Kai, no more. It’s starting to feel cramped in here,’ she said, tapping her head.

He continued to look at her with a carefully blank expression that sent alarm bells ringing.

As much as he tried to shield it, she felt as that fragment of thought solidified into a plan.

She shook her head resignedly, earning a grin from him.

‘Thrain’s going to love this. Three Angels!’ Miah was still shaking her head as she closed the door behind her, obviously not wanting to be caught in the middle should the commander arrive.

‘Great.’ Kess rounded on the two Angels only to have them disappear on her; Kai had a grin on his face that even Conall would have been proud of. ‘No more, Kai, I mean it!’ She yelled into the empty space of her room, cursing as she sensed amusement and determination from him.

Lumiel’s hesitancy to leave was clear, yet she followed Kai, leaving an almost palpable wave of awe in her wake.

‘Bloody Angels,’ she cursed into the empty room.

‘Couldn’t agree more myself.’

Kess’s heart almost jumped into her mouth, as she belatedly sensed Azrin’s presence through the blære. ‘I’m going to have to get you lot to ring a bell or something, otherwise I’m going to end up a nervous wreck from you all popping in and out all the time.’

He grinned at her, eyes sparkling with amusement.

Unable to help herself she returned the look, marvelling at the changes in her bonded Angel in such a short amount of time. She remembered the first time she had seen him, towering over her; icy blue eyes, cold and uncaring, as he watched her dispassionately.

Now a smile brightened his face, transforming it, and laughter lines creased around his eyes which sparkled with warmth and humour.

His grin faltered as he sensed her emotions at the memory of her capture. ‘What is it?’

She looked at him for a moment, deciding whether to broach the subject. ‘Do you regret it?’

Kess saw understanding in his eyes, and knew she didn't have to explain her question. She could feel his emotions, settled and calm, yet a sliver of dread pierced her chest, fearing that the bond between them was unwanted.

'I did–'

Her heart dropped in her chest.

'–at first,' he said hesitating when he saw her dismay. 'Do you remember that first night before the bonding was complete? I tracked you down through our connection. I was seeking to end it, by killing you,' he admitted slowly. 'But then I saw you sleeping, you were dreaming. I felt your fear as if it were my own, and I was worried for you.' He didn't try to hide the amazement from his voice. 'You were right to think of me as the arctic Angel,' he said, referring to how she thought of him whilst she had been imprisoned. 'Feeling your emotions, so pure and strong was an awakening to how far I had fallen. I realised that you gave me purpose again, a cause to fight for. Our bond gives me the chance to atone for all the terrible deeds I have done. I seek my redemption through you. So no, I do not regret what fate has brought me.'

It was the longest speech she'd ever heard him make, but Kess felt his sincerity shining through. Unable to help herself she launched herself into his arms, surprising him.

I am glad we are forbandt. She thought back to him.

In response, he wrapped his arms around her, squeezing her tight.

'Am I interrupting something?' Thrain's voice was hard.

Surprise and faint guilt made her try to jump back from Azrin, who, not having the same reaction, took his time to release her.

Kess felt her cheeks redden as she faced her Guardian. 'You should be resting. What are you doing out of bed?'

Thrain glanced from her to Azrin, who stared back challengingly.

She half expected them to start circling each other snarling, like two wild cats.

'I have rested enough,' he said flatly, pulling his eyes from her arctic Angel, who decided to flop down on her bed, making a show of lounging back on one arm.

She looked over her shoulder at him, saw the insolent look on his face. *Really?* Kess thought, forehead pinched with annoyance.

He gave her a sultry smile, which, while it may have beguiled some mortal women, only served to increase her frustration. What was it with Angels and Guardians? It was worse than the friction between the warriors and Chroniclers, and that was no little thing.

'Have you come here with actual news or have you just come to practice your posing?' Thrain's tone was as cold as his expression.

Unperturbed by the commander's frosty demeanour, Azrin remained sprawled on her bed. 'I do have some news you may find interesting.'

Thrain's withering glance spoke volumes about how interested he was in anything Azrin had anything to say. He had voiced his doubts that the forbandt bond had changed the Angel so intrinsically, and obviously believed he was going to double cross them.

'I made contact with the demon I was dealing with.'

'What?!' Kess shouted. 'You could have been hurt!'

She saw Thrain move out of the corner of her eye, one hand coming to rest on his axe, the other idly placed on his blade. 'Demons.' He twisted the word, making it sound like a profanity. The tensed Guardian glanced at Kess, clearly assessing his chances of getting her out of the room without the Angel interfering.

She sought Azrin's bond, unwilling to believe he would betray them, and found it calm and quiet like the night before. He was radiating a sense of purpose but nothing that inferred any sinister intentions.

'Thrain.' She shook her head, pointedly glancing at his weapons.

The blonde–headed warrior raised an eyebrow but otherwise remained motionless, hands still firmly gripping his weapons.

She shook her head in annoyance. 'You're going to have to get along one day.' Turning back to her blue–eyed Angel she said, 'So you made contact.'

'Yes,' Azrin said with an amused smile, pointedly looking at Thrain. 'Do you want the others to hear this?'

Thrain stared at the Angel unblinking for several long moments. Just as she was about to tell Azrin to leave, the Guardian finally nodded. With a final glare at the Angel he strode to Kess, grabbed her arm, and walked her out of the room. He clearly didn't want to leave her alone with Azrin, whom he trusted as much as a lion with a newborn babe.

Once in the lounge, he released his grip on her, and opened to the back door, giving a short, incredibly loud whistle. Lounging back against the frame, he crossed his arms about his chest, and watched the Angel, waiting for the others to arrive.

'They will never trust me. Not after what I did to you,' Azrin said softly, as she moved beside him, giving what she hoped, was a clear display of her faith in him.

'That was before.'

Azrin looked down at her, an unfathomable look in his eyes.

She sought his bond, and found tentative hope emanating from the blære.

'You truly forgive me, don't you?'

Instead of answering Kess held up her palm, revealing their forbandt mark.

A soft smile touched his lips, as he looked at the symbol mirrored on his own hand. He stared fixedly at it, until movement near the doorway caught his attention as Miah strode through. She was followed swiftly by the other two who entered like silent shadows, making as little noise as stalking cats.

Looking at the three of them, Miah took a seat, then looked to Kess questioningly. 'You wanted to talk to us?'

'Actually, this was Azrin's idea.' She inclined her head towards the Angel who seemed uncharacteristically hesitant around the assemblage of Guardians.

'You were saying how you were working with demons,' Thrain interrupted, voice dangerously flat.

Kess saw the three other warriors tense, looking at Azrin like he'd confirmed all of their heinous suspicions of him. She watched them carefully ready to warn the Angel to leave, if they made any sudden movements.

Azrin didn't appear to notice. His eyes had taken a faraway look. 'During the war in Heaven there were Angels which suffered what you would term "friendly fire". Caught in the midst of the purification, they were expelled with those responsible for the unrest, for no other reason than they were in the wrong place at the wrong time. I blamed mankind for my exile, and uncaring about their motivations or goals, I worked with demons. I have done terrible things,' he whispered. 'But I cannot undo the past, I can only remedy the future which you made clear for me,' he searched out Kess's eyes, seeking her understanding.

She held his arm, and knowing her words would fall short, sent him her understanding and unequivocal support through the bond.

'As touching as that is, it doesn't change the fact that you work with hells spawn.' Sarcasm tinged hostility oozed from Thrain.

'Worked,' Kess amended.

'Yes.' The Angel confirmed speaking at the same time.

'What are they after?'

'I worked with them on occasion, but that doesn't mean I was privy to their grand plans.'

'You want us to believe that you don't know anything?' Thrain's voice was rock hard, disbelieving.

'Believe it or not, I didn't care what they were doing, or why. I just wanted to hurt mankind whom I blamed for my exile from everything, and everyone I had ever known, and loved.' Anger and remorse flared through the blære in equal measures.

Kess stepped forward trying to diffuse the situation. 'This is not getting us anywhere.' She turned to the blue–eyed Angel. 'When you captured me, you kept asking where "He" is. Who did you mean?'

Sorrow filled his eyes. 'I am sorry for the pain I caused you,' he looked down, not wanting to meet her gaze.

Kess's own anger flared. Azrin had changed from the Angel he had been, and was tormented by what he'd done not only to her, but others.

'That was before we were forbandt. You wouldn't do that, now would you?'

'Of course not!' He nearly shouted, fingering the mark on his hand.

'So, who did you mean? Kai?'

He shook his head. 'I was visited, by one of the Host, someone I used to work with on occasion when I was still in Heaven. I was told to find the Morning Star. He said if I did he would help me return home.' Yearning filled his voice, and desire ripped through the blære, so strongly it wiped away any other thought in Kess's mind, until he suppressed it, shutting away the one thing he wanted more than anything else. An overwhelming desire which hadn't dulled over the immense passage of time, but had only grown stronger.

'Who approached you?' Miah asked intently.

Azrin's looked blankly at the brunette warrior, before he regained his composure. 'Gabriel.'

Kess was too stunned to pay much attention to what they were saying. Of all the people, or Angels he could have been searching for, the former right hand of God, instigator of the Heavenly War, was the last one she'd expected to hear.

'The devil?' Kess interrupted, not hearing what the others had been saying. 'Why would you need demons to search for their maker. Surely he is in Hell, Hades, the Underworld, or whatever it is you Heavenly beings call it. If Dante is to be believed you can find him frozen in the centre of the ninth circle.'

Azrin shook his head at her outburst. 'Dante saw only what he had been designed to see. Apparently, the Morning Star is missing and has been for some time. Both Heaven, and Hell, are rather keen to find him.'

She wondered idly how many years, or centuries, an Angel considered to be "*some time*". 'Wait – you're saying Dante actually descended into hell?'

The arctic Angel nodded. 'To my understanding, yes.'

'How–' She was interrupted by Miah, whose icy demeanour towards her forbandt hadn't defrosted an inch with this revelation.

'Why did you think Kess knew where he was?'

‘I didn’t. Her name was on a list of humans who may have had contact with Angels and potentially possessed information.’

‘How did my name get on a list of people who could know the damned devil? I’m not a Satan worshipper, or–’ she floundered for a moment, ‘Marilyn Manson. I’m, well – nobody. Why would anyone think otherwise?’

Her mind raced. *Who made this list? How did someone like that even know she existed, let alone had any contact with Angels?*

Would they come again? Keep coming, until they had what they wanted or she was dead?

At that time the only Angel she had met was Kai – that she knew of anyway – could he have something to do with this? Her brain hurt with all the questions flying around.

Zuri coughed, none too subtly. ‘I would hate to see a somebody, if you’re a nobody Kess. Look at what you can do for Angels’ sake.’ Kess loved her newest Guardian’s straightforward attitude – usually.

‘You followed me,’ Kess said flatly.

Azrin nodded uncertainly, catching wafts of her tumultuous emotions.

‘Did you come into the Haven as well?’

Azrin’s brows lowered quizzically. ‘What do you mean as well? Who else–’ he cut off as an understanding light entered his eyes. ‘Kai.’ However instead of looking sated by the knowledge, he looked troubled.

What is it? Kess thought, catching his turn of emotion.

Maybe nothing, he said, trying to calm the worry he couldn’t hide from her. *Leave it with me for now. We have more pressing issues to deal with before us.*

Kess realised the room had fallen silent and turned back to see four pairs of eyes watching them.

Azrin continued the previous thread of conversation, aloud for the benefit of the others. ‘Most of the people on the list were delusional, and were obviously not in contact with any of the Host. You piqued my interest.’

A spasm of pain tore through her chest as she thought of Conall; how, now with everything that had happened, his death had become meaningless. Glancing at the Angel to her left, she tried to banish the thought, and squashed down on her emotions, but the rush of sorrow which came from Azrin, revealed he knew what she had been thinking about.

'I met with my contact and told them that you'd had no association with any Angels, and were of no consequence. They may figure it out eventually, but for now they are looking elsewhere.'

'Thank you,' she said softly, knowing the risk he took in returning to the demons, even if only briefly.

Miah narrowed her eyes, then to Kess's surprise she said approvingly, 'You have our thanks for protecting our charge An– Azrin,' she looked towards Kess as she finished speaking, giving her a small smile.

Zuri and Kisho gave him approving nods.

She looked to Thrain and found him staring not at Azrin, but at herself.

She met his stare, daring him to say anything against her forbandt.

He pushed himself away from the wall and stalked towards where they stood, halting a few feet away. He turned his attention to Azrin, looking up at the Angel who stood at least a head taller than him.

Kess braced herself, unsure what to expect, so when she saw him extend an open hand, and clasp Azrin's forearm, she sighed in relief.

'Well that's a start,' she muttered to herself, earning a grin from Azrin and a glare from Thrain.

One step forwards.

'I understand that you don't like or trust me because of what I did to Kess, but there is something you should know. I didn't send the dragkheir after her. They aren't supposed to exist anymore,' he brow furrowed as he shook his head. 'I brought the two hells spawn to occupy the Guardian while I captured Kess.' Azrin looked to the warriors. 'Someone else sent the dragon.'

'Who?' Thrain demanded.

As Azrin shrugged she felt his worry through the bond. 'I don't know. I have made discrete inquiries, but no one else seems to know either. The only thing I found out was that dragkheir answered only to the Legion – or Satan,' he said grimly, fixing Kess with a look filled with dread.

As the Guardians expressions hardened he said, 'I will keep searching.'

CHAPTER 22

A Guardian's Life

As Azrin disappeared she looked at her Guardians who for some reason still appeared tense.

'Is everything alright? You understand, that Azrin would never do anything to hurt me now, don't you?'

'This has nothing to do with your Angel,' Thrain said stiffly.

'Then what does it have to do with?' She crossed her arms about her chest.

'There is something we need to talk to you about.' His words came out slowly, as though he were reluctant to say anything at all.

She watched waiting for him to continue, but he stood there, weighing her with his thoughtful gaze. Her head tilted as she ran through the events of the last few days, trying to think of something she may have done wrong.

Miah stepped forwards. 'It is nothing that you have done, Kess. This is something about us,' she said, seeming to be able to read her thoughts.

Kisho sobered instantly. 'It is time?' Dread and anticipation were thick in his voice. He sat on one of the sofas and patted the cushion next to him. 'You may want to take a seat.'

Wordlessly she sat back against the firm cushions, consumed with worry. *What could they tell her that was so awful, that they, hardened warriors, were all dreading?*

'What do you know about Guardians?' Miah asked, as she settled into a chair she had dragged in front of the sofa.

‘Not much,’ she admitted, realising how incomplete her lessons at the Haven really were. She knew nothing about the Guardians, beyond what she, herself had gleaned, or had been told by the warriors themselves. But then again, how much did she really know about Chroniclian history?

Again they remained silent, glancing around the circle, until all eyes came to rest on Thrain, waiting for him to speak.

‘We have all been doing this for a long time.’ Thrain’s gaze concentrated on her, monitoring her reaction.

‘Long. As in what ten years?’ Silence. ‘Twenty?’ Kess said jokingly, thinking how young they’d had to have been when they started training. Yet no one said anything.

‘A bit longer than that,’ Kisho said quietly. The normal exuberance in his voice was missing, which added to her worry. ‘This may be hard to hear, Kess, but we have guarded many Chroniclers during the last few hundred years, or so,’ he said, adding the last two words belatedly.

‘Few hundred,’ she whispered, looking to Miah, for confirmation; sure she must have heard Kisho wrong.

The dark–haired warrior held her eyes, before nodding.

‘How old are you all?’ Kess whispered, heedless as to whether or not it was a rude question.

Zuri, the least reluctant, spoke first. ‘I am the youngest here. I was a pirate sailing the waters of the Caribbean in the year 1701 when I first heard the call. It was lucky for me I did,’ she said grimly, ‘otherwise I would have ended up hunted and killed like Blackbeard and the rest, when the Royal Navy started to actively enforce anti–piracy laws.’

‘1701,’ Kess repeated numbly. ‘Wait that would make you–’ She paused trying to add it up.

‘Careful there, it’s not polite to declare a lady’s age,’ Zuri chimed in, smiling at her trying to lighten the moment.

A numbed shock settled around Kess making her incapable of returning the smile. ‘What’s the call?’

‘If an individual has the potential to become a Guardian they hear, what we describe as ‘The Call’. This usually happens when another Guardian is nearby; they are drawn to them. Though like Chroniclers it is not usually until they reach a certain age.' Thrain spoke slowly, trying to ensure she understood, and retained the information through her poorly contained shock.

'What about the rest of you?'

Kisho drew breath, but she cut in before he could start. 'Let me guess, you were a samurai.'

His dark eyes sparkled in delight. 'I became a samurai near the end of the great era, but had the privilege to study under Miyamoto Musashi at the Individual School of Two Skies in the early 1600s.' Seeing the pinch of confusion in her eyes he explained further. 'Musashi is believed to have been the best samurai warrior ever to have lived. He founded the school, teaching there for a few years. But he was a rònin; a wandering warrior, and was not suited to a confined academic existence. I was one of his first pupils and travelled with him for many years after he left.'

'So that would make you–' Kess tried to work out the maths quickly in her head.

'Nearly four hundred and twenty. But they say you're only as old as you feel,' he added with a grin.

Her head rose and fell in a very exaggerated nod, while she tried to comprehend what he was telling her. Four hundred and twenty! She shifted her focus to Miah, figuring, like a plaster it was best to get this over with quickly.

'I was a merchant's daughter, in an area now known as Juen, in Spain. My father owned a moderate–' She halted, narrowing her eyes at Thrain who shifted in his chair. He was looking down at his hands, but Kess was sure she saw the curl of a smile on his lips. 'a moderate–sized olive orchid,' she continued, 'the fruit of which was pressed to produce oil. Thrain found me one day when I was in the market at our family stall, and convinced me of who I was.'

'As I recall you didn't need much convincing to leave.' His voice softened, remembering a time fondly, that she couldn't even begin to understand.

A muscle spasmed in Kess's chest. 'You have known each other a long time.' She was not sure why this information seemed worse than the rest.

Miah looked towards Thrain with respectful affection. 'He's the stern uncle I never had,' she said, trying to hide the small grin on her face.

'Stern uncle?' Thrain's eyebrows rose. 'That would make you the wilful niece?' He jested, displaying a rare glimpse of humour.

The tightness in her chest released its painful grip. Kess rubbed the spot between her ribs, wondering how many more shocks; emotionally and physically; her body could take before it decided to pack it in. 'So where do Guardians come from? Originally I mean?'

Thrain shrugged. 'No one knows. We have always been, as far back as memory goes.'

'If there were any records, they have been lost, or destroyed over the course of time.' Miah fell silent and turned to Thrain clearly passing the lead over to him, yet he just looked at Kess, his grey eyes piercing deep within her like he was trying to read her soul. He, of all of them, seemed the most hesitant to reveal his past.

She decided to ask a question of her own to give him more time. 'So you live forever? Immortal?' A flash of red hair floated before her eyes. 'No, you can be killed,' she said softly.

Kisho's face became sombre as he followed her thread of thought. 'Yes. We can die, but as Guardians we become more resilient, surviving wounds, infections, and illnesses normal folk would succumb to.'

'How long do you live?'

'No one knows. Longer than the average human,' Kisho shrugged, not adding anything further.

Thrain spoke, surprising her. 'I believe I am one of the oldest who remain.' His words were matter of fact, yet she could see how difficult this was for him to admit.

She waited for him to continue, wanting to hear his story, but again he fell silent.

'Guess Kisho really wasn't kidding when he called you an old man.'

She was rewarded with a bark of laughter from the warrior she had once thought of as a block of granite.

'Do you tell all of your Charges?'

'No,' Thrain said. 'We have never told anyone else. You are a – special case.'

'We decided it only fair that you are aware of our abilities, since we are aware of yours,' Zuri said, in a way which made Kess think she had been the instigator of this decision.

'Is there anything else?' Even to her, her voice sounded as tired as she felt. 'Any other mind shattering revelations that you'd like to tell me about?' Kess included the four of them in her glance.

Thrain answered her. 'If you're asking if that is all you need to know about us; then the answer is no. There is much for you to learn, about Guardians and Chroniclers. About yourself.'

'If you want to know anything just ask, otherwise we will let you know things as they become relevant.' Miah absently pushed a strand of hair which had become loose back behind her ear.

Kess nodded absently overwhelmed by the revelation of their longevity. No wonder they were all so good at martial arts. They'd been practising for hundreds of years.

She looked over to Kisho. 'If you're over four hundred years old, why do you look like you're in your late twenties?'

'It is part of what makes us Guardians. Once we hit our optimum physical peak, we stop aging. There would be no use having a warrior who has become slowed with age.' He watched her carefully.

They were all looking at her like she might crack at any moment. She wasn't so sure that she wouldn't.

'How?'

'No one knows,' Zuri said.

'How long do Potentials train for?' she asked using the term she had heard mentioned for the warriors in–training.

'Until they are ready,' Thrain said in his usual forthcoming manner.

Miah provided a bit more information. 'Because their agelessness will kick in at some point, they train until they can pick up any weapon and use it proficiently. Until their mentors deem them capable of passing the trials.'

'The trials?'

'A number of tasks to test a Guardians weaponry, temerity and wits,' Thrain said flatly making it clear that was all the information she was going to get out of them about their secretive warrior society.

'Do you even exist?' She glanced around their bemused faces. 'I mean, not existentially – as in are you a figment of my imagination – but do you have a driver's licence, or a NHS number? You must have passports; how else could you travel overseas?'

'Of course we exist,' Miah said with a laugh. 'We have passports and all the things normal people need to function in society.'

'How do you get around the not aging thing. I'm sure someone will eventually click that you have the birthday of say an eighty–year–old but only look a fraction of the age. Or is this one of those connections things?'

'We do have contacts in places, however some of our younger generations have proven adept in this area in recent years and now generate the majority of the documentation that we require.'

'But surely you need more than just documentation,' Kess said confused. 'Databases now have people's histories in them, their bank accounts, previous addresses, associates,' she said thinking of all the police television drama's she'd watched.

Kisho laughed. 'We have it covered, Kess. We've been doing this for a while now.'

'What about you?' Kess asked Thrain directly, curious about how he became a Guardian.

'Another time perhaps. This was supposed to be a meeting about your Angel, not a gossiping WI knitting circle.' He finished gruffly, earning a bark of laughter from Kisho, who tried unsuccessfully to cover it with a cough.

Kess knew that arguing with him was pointless. He wouldn't tell her anything about himself until he was ready, and no amount of needling from her would change that.

The reality of what they had just told her, started to sink in. She was sitting in a room, surrounded by four people who claimed to be hundreds of years old, immortals for want of a better word.

Kisho nudged her, rocking her back into lucidity.

She looked about, aware that the conversation had come to a halt, and her Guardians were staring at her with concerned expressions on their faces. Belatedly, she realised she'd been staring at a square on the couch near her leg.

'Kess, are you alright?' Kisho's voice seemed to come at her from a great distance; like he, or perhaps she, was far away.

Her body felt abnormally warm, yet her face was cold and clammy. She gulped in a breath, opened mouth; for it seemed that she wasn't getting enough air breathing through her nose.

Voices bubbled around her but she couldn't seem to make sense of what they were saying. '–in shock–'

'–told you too much–' Another voice, higher in pitch, full of concern.

Their conversation plucked at her, rousing her back. Her thoughts whilst sluggish, started to work again, piecing together the snippets of conversation she'd heard. 'I'm fine – or at least I will be.'

So unlike the cold, contemptuous warrior she had first met; the genuine concern on Miah's face, highlighted the transformation in the Guardians attitude towards her.

'You were right to tell me. It's better that I know.' She looked around the group, and saw worry still dominating their faces. 'It's just a lot to take in. I just need–'

Miah stood. 'What you need is a good run to get your blood circulating again. You're as pale as an Eskimo's backside.'

Whilst she stared at the warrior in amused shock, Kisho jumped up, offering his hand to help her to her feet.

When Thrain stood as well, Miah turned to face him, hands on hips. 'Not yet, Commander.'

'I'm not an invalid,' he said gruffly. Then seeing the brunette's raised eyebrow, continued, 'But neither am I a fool. I will oversee your exercise.'

Kess followed the warriors as they filed out of the house into the muted light of the autumn afternoon. Winter was approaching fast this year, already spreading her icy fingers to chill the afternoons and mornings.

Miah came up beside Kess and grabbed her elbow, pulling her into a jog.

At first her steps were sluggish, but she soon lost herself in the rhythm of their footsteps pounding against the hard ground. Other steps joined theirs, as Zuri and Kisho followed behind.

Arms crossed about his chest, Thrain watched them depart from the doorway of the cabin.

They ran the perimeter surrounding the house, increasing their pace with each lap until Kess's heart galloped in her chest, and her breath came in short gasps.

As soon as Miah called a halt, she put her hands against her knees trying to catch her breath. She was only given a few moments before the brunette warrior grabbed her arm again, dragging her towards the tree line.

Thrain walked towards them, and although he tried to mask it, she saw the stiffness in the way he held himself and moved; obviously his wound was bothering him more than he admitted. *And he'd accused her of being stubborn!*

Kess followed suit as the others lay back against the soft green grass which felt like a wonderfully soft cushion beneath her.

'Sit ups. Forty,' Thrain barked, launching the trio of warriors into immediate crunches.

Although Kess finished last, she was pleased when she completed hers soon behind the warriors.

'Push ups. Twenty.'

The Guardians flipped over, hands and toes pressed against the ground, their bodies taut and level, and began pushing themselves up and down.

Kess followed suit, but quickly realised how easy the warriors had made it look. She soon stopped paying attention to how the others were doing, and concentrated all of her attention on her own action – up, down, up –

Her arms, unused to this particular exercise, were trembling beneath her as she finally reached twenty. She pushed herself back resting on her heels, and shook out her arms trying to loosen the muscles.

The others had of course finished and were waiting on her.

'Repeat.' Thrain barked. 'Faster!' The others flipped over immediately and began the set again. Although she tried to keep pace with them through this round, her strength – or lack of it – in her upper body let her down again when it came to the push ups.

'Come on, Chronicler,' Thrain growled as she began to flag.

Her arms felt like jelly when she finally reached twenty, yet this time she was given no respite.

'Run.' Thrain barked at the others sounding like gruff old army sergeants did in the movies.

Kisho and Zuri sprinted away, while Miah trailed behind clearly waiting for her to catch up. With a groan, not quite loud enough for Thrain to hear, she ran with the Guardians until her legs gave out.

Hours later Kess stumbled into bed, hair still wet from the shower, and fell into a deep sleep. Her last thoughts skittered around what she had been told.

It wasn't possible, was it? To live that long?

CHAPTER 23

Yet Another Oddity

Kess groaned as she opened her eyes to the beginnings of daylight, morning always came too quickly.

Remembering the events of the previous day, she tensed her legs, prepared for the ache of overworked muscles, yet was amazed when she felt only small twinges.

Not wanting one of the warriors to burst in and catch her in bed, she threw back the covers and stared at her arms in shock.

They were covered in writing. Not a texter or pen; like someone had drawn on her while she slept, but etched into her skin like ink on parchment from an old faded book. The cuneiform was unlike anything she'd ever seen before, comprised of great flourished strokes, but was totally illegible to her.

She twisted her arm around, looking at the inside of her forearm and saw words disappearing under her sleeve, continuing up her arm.

Her heart began to thrum as she drew the hem of her shirt over her head, and walked to the long rectangular mirror which hung on the wall.

Eyes wide, she stared at a body she barely recognised as her own. Her skin was almost obscured by the strange script, which was more silver than grey in colour.

The writing flowed from her jugular, down to the hollow of her neck in the shape of a 'v', over the ridge of her collar bones, the swell of her chest and crossed the planes of her abdomen, running down to where her track pants sat low on her hips.

She twisted, trying to glimpse her back in the glass, and saw that the writing continued right to the protruding bone at the base of her neck.

She was one giant canvas.

Kess was sure if she removed her pants she would see it covering her legs as well.

Looking at her arm again, she tried to make sense of it – beyond that she had totally and completely lost her mind. The marks shimmered, then as if someone had turned a page in a book, the words changed.

She was still examining her arm when the door flew back, giving her no chance to cover herself.

'You know there is no decent food in this place. What do you want for breakfa– what are those?' Zuri demanded from the doorway; all complaints about breakfast forgotten.

She turned toward her Guardian, eyes wide. 'I don't know. I woke up and–' she shrugged her shoulders, then realising she was just wearing a sports top and pants, grabbed a shirt off the bed, hastily donning it.

Her dark–skinned Guardian flipped out her mobile. 'Thrain, you need to get here. Now,' she paused listening. 'No, Kess is safe. There's something–' She pulled the phone away from ear, looking at it with exasperation. 'Just get here,' she barked, then pressed the end call button.

Pocketing the mobile, she grabbed Kess's arm examining it. 'I have never seen anything like this before.' Zuri looked up and saw something in her charges face.

Dropping her arm, she sat on the edge of the unmade bed watching Kess closely, who, at a loss for what to do, stood in the centre of the room.

'You know–' Zuri started, but was interrupted as Thrain burst into the room, flinging the door back so hard that it left an indent in the wooden wall.

Close on his heels, Miah and Kisho skidded to a halt behind him.

'What's going on?' He demanded, glancing around like he expected a demon attack, then froze as he caught sight of Kess's arms.

Thrain stared at her, and for the first time since she had met him, his emotions were clearly visible on his face – fear. Wide–eyed, he stopped a foot in front of her, as if he dare not approach any further. 'May I?'

She nodded and held out her arm, beginning to feel very self–conscious with four sets of eyes trained on her.

Holding her fingertips, he stretched out her arm, so he could see its length, and pulled up her sleeve. Her skin shimmered as he lifted it into a ray of sunlight. She watched as his eyes darted back and forth, scanning the length of her arm, but couldn't tell whether he was able to translate the strange writing.

'Is it just on your arms?' Miah asked, standing beside Thrain.

Kess shook her head, and raised the hem of her shirt to show her stomach, then twisted, showing them her back. She turned around again, pulling her shirt back into place as she looked at her stunned Guardians. 'Why does it look like someone took an ink gun to me while I was asleep and covered me in writing?' She quipped, trying not to let the apprehension which had started to form when she saw the marks on her skin, escalate into full scale panic as she waited for one of them to respond.

Thrain looked at her with such a wide–eyed expression, that it made him look younger and more vulnerable somehow. He shook his head wordlessly, seeking out Miah who shrugged her shoulders indicating her ignorance. 'I – we – don't know.'

'Maybe you should call your Angels.' Zuri spoke up. She alone seemed more willing to accept her forbandt.

She waited for agreement from the others before she closed her eyes and concentrated on the three bonds nestled within her mind. As she opened them again, blinking to clear her vision, she saw her trio of Angels appear.

'Are you alright?' They asked almost in tandem as soon as they materialised. She noticed the others showed no surprise to the presence of the pale Lumiel.

'What do you know about this?' She stepped away from her Guardians, and walked into a sliver of sunlight shining into the room through her small window, holding out her arms. She met their eyes hesitantly, fearing their response.

Lumiel looked shocked and seemed unable to take her eyes from the marks.

Kai and Azrin looked at each other, then to Lumiel who reluctantly drew her gaze away from Kess, meeting their serious stares.

She felt fear from them – clear and strong.

Her own dread rose up in response, to a nearly choking intensity. 'What is it?'

It was Azrin who spoke. 'I don't know. I've never seen its like.'

Kai stepped towards her. 'Has anyone else seen these?'

'Apart from the eight of us?' Kess said, doing a quick count. 'No, how could they?'

'You must never show these to anyone,' he said urgently, worry quickening his words. 'I don't know what they mean either, except that they are dangerous, perhaps beyond what any of us can fathom.'

She looked wildly around the room, unable to stop the shaking which racked through her body. Demons were already after her. If these marks meant even more danger, what chance did she have?

'Are they going to fade?' She didn't try to hide the panic in her voice.

'I don't know,' Kai answered, looking to Lumiel, who had remained quiet.

She shook her head a fraction, not able to add anything further.

'Do you know what language it is?' Miah directed her question at the three Angels.

Kai shook his head slowly as he looked at her arm. 'No.'

Something snapped inside Kess, and rationality fled. 'I have to get this off. How can I–' She ran to the bowl which made do as a small basin, and began scrubbing at her arms with a flannel yanked from the rail, trying to remove the marks, but all it did was make her skin red, emphasising the silvery writing even more.

Her body shook uncontrollably as she scrubbed harder, all focus on scouring her skin clean.

One of the newly healed scabs on her arm split open, trickling blood. She kept rubbing, desperately trying to make the writing go away.

A hand grabbed wrist, stopping her. She looked up into Thrain's grey eyes, usually distant and cold; now pinched with concern. 'Kess, stop.'

'This,' she said looking down at herself, 'is not normal.' Her eyes returned to the mirror. 'Look, it's everywhere.' The writing was clearly visible above the rounded neck of her shirt, extending halfway to her jawline. 'I can't walk around like this,' her voice rose a few octaves to a near screech.

'I don't know if it will go away, or not,' Thrain said in a slow calm voice, like she was a wild animal he was trying to tame. 'But this changes things. If your Angels don't know what the markings mean, then I am not sure where we go from here,' he shrugged. 'I do believe them when they say these marks mean danger for you. That there could be those who would kill you for the possibility of what it could mean.'

Kess's head began to spin and her throat burned as bile rose high enough that she could taste it in her mouth. *Why would anyone be after her?* She was a nobody, despite what Zuri thought.

'Demons, Fallen Angels, even some Angels. They could kill you to obtain whatever this is, or to conceal it,' Azrin answered her unspoken question.

'So, what do we do.'

Hands on hips, Thrain gave her a serious look, spoilt slightly by a wince of pain. 'We stay here until we figure out whether this is going to fade or not,' he gave her a slow measured look. 'And find you some clothes which cover the writing.'

'We will see if we can find out anything,' Kai said, as her three worried Angels disappeared.

~

Miah trod quietly into the room, making as much sound as a stalking lioness.

Kess looked up from where she sat staring at the writing on her forearm, to the Guardians full arms.

'This is the only clothing Zuri and I could come up with.'

She dumped the pile onto the mattress next to her charge. Crouching down beside the bed she reached out touching her arm. 'I know the last few weeks have been tough, but we will work this out. I promise.'

Kess nodded, not at all sure how they were going to "work it out". It had been hours and the writing hadn't shown any signs of fading. She felt the bubbling rise of hysteria, but pushed it firmly down and tried to concentrate on something else. 'Can I ask you something?' She waited for Miah's cautious nod before continuing. 'What is this fatalistic attraction to Angels that everyone is so worried about?' The question had been bothering her, since her talk yesterday with Thrain.

Miah studied her carefully surprised by the change of topic. 'Angelic beings emit a resonance of sorts, which, for humans, beguiles them and makes them susceptible to whatever it is the Angel wants. Prolonged contact can result in that attraction turning to love and obsession.'

She thought about her trio of forbandt, but felt nothing but fondness. There was definitely no infatuation or compulsive desires lurking within her for them. 'I don't feel any of that.'

'No. You do seem to be immune.' Once again, she got the impression that while her Guardian was relieved, there was still concern as to why she didn't feel the same emotions around Celestial beings as everyone else.

'Do you feel anything?' Kess asked, curious.

'There is always a strong pull to them whenever they are around, but part of Guardian training focuses on techniques on how to ignore that lure. Normal people don't have that training and only a few possess the innate strength to resist them. You may be one of them,' she said sceptically. 'Get dressed.'

Miah stood and walked from the room, shutting the door as she left to give her some privacy. Knowing she couldn't sit in here all day she rummaged through the clothes and sucked in a breath, as she realised what Miah had brought her.

~

Kess propped her leg up on the bed slipping the last boot on and reached down pulling the zip up her inner calf, to her knee. Turning, she caught sight of herself in the tall mirror.

Dressed in Miah's spare uniform she looked like something she wasn't – a Guardian.

The high firm neckline of the shirt hid the writing covering the sides of her neck and the long sleeves left only the back of her hands exposed. The rest of her was wrapped in leather, from the tight looking, yet surprising pliable pants to the tall snug fitting boots.

She jumped, startled by the soft knock at the door. 'Yes?'

The door opened and Thrain stalked in, halting mid stride as he saw her. His eyes widened and mouth parted with a sharp intake of breath.

He stared at her unmoving.

She waited for his explosion about her wearing clothing she had no right to. 'I know I'm not a warrior, but I needed a change of clothes. This is the only thing Miah could find that covered the marks.'

His silence and continued staring, made her uncomfortable.

'I will find something else,' she started to turn away but stopped as he grabbed her wrist.

'Wait.' He pulled gently on her arm, turning her back towards him, and reached out towards the high collar but stopped just short of touching her. 'Don't. It suits you.'

She glanced back at the mirror. The outfit made her look as lethal and dangerous as it would a real Guardian, but she felt like a fraud. A nervous fraud. 'I can't wear this forever though.'

'We will work something out,' he said with a confidence she didn't feel as he led her out into the main room where the other Guardians were waiting.

She strode into the room ignoring Zuri's wolf whistle and Kisho's appraising glance. 'We have to go back to Athenaeum.'

All four Guardians began speaking at once. Kess couldn't hear their individual words but she didn't have to, their tone and gesticulating arms all indicated the same thing; their disagreement.

'Havens have some of the largest caches of books anywhere in the world. Where better to find information about what these mean?' She indicated the marks, concealed by the warrior's uniform.

'You've been ambushed there already. What's to stop another demon, or ten, from entering and attacking?' Miah challenged.

'You mean besides my Guardians?' Kess asked sarcastically. 'What's to stop them from attacking us here?' she said seriously, looking Thrain and Miah in the eye. 'Here they can come in their hundreds with nothing to hinder them. The Haven, while apparently not flawless, has stopped any other demon incursion.'

'How are you going to hide those?' Kisho asked.

She shrugged. 'It's coming into winter, I can get away with covering up. Besides I'm still hoping it will fade,' she tried to ignore the doubtful looks that settled on the faces of the warriors.

Thrain, face set in the stern countenance of disapproval; eyebrows furrowed closely together and mouth drawn, remained silent, hearing her out.

Miah however didn't exhibit Thrain's composure. 'Are you insane or have you been bitten by one too many demons recently? There is something not right in Athenaeum. Don't tell me you haven't noticed it.'

'Yes I have, but it still doesn't change the fact that it's the best place for me to get information. I need to find out what I am. Why I can bond Angels,' she said emphasising the plural form of the word. 'Why I'm a human manuscript,' she looked at each Guardian in turn. 'Please.'

'Well if we can't protect you there, then we can't protect you anywhere,' Kisho conceded. 'Besides there we will have the rest of the battalions.'

A smile of relief formed before she quickly smothered it; they were considering her proposal. She decided to take a chance while they were in a listening mood. 'I want to take a short walk. By myself,' she amended as Miah started to rise from her chair.

'Not a chance,' Thrain said flatly.

'So, what, I'm never allowed to go anywhere by myself anymore? Next you will be telling me it's too dangerous to even shower by myself,' Kess yelled angrily.

A strangled sound emerged from Thrain's throat, whilst his eyes widened almost to the size of fifty pence coins.

Zuri however crashed back in her chair, slapping her thigh as she roared with laughter.

'I didn't mean – you know what I meant,' Kess flustered, trying to ignore the red creeping into her cheeks. 'I just want to go for a short walk. We are out in the middle of nowhere. Nobody knows we are here. With everything – I just need – I won't go far,' her statement ended sounding more like a plea.

She had always found walking amongst the green of Primrose Hill calming, and she needed some of that right now. She forced herself not to look down at her covered arm, at what she knew lay beneath the thin layer of material.

Miah stood, hands on hips, a scowl furrowing deep lines down her forehead. It was clear what her answer would be.

But it was Thrain who spoke, regaining his composure; his eyebrows had lowered and his grey eyes were as hard as steel. 'No.'

'Please.' Kess knew she was pleading now, but short of climbing out of her window and hoping she could avoid their patrols, she had to try to convince them.

'No,' Miah and Thrain spoke together, then glanced at each other, their looks mirroring the others; intransigent and definitely not willing to even potentially risk their charges safety on a whim.

Without another word, their hard gazes returned to her, waiting for her to back down.

'You can go with a guard,' Thrain said, surprisingly trying to compromise with her.

She shook her head stubbornly, not feeling like company. 'Forget it.' She spun on the heel of her boot and stalked back to her room, infuriated at how restricted she once again felt.

She had forgotten how liberating it had been to escape, if only temporarily, the fettered nature of being a Chronicler, yet now found herself bound not by books, but by the zealousness of her companions.

Part of her understood that the Guardians were just doing their job, but the other part of her – the more dominant part at the moment – wanted freedom.

She slammed the door behind her, knowing it was childish, then paced the five steps of her room. Her focus kept returning to the window, which was only two tantalising steps away.

She looked around her small room lined with timber, and for a moment she was back on the ship, trapped in that wooden room, disorientated, and in pain. She shook her head trying to clear the image but the walls appeared to move inwards, leaning towards her.

Kess's heart raced and her mouth was suddenly as dry as a cotton wool ball. She needed to get out of there.

Glancing over her shoulder to the shut door, she fought with the little devil on her shoulder, but her sudden claustrophobia tipped the scales, and recklessness won.

She lifted the latch and carefully opened the casement style window, like two miniature doors, fearing any squeak which would give her away. They opened smoothly and with an easy movement her legs were over the frame and she had pushed herself away from the sill, landing on the green grass below.

With a quick glance to either side she took off at a run heading straight for the woods. Despite the unfamiliar clothing she maintained the pace easily, reaching to covering of the tree line within seconds, and more importantly undetected.

She knew one of the Guardians would check her room soon, find it empty and follow.

But for the moment she was alone.

CHAPTER 24

If You Go into the Woods Today

'For every action, there is an equal and opposite reaction.'

Newton's Third Law of Motion

Running through these woods reminded Kess of her morning jaunts in Athenaeum, leaping over tree roots, and ducking under overhanging branches.

She could almost pretend that nothing had changed.

The funny thing was that she had wanted that change. Hadn't wanted to be hemmed into the restrictive Chronicler existence. Now there was barely anything recognisable in her life. Something her mother used to say to her floated through her mind – *Be careful what you wish for*. Whilst she wasn't so superstitious as to believe that she had caused these changes to occur in her life because of her desire for that change, it was unsettling to find herself now wishing for her old life back.

She was so lost in thought and distracted by the rhythm of running that, at first, she didn't hear the crashing following her through the woods to her left. When she finally noticed, she thought, for a split second that it was one of her Guardians catching up, but quickly realised they wouldn't make so much noise.

She stopped and listened. Dread settled heavily within her as she confirmed the crashing was definitely heading towards her, and was approaching fast.

'Satan's horns.' She swore, as she drew her Angelic blade, cursing at the injustice of her luck to run into a demon within minutes of absconding, when the several previous days of Guardian patrols hadn't come across anything.

If the demon didn't kill her, Thrain would.

The cracking of branches grew louder, then with a deafening roar, a demon jumped out of the woods, several metres in front of her, blocking the pathway she'd just traversed.

It was huge, standing over seven feet tall with large pointed ears like a bat and folded flaps of pale skin where its nose should be. The resemblance to the nocturnal creature ended there, however, as its torso more resembled an insect's carapace than a mammal's furred body.

The hells spawn scented the air, nose flaps quivering grotesquely, as its oversized ears swivelled about like radar dishes, clearly seeking her through vibration or sound.

Holding the blade up in front of her she drew the knife as well, feeling steadier with the two weapons in her grasp.

As the knife slid from its sheath, its small beady eyes fixed on her, and a large pair of retractable fangs descended from the demon's mouth, extending nearly half a foot in length.

Even from this distance she could see their serrated edges, which ended in wickedly sharp points. Kess tried to banish the vivid image of them tearing through her flesh with ease.

The hellion tilted its head from one side to the other, like a dog, considering her. Then with an ear–piercing shriek, it charged forwards, covering the distance between them in hop–like strides.

All she had to do was keep it at bay.

A few minutes had passed since she'd stupidly left the cottage, and knowing the vigilance of the warriors they would notice her absence soon – if they hadn't already – and come looking for her.

Just keep it at bay. Easy as pie.

A grasshopper–like leg, complete with long sharp spines raked the air in front of her face, only missing as she threw herself backwards at the last second, thumping instead into the thick tree trunk to her left.

The demon swiped at her again, scoring deep fissures in the flaky bark beside her cheekbone. Thick orange sap oozed right next to Kess's head, smelling strongly of bitter resin.

She thrust her sword up trying to impale the bat demon, but it moved, blurringly quick to the side. Kess overextended herself as the thrust missed, and she lurched forwards almost losing her balance.

With another ear–piercing shriek, the hells spawn tilted its head back exposing the full length of its fangs as it pounced seeking her throat.

She slashed out wildly with the dagger in her right hand, and was rewarded as her blade grated against the plating of the demon's neck. It lurched backwards, giving her time to raise her weapons again.

She knew her time must be running down. She just had to keep it busy for a short while longer. But her limited training had left her unprepared for single combat against such an agile foe. If she could strike a decent blow with the Angel blade she might have a chance, but the damned thing moved so fast.

The creature stared at her impassively.

Goosebumps prickled her skin as she looked into the face of the demon and saw her death reflected in its cold, black faceted eyes.

Unless some miracle happened, she wouldn't live long enough to see her Guardians. The hells spawns speed would tip the advantage in its favour.

Strangely, instead of fear, she felt regret, and anger at herself for her rash impulsiveness, even though all she had wanted was some time alone.

The grotesque folds of skin where the bat demon's nose should have been quivered again, giving her a second's warning before it launched.

Yet the hellion hadn't moved more than a step forward, when it gave a violent shudder and collapsed; almost landing on top of her. If a demon could show emotion she would have said that it seemed surprised.

Carefully disentangling herself from the spiny limbs of the grasshopper demon, she stepped back as hells fire consumed the corpse, and brushed the dirt from her clothing.

The thanks she'd been ready to give to the Guardian who'd saved her froze on her tongue.

A tall lizard demon towered several feet above her. Blue–tinged saliva glistened in dangling globules from the multiple rows of teeth within its mouth. It looked like photographs she'd seen of a chameleon, with large eyes near the sides of its head and a thick ridge protecting the back of its neck.

Stunned, she stood there, weapons raised, but unmoving. A demon had saved her?!

The lizard's head tilted to the side giving it an oddly feminine cast.

She had never thought of demons as being male and female, or being anything beyond mindless killing machines. Yet intelligence gleamed in its eyes. It was clearly assessing her, just as she was it.

'Thank you for saving me,' she said when the creature showed no inclination to attack.

The chameleon remained silent.

'Are there more demons out there – apart from you?' Kess wasn't sure she really expected an intelligible response, so when it answered she felt like her whole world view had shifted.

'The Vowen is solitary and territorial. Its lair will be nearby.' The words, perfectly formed, sounded strange coming from this creature.

'What do you want?' Kess couldn't believe she was asking this of a demon.

'To be freed.'

'Freed? From what?'

'We are bound to the Dark One. To serve and suffer for all time.'

Kess stiffened in surprise. Every book she had read, any person she had talked to said the same thing; demons enjoyed killing, lived to do nothing else, yet this one didn't seem to fit that mould.

She lowered her weapons to her sides, not wanting to have a conversation over them, yet remained wary; how could she not be around a demon.

'Are you the one?' The demon asked, sniffing the air above Kess's head.

‘The one?’

‘The one who binds Angels?’

Kess felt as if she’d been plunged into an icy river. ‘How do you know about that?’

‘Are you her?’ The creature ignored her question.

She could have lied but again curiosity, perhaps unwisely, overrode her caution. ‘I am.’

The creature blinked slowly, then knelt down in front of her, lowering its head. The pose was entirely submissive, placing its trust, and life completely in Kess’s hands. ‘Bind me.’

‘What?!’ Her voice rose to a near shout before she calmed it. ‘You’re a demon!’

‘Not all are like the Badenoch or the Rask.’ Kess had never heard of the first demon, but the second she would always bear the scars from.

‘What’s your name?’

‘Treilithdrijar.’

‘Treil.’ She shortened the name to something manageable, and waited for the demon to nod. ‘I am not sure it would work with one of your kind.’

This was madness!

When did she even begin to consider this to be a possibility?

Yet she was.

She could bond members of the Host, why not hells denizens? Her mind whirred with the possibilities of having one of them on her side.

Miah emerged from behind a tree as Kess reached out to grip Treil’s arm. ‘Are you sure about this, Kess?’ Her Guardians voice while calm, was betrayed by the deep creases around her eyes which held concern, but also simmering anger.

Kess spun towards her voice, heart thudding crazily in her chest. ‘How long have you been there?’ she asked, surprised that her dark–haired companion would be this close to a hells spawn without killing it on sight.

Ignoring her question Miah said, 'Long enough to see it kill the other demon. Long enough to hear it talk to you, rather than attack. But consider what you are doing. The bigger ramifications.'

'You would have me turn away a possible ally? Someone who wants something different from the fate they have been dealt?'

'Your greatest weakness is your empathy. Your belief that those about you would act the same way as you.' Miah shook her head. 'Not everyone is like you. Most would seek to exploit any perceived vulnerability. You see the goodness; the strength of character in the most unlikely of companions. That is why you are special. It is a vital part of what makes you, you. What makes you worth protecting. At any cost.'

'And you would have me change that?'

Miah sighed. 'No, I would not change who you are. I doubt I could even if I wanted to. I just seek to warn you, to be your reason.'

Kess nodded, and turned her attention from the Guardian to Treil, who waited, arm extended, for her decision. Without giving herself time to think she reached out and gripped the demon's arm. Though she'd made her choice, she still had to fight to suppress the trepidation which surged through her at willingly being this close to a demon.

The reptilian skin that met her fingertips was as rough as heavy grit sandpaper and covered in thousands of tiny bumps.

Treil glanced up at her movement, but remained still, watching Kess intently.

She looked up into eyes blacker than the darkest night and was torn away from herself – not in a whirl of wind but a tornado of fire. The heat seared through her, warming her skin to an almost unbearable heat; imprinting her bones with flame.

Treil stood in front of her, amidst the flames but untouched by them.

Kess stepped towards her – she had been right about the demon's femininity – as she moved closer images appeared all around her; beings writhing in torment, covered in chains; creatures being torn apart limb from limb and eaten by horrifically mutated animals; hellions with strips of torn flesh hanging from bodies; others burning in unquenchable pits of fire; more tortured in devices so extreme, she could not conceive what they did other than inflict excruciating pain.

She reached through the tornado touching the demon's outstretched clawless hand and came back to her body. 'Who were those creatures?'

'My kin,' Treil said sadly. 'Imprisoned by The Highest. Tortured for amusement, as well as punishment.'

'The Highest?'

'Whom you call the Devil,' she looked intently into Kess's eyes. 'They would also seek bond to you if they could.'

Kess could feel sincerity pour through the newest blære which had formed in her mind. She held up her hand, showing the bonded brand. The demon copied the movement and Kess saw not a silver mark like hers but a fiery red one etched into the tough skin.

A dangerous mark for you to have. She thought, curious as to whether a demon bond was like the one with her Angels.

Surprise flared in Treil's bond. *It would be, had I not the ability to conceal it.*

Kess watched as the brand dimmed then faded from sight. 'How did you do that?'

'My skin is similar to something you call a chameleon in this realm.' Treil raised herself up from the ground, towering over her.

'You actually bonded the demon.' Miah looked at Kess, a tangle of emotions flitting across the warrior's face that she couldn't begin to unravel.

'She asked me to.' Kess knew that wasn't what her Guardian meant, but chose to misunderstand.

'She?'

'Yes, can't you tell?'

With a pinched, suspicious look, the warrior peered past Kess to where Treil's head towered above hers. 'No,' she said finally, 'all I see is a kîngkã demon,' she shook her head disbelievingly. 'A demon! Thrain's going to love this.' Sarcasm dripped from Miah's voice.

Mention of the blonde–haired commander sent a stab of alarm through her. He would be furious at her already for leaving the house unguarded.

Miah was right, he wasn't pleased with her bonding Angels, let alone a demon.

'We have to get back.' Miah looked from her to Treil. 'Thrain and the others will be searching for you.'

'I will patrol the woods. Make sure no demons enter it.' Treil melted into the surrounding trees, disappearing within seconds.

Kess felt her move away through the bond. Sighing, she turned back to her Guardian, knowing she was in trouble.

~

The walk back to the cabin was made in silence, though she caught the dark–haired warrior glancing at her from time to time, with an unreadable expression on her face.

'Thrain is not pleased,' Miah said finally when the log building came into sight.

'I'm sure that's the understatement of the year,' Kess grumped, but annoyingly felt a stab of angst at earning his disapproval.

'You left!' Miah growled. 'After we told you not to. Even after all the attacks–'

'Thank Izanagi you're alright,' Kisho exclaimed, invoking a Japanese God, as he materialised from the woods several metres in front of them. He surprised Kess as he pulled her into a fierce hug, like she was a younger sister who'd gotten lost. 'Are you alright?' He pulled back, gripping her by the shoulders.

Before she could say anything the door of the cabin flung back so hard the crash made Kess jump. She wouldn't have been surprised to see it fall from its hinges.

Standing in the doorway, Thrain's usually blank face, was wild; like a tempestuous sea during a hurricane. Charging forward he met them several paces from the cabin, heading straight for Kess.

She held herself straight, determined to receive whatever punishment he issued, yet as he raised his hands, she couldn't help but flinch.

Something flitted across his eyes too fast for her to catch, then the wildness was gone replaced with a cold fury; which was unmistakable. He lowered his arms to his sides, hands clenched in fists so tight the veins stood out, vivid against the paleness of his bloodless skin.

'You left,' his voice was flat, tinged with fury.

'I'm sorry,' she said softly, and she was too. Sorry she had ever climbed out of her window. Mortification rose within her at her actions, she wanted to be like the warriors, yet at the first hardship, had shown herself to be nothing more than a petulant child throwing a tantrum and running away.

'I–' she cut off as he turned his back on her and walked away. His last look was not of anger but of disappointment, which was so much worse.

An angry Thrain she could deal with, but having him disappointed in her was like a knife twisting in her belly.

Unable to watch him walk away she turned to her companion. 'He's never going to forgive me, is he?'

Miah, who was still watching the blonde–headed warrior, spoke without looking in her direction. 'When he calms down he will. When he found your room empty he went wild. You scared him.'

'Thrain's not afraid of anything.' Her surety wavered as she saw Miah's solemn face.

She had made a big mistake.

~

She found Thrain out the back of the cottage, sharpening the blade of his sword, which clearly didn't need it. His movements faltered as she sat down beside him, then picked up their rhythm again. His focus was on the motion of the blade, so, not wanting to interrupt, she leant back against the post and closed her eyes finding the rasping of the metal on the stone calming.

'Becoming a Guardian, you learn to follow orders from your superiors without hesitation, believing in the fact that they have more information about the situation than you. When Miah agreed to train you, you swore to abide by that precept.' His voice was even as he continued the steady movements of honing his blades edge.

'I know I stuffed up,' she pushed herself away from the post and looked at his lean face, which remained turned away. A soft sigh escaped her lips, she knew she had to say more, explain; but was reluctant to do so. She had never been good with opening up. 'When I first came to Athenaeum to be a Chronicler I was excited. Their – our,' she amended, 'job sounded important, a worthy thing to do. But of late I've felt like I wasn't meant to be there. That I'm not meant to be a Chronicler. I don't think the same way they do. I'm not satisfied with the scholarly lifestyle they delight in. I wanted more. I wanted adventure and excitement. I wanted to be a Guardian,' she admitted softly, refusing to look in his direction. 'I guess I got it in spades. Demon attacks, what happened to Mum,' her voice cracked but she continued on, unable to stop now.

'I forgot in all of that, how lucky I am to have Guardians beside me, protecting me, even against myself.' Kess trailed off again, looking out across the small clearing into the darkness of the wooded area ahead, needing to focus on something else to continue. 'I know I let you down. I was overwhelmed with all this,' she held out her covered arms, 'and just wanted to run, to forget it all if only for a short while. But running isn't the answer. I need to stand and face whatever comes and hope that after all of this, I still have my Guardians beside me. If I haven't completely screwed up that is,' she finished in a rush and looked hesitantly at Thrain who stared silently at his blade, sharpening forgotten.

As the silence dragged on, she cleared her throat uncomfortably and started to stand. 'I just wanted to tell you that I was sorry. That I will follow what you say in the future without question. Or complaint,' she added the last quietly and was rewarded with a soft chuckle from Thrain.

'Don't make promises you can't keep,' his words were light, not containing any malice.

'I won't,' she started indignantly, then grinned, 'I will try not to question you.'

He turned to her then, a haunted look in his eyes. 'You scared me,' he looked away from her out into the woods again, changing the subject. 'Are you sure you want to do this? Go back to the Haven?' He shifted his body around so that he was facing her. As he moved, his leg brushed hers, the brief touch radiated warmth through the skin–tight material making her realise how cool the afternoon was becoming.

'How else can I find out what all this means?' Kess pushed down the fear building inside her again. She had lost count of the amount of times she'd had to do that since she'd woke this morning and found herself covered in the weird markings.

His eyes softened as he looked at her. 'What if it's not anything to do with your Chronicler history?'

'What choice do I have?' She met his eyes with a steady gaze, belying the fluttering of worry which had started in her stomach at the thought of returning to Athenaeum. 'There's something I need to tell you that you're not going to like.' Kess's stomach lurched in dread, but knew she didn't have any choice but to tell him.

Thrain's gaze hardened immediately, as he once again became the stone warrior.

'I ran into a demon in the forest.'

The blonde Guardian started to rise but she grabbed his arm, stilling his movement. Beneath his leathers his arm was granite hard with corded muscle.

'It's dead.'

His eyes already upon her, focused sharply. 'You killed it?'

'No,' she said softly.

'Miah?'

Kess shook her head.

'Your Angels?'

Again, she shook her head.

'Well who then? Demons don't just combust themselves.'

She hadn't let go of his arm and unconsciously squeezed her fingers tighter about his forearm in her hesitancy to tell him. 'It was another demon. She saved me.'

His eyebrows furrowed. 'Demons are not male and female. They are just Demon. Not born of living flesh but formed from hatred and darkness. If it killed the other hells spawn, it wasn't to save you, but because of a predatorial, or territorial instinct.'

She had started to shake her head as he spoke.

'Stop shaking your head at me,' he growled. 'If there's one thing Guardians are well versed in, it's demonology.'

'Her name is Treil. And she saved me because she knew who I was. She asked me to bond her, to free her from the devil – the Highest – as she called him.'

Thrain broke his arm free of her grip and rose to his feet. Towering over her, he glared down at where she had tilted her face up to see him. 'Wake up, Kess! Demons are pure unadulterated evil; distilled and condensed until that is all they are. Rage and hatred consume them; pain and torment feed them. They are not like beings of this realm which inherently contain a spark of goodness,' he looked at her for a moment and saw something in her face. 'What have you done?' he yelled, grabbing her by her upper arms and dragging her to her feet.

His fingers were like bands of steel on her skin, but she didn't flinch as he tightened his grip, shaking her, in his anger. As he realised what she'd said, he stilled, glaring at her. 'You talked to it.'

She didn't answer.

'You bonded it, didn't you?' Disbelieving horror filled his voice.

Kess opened her mouth, but stayed silent, unnerved by his anger which he seemed barely able to control.

Thrain looked at her with such a tangle of emotion that Kess couldn't start to unravel.

'How could you! Do you know what you have done?' he spat, shaking her again.

'Thrain!' Miah's voice thundered from behind the commander's back. 'Let. Her. Go.' She enunciated each word, letting her own anger and disbelief fill them.

The sound of her voice cleared some of the undisguised fury from the commander's eyes, and his gaze fell to his hands that still gripped her tightly. He let her go so forcefully that Kess stumbled back a step, before righting herself.

She watched him, taken aback by his hostility.

He refused to look in her direction; but whether that was from anger at her actions, or his own, she didn't know.

Miah strode over placing herself so that she stood a shoulder in front of her charge.

'You knew about this!' Thrain turned on Miah.

'Yes,' she answered defiantly, hands on her hips.

Not unfamiliar with the Guardians mannerisms, she noted the way Miah stood protectively in front her, balanced on the balls of her feet and realised, with alarm, that the brunette thought she may have to protect her from the commander – and worse – that she was prepared to do it.

'How could you have allowed this?' Thrain thundered on, not showing any reaction to the sub–commander's defensive posturing.

'In case you haven't noticed our young Chronicler has a mind of her own and a strong will. You weren't there, Thrain. The kîngkã saved her; talked to her.'

'It lied!' he roared.

Kess flinched. She'd never before seen him so consumed with emotion. Her disappearance, and this news seemed to have put him near the edge of losing his rigid self–control.

Miah stepped fully in front of her now, blocking her from Thrain's view. Without glancing around, she said, 'Kess, call her.'

I am here. The words floated through her mind.

'She's already here,' Kess said softly.

To her relief Thrain didn't immediately draw his weapon, though he did peer about behind him searching.

Treil materialised beside Miah who apart from stiffening slightly, remained focused on her commander.

'Greetings, Guardian,' the demon stated formally, lisping only slightly on the 's'.

A deep crease appeared between Thrain's eyebrows, and his hands which had come to rest on his weapons at the kîngkã's arrival twitched, yet he made no other move.

Kess looked to Treil who sensed her attention and sent. *It is well, Bondmate. His concern is only for you.*

Kess's focus returned to the warrior in front of her.

The Chameleonesque demon drew herself up to her impressive seven foot of height. 'I am Treilithdrijar, born of Onalithiel, born of Gilawywiel. I am Kîngkã. Born into damnation in Ereshkigal, in servitude under rule of the Highest. My grandsires, one of my sires and most of my hatchmates are dead; tortured and killed under order of the Highest and his Legion for amusement, imagined slight, or perceived infraction. There are many others, demons you would call us, who want their freedom. We have been searching for Kess. We believe she can save us.'

'And how would she do that?' Thrain demanded, suspicion lacing every word.

Kess saw how rigid the commander was, but at least he hadn't attacked – yet.

'By bonding us. I volunteered for the trial, to see whether it confirmed our belief. And it does. The bond between us breaks the hold of slavery from the Highest.'

Kess stepped back, away from the kîngkã, surprised by this revelation, amazed that Treil had taken the risk in approaching her. 'You took the chance of me not killing you on sight?'

'The freeing of our kind is worth the sacrifice of one,' Treil stated, unfazed at the thought of possible death.

'How can I bond them?' Kess asked, confused. 'They are imprisoned.'

'Yes.'

'You want me to go to hell,' she said as realisation dawned.

'Enough! I will hear no more of this madness!' Thrain barked, slapping his hand against the verandah post. 'Even would we allow it, which we wouldn't, it is impossible for a living being of this realm to transverse the barrier and enter Ereshkigal.' He gritted his jaw so tightly Kess thought she could hear the creak of his teeth in protest.

Glaring at Miah, Treil and herself, he stormed away.

Wisely, the demon remained silent, bidding Kess farewell as she blended into the forest, presumably to resume her patrol.

With a sharp look, Miah followed Thrain, leaving Kess missing the simplicity of her old life.

CHAPTER 25

Not As She Imagined

As Kess left the cabin, she looked back fixing its location in her mind. A secluded cabin, that no one knew about, could come in handy one day.

She approached where Kai waited with the others, catching the tail end of what Miah was saying, '–still haven't said why you didn't come?'

'Because,' the Angel sounded exasperated, like he was repeating something not for the first time, 'she wasn't scared or terrified. If I had felt that I would have come. All I could sense was determination, mixed with anxiety and regret,' he said the last, looking towards Kess as he felt her approach.

Miah turned, catching the shift in his focus and aimed an intent stare at her. 'Ready?'

Taking a deep breath, she nodded. This had been her idea, and it was too late to second guess it now.

The dark–haired warrior made a show of looking around Kess. 'What no more additions?' A small smile lightened Miah's words, yet she still felt shame about yesterday.

'Not today,' she said as she turned back to Kai, who was looking at her thoughtfully. He, more than the others had been incredulous at Kess's claim of bonding a demon. Something he had flatly told her was impossible.

'Remember not too close to the walls. I think the gate Guardian would freak if we appear out of mid–air with you at our side,' she smiled winningly, at her clearly exasperated Angel.

She looked towards her Guardians. 'You never have told me how you can tell someone is an Angel. You seem to know at a glance.'

Zuri answered her. 'They glow.'

'What like one of those worms?'

Kess heard a disgruntled sound strangle from Kai's throat. Thrain barked a laugh, which she took as a good sign that he might be forgiving her. Whilst Zuri, broad grin on her face, clarified, looking at Kai as she described it to her. 'There is an outline around their bodies. Like when someone stands in front of the sun, and the golden light shines around them.'

Kess turned back to her forbandt, but all she saw was the tall, muscular, twilight blue eyed man. 'I don't see it.'

'You wouldn't. That is one of the gifts of becoming a Guardian,' Kisho said, giving her a smile. She thought he looked a bit better today, not as drawn or pale, and his eyes had lost some of the redness which had rimmed them for days.

'One of the gifts? What else is there?' They had always been so tight lipped about Guardian ways. But after their big revelation the night before, maybe they had decided to open up a bit more.

'It's time,' Thrain said, ending their conversation and Kess's hopes of finding out more about the warriors' secretive society.

Kai rolled his eyes, sensing her frustration, then held out his arm for the Guardians to grab. For Kess, he held out his other hand which she grasped firmly, savouring the closeness which enhanced their bond.

Having travelled this way a few times, she remembered, just in time, to close her eyes against the disorientating rush of air around them as they were transported to the outskirts of Athenaeum.

As soon as they could the Guardians let go of Kai's arm, on the prefix of scanning the woods around them.

'We're about a half a mile out,' Miah said, recognising the area.

I'll be close by, Kai thought before he disappeared. *Stay safe. And keep those marks hidden.*

She tugged at the sleeves of her shirt making sure they covered her wrists. For a brief moment, she had actually forgotten about the silver writing covering her.

The familiar cocktail of worry, mixed with disbelief and simmering fear swirled within her before she stomped it down.

Their entrance back into Athenaeum was as quiet as their departure, with only the gate Guardian noting their arrival. His sharp gaze took in the entire group then flitted back, watching her more closely than the others. Two more steps forward and she knew that he had figured out she was not a Guardian, despite the clothing.

She glanced at her companions out of the corner of her eye, and saw what had given her away. Surrounded by the loping saunter that all Guardians mastered that graceful gait that was part dance, part stalk – she looked like she was stomping through a field of mud.

'Bannen,' Thrain said in greeting, yet the lilt at the end of his name was a clear inquiry for information.

Bannen had the lean physique of someone who trained rigorously, the hard lines of his face were made even sharper as his chestnut brown eyes narrowed looking at her, and mouth thinned with undisguised reproof at her presence.

'Guardian, report,' Thrain demanded, anger clipping his words.

'Where is Samael?' Kess interrupted, concerned about his absence. It was Wednesday. In all the times she'd had her hospital visits, he'd never missed a shift.

The sandy–haired Guardian glanced in her direction then pointedly ignored her, looking back to the others. Zuri and Kisho moved to either side, flanking her, showing where their allegiance lay.

'The Chronicler asked you a question, Guardian,' Thrain's voice was low and filled with menace.

A sneer crossed Bannen's face. 'You reporting to Chroniclers masquerading as Guardian now, Commander?'

Thrain moved quicker than Kess thought possible, and punched Bannen in the face.

The gate Guardian staggered back, clutching at his nose which gushed blood all over his hands.

'I said report,' Thrain barked.

Surprised at his violent reaction, Kess looked around the group, yet far from looking shocked at her leader's actions, Miah's face radiated approval.

Drawing himself up, the gate Guardian dropped his hands to his side, ignoring the red stream flowing down his chin. 'Samael has disappeared,' Bannen said grudgingly, making a point of reporting to the Guardian commander and ignoring Kess completely.

'When?'

'Eight days ago. He finished work for the day, was observed heading towards the gym, and then nothing. He was not seen leaving and hasn't been spotted since.' Some of the hostility left Bannen's voice.

'Anything else out of the ordinary?'

Bannen looked at Kess uncomfortably. 'The day before he disappeared we received orders that there would be emissaries that weren't to be questioned, or searched. The orders came straight from Custodian Drazen himself, and without either of you here to countermand–' he shrugged, 'Cadder objected, but was overruled. We didn't have a choice but to let them in.'

'Who were they?'

'Both times I was on duty there was six, but there have been several more visitations. I have spoken with some of the other guards on at those times and they all report varying numbers anywhere from two to nine. No identifications were able to be made as on each occasion they were wearing hooded robes and none of them spoke. Custodian Drazen personally came to meet them each time. And just prior to every arrival, we were ordered away from the gate.'

'After you finish your shift report to me. I want to hear more about this,' Thrain said in a tone which would have had Kess sprinting to meet with him after she'd finished for the day.

A troubled look settled on Thrain's face as they walked away.

Kess glanced back over her shoulder at the sandy–haired gate Guardian, who stood in the middle of the path watching them, and shivered. They had only been gone for a few weeks, yet she was already beginning to question the wisdom in returning.

Something wasn't right.

She could feel it in the very air around them, which seemed to thrum with foreboding.

Her Guardians tensely watched their silent surroundings. Chroniclers should have been walking the paths between buildings. Guardians should have been patrolling or practising in the yard. Yet the walkways and grounds remained empty.

Something was very definitely wrong.

'Kisho, Zuri, take Kess back to her room. External patrol and room check. One Guardian with her at all times until we can figure out what's going on here.' With a nod at Thrain the pair glanced at each other before breaking off to escort Kess back to the room that for years had been her home, but now she felt dread at having to return to.

Her only reassurance lay in the fact that she wasn't the only one who was unnerved. Yet having the Guardians worried, only compounded her fear.

As they entered the building Kisho veered away jogging around the corner out of sight, presumably clearing the area, leaving Zuri to escort her to her room.

They had only been in the room for a few minutes when a sharp rap at the door had her dark–skinned companion eyeing her sharply, and inclining her head towards the corner of the room, away from the doorway.

'I'm looking for Chronicler Grayson.' A familiar voice said as Zuri opened the door a fraction. She blocked the view into the room with her body, holding her thigh against the door as a stop, should the person on the other side try to force their way in.

'And you are?' Zuri asked insolently.

'Captol Wessler. Is she here, Guardian?'

'Zuri, let him in.' Kess could pretend she wasn't here but she knew his timing hadn't been a coincidence, they'd obviously been watched arriving.

The familiar mousy brown–haired, weasel–faced Captol walked into the room, eyebrows lifting as he passed the brazenly feisty Guardian. They rose even higher when he saw what Kess was wearing.

Unwilling to explain herself, and quite frankly not knowing where to start, she crossed her arms about her chest and levelled him with a flat stare that even Thrain would have been impressed with. 'Is this a social call, Captol, to welcome me back?' she asked, knowing that it wasn't.

'While it is pleasant to have you return to Athenaeum, my reason for visiting is not social but rather relates to the Choosing which was conducted whilst you were away. You will be given some time of course to reacclimatise yourself, however Custodian Drazen asked me to personally oversee you and assist in your choice upon your return.'

Kess was definitely beginning to regret coming back. 'Sure. Some time would be great,' she said hoping to stall that decision for as long as she could.

Her only purpose in returning was to find information about what was happening to her. She had no desire to choose a faction and be tied down again. She knew the Chapters kept an eye on their new members, assigning them mentors to advise them and ease their transition into their ranks.

'If there is any way I can assist you just let me know.'

She nodded at him, only partially paying attention to what he was saying. Her mind was already whirring with how to find the information she needed as quickly as she could. She was on a shorter deadline than she thought she would be, and it seemed like she'd already obtained a chaperone.

Sensing her lack of attention, he finished up. 'Right, well you must be tired from your journey. Rest up and I will see you tomorrow.' He headed for the door, pausing before he reached for the knob. 'Kess,' he hesitated, and with a glance at Zuri as she shifted, changed what he'd been going to say. 'Never mind.'

'That was weird,' Kess muttered, as he left the room. Not only had he seemed friendly but he'd never referred to her as anything other than Chronicler Grayson before.

'Want me to take care of him for you?' Zuri asked, raising an eyebrow as she twirled her deadly double–bladed haladie around.

'Careful, there's not enough room to swing a hamster around in here, let alone that thing,' Kess said, quickly stepping out of the way.

The dark–skinned warrior laughed, twirling the weapon about her faster and faster until the blades were only a shiny metallic blur.

'Alright, alright, I get it,' Kess said, admitting defeat. 'You're a Guardian,' she said, knowing that was all that needed to be said about the warrior's expertise.

'Have you thought about your weapon of choice?'

'Chroniclers don't carry weapons.'

'We both know that you aren't just a Chronicler. If you want to have a look at a few different choices, I can take you to Aldoak. Have you seen their weapons room?'

Kess shook her head, having only seen the training room and the small meeting room.

'Now that is something to see,' Zuri said wistfully.

Kess shook her head, thinking she would never understand Guardians and their weapons. 'I'm sure you have more than enough strapped to you right now,' she said wryly, and was rewarded with a throaty laugh.

'If one of you are going to camp out in here for the foreseeable future, we'll need to get a bed and some blankets from somewhere. And don't give me any nonsense about Guardians not needing to sleep, ever. If we are in the same room then it's not like you won't wake up if there's something suspicious going on.'

Zuri listened to her silently, then shrugged her shoulders. 'It's a good idea. I can get a camp bed, if you can rustle up some blankets.'

'I should be able to do that.' She knew the laundry staff well enough that she should be able to get a few more things; winter was coming after all.

CHAPTER 26

A Whole Lot of Nothing

The blade that severed the wings from her back was her own. She knew that, even as she was aware she had never held that sword. The pain from the stumps on her back was excruciating, yet the sight of the soft grey feathers, her wings, severed and lifeless beside her, was unbearable.

A silhouetted figure loomed above her, features darkened by the brightness of the sky behind. The only physiognomy discernible was the bright crimson wings extended to their full span, and the sword raised in the air, ready for another strike.

This being would kill her without compunction or regret, once the downswing began.

The blade glinted in the soft perpetual light.

'Stand with me.' The voice boomed, loud in the silence around them.

'No.' The words formed on her lips, even though she didn't understand what she was rejecting.

Though the face was still shrouded she could sense the sneer in the voice as the Angel spoke again. 'Then die.'

The sword started its descent.

Kess jolted from sleep, back still aching from the loss of her dream wings.

She reached behind her touching her shoulder blades, half expecting the shirt to be soaked with blood, but dry cloth met her fingertips.

The rustle of cloth moving had her looking around in confusion until she remembered her nightly changing, permanent room guest.

‘Kess, you alright?’ Zuri asked, alert even thought she’d just been woken in the middle of the night.

‘Bad dream. Sorry I disturbed you.’

‘No worries.’ The warrior rolled over again, and within moments was breathing deeply again, sending a stab of envy shooting through Kess. Was that something they learnt in Guardian school?

Settling back under her covers she reached out to Kai’s blaere in her mind, needing to feel something other than the lingering turmoil.

Kai, are you there? She didn’t get a response, but there was a fuzziness to the bond, so maybe he was far away.

Wriggling around until she got comfortable she closed her eyes. Her last thoughts were of the strange shimmering writing that covered her body as she entered an uneasy, restless sleep.

~

Several hours later and frustration had made its permanent home inside Kess.

So far, all her research had uncovered was dead ends. Not only were there no leads but the stuffiness of the Archive, and the high necked, long sleeved, total cover clothing she was forced to wear to hide her strange markings, had left her sweaty and irritated.

‘Any luck?’ Miah asked from behind her shoulder. The dark–haired warrior had just replaced Zuri who had briefed her out in the hall about the morning’s events, or rather, the lack of them.

In case she was questioned, the story Kess had concocted that she was interested in researching the history of the Chroniclers – which in a way was true. Only she was looking for any information that hinted to forbandt bonds, not at the formation of the group.

‘No.’ She let out a frustrated sigh pushing the book she was reading across the desk, next to the dozen others which had also proven useless. ‘Nothing has any reference to–’ she looked around and lowered her voice, changing what she had been going to say, ‘what we are looking for. Every source pretty much just says; the Angels descended from Heaven, picked out some worthy humans and made them Chroniclers. What a load of Angel feathers.’

Miah raised her eyebrows, but didn’t comment on her choice of language.

‘I didn’t think it would be as easy as walking in here and finding a dummies guide to being covered in weird writing and what it means.’ She whispered, afraid someone would hear, even though the nearest Chronicler was seated several seats away from them. ‘But I did think we would find – something,’ she exhaled loudly in frustration. ‘I also visited the Vault, and was refused entry because I didn’t have direct written approval from a Head Captol.’

Worry and something very close to panic flared within her again, white hot and constricting. She put a hand to her chest, where it almost physically hurt.

How could she find any information if she couldn’t ask the right questions? What if she couldn’t find out anything about the writing covering her.

Her breaths started to come faster as she fought to control her fear.

How would she explain it if someone saw the strange marks?

Miah’s voice broke through the fog. ‘My, we are grouchy today aren’t we?’ the brunette quipped. ‘Not getting enough sleep?’

Though her Guardian was joking, the sleep comment hit a nerve. She saw Miah’s eyes narrow, catching Kess’s concern, so wanting to avoid that conversation she continued her rant. ‘And since I can’t just go up to a H.C. and say I’m trying to research information on this and show them my *artwork–*’ she hesitated, looking around them again, ‘I don’t like my chances.’

Miah gave her a silencing look, and glared around at the Chroniclers, like they could all decide to make a sudden attack.

'Stop doing that. You're making them nervous,' she whispered, noting the way the closest had shrunk back in their seats, pointedly not making eye contact with the agitated warrior.

She had forgotten what a timid bunch Chroniclers were. Spending so much time around the Guardians had definitely changed her.

Kess stood and stretched her stiff shoulders as she walked back to the desk of the Archival assistant she had spoken to earlier. Still hunched over an open book he looked as though he hadn't moved in the last half hour, except to glare at anyone who interrupted his study.

'Yes?' His bushy eyebrows pinched together forming one great overgrown hedge on his face. Even his voice was dry.

Thumping the book she held down in front of him, Kess pointed to a spot half way down the page. 'You told me this book provided a "wealth of information about the formation of the Chroniclers",' she said mimicking his words, 'but all it has is one lousy paragraph which is mere speculation with not a whiff of factuality.'

Narrowing his aged, filmy eyes at her, he made a show of picking up the volume she had dropped and placed it to the side, away from what he was reading. 'What more do you need to know?' The Archival assistant asked as he examined his book for damage.

The careful, casual way he said it, had alarm bells ringing in her head, even before she felt Miah's warning jab in her ribs. 'Ahhh, nothing I guess. Thanks for your help.' She turned, leaving the book on his desk and headed with her Guardian to where her belongings were at the back of the room.

She gathered the discarded books into piles at the edge of the desk, ready for collection by the assistants, then turned, almost bumping into Wessler who grabbed her by the back of the arm steering her a few steps away.

Miah, ever alert blocked his path, arms casually folded about her chest, eyebrow raised as she looked pointedly at the hand which held Kess's arm.

'Kess, you must be careful. The questions you're asking; what you're researching, you have to take care,' he whispered releasing his grip. He stepped a pace away from Kess looking at the warrior for confirmation that his distance was sufficient.

'How do you know what I've been looking for?' She couldn't help but glance towards the old Chronicler who had forgotten his work and was staring at her. She whipped her eyes back to Wessler.

'Too many people do. Look we can't talk here, it's not safe.'

Kess looked around at all the Chroniclers hunched over their work imagining every one of them straining to listen.

She glanced at Miah, who gave her a nod. 'Come to Aldoak tonight, Ten o'clock.'

The weasel nodded, then raising his voice admonished, 'If there is one more infraction I will have no choice but to inform H.C. Brennan, are we clear, Chronicler Grayson?'

'Yes, Captol Wessler,' she said in her humblest voice, trying to look chastised.

Wessler nodded, satisfied at her denigration, then walked away.

Several younger Chroniclers seated nearby who had put their noses deeper into their books trying to avoid drawing his attention, looked sympathetically in her direction once he left. She noticed the way their gazes flitted between her and Miah, no doubt wondering about the warrior's company.

Miah touched her arm, signalling it was time to leave.

Having had more than enough for the day, Kess gladly followed the warrior out of the Archive, empty handed, much to her disgust.

A dark–haired girl caught her eye and nodded at Kess as they passed.

Surprised, she bobbed her head in return, not really sure what she was acknowledging.

CHAPTER 27

Secrets Within Secrets

Ten o'clock found Kess waiting, hidden amongst the columns with Kisho, near to the place where Miah had stood waiting for her, only a few weeks earlier. So much had happened since then that it seemed like a lifetime ago.

Wessler was late.

'How do you know you can trust him?' Kisho whispered, asking yet again.

'I don't, not for sure. Something tells me I can.'

'So, you've become divine now as well as an Angel magnet?' Kisho quipped, then tilting his head to the side said softly. 'Someone's coming.'

Kess listened, and picked up the faint crunch of feet on gravel. 'Nice warning system.'

'It's low tech but it does the trick,' Kisho whispered as Wessler came into view clutching at a satchel strapped to his chest, and looking over his shoulder. They waited until he was several steps away before revealing themselves.

The nervous Captol jumped in surprise. 'Sorry I'm late, I thought I was being followed so I took a nice circuitous stroll around the woods until I lost whoever it was.'

'Did you see who was following you?' The usual humour in her Guardians voice had vanished.

The Weasel shook his head. 'I just heard steps behind me, and saw a shadow a few times. I lost them on the path in the woods.'

'I'll go have a look,' Kisho said. 'You know your way?'

She nodded. 'Be careful out there.'

'Always.' He smiled, humour back now that there was potential danger and ran off disappearing into the dark after a few steps.

'Come on, let's get inside,' she ushered Wessler through the large doors, and led him to the small meeting room where Miah and Thrain waited.

Wessler started when he saw them. 'I assure you I pose no threat.'

'They're my Guardians, where I go they go,' Kess replied shrugging.

Wessler gave her a considering look. 'They haven't been assigned to you.'

'We assigned ourselves,' Miah stated flatly, arms folded about her chest.

'Interesting,' his gaze flitted between the three of them.

'What did you have to tell Kess that was so important to risk a meeting?' Thrain asked gruffly.

'Right, yes. Straight to the point,' he glanced at the two Guardians. 'You may want to take a seat; this could take a while.' When they didn't move he shrugged, then looked at Kess. 'Around two hundred years ago a secret group was formed within Chronicler ranks to monitor the world for signs of increasing demonic activity, which is one of the precursors to the Apocalypse. The group started off small but over the years we have grown and now have members in all four Havens,' he paused, looking intently at Kess. 'What do you know about your mother's work, before–' he hesitated, looking at her sadly.

'Before she went insane?'

Wessler shook his head, sending his wavy brown hair cascading around his eyes. 'She didn't get that way by herself.'

'What do you mean?' Kess towered over Wessler having risen from her chair. She felt a hand on her shoulder, and looked at Miah before sitting again.

'What do you know about what your mother did?' the Captol asked, unperturbed.

'What do you mean what she did? She was a Chronicler.'

Wessler shook his head again. 'She wasn't *just* a Chronicler. She was on assignment when she was taken. Your mother was a member of L'Ultima Luce; as am I.'

Kess sat up straighter; Wessler had her full attention now. 'You said she was taken?'

'Your mother was kidnapped.'

'By who?'

He looked at her with pity in his eyes; pity and something else. 'By demons,' he said softly.

Kess joined the dots. 'They made her the way she was.'

Wessler was clearly reluctant to reluctant to be the bearer of this news. 'They tortured her for information.' He paused looking at the paleness of her face, waiting until she met his eyes before he continued. 'We rescued Anna, but by the time we found her, it was too late. Her mind had been broken.'

'How long was she there?'

Again, Wessler faltered. 'Two weeks.' The words dragged from him reluctantly. 'We searched for her, day and night, but it was like she had disappeared from the face of the Earth. I was Anna's friend, but we failed her.' Guilt laced his voice. 'Only a few of us knew the truth about your mother's condition. Everybody else believes she had a breakdown as a result of stress. It was safer that way.'

Horror at what happened to her mother, warred with the guilty relief that surged through her, that the madness her mother suffered wasn't a hereditary illness, like she'd feared. 'Safer for whom?'

'Our group. Your father. Your sister. You. If someone thought she had valuable information worth killing for, then you would not have been safe.'

'There is no way Chroniclers rescued anyone from a nest of demons.' She turned looking accusingly at her two protectors. 'Did you know about this?'

Miah shook her head, apparently as stunned as Kess.

Thrain remained silent, meeting her eyes flatly.

Whether or not he knew anything more wasn't obvious. Having other questions for Wessler though, she filed it as something she'd have to ask him another time.

'Why was she captured?'

Wessler stared intently at her. 'Because of what we were looking into.' His eyes flickered to the Guardians flanking her, then focused on her again. 'We were trying to uncover the *Verità Scuro*; which is Italian for the "dark truth",' he clarified when she opened her mouth to interrupt, 'within our ranks.'

'Within the Chroniclers?'

'Chroniclers, Captols, the Consilium. *Verità Scuro* infiltrate all ranks, including the Guardians,' he pointedly avoided looking at the two warriors standing behind her.

Kess could almost feel the pair bristle, ready to defend their brethren.

'My mother was betrayed?' Kess asked hesitantly.

Wessler nodded. 'Somebody outside of our group found out what we were doing.'

'How do you know that *somebody* wasn't part of your secret club?' Miah asked softly.

'Because some of them died trying to save Anna, even more in the fight against darkness over the years. They, we–' he amended, 'are trustworthy,' his tone was intense, matching the focused look in his eyes. 'Your mother asked me to keep watch over you, should something happen to her. She said that you were special, and because of that, would be in danger.'

'Danger, from whom?' Kess asked at the same time Miah said, 'What do you mean special?'

He ignored both questions, instead pulling the satchel he'd been carrying onto the table, opening the straps.

Miah leapt forwards pouncing on the bag before he could undo the latch. She hadn't drawn a weapon, but the look in her eyes made it clear she didn't need one.

'You will have to mind my friends here, after several demon attacks, they are a little touchy.'

'Demon attacks? They've come after you?' Wessler's hands faltered, clearly stunned.

Kess followed suit, leaving his questions unanswered. 'What do you have in there that's so important?'

'A letter from your mother.'

Miah released her grip on the bag, but stood over the Captol as he opened the flap and pulled out a sealed envelope. Wessler handed it straight to the dark–haired warrior, who turned it over in her hands before handing the paper to Kess, deeming it safe.

'When did she give this to you?' Kess held the envelop in her hands unopened. As much as she wanted to read the letter from her mother, she wanted answer from Wessler more.

'Before her last mission nearly ten years ago. She was rather agitated when she came to see me. She was very insistent that I hold onto this letter, in case something happened to her. She said that I was to give it to you just before your choosing.'

'Why then?'

'That is when Chroniclers are recruited into *L'Ultima Luce*.'

Luce was Italian for light; she knew that much. But as to the rest she could only guess.

'The Last Light,' Thrain said softly, earning an approving nod from Wessler.

'You were to be approached, for recruitment. I was the one assigned to observe, and assess your fitness to join us.'

'That's why you were always watching me. I thought I had done something to annoy you,' she peered at him suspiciously. 'You know everyone thinks you watch everything to report to the Head Captols.'

'It's the perfect cover,' Wessler shrugged. 'One that took years to cultivate. If a snivelling *weasel* is all people expect to see then they won't look for anything else, will they?'

Red flashed along Kess's cheeks as he used the nickname well known, and often used, particularly amongst the younger Chroniclers. 'Who else is in this secret club of yours?'

'I can't tell you that. Not until you join us.' As he had spoken he had lost the pinched secretive look on his face, transforming his features into someone barely recognisable. His cover apparently included modifying his appearance to "play" the part of the fictional weasel he had created. 'And it's not a secret club,' he said, in an offended tone. 'We are a covert group dedicated to uncovering the corrupting influence of the *Ver*ità *Scuro*. Amongst other things.'

'How is that different from what I said?' Kess heard Miah chuckle behind her, but didn't turn around, trying to maintain a straight face. He was as much fun to tease as Thrain was with his secret hideouts.

'You think we would allow our charge to join this group of yours? That we would let her vanish off with you, the Angels only know where?' Thrain, as always, didn't see the humour of the situation, just the potential danger.

'Your presence does complicate things,' Wessler admitted seriously, ignorant of the scathing looks he received from the warriors. 'But I still want to recruit you. You would be an excellent asset.'

'What do you mean asset?'

'You killed the demon that got into the Haven, didn't you?'

Miah and Thrain were suddenly at his side, as if they had materialised there. No weapons had been drawn but the air of menace about them was unmistakable. Wessler looked first at Miah to his left, then at Thrain, looking completely unruffled by their very close proximity.

A satisfied look settled on his face, as if their reactions confirmed his suspicions.

'Why would you say that?' Kess asked, keeping her expression carefully blank.

'I pay attention when others assume or ignore. If you had not killed that creature, then I doubt you would have been escorted here that night, nor have had so close an eye kept on you by the Guardians in the days since then.'

Miah gave Wessler a considering look, losing some of her hostility.

'Your mother told me you were special, Kess. How much remains to be seen. But I believe you will play an important role in the events to come. Already your actions have had ripple effects, like a pebble thrown into a pond.'

'What is it that you think I've done?' Kess demanded, unsure what he was talking about. She wasn't special and didn't want to be. All she had wanted was to not be a dull, boring Chronicler.

'You have been back for not even forty–eight hours, yet already I have seen some of the younger Chroniclers following your example towards the Guardians. For the first time in many hundreds of years, they have been mingling, actively seeking out, and interacting with the warriors rather than trying to avoid them. You are responsible for that, maybe not by direct action but by being out with your guards and talking with them, laughing. Not caring what anyone thinks.'

Wessler sat forwards in his chair, and held his hands up in front of her counting points on his fingers. 'You do not fit into the conventional mould of what a Chronicler "should" be. You are unable or unwilling to pick a Chapter to belong to. You asked to train with the warriors. You killed a demon. Guardians have assigned themselves to be your protectors. Since your return, the warriors have not left your side, even for a moment, suggesting fear of attack. I am sure they are but the tip of the iceberg that I am yet to discover about you.' Lowering his six raised digits, Wessler looked closely at her, like he was hoping she would confirm some of his points, or add to them.

Kess shifted uncomfortably in her chair, looking down, unwilling to meet his eyes. Her hands twitched, itching to check the stiff collar of her shirt, to make sure it was still covering the strange writing decorating her, but didn't want to rouse his suspicions any further. He was already paying too much attention to her, and had pieced together far too much for her liking. She pushed her fingertips under her legs, making sure they wouldn't stray, and give the deadliest of her secrets away.

How did he know she had approached Miah for training? Was he the one who told Drazen? She looked at him again, but didn't think she was wrong in her assumption that he liked Drazen as little as she did.

When she remained silent, he sighed and leant back in his chair. 'You have been told more than any other. The decision is now yours to make. To join with us and fight the growing darkness; something I have the feeling you are already doing. Or not, and join one of the usual Chronicler Chapters for a quiet life of study.' The smile he gave her said he knew what her choice would be.

'Will being part of the *L'Ultima Luce* allow me access to the Vault?'

'It can be arranged.' A grim smile lit Wessler's face; he knew that he had her.

'What do I have to do?' Kess said, ignoring the concerned looks of her Guardians.

'I will need to meet with the others, and let them know your decision. Then there is the initiation and following that you will be introduced to some of the other members.'

'And what does this initiation involve?' Miah asked suspiciously.

'Nothing I haven't undertaken myself, *Praeses*.' Wessler called the dark–haired warrior something Kess didn't understand. It sounded like a title, rather than something derogatory. The Captol, unlike most other Chroniclers didn't treat the warriors with disdain.

Both Guardians looked at him in surprise at his use of the word.

Miah moved to the door, and opened it, signalling the end of their conversation.

Wessler hesitated only long enough to say, 'Look after yourself,' then he walked out the door, escorted by Miah.

She turned to Thrain who stood in the same spot at the edge of the table, looking out the door, as if lost in thought. 'What was the word that he called you?'

'Praeses,' Thrain said, his tone was wistful, eyes distant. 'It was from a time when Guardians were honoured in duty, and for the sacrifice they made.'

'Sacrifice?'

‘To give their lives in protection of their Charges. It is the oath we make when we become Guardians.’ He moved around the table, to within a foot of her.

‘I am the sword and the shield
I am the dagger and the bow
I stand till the last
And to the last I fight
My final breath given freely,
To protect the light and the lights flesh.’

Thrain finished, his grey eyes staring hard at Kess as if making the oath to her. She almost expected him to drop to his knees like the ancient knights did when swearing fealty, but with a ‘hrrmff’ clearing of his throat, he said, ‘I assume it would be a waste of time trying to talk you out of this.’ He said it as a statement, but the pause was a clear space for her to jump in.

When she stayed silent, he turned to Miah who had stepped silently back through the door. ‘You stay with Kess until we have a time and location for this initiation.’

CHAPTER 28

Initiation

Kess sat on her bed, staring at the blank envelope, turning it over and over in her hands, hesitant to read her mother's final words to her.

It had been nearly a day since Wessler had given it to her, yet the letter was still sealed with a blob of red wax.

She tilted it towards the light and saw a dove pressed into it, like a family crest. She recognised the faint outline, from the pendant her mother had always worn around her neck. With a pang of sadness, she picked at the seal ripping open the envelope.

Inside was a single folded sheet of paper, with writing covering both sides. Her hands shook as she unfolded the page.

Kess,

If you are reading this letter, then something went wrong during my last assignment.

I have entrusted this letter to Tomas Wessler, and have asked him to watch out for you when you come to Athenaeum. He would have explained to you by now that I am a member of L'Ultima Luce, a group dedicated to fighting the growing evil in the world.

I have no doubt Wessler will have asked you to join the Luce, to fight against the rising darkness. The choice is yours. But perhaps it would be better for you to remain hidden.

There is a truth I must tell you, yet there is no easy way to reveal this, especially on paper, but I fear it is something that will bring you trouble, later in life.

I had always planned to tell you, but I believe am on the verge of uncovering a truth that the Verità Scuro have gone to great lengths to keep hidden. So, I must write to you instead, in case something should happen.

Robert Grayson is not your biological father.

Kess's heart stopped and she blinked, carefully rereading that last line, sure she must have misunderstood, yet the line remained the same.

Robert Grayson is not your biological father.

I was on assignment in Manilla, where I met a man, unlike anyone I had ever known. Little did I know that he was one whom I should have stayed away from, one who was forbidden. An Angel. I know what you must think as you read this, an Angel, they don't exist, but my darling they do.

As soon as I found out what he was I left, not knowing the wonderful gift he had given me.

You.

I met Robert years later, just before you turned three and fell in love with him. He raised you as his own, knowing the truth about your patrilineage.

You are a forbidden hybrid of man and Angel, yet you are also Chronicler-born, a mix which to my knowledge, has never been known.

Tell no one that you do not absolutely trust about this, because you will be putting your life into their hands. There are many that would kill you without hesitation, if they even suspected what you are.

As a mother, I know I should tell you not to be afraid of the dark, but be careful, there are monsters out there, and they will come to find you.

You are special my beautiful girl, and I fear all too soon others will recognise that in you as well.

Don't give your trust lightly. Follow your instincts, for they will help warn, and protect you.

Hopefully you need never read this letter, but if you do then please forgive me.

Know that I love you.

Mum.

Kess carefully read the letter again, then walked to where Miah sat on the camp bed sharpening her knives, and held out the sheet of paper.

'Your mother's letter?' Miah took the letter but looked to her charge. At Kess's nod she unfolded the note and read.

She could tell the moment the warrior read the truth of her parentage when her eyes whipped up, round and wide, mouth parted in shock. 'That explains a lot,' was all she said though, before continuing reading.

A small smile reached Kess's mouth as she shook her head – Guardians were never surprised for long.

'You never knew?' Miah asked as she handed the sheet back.

'That my father was an Angel? No of course not.'

'Shh,' Miah warned, looking around the room suspiciously. 'You must *never* say that aloud, even when you think you are alone.'

A stab of white hot fear flashed through her. *Was it that dangerous for her to be what she was?*

'You trusted me with this?'

'Of course. You are my Guardian,' she replied in all seriousness.

A smile reached the warrior's face. 'Not long ago we were strangers.'

'We've been through a lot since then. I trust you four completely.'

A satisfied look settled on Miah's face. 'About time,' her small smile, vanished quickly. 'You must *never* tell anyone else about this. Or even we may not be able to protect you.'

The seriousness of Miah's voice, the obvious fear which flitted through her eyes, before she carefully masked it, sent a flush of panic through Kess. She was already being hunted by demons. If they found out about her being part Angel, covered in strange writing, and who could bond multiple beings – who knows how many would be sent next time.

The fear in Miah's eyes, suggested something worse than demons. The Angels only knew what that could be. She definitely wasn't in any hurry to find out.

'You will have to destroy that letter. If anyone found it–' Miah trailed off letting her words hang ominously in the air.

Kess nodded absently, knowing that would be the smart thing to do, but it was one of the few things she had left from her mother.

'Thrain has to be told.' Miah turned from her and switched on the desk lamp, shining it directly out the window.

The worry Kess felt settled in a cold ball within her chest. She was dreading the conversation with Thrain that much, that she didn't even make a crack about Miah using a bat signal to summon him.

A soft knock at the door a few minutes later had Kess in a jumble of nerves. Miah opened the door letting him in, and with a glance outside to make sure no one was within hearing distance, firmly shut the door. Leaning back against the wood she handed the note to Thrain without a word.

The blonde warrior took the letter, looking to Kess for explanation but when none was forthcoming he looked down, eyes darting back and forth as he scanned the contents.

When he got to the bit Kess was dreading he sucked in a breath. 'That's impossible. It is Forbidden.' The way he spoke you could hear the capitalisation in the word. Thrain scowled, glaring at Kess like it was all her fault. His voice was cold and steel hard clearly expressing how much of a sin he believed her existence to be.

Forbidden.

Not unheard of, or rare. But forbidden. Something which should not be.

Her.

She recoiled a step, his words hitting her like a slap in the face.

'Forbidden or not, Kess's father is an Angel. It is the only explanation for her abilities.' Miah put her hands on her hips. 'You know it's true.'

Thrain shook his head wordlessly, anguish plain on his face. 'She can't be–'

'Who her parents are is no fault of hers. You know the person she is.' Miah was interrupted from saying anything more as a knock sounded at the door.

Thrain flung back the door, glaring at the Captol standing on the other side.

Wessler's eyes widened, and he took an involuntary step away from the angry commander. Peering around the warrior he saw Kess, and visibly relaxed, obviously fearing something had happened to her. 'It's time.'

Kess grabbed her coat and hurried out the door, glad to have an excuse to leave.

She caught Thrain looking at her, and wondered if he would ever see her the same way again. That the Guardians disliked Angels was no secret, but she didn't think he would classify her in that enmity. But the way he looked at her now was different, like she had deceived him in some way.

But how could she have, when she'd only just found out herself.

Without looking in Thrain's direction, she stalked from the room, relishing the chill night air as it hit her flushed face. She breathed in the crisp freshness, calming herself.

Zuri emerged from the shadows but Kess glanced away, not wanting to see the change in her Guardians behaviour when told what she really was.

Her vision blurred, but she refused to let the tears fall. After weeks with the warriors she'd thought they'd diffused any Guardian–Chronicler issues, that she could consider them friends. Well maybe not Thrain, she doubted he had any friends, but the others certainly.

Would they walk away from her after finding out what she was?

She waited for Wessler to take the lead and followed him, not looking back to see where the warriors were. A rustle of movement beside her had her reaching for her weapon, pulling the blade half from its sheath before she saw Miah's slim form.

The dark–haired warrior raised an eyebrow at her, but said softly. 'We are your Guardians, nothing you could reveal about yourself will change that.'

'Thrain certainly doesn't seem to feel that way.' There was bitterness in her voice that she didn't try to disguise.

He will come around. He's just – surprised.' She was obviously as annoyed at the Commander's attitude as Kess.

'He's surprised?' Kess's voice rose an octave, loud enough that the other Guardians glanced in her direction. 'Imagine how I feel,' she said, lowering her voice again.

Miah gave her a small smile. 'Do not think we will turn away from you. Ever.' With a slight squeeze of her arm, the warrior fell back resuming her scan of the area.

The tightness which had clamped around Kess's heart loosened. She turned her head, risking a glance at Zuri, who met her eyes and gave her a nod. She'd obviously been told, but was showing Kess she didn't care. She felt her eyes tear again, this time with overwhelming relief.

'Kess,' Wessler said softly. 'There are some things you need to know before we arrive.' She turned her attention away from the warriors and listened as the Captol explained the details of her upcoming initiation.

She frowned in disappointment when Wessler told her where the *Luce* met. 'What? No secret levers leading to dark staircases, lit only by a torch which you pulled from a bracket in the wall?' She had expected cloak and dagger; hidden rooms and clandestine meetings. Not the teaching room in the Archive.

Wessler looked at her sideways, a slightly exasperated look on his face. 'Sorry to disappoint.'

She heard Zuri laugh softly behind her – didn't anyone know how a secret society was supposed to meet?

Their unusual entourage cleared the path of any oncoming Chroniclers, who gave them wide berth. Considering the time of early evening, there seemed to be quite a large number of people about.

A pair standing at the side of the path however gave her pause, drawing her gaze. A young female Chronicler was standing with a similarly aged Guardian, talking. The raven–haired girl looked in Kess's direction, staring intently back at her before giving a slow, deliberate nod. Like the Chronicler had in the Archive.

What was going on?

Wessler pulled a set of keys from his pocket and unlocked the Archive door, ushering them past him with quick hand movements. As soon as they were all inside he slipped in, locking the door behind him.

With sure steps, he hurried to the rear of the large room, and paused in front of a closed door. The Captol pulled up a hood she hadn't noticed before on the back of his cloak and knocked once, paused for a moment, then knocked again rapidly, three times.

The deep boom of his knuckles on the wood echoed loudly through the silent space. Kess turned – nervous the sound might draw unwanted attention – but breathed a sigh of relief when no one flung open the front door demanding to know what they were doing in the closed Archive at that time of night.

The door in front of Wessler swung silently open, revealing a dark interior within. The Captol strode through, obviously assuming they would follow.

Kess's eyes took a moment to adjust to the dark room, which was lit only with a few sporadic candles. She saw, with some satisfaction that everyone in the room wore a hooded robe which hid their faces deep inside, concealing their identity.

Wessler shut the double doors behind him and barred the door with a heavy looking length of timber.

'Who comes before us seeking admittance?' A deep voice boomed out.

Kess sought the owner of the voice, and found him standing in the centre of the room, backed by a crescent of four silent hooded figures.

'One who is worthy,' Wessler stated coming to stand beside her.

She looked around and saw the Guardians had taken position around the room. Their condition of entry had been to remain inconspicuous – as inconspicuous as four leather clad, heavily armed warriors could be amongst a group of robed figures.

'One who seeks to join the fight against the darkness.' Her voice rang out clear and steady, saying the words the Captol had drilled into her on the walk over.

'Does she covet the light?' One of the hooded members in the crescent asked. The voice was female, her cockney accent clearly identifying her from the suburbs of southern London.

Wessler spoke again. 'She walks in the light denying the shadow,' he stated, completing the ritual words. Then with a quick glance at her, continued. 'She has already fought and killed hells spawn both within the Haven and without.' A murmur ran through the group, quickly silenced as the leader held up a hand. 'Her mother Anna was one of our own,' Wessler continued. 'She is worthy,' he repeated.

Kess wondered why Wessler had deviated from what he had told her was the standard ritual, adding the stuff about the demon killing and her mother.

The man in the centre remained silent, considering the Captol's words. 'You bring her before us affirming her path in the light?'

‘I do.’

That was her cue to walk forwards and kneel before the crescent. The ground was hard under her knees as she waited for their acceptance or rejection.

‘Do you vow t’ always walk in t’ light?’ A man’s Yorkshire accented voice rang out, he stepped forwards breaking the crescent, stopping a pace behind the leader’s right shoulder.

‘By the Angels I so swear,’ she said solemnly.

‘Do you swear to always fight the forces of evil?’ The cockney woman stepped forwards, to the leader’s left.

‘As long as the Angels will it, I will fight,’ she stated.

‘Do you promise to protect the identity of your brethren unto death.’ The third hooded figure in the line asked, taking a step forward to form the back left of the vee, behind the Londoner.

‘Unto death and beyond. By the Angels I so swear.’

‘Thrice she has sworn by the Angels,’ the fourth man stated. ‘Thrice you are bound. In the now. In the future. In the hereafter,’ he intoned taking the last place in the five–figure vee.

Now came the bit she’d been dreading. Kess held out her left hand, and waited, heart fluttering.

When nothing happened, she glanced up and saw a ginger haired woman standing in front of her. Hood thrown back revealing her pale heavily freckled complexion, she hesitated, holding the glowing red brand inches away from her skin.

The heat radiated from the molten metal, curling the hairs on the back of her hand. This close she could see the bright red of the tip, shaped in a half crescent moon with a large dot in the centre – the mark of the Luce.

The moment dragged on, and she wished the woman would just get it over with. She remembered being told once that fear of an event was sometimes worse than the actual thing. She didn’t hold much hope that the scalding metal burning a brand into her skin would be anything but horrific.

‘We usually choose somewhere more concealable.’ The woman said softly, glancing behind her for confirmation.

Kess hesitated, then pulled the high collar down exposing a slightly larger patch of skin, under her hairline where her spine met skull. She was careful not to reveal the strange writing that started at the large protruding bone at the base of her neck, as she pulled her hair out of the way.

Without warning the woman plunged the metal down onto the sensitive skin. She jumped unintentionally at the searing intense pain that felt like it was scalding her bones, but remained silent.

Hearing the sizzle of her flesh was disconcerting, but it was the smell, like a steak cooking on a hotplate, which was almost worse than the pain itself. Her stomach flipped at the image, and for the first time in her life considered becoming a vegetarian.

Thankfully the heated metal pressed against her skin for only a few seconds, enough to mark her but not do any permanent damage.

‘Welcome, Sister.’ A dozen voices rang out, and as one every member flung back their hoods revealing their identities. There were many faces that she recognised, but just as many were unfamiliar.

‘Here let me look at that.’ Miah was suddenly at her side, helping her to her feet as she inspected the burn on her neck.

Knowing it would do no good to argue, she let the warrior examine the blistered skin, glad it was over. Thankfully her vivid imagination was worse than the actual experience – not, that she wanted to do it again though.

Miah released her arm as Wessler walked over. ‘Welcome to *L’Ultima Luce*.’ A broad grin lit his face, which was now uncovered. ‘Kess, this is Custodian Partan, from Asile, the Canadian Haven,’ he introduced the unfamiliar man standing behind him. ‘He remained here after the Quaternary council finished sitting to see what help he could give us. He is of course a member.’

‘Kip, please.’ The Custodian’s light brown eyes held a kind twinkle which immediately engendered Kess’s trust. She couldn’t have put an exact age to him, older than forty, but how much so she couldn’t guess.

Partan held up his sleeve revealing the mark, identical to hers on his inner arm right near his elbow. Unsure what the protocol was for secret clubs, she nodded at him, not bothering to expose her own which he just saw branded.

With a small incline of his head Partan made his way towards the seats in the corner of the room. Wessler ushered Kess in front of him sitting in the chair opposite her, next to the Canadian Custodian.

She waited for him to speak unsure where this was heading.

'As you know the Council recently convened on a number of issues, but there were two main topics of agenda. The first was the dramatic decrease in Chronicler initiates over recent years which has shown a further significant reduction this year. This decline is totally in contrast to the Guardians who have had several thousand new recruits between the Havens in the last six months alone.'

'And the second?' Kess asked, trying to keep him on point.

With a slight downturn of his eyebrows he cleared his throat. 'Ahh yes, the second were the attacks on Chroniclers which I'm sad to say is on the increase. There was another occurrence two weeks ago in Mexico.'

Wessler spoke, with a quick look to his left. 'What can you tell us about the demon attack here?'

She had already discussed, with Miah and Thrain, the likelihood of that question being asked, and they decided that she would answer truthfully, in the hopes of figuring out how the demon got in, to which Thrain was especially interested. 'I visited my mother earlier that day at the hospital.'

'Her mother is a resident of St Anne's, a psychiatric facility near here,' Wessler explained to Partan.

'She was acting strange, talking about weird things and then she attacked me.'

'What did she say?' Wessler asked.

Kess's eyes unfocused, not really seeing him, as the words came back to her. 'Her last words to me were – I'll see you screaming, soon.'

His eyes widened in shock, even Miah standing beside her looked a little surprised. She hadn't told them everything that her mother had said; at the time it had been too painful.

'Later that night I was walking back to my room when she appeared out of the darkness and grabbed me. She transformed into what I was later told was a Rask–'

Partan sucked in a breath, eyebrows rising high on his face.

'It attacked me and I killed it,' she continued quickly, not wanting to relive that moment again in detail.

'That simple.' Partan scoffed, earning a hard look from both Miah and Wessler.

'Beheading usually is.'

'You killed it? Not the Guardians?' Partan asked, sweeping a hand through his artfully swept back hair, which had more than a few grey hairs peppering through near his ears.

'They didn't arrive until later.'

'I knew it,' the Captol said softly. A strange light had entered his eyes, confirmation of his suspicions about her no doubt, but there was also something else – wondering.

Kess looked away, afraid he would see some truth in her eyes; figure out things she wished to keep hidden.

What else could he know?

'Well you are a very lucky young lady to have survived an attack from such a demon.'

She touched her sleeve where the scars lay. 'Not that lucky,' she retorted. 'It killed my mother.'

'Anna's dead?' Wessler looked horrified.

'Yes,' Kess said thickly, eyes flitting to Miah whose concerned gaze was upon her. 'The demon used her life force to gain entry to our realm.'

Wessler thumped back in his chair, face pale.

'You didn't know?'

'No.' He shook his head, clearly distraught.

'Drazen believes that the demon went to the hospital and killed her. We didn't bother enlightening him.'

'He knew?' Wessler said flatly.

Kess nodded. 'Do you have any idea how the demon got into a Haven in the first place?'

'We've been making some inquiries into that, and it appears that the Obiex was tampered with in the hours preceding the attack.'

'By whom?' By agreement Kess was to ask all the questions. Miah's thinking was that she would be able to gain more information from the Chroniclers than a Guardian would.

Wessler ignored her question asking one of his own. 'How much contact have you had with Drazen?'

'Little.'

'Care to elaborate?'

Kess shifted irritably, frustrated by how little she was finding out. 'I'm the one answering all the questions here. You aren't telling me anything I didn't already know. Why are you so interested in Drazen, or what I know about him?'

She met their silent stares with one of her own, unwilling to be the one giving all the ground.

With a deep inhaled breath, Wessler muttered something that sounded like '*as wilful as Anna*' before turning to Partan, who grudgingly nodded.

'What do you know about Drazen's activities?'

At her continued silence he added, 'Just humour me for a moment.'

She shrugged. 'I heard he gave the gate Guardians an order they didn't like.'

Partan looked at her expectantly, clearly waiting for more.

With a sigh, she leant forwards resting her elbows on the table. 'I don't know. We don't exactly hang out together. He was there right after the demon attack, with you,' she said, looking at Wessler. 'He didn't want to let me leave the Haven,' her voice trailed off again as she tried to remember anything else strange. 'He didn't seem in a hurry to tell the other Custodians about the attack. A Guardian vanished not long after Drazen's strange orders were issued.'

The two watched her silently, clearly waiting for more.

'I don't know what you're expecting me to say. It's obvious you don't think he's pukka,' she said, using one of her favourite DelBoy sayings, 'but I don't understand what you think I know.'

Grim lines creased Partan's otherwise youthful looks. 'We are unsure whether his conduct is a result of him merely seeking to further his own agenda, or whether his actions have deeper ramifications.'

'What are you really doing here?' Kess asked Partan.

Wessler made a choking sound at the directness of her question, which with retrospect, possibly bordered on rudeness.

The Canadian Custodian laid a hand onto the Captol's arm patting it lightly. 'It's alright, this young lady has been through a lot, and from what you've been telling me about her associations, it seems as though the Guardians directness has rubbed off on her. I must say, I prefer a straight shooter over a smooth tongue.' He gave her a charming smile which again, almost against her will, had her grinning back at him.

'We are worried at the apparent increasing number of *Verità Scuro* within our own Haven. Tomas confirms similar incidences here as well. The *Scuro* are a furtive group, and like an insidious worm burrowed within a ripe apple, we are finding it hard to dig them out.'

'Maybe I'm dense but I still don't understand. How you think I can help,' she asked, looking to Miah and Thrain to see if she was missing something obvious, but their faces remained carefully blank, watchful.

'As I said the figurative worm is buried, but we are unsure how deep the corruption goes. We are trying to identify their members that we may either infiltrate them or use one member to find another, and so on. You have had a number of dealings with Drazen. We just wanted to find out what you knew.' Partan gave her a direct stare that seemed as though he was trying to scry the information he was looking for from her mind.

'I'm not sure what I am supposed to be looking for, but I will keep an eye out.' Kess looked across the table at the man who was one of the leaders of the Asile Haven, and who was clearly well placed within this secret organisation. 'If the Luce watch for signs of the Apocalypse, what is the purpose of the Scuro?'

Partan's eyes softened as he looked at her. 'There has always been corruption in the heart of man, perhaps since Eden. The Scuro capitalise on that weakness to further their own dark agenda.' The Custodian looked at her speculatively. 'You seem a very capable, resourceful young woman. Should you find yourself in the neighbourhood, or want a change of scenery, you would be welcome at Asile. You may find our Vault contains some tomes as interesting as the ones here.' Seeing her about to reply, he continued, 'Don't make up your mind now. Should you decide to accept, ask for my Secretary Elin, tell her I offered to mentor you.'

Kess nodded, taken aback by his offer. 'Thank you.'

'Ah, I see someone I need to talk to. Chronicler Grayson it was a pleasure. And please consider my offer.' With that he walked away, eyes twinkling as he strode across the room.

'Do you trust him?' Kess asked Wessler who had remained behind.

'Without hesitation,' the Captol said seriously. 'He joined us after his daughter was murdered by the Verità Scuro.' Seeing her eyes narrow sceptically, he added softly. 'He almost died protecting me, the day we recovered your mother.'

Not knowing what to say to that, Kess opted to remain silent.

'There are many who will be wanting to welcome you and I'm sure they're chomping at the bit, waiting for me to leave.' Wessler rose and walked across the room in the direction Custodian Partan had taken.

The moment he vacated the table she found herself surrounded by a group of three robed Chroniclers.

With a quiet sigh, she put on her brightest smile and tried to listen attentively to a bird–like man who'd taken her hand in his excitement, or perhaps, to stop her leaving now that he finally had a chance to talk to her.

~

Kess failed to stifle the yawn which was the third in as many minutes. Hiding her mouth behind her hand, she nodded politely at the middle–aged Chronicler who was still, after several minutes, telling her how glad she was to have Kess initiated.

‘Kess,’ Miah interrupted, causing the woman to halt mid–sentence.

‘Excuse me please,’ she told the Chronicler, who with a polite nod and one last smile walked to a small group huddled not far away. ‘Thank you. Let’s get out of here before anyone else tries to accost me.’

Walking quickly towards the door, she saw Wessler look over and nod at her, not quite managing to hide a smile, as he saw her escaping. She returned a relieved smile, amazed at the transformation in him. She no longer thought of him as the Weasel – the visage he maintained in public – he was someone she was quickly coming to trust and could go to for advice. Certainly not about everything, not yet. She tugged at her sleeves consciously, pulling them down.

They were met at the door by Thrain and Zuri who led the way, letting Miah guard the rear. She fell in with them, not questioning their actions any more, knowing whatever they did was to protect her.

Their escape was halted when they got to the locked Archive door. She looked back towards the room, hesitant to go back in, for fear of not being able to escape again, when she saw a Chronicler, who looked younger than herself, walking quickly towards them.

‘The Captol sent me to open up for you.’

Relief rushed through her. ‘Thanks–’ Kess paused, not knowing the girls name.

‘Lacy,’ she supplied.

‘I’ve seen you around, haven’t I? You work in the Archive? I’m Kess, by the way.’

Lacy smiled brightly, clearly surprised Kess had noticed her. ‘I know who you are,’ she said softly, ‘and yes I do work here.’ She pulled out a key and unlocked the door swiftly. ‘Good night,’ she included the Guardians in her salutation, then shut the door firmly behind them.

Kess heard the lock click again as she fell in behind Zuri who led the way back to her room.

~

‘You’re guarding tonight?’ Kess asked, surprised when Thrain followed her through the door. He seemed to have calmed down from earlier and was looking at her again, though he still seemed distant – more so than usual.

‘Yes,’ he focused on her, only giving the room a cursory glance, ensuring they were alone. ‘Is that alright?’

She nodded, not sure what else to say, then sat on the bed, feeling self–conscious about him being in her room. She could joke around with the others and felt more comfortable spending one on one time with them, even Kisho, whom she thought of as an older brother.

Thrain in contrast was always serious, never losing the Commander persona. The last time she’d been alone with him was after she had run off, she still felt horrible about that, which added to her awkwardness.

Yet he seemed hesitant around her too, making her remember the way he had lost control of his rigid emotions that day; the wild look in his grey eyes as he gripped her arms, so tightly she’d later found handprint bruises on her upper arms.

She hadn’t told anyone, afraid it would cause more friction between her Guardians and with all the clothing she’d had to wear to cover her markings, no one had noticed the purple contusions which had now faded to mottled yellow.

‘How is your neck?’

Reminding Kess about the burn made it flare with pain, but she pushed the feeling away. She’d had a lot of practice at that lately. ‘It’s alright.’

Without a word Thrain looked around her room, gaze settling on her desk where the tub of salve lay. He picked up the container and stepped behind her lifting her hair carefully, and with a touch as gentle as a summer breeze rubbed salve over the burn.

While focused on his task, she took the opportunity to study him, out of the corner of her eye. Whilst he looked healthy again, recovered from his injury, she saw with concern, the dark smudges marring the skin beneath his eyes and the weariness which seemed to have etched itself into his skin.

Thrain looked up from his ministrations, and caught her staring. His grey eyes, which she had learnt conveyed his emotions, were calm, studying her as she did him.

As she stared into his slate gaze, she felt a sensation she was becoming all too familiar with; a whirlwind, trying to pull her towards it.

She pulled away from him, surprised.

He tilted his head, watching her, calmly replacing the lid of the container, and putting it back on the table top.

'Did you–' she halted, unsure how to explain to him what she'd felt. Was it possible that she could bond Guardians as well as Angels and a Demon? 'Never mind,' she said, realising he would have said something if he'd felt the whirlwind as well. 'I guess I'm more tired than I thought.'

She had no idea what the time was but thought it had to be after midnight. It seemed like all the *Luce* members in attendance had wanted to have their chance to talk with the newest initiate, not allowing her to escape any sooner.

Grabbing clothes from under her pillow, she walked to the bathroom, more than ready to crawl into bed.

Thrain averted his eyes, when she walked out, making her feel self–conscious even though she was wearing track pants and a shirt. Though she was hardly scantily–clad by any stretch of the imagination, his reaction unsettled her.

While she couldn't imagine Thrain wearing pyjamas, she saw that he was still wearing his Guardian issued pants with a black T–shirt, which surely wouldn't be comfortable to sleep in. She was also sure he was armed, but didn't bother trying to dissuade him. She'd have better luck trying to talk a tiger into giving up its stripes.

She noticed with some amusement, his shoes placed neatly at the foot of the camp bed, his jacket folded neatly atop her desk, everything neat and orderly reflecting the man himself. Whilst she was more than contented to leave her clothes in a crumpled heap atop her washing basket until the morning.

'Ready?' Kess asked, hand pausing before turning off the light.

With a final look around the room, he nodded, settling on top of the blankets of the makeshift bed. 'Wait,' he said suddenly as she reached for the switch.

She turned half expecting something to be wrong yet his gaze was fixed upon her, on the marks on her arm which his keen gaze had spotted.

He stood hesitantly and walked towards her pulling her sleeve higher as his other hand lifted her arm towards him. 'Is this–'

'It's nothing,' she said trying to pull her arm from his grasp.

He didn't fight her, just let his arms drop to his sides.

'I'm fine,' she said again, as she saw guilt swirling in his eyes. She cursed herself for letting him see the faded bruises. Not wanting to talk about it she said instead, 'What I found out today–'

'Let's just forget it for the moment,' he said sounding very unlike the face–a–problem–head–on commander she had come to know. 'Sleep well, Kess.'

'Goodnight,' she replied, realising that like her, he too needed time to process the huge revelation of her parentage.

She lay down, conscious of the sound of Thrain's steady breaths, and closed her eyes, drifting immediately to sleep.

CHAPTER 29

A Softening

She felt the panic of the mob around her, thick in the air like a heavy fog on a winter's morning – so dense it was hard to breathe.

Thousands of people lined the street, desperately trying to escape, but the press of bodies crawled slowly forwards, allowing no movement faster than a steady walk.

Some had taken to the rooftops seeking a quicker way, but the steeply sloped roofs offered precarious footing, and more than one unlucky soul had slipped to their deaths already. Yet more and more took the risk, desperate to get away, willing to take their chances.

A cataclysmic boom exploded in the distance, disintegrating the angry volcano in a torrent of molten lava and house sized chunks of earth thrown high into the air.

As a blast of hot air pummelled across the city, almost levelling everyone in the street, the mob, temporarily frozen watching the chaos, surged forwards. Their desperation to leave, turning to panic to escape, as they saw the rapidly approaching cloud of deadly sulphuric gasses descending upon their decimated city.

People pushed forwards, elbowing anyone in their way, fighting to escape the impending destruction raining down on their once beautiful city. Men, women and children fell under the press, and were trampled by the stampeding feet of those around them who were unwilling, or unable to help.

She could taste their fear as reason was lost and primal instinct – the need to survive – reigned.

'Kess.'

She looked around the street, seeking the source of the familiar voice, yet all she could hear was the screaming of thousands of voices, crying infants and children, and the rumble of the approaching violence.

'Kess!' The voice intruded again, clearing her mind.

This is a dream. She said the words aloud, noticing how the people around her didn't react. She stopped struggling against the press of bodies and tried to shut out their panicked screams, their terror. Tried to ignore the crashing of debris raining down on the buildings around her.

This is a dream. She whispered the words to herself, trying to make herself believe them.

A dream.

A hot blustering wind buffeted against her knocking her back into a wall, bashing her head sharply against the granite. She raised a hand to her head which pounded with pain.

A dream.

She struggled to retain her thoughts as she felt the dream try to suck her back in and claim her.

Utterly terrified she fought against the whirlpool, becoming frantic as she continued to lose ground. The panic of the people surrounding her filtered through, filling her as if it were her own.

'Kess.'

She heard her name again, and with it a warmth; a strength which steadied her against the overwhelming current of the dream. She clung to it like an anchor and slowly pulled herself free.

She opened her eyes and saw a face, etched with concern, inches from hers.

'Thrain?'

His hand cupped her face.

She recognised the warmth as the lifeline that helped her escape. 'You helped me get back.' Her chest heaved in deep breaths of fresh air.

'You cried out. I thought someone was in here – but you were dreaming.'

'It wouldn't let me go. I couldn't escape.' She felt a tear glide down her cheek and started to turn away from him, embarrassed.

He held her chin firmly so she couldn't turn away and gently wiped the tears from her skin with his thumbs. 'Your dreams are not to be feared. They teach, guide.' He wiped another tear with his thumb.

She had never heard him sound so gentle before.

The moonlight streamed through her window casting a gentle glow throughout the room. In its light, she saw *him*. The grim exactness he carried naturally was softened making him look younger and less forbidding. With his glowering and usually hostile layers stripped away, she realised for the first time how good looking he really was.

Her face warmed as she realised how close he was, seated on the edge of the bed, leaning over her, one hand holding his weight denting the pillow beside her head. The other still held her face. He was so close, his warmth seeped into her fear soaked body.

Seized on impulse, her hand moved, trying to free itself from the covers, to touch the hand that held her cheek.

Mistaking her movement, he dropped his hand, and slid his body backwards on the bed increasing the gap between them.

She felt coolness where the warmth had been, then a flush of embarrassment as she realised what she had almost done. Thank the Angels he'd mistaken her movement. She'd never be able to face him again if he had realised she had been trying to touch him when he was just doing his job watching over her.

'Thank you,' Kess said trying to diffuse her chagrin.

'Remember what I said. Don't fight your dreams,' he stood, looking down at her for a moment, before settling back on his bed.

She tried to ignore the conflicting emotions fighting within her, focusing instead on her dreams. She hadn't told her Guardians but they were obviously aware of her rough nights. They'd also apparently discussed it amongst themselves since Thrain hadn't seemed surprised at her restlessness.

Thinking of Thrain brought a flush to her cheeks again and she was thankful the room was dark enough to hide her blush.

She could still feel his hand against her cheek, but tried to banish the thought.

He was Thrain. The hard–ass head of the Guardians. Not someone to be thinking about in any other way.

CHAPTER 30

An Unveiling

The bed Thrain had slept in was empty by the time Kess woke. Hurriedly she threw on a change of clothes, and had just straightened from tying her shoes when Kisho walked into the room, throwing a brown paper parcel at her.

She caught it as it hurtled towards her stomach. 'Jeez, you could have warned me.'

'Guardians have to be ready for anything, at any time.'

'But I'm not a Guardian,' she said giving the bulky package a squeeze trying to figure out what was inside.

'Do you want to be?'

Parcel contents forgotten, she stared at Kisho who was looking at her intently. 'I was told once, "Chroniclers are born. Guardians are born. They do not, have not, ever swapped sides".'

'Thrain?'

Kess shook her head smiling, though it did sound like something he'd say. 'No, Miah. How can I *become* a Guardian? I imagine there are very strict laws about that.'

'I don't think those rules apply to you.' He shrugged. 'You seem to be outside of what we believe to be possible, so why not this?'

She looked at him sceptically. 'Was this your idea? I doubt Thrain would agree with you.'

He shrugged his broad shoulders again, but didn't say anything further, apparently content with planting the seed of possibility in her mind.

‘What’s in here?’ Kess asked shaking the heavy brown package.

‘Something from Zuri.’

Setting it on her lap, she pulled the tail of the string bow tied about the package, undoing it. Bundling it up, she put it on the bed beside her, then unwrapped the crinkly paper revealing a pile of neatly folded outfits.

She held up a dark green shirt sitting on top. The style was obviously bespoke, with a high firm neck collar that opened at the front in a narrow vee. The tops of the shoulders had the familiar raised pattern to them that the Guardian outfits sported, and yet the front of the shirt was also panelled into three vertical segments allowing for a slim fitting design that would sit against her body like another skin.

Carefully folding it back up, she placed it on the bed and looked at the rest of the stack. A trio of similarly designed shirts in black, dark brown and blood red were quickly placed to the side, atop the first.

Unsure what the next folded up bundle of material was, she shook it out, and found what she was sure would be very tight–fitting pair of dark coloured pants, with an array of pockets down the side of the legs, also similar to Guardian issue. A second pair of pants followed the first onto the growing pile on the bed, leaving two items.

She looked up at Kisho who watching her silently not offering any comment.

At his shrug, she picked up the inch–wide black leather belt, staring at it in wonder when she saw her forbandt mark stitched along its entire length.

Kess looked closer at the wide oval shaped buckle and found two small throwing knives that could be unclipped from each side of the metal clasp. A wide grin lit her face, trust Zuri to mix fashion with weaponry.

The last item was a pair of soft, short heeled, black leather boots. Not that she knew anything about leather, but they appeared to be well made, but heavy. Frowning, she undid the full–length zip and saw a pouch sewn into the lining on the inside panel of the boot, and poking from the top of each, was a small hilt. She pulled the knife from the hidden pocket finding a fat fish–shaped blade in each.

‘Throwing knives,’ Kisho told her, holding his hand out for one of them. ‘Excellent weight,’ he said twirling it around him like a performer from a circus act. He gave her a cheeky smile, and a small bow at her clapping, then handed the blade back to her hilt first.

'Why would she do this?' she asked indicating everything on the bed.

'You have made quite an impression on her, on all of us.' Kisho watched her closely. 'Go on,' he indicated his head towards the bathroom.

~

Kess looked at her reflection in the mirror and saw someone she barely recognised. Hair tied back in a ponytail, she looked different – or thought she did.

The outfit was as tight–fitting as she had thought it would be. She didn't know what the material was but it was light, yet snug without being too hot. The long sleeves fanned across the backs of her hands in the shape of a spade, covering her marked skin perfectly. And even the boots with their hidden weapons didn't restrict her movement and were comfortable to wear.

She emerged from her bathroom to find Kisho lounging on his makeshift bed.

'May I be the first to say mrow,' he waggled his eyebrows at her suggestively. The broad grin on his face took away any lewdness from his comment.

She held her arms across her body in a self–conscious gesture.

'Don't,' he said rising from the canvas frame which creaked alarmingly as he moved. 'It suits you. Own it.'

At her grimace, he laughed. 'Now let's get you out to see that Angel of yours.'

Kess closed the door behind her, and started walking down the hall beside Kisho.

'So it's true.' A familiar female voice rang out. 'You've finally come back.'

Kess turned and saw Lisbeth standing in the doorway to her room, arms crossed – a look of disdain was plastered across her porcelain–fine features. 'What, you're away for a few weeks and now you think you're one of them?' she mocked, lips curled in an ugly sneer.

Kess was glad Zuri wasn't on duty this morning; she would have delighted in wiping that look from her face.

'Nice to see you too, Lisbeth,' she said calmly. 'I thought with the Choosing over you would have moved to the Linguist Quarters already.'

The blonde sniffed. 'I'm cleaning out the last of my things. Where did you go?' Lisbeth demanded. 'I was worried,' she added belatedly, totally at odds with the snarky way she was acting.

'Yeah, it seems like it,' Kess muttered.

Lisbeth's eyes narrowed, but the comment must have been too soft for her to hear. 'It's not bad enough that you run around wanting to be a Guardian, now you're dressing like them too?'

Kess looked down at her new clothing. 'It was a gift.'

'What from lover boy here? Don't think everyone hasn't noticed you having a different man, or woman,' she sneered, 'in your room every night.' She shook her head mockingly. 'You are getting quite the reputation.'

Kess's cheeks heated at the remark. 'I have to go.'

The look in Lisbeth's eyes was cold. 'You never were suited to being a Chronicler. Go pretend to be a warrior, maybe you'll be better at that.' She fluttered her slim hands out in front of her, shooing the pair away.

Kess shook her head, unsure where all this hostility had come from, especially from someone she'd thought was a friend. She watched the blonde for a moment longer before falling in behind her Guardian.

'Well she's delightful. Good friend is she?' Kisho quipped, trying to lighten her mood.

She looked at him sadly. 'I thought she was.' She guessed she wasn't that surprised, Lisbeth had never condoned Kess's actions whenever they differed from whatever she felt a Chronicler should be. But she'd never been outwardly aggressive before.

Kisho watched her face, taking Kess's silence for sadness. 'Some people can't accept life outside their little box of normality. Anything different is a danger, a threat to their fragile little world.'

A horrible thought occurred to her. Lisbeth had known about Kess going out of a night and had assumed it was to meet a guy when she was really training with the Guardians. But she had known. *What if Lisbeth was Verità Scuro and the demon attack hadn't been random?*

She hadn't realised she'd spoken aloud until Kisho whistled sharply through his teeth. 'That's one hell of a bestie you have there.'

'Bestie?'

'What?' A mischievous smile lit his face. 'I'm up with all the hip terms.'

Kess's laughter sounded loud in the quiet of the morning, and drew the attention of a group of young Chroniclers who watched the pair walk by curiously.

Just before they got to the gate, Thrain caught up with them.

With a last cheeky waggle of his eyebrows Kisho jogged back towards Aldoak.

'I thought Kisho had relieved you,' Kess queried.

'I had something to attend to,' he said gruffly. 'If you would prefer he escort you, I can call him back.' He turned around looking at Kisho's disappearing form.

She laid a hand on Thrain's arm, stopping him and felt the hard lines of corded muscle tense at her touch. 'I was thinking of you,' she said softly, 'you look tired.'

He shifted back towards her, coming closer as he did, until they were almost touching. 'I am well,' he said softly. She looked up into his grey eyes and saw a brightness to them that hadn't been there before.

'Let's meet your Angel,' he said, diffusing the moment, before striding away towards the gate.

Technically whilst not against any law, regular departures from the Haven weren't tolerated, however having the Guardian Commander as escort did have its perks.

‘Bannen.’ She nodded to the gate Guardian who since their arrival had been nothing but friendly to her.

Instead of answering, the warrior stared at her, with a gleam in his eyes.

‘Are you going to tell me I don’t have the right to wear something like this?’ she asked unable to forget his hostility towards her when they’d arrived.

‘Not what I was thinking at all,’ he said with a flash of white teeth, making a show of looking her up and down.

Thrain standing next to her harrumphed, and with a final glance in her direction Bannen returned to his post.

Kess felt her face heat and knew that Thrain was watching her. Without waiting for encouragement, she leapt through the barrier glad for once of the iciness to cool her inflamed cheeks.

As soon as they reached their designated meeting spot Kai appeared. With a nod in Thrain’s direction he turned his attention back to her. ‘I have new recruits.’

‘Kai!’

With a shrug, he grinned. ‘This is important, Kess.’

Before she could form a witty retort, three figures materialised.

Kess stepped forward determined to have some control over the situation. ‘Do you know what you are signing up for?’

The trio nodded simultaneously.

‘Kai has spoken with us.’ A beautiful blonde told her. With hair the colour of a bar of gold and eyes that matched, she stood a head taller than Kess, close to six feet tall.

‘At length,’ another Angel said wryly, shaking her midnight coloured hair sending it cascading around her like a curtain of silk.

Kess spun around facing her forbandt. ‘What are you Jehovah witness now?’

Kai looked at her blankly, clearly not understanding her reference.

‘They come to your door and try to convert you–’ his blank look continued. ‘Forget it.’ She turned back to the waiting Angels. ‘Any questions?’

The trio remained silent.

‘Who’s first then?’ Kess asked extending her hand.

The Angel who had remained silent stepped forward. His dark brown hair curled about his head looking like he’d just had them artfully arranged in one of London’s high street salons.

Reaching out, she met his soft brown eyes, and was whipped away from herself.

Moments later the three bonded Angels; golden Caliel, topaz eyed Nakir, and the raven–haired Kasbeel stared at their marks.

‘Anyone else?’ Kess asked sarcastically.

‘Not today,’ he said with a bright smile.

A rush of tiredness hit her; a culmination of interrupted sleep and the events of the last few weeks. ‘Kai, no more.’

The blue–eyed Angel looked at her with concern, feeling what she felt. ‘Are you alright?’

Thrain tensed immediately, scanning her face to see what was wrong.

‘I’m fine,’ Kess told them both. ‘No more for a while though, alright?’

‘We’ll see what the wind brings.’ Kai grinned at her, but the mirth didn’t reach his blue eyes which had darkened with concern. ‘Get some rest.’

‘When I get time.’ She reached out for his arm, seeking to reassure him.

The skin to skin contact increased her awareness of him through the blære, making her keenly aware of its gaping absence over the last few days. It also, unfortunately allowed him to feel the depth of her weariness.

Have you been alright? Kess asked through their blære. *I tried to contact you over the last few days, but could barely sense you.*

A wave of frustration hit her. *I think the Haven’s protective barrier is interfering with our bond.*

She nodded, thinking his hypothesis made sense.

Stay safe, she thought as she dropped her arm, hoping he would let the matter of her tiredness rest.

Turning to her blonde Guardian she saw a similar concern mirrored in his eyes. 'I'm fine. Let's get to the Vault.'

Not giving either of them a chance to argue, she started to walk back towards the gate.

As they crossed the border, Thrain said, 'Miah's your second today, she'll meet us along the way.'

Kess nodded, mind already focused on her next task; finding information about what was happening to her.

CHAPTER 31

The Turn of the Tide

Kess clutched at the note – silently thanking Lacy who'd found them heading towards the Archive, and handed her a slip of paper signed by Head Captol Kentia granting her access to the Vault. The small note attached to the slip which had read, "Enjoy. W." was now safely in her pants pocket.

The Chronicler at the door, read the missive twice before letting them in. As Kess passed by, Guardian in tow, she tried to ignore the considering look the woman was giving her.

She looked around in wonder, at the room she'd stepped into. She had expected the Vault to be, as the name suggested, a metallic small confined space crammed with tomes. So the high vaulted ceilings painted with bright murals, the dark wooden arches spanning gracefully across the breadth of the room carved with intricate designs, and the light–coloured tiles forming decorative patterns across the flooring, had her gobsmacked.

It was beautiful.

A middle–aged woman wearing formal robes approached them, with only a quick glance at her Guardian she focused on Kess. 'I am Head Chronicler Amaya. How may I be of assistance?'

'I seek information about the foundation and history of Chroniclers,' she ignored Miah's sharp look, focusing on the woman in front of her whose shoulder length hair was more silver than blonde.

'Of course. If you will take a seat at one of the tables, I will find some references for you.' She pointed a long bony finger to the right of the room where there were several empty desks.

'Thanks.'

The H.C. nodded her head demurely before departing.

'Do you think it wise to reveal what you are after?' Miah asked.

'I don't really have a choice. There are tens of thousands of volumes here. It would take a lifetime to search through them without knowing where to look.' Her Guardian grudgingly agreed, then stood behind where Kess had taken a seat.

Fifteen minutes later, Miah stretched back in the seat Kess had managed to talk her into taking, whilst she fidgeted impatiently in hers.

Kess's relief as she saw the gaunt woman heading towards them faltered, when she saw the trolley H.C. Amaya pushed, mounded high with books.

'These will provide a start for your research,' she said as she transferred them to the table top, soon obscuring Miah from Kess's view. 'You may leave them piled neatly to the right should you wish to retain them for tomorrow, or the left should you wish to return them.' With that short explanation she left, pushing the trolley back the way she had come.

As Kess pulled the top book from the large stack, she heard Miah mutter, 'This is just a start?' The warrior grabbed a large red leather volume and grimaced as she saw Kess grinning at her. 'You're lucky I like you.'

Smiling Kess opened the front page and began reading.

Thrain, while refuting her insistence that he must have better things to do with his time, spent his shift roaming the grounds outside the Vault, periodically checking in with them.

It was no more than a line in the paragraph filled page, so small and inconsequential that after hours and hours of reading, to the point where her eyes were starting to blur, she had almost missed it. Kess had skimmed over it, and had turned the next page before she realised what she'd just read. 'Listen to this,' she said to the Guardian whose eyes looked as glazed as hers had felt.

'Whilst no factual evidence could be obtained to support this, a man within the small township of Havenport claimed that a story had been

passed down to him, that his great, great, grandfather had met one whom he called Angel and with whom he had formed a connection.'

Kess glanced up excitedly, to a very underwhelmed looking Miah.

'Not much to go on though is it.'

She didn't let her Guardians lack of enthusiasm damper her excitement. 'It is the only reference we have found that has made any mention of Angels in anything other than a fictional sense, and the word "connection" is used, that could mean a bond.' She had lowered her voice to a whisper, but refrained the urge to look about her, knowing it would look suspicious and would gain more attention than their lowered voices.

Miah raised an eyebrow sceptically but didn't argue with her charge further.

~

A loud thump out in the hall drew Kess's attention.

Miah quicker than her, had already made it to the bedroom door and with a quick glance to see that her charge was out of the way, flung back the door ready to launch out.

The knife which had found its way into the warrior's hand vanished back up her sleeve with a quick movement. She looked back inclining her head for Kess to have a look.

Unsure what was going on Kess hesitantly made her way to the door and peered around her Guardians shoulder. Thrain – who had continued his external patrol – had a young dark–haired man bailed up against the wall, sword pointed at his stomach. The Chroniclers eyes looked ready to pop out of his head and Kess could see his hands, which were raised above his head, were shaking.

'Thrain, I don't think they–' She included the caramel–skinned girl, who had obviously been knocked to the ground, and decided that was the safest place to stay, 'are any threat.'

Thrain gave the two another long look before sheathing his sword, the metal hissed as it returned home, which did nothing to soothe the pair.

Kess turned to the girl who had started to climb to her feet. ‘Are you alright?’ She included the young man in her glance, who had deemed it safe to lower his hands, crossing them about his middle to hide their shaking.

‘We – we came to see you,’ he managed to get out, casting a quick glance to Thrain as if making sure he wasn’t going to attack him again.

‘Come in then, there’s no use milling about in the hall.’

The young girl, whose caramel–coloured skin matched the soft brown of her eyes, aimed a not so timid glance at Miah as she walked through the doorway into Kess’s small room. The pair stood in the middle of the space, looking about nervously.

‘Have a seat,’ she pointed to her bed, the only place for them to sit. ‘What have you come here to talk to me about?’ Kess was curious as to what could induce the Chroniclers to brave a run–in with the warriors.

The boy took the lead, more sure of himself now. ‘We want to join you.’

‘Join me in what?’ Kess asked confused.

‘The fight,’ he stated as if it were obvious.

‘And what fight would that be, Chronicler?’ Miah interrupted. She remained standing watching the pair as if they might transform into hells spawn and attack at any second.

‘Against the demons.’ The caramel–skinned girl spoke eagerly, leaning forwards. ‘We’re not the only ones either.’

Kess held her hands up, stalling their growing excitement. ‘First things first. I’m Kess, and you two would be?’

‘We know who you are,’ the boy said, as if that were the most obvious thing in the world. ‘That’s Leora,’ he pointed out the girl. ‘And I’m Abram.’

‘How is it that everybody suddenly knows who I am?’ Kess asked no one in particular.

The look the pair shared was incredulous. ‘You killed a demon! You dress like a Guardian! You’re friends with them,’ his voice rose excitedly as he spoke, until he glanced at Miah, which tempered his enthusiasm.

'Was there a demon killing bulletin I'm not aware of? How is it that everyone knows about this?' Kess looked to Miah who shrugged her shoulders, obviously as clueless as she was.

Thrain stood with his back against the door glancing at the pair.

'People talk,' Leora shrugged, 'especially about things that are out of the ordinary.' She studied Kess as she might a newly discovered species. 'And you are definitely not ordinary.' She spoke in such a way that made Kess forget how young she was, sounding much older than her nineteen or twenty years.

'Why have you decided to join us now?' Kess interrupted, tired of hearing how different she was from everyone else.

'I overheard the conversation you had with your *friend* in the hall this morning,' Leora said, unabashed at admitting to eavesdropping.

'What has that got to do with anything?'

Leora and Abram shared a look, clearly deciding whether to tell her something.

'Spit it out,' she said, not having any patience for tip toeing around unpleasant truths any more.

'Your former *friend*,' again Leora said the word sarcastically, 'always warned away anyone wanting to talk to you, or befriend you. Forcefully if necessary.' She shrugged, before continuing, 'Until no one was game enough to try to talk to you.'

Kess had been shocked at Lisbeth's transformation, but this information left her stunned. 'She hurt people?'

'Well Gerik didn't fall down the stairs by himself and break his ankle,' she pronounced the boy's name GEH–RayK, drawing it out.

Kess remembered a fine featured, boy – whose hair was so blonde it was almost white – using crutches earlier in the year, had even commented to Lisbeth about him, wondering how he had hurt himself. Lisbeth's reply came back to her, stuck in her memory because she hadn't understood it at the time – *Doing something he shouldn't have I suppose.*

'That was her? You're sure?'

'Yes,' the pair said in unison.

‘She did it in front of two of his friends,’ Abram said quietly. ‘Then said they’d be next if they told anyone.’

‘Why didn’t you tell somebody anyway?’ she demanded, unable to believe they had done nothing after such a malicious attack.

‘She warned that any of us informing anyone of higher rank, may not find a sympathetic ear. We didn’t know who we could trust.’

Kess looked wordlessly to Miah whose eyes softened with sympathy. ‘All this time. I thought I was lucky to have a friend like her because no one else seemed to want to know me,’ she said, more to herself than the others. ‘How could she hurt people?’

A maelstrom of emotions stormed through her threatening to engulf her. She pulled all the hurt and anger at the betrayal, and guilt for not figuring it out sooner; into a ball, imagining it tight within her chest, and used it instead to fuel her determination.

She stood drawing the attention of everyone in the room. ‘The *Verità Scuro* need to be eradicated. Its poisonous influence *has* to be removed from our Haven.’

Abram and Leora exchanged excited grins, whilst Miah and Thrain shared the same concerned look – how to keep her safe while she waged war on an evil secret society.

CHAPTER 32

A Warrior's Heaven

Zuri sauntered into her room a few hours later, after the pair of Chroniclers had gone to "spread the word" as they called it, seeking more allies for her.

Miah and Thrain, having Guardian issues to deal with, had briefed Zuri on the day's events before leaving for Aldoak.

'Thank you for these,' Kess told Zuri as she saw her appraising the new clothes. After spending all day in them she loved them even more than when she put them on that morning, and her concerns regarding the comfort of wearing the weaponised boots all day had proved unfounded.

Zuri made a show of looking her up and down then made a circular motion in the air with her finger. Kess complied by turning in a circle, knowing that if she didn't the Guardian would ask for something worse. The warrior had not a shred of self–consciousness in her, often walking in when she was in the shower to ask her questions.

Zuri did it on purpose now after the first time Kess had screeched in embarrassment, and flew for a towel to cover up.

'They suit you,' her words carried more weight than an idle comment.

'You were saying that I should have a weapon?' Kess asked, changing the subject before she was asked to model the other clothes.

Zuri's eyes lit up with excitement. 'Let's go.' The warrior grabbed her arm, and dragged her out of the door, barely giving Kess enough time to shut it behind them.

‘Are you sure you won’t get in trouble for letting a Chronicler into your weapons room?’

The dark–skinned warrior glanced at her. ‘Not now.’

Kess raised an eyebrow questioningly.

‘Thrain has given a command that you are to be granted unrestricted access to Aldoak. Every Guardian was informed that should you require aid we are to give it without question.’ She saw the surprise on Kess’s face. ‘He gave the order the night we got back.’

‘Why would he do that? He has no love of Chroniclers.’

‘You’re not really a Chronicler anymore are you?’

‘What am I then?’ Kess asked more to herself.

‘That’s what we’re here to find out.’

As they talked they climbed the steps into Aldoak, and wound their way through corridors Kess hadn’t seen before, until Zuri stopped so suddenly that she almost ran into the warriors back. With a great heave, the dark–skinned Guardian pushed open one of the massive double wooden doors. ‘Welcome to Heaven,’ she said in such a way that Kess knew that this was the warrior’s ideal of what the afterlife should look like.

The room was massive with great vaulted ceilings that loomed high above her. Lit only with artificial lighting, it was enclosed within walls constructed of stone, which Zuri had informed her on their walk over, were two metres thick, providing an impenetrable refuge. The door of course wasn’t just an insanely heavy wooden door but was plated with a backing of thick steel. And if that wasn’t enough there was also an iron forged portcullis which could be lowered and secured from inside the room, similar in design, she realised as the great front doors of the Aldoak building.

The defences were impressive, yet it was the walls lined with weaponry that stopped her in her tracks. Open–mouthed she looked in wonder around the room. Every surface was lined with weapons and stands arranged in rows almost the entire length of the hall, like a medieval weapons library. Shields hung in the available gaps on the walls like photo frames would be in anyone else’s house.

Kess walked along the closest rack which held a variety of swords, some of which stood nearly as tall as she did.

Beside her Zuri advised what she was looking at. 'These are the great–swords including the claymore.' She indicated the next size down. 'The long–swords and the heavy swords such as cutlasses and broadswords,' she pointed to the ones at the end of the rack. 'These are the sabres and scimitar. They're classified as light swords, but if you are interested in a sword then the short swords would suit you best. This,' she said, picking up a short stocky weapon from the end of the rack, '–is a Gladius, and is an excellent weapon for stabbing,' Zuri thrust the weapon forward in a jabbing type motion, 'and slashing.' She whipped the sword to the side. 'Thrain would be the best one to teach you this weapon. You could also go for one with a longer reach while still being light. The rapier is perfect for speed whilst still being deadly.'

When she showed no interest, they continued onto the next stand. 'These are staves, spears, pikes, pole–arms and halberds.' She pointed to something which looked like a spear with an axe attached to the top. 'Handy for long distance throws but rather useless for a close melee, as you don't have enough room to swing them.' They continued further down the wall.

'These beauties,' she stopped at the deadliest looking weapons yet, 'are maces. You can see the differences in the weight from the heavy style with the big chunky ends, to the lighter fluted varieties, and the ones with spiked balls on top.' Moving along the rack she stopped again. 'These are flails,' she caressed one of the shafts with a lethal looking ball on a chain attached, 'and a morning–star. All extremely deadly when wielded correctly.'

Kess walked to a table in the middle of the room which had weapons strewn across the top. She picked up one which looked like a three–pronged fork.

'Ah, the sai, excellent choice. They are light and versatile for defence as well as attack. These differ from the standard variety as the sai,' she pointed to the central tip of the weapon, 'is sharp not rounded as is usual. This makes the weapon more lethal, as the strike can penetrate the hard outer skin, carapace or armour of the demonic creatures we fight.' She twirled the sai around in her hand. 'They are typically used as a pair in fighting, one for each hand.' She grabbed the second from the table, and gripped the handle of one, so that the blade of the weapon protected her inner arm. 'This is the defensive position,' she said holding out the arm with the blade protecting it. 'This is the attack position,' she held out her other hand which held the grip forwards so the weapon pointed out. 'Note the yoku,' she pointed to the two smaller prongs, 'can be used in defensive moves to catch your opponent's weapons. You can then use the other sai to strike, or just block or defend.' Her tone left no doubt as to which option she would take.

She handed the weapons to Kess who held them feeling their weight studying them as she lifted them higher.

They were made from metal which was golden in colour, but she didn't think they had been made from the precious metal which was soft and would dent easily. What it was made of though she couldn't tell. The sai and yoku – as Zuri had called them – had symbols, which looked like something from an ancient civilisation, etched along their lengths.

She reached forward to place them back on the table, but stopped when Zuri spoke. 'Keep them for now if you like.'

Nodding, Kess kept them in her hands, liking the way they felt.

Zuri gave an approving nod, then pointed out some of the other items on the table top. 'This is a ring sword or chakram.' She pointed to a circular ring of metal which looked wickedly sharp. 'They are deadly but very difficult to learn how to use safely. These as you know are katars.' She reached out touching a strange looking weapon that looked like a dagger blade attached to a square hand grip, similar to the ones Zuri sometimes carried.

On the next table, Kess saw a number of whips ranging from the infamous cat o' nine tails, with beads threaded into each of the multiples tails, to a whip where the braided thong was several metres long but was no thicker than a piece of yarn.

Zuri pointed out another table with nunchucks, something Kess had no wish to learn how to use.

Walking towards the far wall, Kess looked at the weapons on another rack. She reached her hand out, stroking the belly of the axe handle which had leather criss–crossed around the butt of the axe head to half way down the length of the handle. She picked it up, removing it from the stand, and was surprised how light it was.

'Battle axes are lighter than wood axes, the blades are also thinner which allows for more damage when attacking. The lighter weapon also means that it is quick to swing, and you can fight for longer without tiring. In the Middle Ages, they were more popular and more readily available than swords, for those reasons, and also because they were multi–purpose.'

'What, you could hack your way through a battle, then chop a log for a fire that night?' Kess joked as she slotted the weapon back onto the rack.

'Precisely,' Zuri answered in all seriousness. 'As you can see, there are many different types of battle axe. The handle length indicates whether it is a cleaving weapon more like a pole–arm, versus a shorter handle which can be found on the throwing axes and hatchets.' She pointed out the far end of the rack which held axes with curved blades. 'These are the double handed great axes, single spoked battle axes, and Dane axes.' The last was identical to the one that Thrain carried.

She picked up an axe that was a little longer than her arm, the small metal head made the weapon very light.

'You will find that the hammer at the back of the poll,' she touched the small weight on the back of the axe head, 'will balance the tomahawks weight when throwing.'

Kess added the small throwing axe to her pair of sai and walked on past the rows of crossbows and bows, arrows, bolts, and every conceivable piece of equipment you may need to use for either. She even saw a scythe and something that looked like a heavy wooden club.

'No guns?' She wasn't that surprised, she had never seen any of the Guardians armed with any kind of modern weapons.

'Guns?' Zuri asked affronted. 'Where is the skill in them? These,' she said waving her arm around, 'require years of dedication and skill to master.'

Kess held out the two weapons she had picked. 'These.'

'Good choices,' Zuri nodded approvingly. 'Now we need to get you trained up with them. As well as that short sword I've seen you waving around.'

Kess's cheeks reddened, she thought she had done alright – that "waving around" as Zuri called it had killed demons.

She was saved from answering when Miah sauntered through the door, walking directly towards them. The soft creak of her leathers was familiar now and reassuring somehow.

The dark–haired warrior looked at the weapons Kess held in her hands and nodded in approval. 'They are well chosen, perfect for your size and fighting style. Come, we have something to discuss with you.'

Kess looked at the weapons in her hands, and walked reluctantly to the nearest table ready to put them down.

'Keep them, they are your weapons now. I will find cases for you.' Zuri laid a hand on her shoulder, and something sounding like pride had entered her voice, bringing a smile to Kess's face.

Miah was quiet on the short walk to the meeting room, one she could find now without any help. Thrain and Kisho were already in the room.

The commander had his arms crossed about his chest in his usual stern pose, and stood in the corner so he could watch the door. Completely at odds with Kisho, who, looking totally at ease, tilted back in his chair, boot heels resting on the table.

Kess made her way straight to the table, and focused her attention on placing the weapons carefully down, trying to ignore the stab of embarrassment she felt when she looked at the blonde warrior.

'We want you to move in here.' Miah who had taken a seat beside her, looked to Thrain as she spoke.

'What?' Kess was glad she was sitting down, otherwise she may have fallen over in shock.

'You will be easier to guard if under the same roof as several thousand Guardians,' Thrain stated as if it were the most logical thing in the world.

'Do your brethren share your open attitude to cohabiting with a Chronicler?' she asked Miah, worried at the thought of alienating that many warriors.

Miah glanced to Thrain, who nodded. 'The majority have agreed,' she said reluctantly.

‘What about those who didn’t?’

‘They pose no threat,’ Thrain said, in such a tone that she was surprised anyone had dared to disagree with him.

‘Won’t it look strange to everyone else then? Me moving in here?’

Miah raised her eyebrows. ‘Since when do you let what others think dictate your actions?’

She sighed, not able to find a reason to fight them on their suggestion, it was a practicable solution. ‘At least it will mean the four of you don’t have to take night shifts anymore.’

‘Actually–’ Miah started to respond, before Kess cut her off.

‘You don’t think I will be safe, even here?’

‘Wessler confirmed what we feared, that the *Ver*ità *Scuro* have infiltrated all ranks and, while I would like to consider Guardians immune to such an allurement, it would be a foolish and potential fatal assumption.’ Thrain didn’t look happy to be admitting that his warriors weren’t infallible.

‘You will still have a rotating night guard,’ Miah stated, answering her question.

‘I won’t have to sleep in the weapons room, will I?’

Miah gave a short laugh. ‘I’m sure we’ll find somewhere for you.’ She turned to Thrain, a cheeky smile on her face. ‘Any suggestions?’

Thrain refused to answer, yet she thought she saw a tinge of colour in his cheeks, at his companion’s jibe.

‘There is something else we need to talk to you about.’ The hesitancy was clear in Miah’s voice.

‘Wait for Zuri,’ Thrain said halting what Miah had been going to say.

The silence in the room was almost more than Kess could bear, when seconds turned into minutes as they waited for the dark–skinned warrior to join them. Finally, she strode into the room, and took a seat, placing a thin black rectangular case, and three large belt loops onto the tabletop. Miah waited for them all to settle before she continued speaking. ‘We are concerned about you.’

'Concerned?'

'Your dreams, Kess,' she said softly. 'The ones that wake you every night now.'

She looked around the table, not knowing what to say. How could she explain something she didn't understand?

'They are getting worse, aren't they? We have all seen that.'

Kess sighed as she realised she should have told the warriors about her dreams weeks ago, but had been afraid because of what they could mean. That shouldn't really matter anymore though, weird was becoming common place for her. 'I have been having dreams for months but I was never able to remember them, until the day we left on the train for London.'

'What have you seen?' Kisho's voice was serious, lacking his usual playfulness.

'The first dream I had, I was falling. I don't know what happens before or after. There is just overwhelming sadness and pain.'

'Is that what happened that night on the roof when Conall found you?'

A stab of sadness, mixed with guilt flooded through Kess, at the mention of her fallen Guardian.

Zuri tilted her head, clearly unaware what had happened.

'Kess nearly took a stroll off the top of one of the towers,' Thrain said wryly.

'I don't know what happened that night.' A thought occurred to her. 'Is that why you insist on staying in my room with me? Because you're afraid I might dream–walk again?'

'That's one of the reasons.' Miah looked at her raising an eyebrow, as if daring her to challenge them.

Thrain leant forward intently. 'You said the first dream, meaning you have had others.'

She nodded her head. 'That was the first. But they have changed now. They are different most nights, but they always involve death and destruction of some kind – decimated towns, burning cities, people dying in my arms, a man trying to kill me with a sword.'

Miah spoke first, breaking the deafening hush which followed Kess's explanation. 'It is not usual for Chroniclers to have dreams of this kind.'

'How unusual is "not usual"?'

'We have looked after many in our time.' Thrain spoke slowly, unsure how she would receive the information. 'But you are the first we've heard of who has dreams of these kind.'

'Does that surprise you?' Bitterness tinged her words. 'With everything else I can do that is supposedly impossible, and this weird writing,' she pulled up the sleeve of her shirt rubbing her right wrist hard with the palm of her other hand.

A strong hand gripped her wrist stopping her from trying to rub the writing off. She looked up into grey eyes. 'You are special. It is why we protect you. Why we would give our lives to protect yours,' Thrain said softly.

'I don't want anyone else dying because of me,' she said fiercely.

'We protect you not only because it is our job, but because we see something special in you.' Zuri had been unusually silent but her words were spoken firmly, enforcing the depth of their commitment to her.

Thrain leant back against the wall watching her. 'Are you going to sit there all night, Chronicler?'

'You want me to move in now?' She glanced at the watch on Kisho's arm, craning her neck to see the face.

'Yes,' Thrain said simply as he crossed his arms, signalling the end of the conversation.

Zuri stood first, stretching her arms and arching her back like a cat. 'Come on, I will walk you back.'

Knowing there was no getting out of it, no matter how ridiculous a time it was to move, she stood, following her dark–skinned companion out of the room.

~

It didn't take Kess long to pack, she didn't own many things, two bags and a backpack, and she was done, most of which was the new clothes from her Guardian. She looked around the room, which had been her home for several years, yet felt no attachment to it.

'Ready?' Zuri asked brightly.

'Yep.' With a small pack on her back, and a barrel bag on one shoulder, Kess struggled getting the last bag onto her other shoulder without overbalancing.

With an amused grin, Zuri held out her hand for it.

'Thought you'd want to keep your hands free.'

'Anything can be a weapon,' the warrior stated in a tone that said that should be obvious, as she grabbed the remaining bag.

'So how do we find my new room? I don't really have to sleep in the weapons room do I?'

Zuri laughed. 'You worry too much.'

Kess raised an eyebrow, a Guardian lecturing her about worrying about things.

With a martyred sigh, she said, 'Miah will meet us.'

As the two of them walked out of the building Kess felt a prickling between her shoulder blades. Glancing back, she saw the caramel–skinned Chronicler, Leora, staring out of her second storey window.

Seeing Kess turn, she raised her hand in a forlorn farewell.

Kess felt a surge of guilt flood through her. *How could she leave for the safety of Aldoak without feeling like she was deserting those who had come to her for help?*

~

True to her word, Miah met them at the entrance to Aldoak, her new home. 'Are you sure I will be welcome here with the other Guardians?'

'You will be fine,' the brunette warrior stated as she walked off.

They followed her deep into the heart of the warriors' abode, walking down the corridors, turning this way and that, until Kess despaired of ever finding her own way out again. She bumped into Zuri who'd stopped suddenly in front of her. 'Sorry.'

The tall warrior looked at her, and, like Miah always seemed to understand her worry. 'You will learn your way quick enough,' she said with a reassuring smile.

'Here we are,' Miah said brightly. 'Your new home,' she stopped at the side of the doorway letting Kess enter first.

While the room was small, it was not the size that captured her attention, but the second bed on the opposite side of the room. 'You really weren't kidding about me not being safe even here, were you?'

The look Miah gave her said volumes about the lengths they would go to keep her safe, even if it meant siding against their brethren. She wondered, not for the first time, what she had done to earn such loyalty from the warriors she'd only known for a short time.

Kess threw down her bags onto the bed, and turned back to her Guardians. 'What now?'

Miah peered at her closely. 'You're tired. Between that Angel of yours trying to single–handedly build your *special* army, and your need to push yourself searching for answers, you're exhausted. You need sleep.'

Kess shuddered, sleep always brought dreams, and they were getting increasingly vivid and it was becoming harder to withdraw herself from them. She knew that her reluctance to rest wouldn't go unnoticed, but the thought of closing her eyes, getting sucked into another dream which didn't want to let her go again, terrified her. 'I'm fine.'

'You're not. You are pushing yourself too hard.'

The pounding in Kess's head confirmed her Guardians worry. She was tired, but there was always something to do; research, bonding angels, weapons practice, there weren't enough hours in the day.

Worryingly, after the addition of the last three forbandt bonds, she had begun waking up with a pounding pressure in her temples and behind her eyes, which continued to build throughout the day into raging headaches.

At first she thought it was because of the lack of sleep from her restless nights, but each day now it was the same.

She also found, that while she had been able to completely shut off a few bonds, the culmination of so many within her mind was making it increasingly difficult to fully wall herself away from all the incoming thoughts and emotions.

At times it became hard to think over the babble in her mind – there were too many people in her head. She had started trying to avoid being around groups of other people as the noise became overwhelming.

Seeing something in her eyes Miah relented. 'Come on, let's train.'

Kess gave a small laugh as Zuri's eyes lit up. 'I take it you'll be joining us as well.'

~

'You still need to choose a Chapter to belong to.' Wessler spoke softly as he leant across the table towards her.

He had found her in the Vault, the place where Kess spent every available minute when she wasn't training or meeting with Kai; pouring through book after book, looking for something, anything that shed some light about her abilities.

'Being a member of the Luce doesn't preclude you from that, if anything it makes it more imperative for you to blend in.' Seeing Kess's look of frustration he added, 'Seren Pendry is the head of the Historicals and also a member of the *Luce*,' he said lowering his voice. 'It is also the Chapter I belong to. I will speak to her if that suits.' The moment she nodded her agreement Wessler rose, and with a 'Wait here', walked towards the exit.

She sat back in her chair, silently cursing herself for not thinking of it sooner. Could the faction dedicated to histories have the answers she was looking for?

Kess pretended to read the book in front of her until she saw the dark–haired Captol, standing in the doorway beckoning her with a crooked finger.

‘We are not dogs to be called to heel.’ Miah arched an eyebrow at him as she sauntered over.

‘That’s why I didn’t whistle and give you a treat for being a good girl,’ he said, straight–faced.

Kess looked from one to the other unsure if she was going to have to try to protect Wessler from an enraged Miah, but judged it safe as she saw humour twinkling in both of their eyes.

‘This won’t be like the last initiation, will it?’ Not that she was scared, she just didn’t want any more markings on her skin. When she was younger she had seen people on the streets of Camden covered in body art – “sleeves” – she’d heard them called, masking their arms and legs completely. She didn’t know how they could stand it. But they had chosen to have the tattoos. She hadn’t. Almost in response to her thoughts, she felt the familiar tingle all over her skin, like muscles awakening from pins and needles, and knew the writing was changing again.

‘Kess?’

She looked up to find two concerned sets of eyes watching her closely.

‘Are you well?’ Wessler asked.

The question reminded her of the dull throb in her temple and left eye which hadn’t gone away for days. ‘I’m fine.’

Miah’s eyes narrowed.

‘I’m just a bit tired.’

‘Yes, we do have to talk about that,’ Miah said ominously.

CHAPTER 33

A Request for Sanctuary

Kess had just eased herself onto her bed when loud banging rattled the door in its hinges. For a wonder, she was actually alone in her room, so she answered the door herself. Groaning with the effort of muscles strained from too many recent training sessions, she made her way to the door.

Kisho stood outside, breathing a little heavier than normal; clearly he had just run here from somewhere. 'You'd better come see this.' Not explaining further, he ushered her out of the room, and up the hall to the large wooden front doors, one of which was partially open.

'What's going on? Is there an attack?' Her hands sought her sai which rested comfortably at either hip, sitting in the belt loops Zuri had found for her.

Kisho shook his head, and gently pushed her forwards out through the narrow crack. She blinked, trying to clear the bright spots which danced before her eyes as she emerged into the bright afternoon sunlight.

Thrain stood outside, hands on hips, scowling; in other words, being his normal intimidating self, however even that wasn't enough to scare off the dozen or so young Chroniclers standing on the steps below him.

Walking up beside the blonde–haired commander she surveyed the group. Several Chroniclers gave her small smiles as they recognised a familiar face.

'They have requested sanctuary.' She knew Thrain well enough now to hear the surprise in his voice. Not that long ago, she wouldn't have picked up on the subtle nuances in his gruff tones.

'Sanctuary? What's going on?'

'We want to join you.' A young man she didn't recognise spoke out.

Kess looked over the group again, and saw two very familiar faces.

Leora returned her look with a defiant one of her own, whilst Abram gave her a broad grin. Clearly he was still thinking this would be some great adventure, like the quests within a Terry Goodkind novel or an Indiana Jones movie. Little did he realise, that adventures weren't as benign as they were in fictional stories, they were often violent, filled with fear and pain, and sometimes the death of friends. It was something she hoped none of them ever had to experience first–hand.

She looked to Thrain who seemed on the verge of exasperated violence, so she took a step to the edge of the stairs and waited until they fell silent before speaking.

'You are all here because you believe things are not as they should be within Athenaeum.' She paused feeling the weight of their stares upon her and strove to find the right words to impress upon them. 'You would be right.'

Her voice was drowned out as the Chroniclers murmured to each other until Leora bellowed, 'Shut it!', halting their chatter immediately.

With a nod of thanks Kess continued. 'But,' she looked at the young eager faces before her, 'that is the reason the Guardians are here, to protect us from danger. We have to trust them to do their jobs.'

'Why are you here living here then?' A raven–haired girl asked, her wide eyes watching Kess with unfeigned innocence. She was petite, and didn't look a day over fourteen, though had to be several years past that.

'I–' she faltered, unsure what to say, without sounding like a hypocrite. How could she convince them it was safe, yet remain living within the protective walls of the warriors' compound?

'Chronicler Grayson is here because there have been several attempts on her life.' Seeing her hesitation Thrain stepped forward coming to her rescue.

The chatter took longer to die this time – clearly the gossip mill didn't know everything about what had been going on – she thought with a morbid sense of satisfaction.

Seeing their excited reactions to the admission of attacks, which showed none of the angst she would expect, Kess tried a different approach. The truth. 'One of my Guardian, a good friend, died during one of those attacks. I held him in my arms and watched as he took his last breath. I couldn't help him. I can't–' she paused as her voice wobbled. 'I don't want to see anyone else hurt. Please go back to your rooms. Trust that we will do everything we can.' She felt the weight of Thrain's eyes upon her, but kept her focus on the Chroniclers in front of her.

For a few seconds, she thought she had swayed them into returning to the rooms, giving up their romanticised fancies of knights fighting honourably; of a world where good always triumphs.

Her hope shattered as Leora stared at her, bold and defiant.

'Bollocks,' she muttered as she watched the young Chronicler's attention turn to Thrain.

'I request sanctuary. Would you deny my request for safety, Commander?' Leora's raised voice echoed against the stone building behind them.

Thrain took a deep breath, clearly debating whether to turn them away. Then releasing his breath noisily through his nose, he said, 'No request for sanctuary has ever been denied.' With a hard stare at Kess, like it was somehow her fault for the new arrivals, he gruffed, 'You can find our *guests* rooms.' With one final glance at the assemblage of refuge seekers he shook his head, then stalked inside without another word.

Kisho walked up behind Kess and leant his arms on her shoulders, resting some of his weight upon her. 'You seem to be having an effect on our commander.'

Before she could question him about his ambiguous comment, he stepped away towards the group of excited Chroniclers. 'I see you came prepared,' he said, glancing at the bags strewn on the ground by their feet. 'Follow me.'

Unable to let Kisho deal with them all by himself she followed at the rear of the group, ensuring no one lagged behind.

Much to her chagrin he led them to an all too familiar corridor.

'This will be your wing. Make sure you remember where it is. If you have any queries or questions I'm sure Kess will be happy to help you settle in. Her room is this one right here,' he pointed out the door they had just passed.

She shot him a venomous look, which he returned with a bright mischievous smile, when she saw the new arrivals taking note of the location of her door.

The first room they stopped at was less than thirty feet from her own. Like hers it contained two narrow beds. Upon seeing the room configurations, the Chroniclers separated themselves with the boys taking the rooms on the right and the girls the ones on the left.

Leora, for all her stubbornness issues with authority, was a born leader herself, chivvying the others into rooms and quickly sorting out any pairing issues which arose. Which left Kisho and herself to watch the process, and quicker than she would have thought possible, order was restored and the hallway was empty.

A quick walk past the open doors showed each setting up their own spaces with meticulous order and efficiency. She poked her head in the door of the room where Leora now lodged with a raven–haired girl – Kadence Worsley – as she had excitedly introduced herself as during the rooming process.

Leora looked up just as Kess was withdrawing and followed her out into the hall. 'When do we start training?'

'What?'

'They're training you,' Leora waited for her to respond but instead Kess folded her arms about her chest and gave the girl her best imitation of Thrain's hard stare. With a visible gulp, the young Chronicler continued. 'Shouldn't we be taught to defend ourselves?'

'Yes,' Kess admitted, then held up her hands forestalling Leora. 'But – that is up to Miah. She's the head trainer so you will have to convince her.'

Kess tried hard not to smile at the look on the young Chronicler's face at the thought of approaching Miah with a request like that. She remembered how it had felt when she'd done the very same thing herself, not that long ago.

'Get settled in first. Give it some time before you go to her,' she advised, though she was sure, with this one, the advice fell on deaf ears.

She started up the hall leaving the Chroniclers to settle in, knowing that her training session with Zuri had started five minutes ago.

'You're late.'

'I had to settle our new arrivals in.'

'Yes, I heard about them. You're starting quite the revolution, aren't you?' Zuri said, smirking.

'Me? *I* haven't *started* anything. Is Thrain blaming their arrival on me?' Exasperation filled her voice, clipping her words.

The dark–skinned warrior chuckled quietly. 'He hasn't said a word. I watch you, Kess. You are like a pebble thrown into a pond. It is interesting watching the ripples you create.'

That was the second time she had heard herself mentioned in that way. Entirely uncomfortable with where her Guardians line of conversation was heading, she pulled the sai from her belt. 'Alright, so how do I use these?'

With a shake of her head, at the noted sidestep in topic, Zuri crossed onto the padded mat in the centre of the room. Balancing on the balls of her feet she produced her own set of the triple pronged weapons as she waited for Kess to join her.

Instead of holding them awkwardly like she did, the warrior twirled them backwards and forwards with a practised ease that made the motions look effortless, which Kess was sure was anything but.

'The sai,' Zuri began, 'is a versatile weapon that can be used in defence or attack. They can be used to stab, parry, block or throw. This,' she clanged the two central prongs together, 'is called a sai. The point is usually blunted; however, we have found that for piercing thick demon hides, a pointed tip is the most practicable. The two side prongs are called yoku and can either be both facing up like these ones are, or can have one prong pointing down, as protection for your hand. The central point between the two side guards is called the moto, and the tsuka is the handle.'

Zuri gave her an intent stare making sure she was paying attention.

'Sai, yoku, moto and tsuka.' Kess named the points, indicating where they were on the weapon.

The dark–skinned woman raised an eyebrow. 'Very good.' She held one hand out in front of her, leaving the sai swinging in the vee between her thumb and forefinger, hilt up. 'When holding your weapon defensively you put your index finger along the butt of the hilt running towards the top.'

Kess moved alongside the warrior to get a better view.

'Your thumb grips under the yoku, while the rest of your fingers come over the top of the other yoku.' She demonstrated by pivoting her palm so it covered the central point – the moto – and then curled her fingers over the curved metal at the base of the other prong.

Kess held out her right arm and copied the placement of the warrior's hand. The sai ran up the length of her arm ending at her elbow. Instead of feeling uncomfortable like she imagined it might, the weapon seemed to mould to her skin, like it had been made for her.

'Good. Now to rotate your weapon from a defensive to an attack position you keep your thumb in place whilst releasing the grip with your fingers,' she held her sai out demonstrating in slow motion. 'Then move your index finger so it is on the same side of the hilt as the thumb, and place your other fingers beside it. Loosen the grip with your thumb, then use your fingers and wrist to pivot the sai and flip the blade around. In the offensive position, your fingers grip the hilt whilst your thumb rests on the moto.'

She held out her hands which had just flipped the weapon from the defensive to offensive positions and rotated her wrist around showing how her fingers were positioned and where her thumb sat on the central point of the weapon where the hilt ended and the prongs began.

'Now you need to be able to grip the weapon defensively and offensively in each hand, and be able to switch without thinking. Research has shown that a movement becomes instinctual – that you can do it without having to think about it – after a thousand repetitions. You have a day. Live and breathe your sai.' And with that the warrior walked away leaving Kess with her homework.

Kess didn't see Zuri leave, instead flipped both sai back around so they rested along her arms and began her first repetition.

CHAPTER 34

Training Gone Awry

It seemed strange to see Chroniclers freely walking the halls of Aldoak. They were always in small groups and although they strode confidently, Kess saw the widening of their eyes as they passed some of the older Guardians, cracking their stalwart facades.

She shook her head as she watched a group walk past, each giving her a nod.

'I wish I had groupies,' Kisho's voice came from over her shoulder.

'They're not my anything,' she scowled at the grinning warrior.

'They are totally Team Kess, look they're even dressing like you now.' Kisho pointed out with much amusement the group who as a whole were sporting clothes nearly identical to the ones that she wore.

'Shut up.'

'Well that's witty,' he laughed.

Much to her chagrin she did have to admit he was right, not that she'd ever tell him that. 'Where did they even get them from? They've only been here a day.'

With a final glance at them, he shrugged. 'Come on. Zuri's waiting in the training room. She won't be pleased if you're late again.'

As soon as she stepped into the room Zuri looked at the clock on the wall, giving a satisfied nod at the hands which showed she still had a minute left until their training session began. Kisho followed her to the centre of the room.

'You're here today?'

'I'm your attacker,' he said wiggling his fingers at her, widening his eyes, in an apparently threatening manner, which lost some of its effect with the broad grin on his face.

'Terrifying,' she laughed as she pulled her sai and faced Zuri.

'Show me what you've learnt.'

For the past day Kess had done nothing but practice flipping her weapons from defence to attack positions and back again, until her fingers cramped and her wrists ached. Gripping both sai in defensive positions she flipped them around fluidly, ignoring the lingering ache in her hands. Despite being left handed, both movements were steady and sure. Satisfaction flowed through her, but she didn't let it show on her face, just concentrated on flicking the weapons.

'Good. Now something harder. Left attack, right defence.'

Kess followed her command.

She had anticipated this and thankfully had practised one handed movements, as her first attempts had been sloppy.

'Left defence.'

She followed Zuri's instructions, sometimes not always as fluidly or quickly as she would have liked, but was satisfied overall with her progress. None of that showed on her instructor's face until her voice rang out. 'Halt.' Then a beaming smile broke out showing the brilliant white of her straight teeth. 'Excellent work.'

Kess smiled proudly at the praise.

'Now, to add in an attacker.'

Her smile faltered.

'We will show you a practice round of how to fight with your sai. Then it's your turn.'

She watched in fascination as Kisho pulled his twin tantou, then attacked his dark–skinned opponent with no warning. They danced backwards and forwards, their weapons moving so quickly at times she saw nothing but a metallic blur as they thrust and blocked, parried and jabbed. Concentration was fixed on both their faces, yet she could tell they were both holding back, restraining themselves for her benefit. At some unseen signal, they both halted and sheathed their weapons. With breathing only slightly accelerated they both turned to her.

'Now while we don't expect you to be that fast – for a few days at least,' Zuri's wicked smile left Kess unsure whether she was joking or not, 'I want you to give it everything you have.'

'Alright.' She tried to sound sure, but really had little confidence in being able to fight competently with this type of weapon so soon.

She faced Kisho, and watched his eyes. A fraction of a second before he moved, his eyes tightened focusing on her left, then he leapt forwards. She thrust her left sai forwards managing to catch the blade in the arch of the yoku. Without warning his other sword screamed towards her. The metal gleamed as it caught the light from the fluorescents high above them.

She saw it and tried to raise her right hand in time to deflect it.

Without warning a blade slid between her and the oncoming weapon, with a squeal of metal, as they clashed together.

She looked up to find Thrain guarding her right.

His head swung towards her, and she saw anger creasing the corners of his eyes. His jaw clenched, showing corded muscle as he tried to control his temper, yet the look he levelled at Kisho could have wilted flowers. 'What do you think you're doing?'

'Teaching Kess how to fight with her sai.' The samurai warrior watched his commander cautiously. She noticed how he kept his weapons out – although pointed at the ground – yet they were an obvious presence between him and Thrain.

'You could have killed her.'

'I know how to fight,' Kisho replied stiffly, for once losing his glibness.

'I will take over from here.'

Kisho opened his mouth, ready to argue, yet Zuri stepped between them. 'We'll see you tomorrow Kess.' She ushered the samurai out of the room, and while Kess couldn't hear them, she could see their mouths moving. Clearly neither were happy at being dismissed.

'You don't trust them?'

Thrain turned his gaze away from the pair and looked at her. 'You could have been hurt.'

'I have been hurt. A few times now. They were teaching me how to fight so that next time, maybe I can avoid that.'

'There won't be a next time.'

'Do you really believe that?' Kess asked softly.

His shoulders sagged. 'No.'

'Then – what?'

'I couldn't stand there watching the blade come towards you and do nothing, on the chance that you managed to block it in time.' The admission dragged from him, and he looked down, unwilling to meet her eyes.

'Thrain.' She paused until he looked up, meeting his steely gaze and saw that look again, the one that she couldn't read.

'Come on.' And just like that, whatever had been in his eyes vanished. 'I'll spar with you. Let's take this nice and slow,' he cautioned.

Thrain brought his sword around, slow enough that he could pull it back if necessary, but quick enough to warrant fast action.

She caught his strike in the guard then twisted the sai wrenching the sword around out of her way, at the same time bringing her other hand around in a jab towards his stomach.

He pivoted to the side narrowly avoiding her tempered jab. Thrain pulled his arm back, hard and fast, almost wrenching the sai from her hand as he pulled his sword free.

A twisted smile broke out on his face. 'You learn fast.'

Not knowing how to respond to his rare compliment, she settled for a small smile.

'You clearly can jab. But have you been taught the other holds for your weapon?'

As she shook her head, he sheathed his blade and stepped closer, holding out his hand for one of her sai.

She reversed the weapon offering it to him hilt first.

As their fingertips brushed static jolted through her, making her fingers and arm muscles twitch. She looked up, hoping he hadn't seen her reaction, and found him studying her.

Instead of looking away he held her gaze steadily, his hand still gripping the hilt. She searched his grey eyes and found them calm, softer than their usual steely hardness.

Then the hilt slid through her fingers and he pulled away.

'The sai is an extremely versatile weapon.' He told her slipping flawlessly back into instructor mode. 'You can use the attack and defence holds that you have been taught or there are a number of other, less friendly options. You can strike the face or neck with the hilt, disorientating or stunning your opponent.' Turning his grip on the weapon so his fingers rounded the moto, he demonstrated aiming first at her throat, then towards her nose.

She stood still, barely blinking as the weapon sped at her.

'Or the less friendly option.' He spun the sai around so the pointed tip rested against the soft skin of her windpipe.

'If you are close enough, you can disarm using the longer reach of your sai or either of the side tips to stab into your opponent's wrist.' He adjusted his grip again so the hilt jutted out past his thumb, the steel poking out the other end of his hand. 'From this position you can slash–' he pivoted his arm around in a clockwise motion using his whole arm to round the weapon, 'or backhand stab with either the pointed or the non–lethal hilt end. The sai can also be thrown like a knife, however this option is not always effective. You have to throw under–handed and often can't generate enough force to penetrate a thick demon hide, especially if more than a few paces away, so this option usually stuns rather than kills.'

He looked up from the weapon and searched her face, seeing if she'd been paying attention. 'Right, your turn. Hilt strike.'

Kess thought for a moment, then gripped her hand diagonally across the moto and jabbed out at an imaginary attacker.

'Hold,' Thrain called as he stepped up to her outstretched arm. He adjusted her fingers slightly realigning them along the curved metal. 'Better?'

She could only nod for fear her voice would betray the quiver that ran through her.

'Wrist disarm,' Thrain barked, apparently feeling none of what she did.

She pushed him from her mind, and flicked the weapon around to the familiar attack position and struck at her imagined attacker again in rapid succession aiming first with the yoku then the longer central blade.

'Good.'

CHAPTER 35

An Awakening

'Kess,' Thrain barked gruffly.

She looked up to find the commander in the doorway, one of his usual glowers darkening his features. She hid a grin at the effect his foreboding stare was having on the two young Chroniclers, who lounged on the bed set aside for her Guardians.

With wide eyed apologetic glances at her, Abram and Leora dashed off, with a quick, 'We'll see you later,' Leora showed none of the moxie she had towards Miah yesterday. Clearly she was intimidated by Thrain and couldn't wait to get away from him.

Not that she blamed them, he did look particularly grouchy, as opposed to any other time when he only looked mildly annoyed.

'Yes, Commander.'

He eyed her sharply trying to figure out if she was making fun of him, but her carefully blank face gave nothing away. 'Come with me.'

She followed him down the hall having to lengthen her stride to keep up. He wasn't hurrying, this was just his usual pace – he wasn't one for strolling.

'Where are we headed?' They had finished training less than an hour ago. She couldn't imagine what he would want, or need, her company for, outside of training or guarding her.

'To view the Obiex.'

Kess barely contained the excited smile which fought to inch its way onto her face. Whilst her research hadn't revealed anything useful, she had read a lot about the Havens and the Obiex which protected them. Most however had been theories about how it worked to create the protective barrier. The only point every author agreed upon was that nobody could determine the origin of the stones, nor definitively prove how the barrier was created.

Not exactly helpful or informative.

They walked in silence, and though she kept glancing at him, she didn't want to talk and run the risk of annoying him and have him decide not to take her after all.

Thrain stared straight ahead, so Kess took the opportunity to glance at him out of the corner of her eye.

'You're likely to trip if you don't look where you're going.'

She whipped her eyes forward embarrassed at having been caught staring. 'Why is the Obiex located here?' she asked, trying to change the subject, as they approached a building she had never been into before. Oddly, a tall bell tower–like structure jutted from the roof, though no bell was visible from where she stood.

He looked at her quizzically. 'You've never seen it?'

'No,' she shook her head.

'I would have thought that would be part of your studies.' As he spoke, Thrain opened the heavy wooden door, and ushered her inside, closing it firmly behind him.

'I did ask when I first got here, but was told by my instructor that "the majesty of the source of our protection was not for the eyes of just anyone, especially an Initiate",' she said imitating the high pitched nasal tone of Chronicler Storro, who had been in charge of her small group when she'd first arrived. 'I'm beginning to realise that a lot has been left out of our education.'

Thrain's eyebrows rose, waiting for her to elaborate, yet she remained silent as she realised the truth of what she'd said. There was so much she'd only recently learnt about Chroniclian history because of the research she was doing. *Why weren't they being taught about their heritage?*

Thrain's voice took on a lecturing tone. 'As you know the stone creates a barrier. But what you probably don't realise is that the Obiex lies at the centre of that. Every Haven's border covers exactly the same area, give or take a few feet.'

As they walked down the corridor she heard a sound, similar to the hum of a bumblebee. She cocked her head, listening.

'What is it?' Thrain scanned the area as he saw her movement.

'Do you hear that?'

His head tilted as he listened but within a moment shook his head, yet surprisingly he didn't dismiss her. 'What do you hear?'

'A hum.'

He listened briefly, before shaking his head again. 'If it changes let me know.'

'You believe me?' Surprise was clear in her voice.

'I have learnt not to underestimate what you can do.' A small smile played on his lips before he moved out of view, continuing along the narrow corridor.

With each step, the buzzing grew incrementally louder, until it sounded like a hive of bees were hovering around her ears.

Thrain's worried face met hers and she saw his lips moving, yet his words were muted like he was standing behind a thick pane of glass. She focused on his lips, trying to hear the sounds and the hum receded a bit, and his voice returned to normal pitch.

'Are you alright?' he repeated.

She nodded as she put a finger in her ear wiggling it around, trying to clear her hearing; though she wondered if that was entirely true.

Why could she hear that noise when Thrain couldn't? Was this just some other oddity about her like her bonding abilities, or the markings which covered her?

Even though she'd recently learnt her mother's mental health issues weren't the result of genetics, after years of worry, psychological instability was always her first concern when something strange happened.

Lost within the noise Kess hadn't realised they'd reached a beautifully crafted wooden door latticed with straps of iron and studded with metal. It looked wonderfully medieval, and appealed to Kess's theatrical sense of propriety for what secret entrances should look like.

With one final glance at her, he knocked on the solid timber.

For a moment, nothing happened then the door eased back a fraction revealing a face pinched with annoyance; clearly at their interruption.

The irritation vanished when the young Chronicler saw the Guardian Commander in front of him, replaced with wary respect. 'Commander. We weren't expecting you.'

'No,' Thrain said gruffly.

The short, dark–haired Chronicler waited clearly expecting more, then coloured as he realised he was blocking the door, and that Thrain, Commander of the Guardians, Last Defender of Athenaeum, was waiting on him. 'Sorry,' he mumbled as the pink in his cheeks escalated to a deep red.

Thrain ushered her through checking the hall one last time before he followed, firmly bolting the door behind him.

As soon as Kess stepped into the room the hum escalated again. She looked at the others who seemed unaware of the noise. She concentrated on it, and realised with a start that the sensation was within her mind, not her ears – and it was urging her forwards.

Thrain busy quizzing the Chronicler; who reminded her of a shorter, geekier version of Harry Potter, didn't immediately react when Kess stepped away, following the pull of the buzzing within her mind. It drew her firmly to the left. She didn't know how, but she was certain that whatever was making the static was behind the wall she now faced.

Thrain stepped up behind her, hand gripping her shoulder as he turned her around. Tightness creased the corners of his eyes but he didn't say anything just led her to a section of the wall a few paces further to the left. His fingers splayed out on the stones, which to her looked identical to every other stone, then pushed. With a subtle hiss, something within the wall released and she saw the outline of a door, which moments before hadn't been there. It had fit seamlessly within the surrounding stone, rendering it still almost invisible, unless you knew where to look. With a rumble, the door swung inwards of its own accord.

The commander raised his eyebrows at her excited grin before striding through the doorway. As Kess followed him through, she glanced to either side as Thrain stood directly in front of her blocking her view. Uncomfortable looking benches lined the walls, stone of course. In fact, that was all she could see, the dull grey of stone from ceiling to floor.

The droning grew louder again, becoming a hive of agitated bees. Her gaze was drawn past Thrain, who had shifted to the side, to the beautiful stone resting on a large plinth in the centre of the room.

It was massive, oval shaped and unlike any other stone she had seen before. It was milky in colour, but even that wasn't right, it was like seeing the sun through fog, the golden rays muted, illuminating the mist around it. She couldn't take her eyes off it.

The intensity of the hum in her mind changed pitch, urging her forward. Her hand rose, palm outstretched.

Something gripped her arm, stopping her.

'Kess,' Thrain said softly.

'The buzz, it's coming from the Obiex.'

His eyebrows furrowed. 'You can hear it?'

Instead of answering she used her other hand to release his grip on her arm. He didn't fight her or try to stop her again, just watched, arms folded about his chest as she extended her hand and touched the stone. Colours swirled under her touch and as the static in her mind stopped, she gave an audible sigh. Beneath her hand the cool stone warmed as colours began to fleck through the mist.

A sense of peace resonated through her and she smiled, looking over her shoulder at Thrain whose eyes were fixed on the stone which now reflected so many colours, that it looked like a rainbow.

Then the tranquillity vanished, and the stone under her palm flexed and suctioned itself to her skin. Panicked, she began to turn to Thrain, when images appeared in her mind.

Hand gripping the foggy stone – the image flicked to another – *a surge of power extending outwards* – flick – *the sense of time passing* – flick –

A serrated blade of pain jarred through her brain, causing her to inhale sharply.

Something laid upon the stone.

She could barely see it, but a sense of pure darkness poured from the deep red stone, a ruby perhaps, something flickered within the blood red stone, something sentient – *discord* – flick – *breach of the walls, pain* – flick –

The flashes ceased as abruptly as they'd begun.

As coherent thought returned, as she realised Thrain was pulling her arm, trying to pry her hand free from the stone. The Obiex released her hand sending them both sprawling to the ground in a tangle of arms and legs.

Thrain's body protected her as his arms wrapped around her, holding her tightly against the warmth of his hard chest. Her head rested in the circle between his shoulder and neck.

'Are you alright?' His breath was warm against her forehead.

She nodded unsure how to describe what had happened.

'I couldn't get your hand free, it merged into the Obiex, and you – you weren't there.' His voice was calm yet she could feel the erratic thump of his heart against her back. The circle of his arms tightened as he talked, then as if realising how firmly he held her, he loosened his grip, yet he didn't let her go.

Though she was covered from head to toe, her skin tingled at the closeness of their bodies which touched from neck to hip. One of her legs rested between his and the other sprawled over the muscles of his thigh.

She couldn't think whilst feeling the contours of his body beneath hers, so, with a reluctance that surprised her, she disentangled herself from her Guardian and stood, pacing as she tried to gather her thoughts.

'The Obiex shared its memories with me,' she said in a hushed voice, becoming aware as she did, of the familiar sensation of another bundle in her mind.

She froze. *How could she bond a stone?*

'I–' She opened her mouth, on the verge of telling Thrain, yet the words died on her tongue. It wasn't possible. Maybe it was just the lingering effects of the visions it had shared with her.

Instead she reached her hand out again, but this time instead of touching the Obiex she held her hand above the surface of the stone. Soft colours swirled reacting to her immediacy.

'What are you doing? You aren't allowed to touch the–' The black–haired Chronicler cut off as he saw the stone. 'What–' He stared at the Obiex, darting glances at her, worry and confusion clear in his eyes. 'How did you do that?'

'I didn't do anything.'

'You did something. I've never seen it glow before.'

She had been so intent on the stone, she hadn't noticed the subtle yet clearly visible illumination coming from the within the Obiex. She looked to Thrain who was watching her with that penetrating gaze of his, yet his face remained unreadable, with no hint of what was going on behind those steel hard eyes.

Without waiting to see if they followed, Kess strode through the secret door, unable to answer the Chroniclers questions. She halted at the beautifully carved door which was barred with several heavy planks of wood and concentrated on the carvings rather than the questions pounding around within her mind.

It wasn't long before Thrain and the Chronicler followed her into the room. The geeky Potter look–a–like pressed the section of stone which swung the secret door shut again, before he walked over towards where she stood.

Clearly, he had questions – they danced in his eyes – and several times his lips parted like he was going to speak, yet he remained quiet. His nearly black eyes watched her carefully, clearly aware that something had happened, but unable to figure out what had occurred, or her involvement in it.

The heavy planks took the Chronicler a moment to shift, and with a 'Fare you well, Commander', the door was finally opened.

Thrain strode through without answering.

Kess was only a pace behind him yet slowed as the Chronicler spoke again, 'Fare you well, Chronicler–' He paused clearly leaving a gap for her to say her name, yet with a quick returned, 'Fare well, Chronicler', she rushed after Thrain. The less he knew about her, including her name, the better.

She kept drawing attention to herself, even when she tried not to. Particularly it seemed, when she tried to keep a low profile.

They walked the hall in silence, each lost in troubled thoughts. She caught the glances Thrain gave her, knew he had to be thinking the same thing as her. *What had she done to the Obiex? Was it the Angel blood in her that had caused it to glow?*

'Are you sure you're okay?'

Kess knew she'd been quiet on the walk back but so had he. She hesitated, wondering if she should tell him about the newest blære nestled within her mind.

'I'm fine.' She settled on wanting for the moment to think about what had just happened, make sure that what she felt within her mind was really another bond, and not something else.

He walked her through the halls of Aldoak to the door of her room.

She had to admit, living in the warrior's complex was much better than the Chronicler building ever had been. As tough as the Guardians were they still had downtime from their training and relished that freedom, congregating together in small clusters or big groups, laughing and mucking around. They enjoyed life in every sense. They were a completely different breed than the Chroniclers who did nothing but study and where fraternising and downtime was permitted, but where it had to be conducted with restraint, and above all quiet.

She opened her door, and saw in amazement that it was empty.

'I am your guard today,' he told her seeing the question in her eyes. 'I have to go to – I will be back soon,' he changed what he had been going to say. 'Will you be alright for a while here by yourself?' At her nod he added, 'Stay here' before shutting the door.

Kess stood a pace within the door frame, eyes staring unseeing at the wall in front of her. *How could she have bonded a stone? Is that even what had happened?* As much as she tried to brush it off as lingering effects of the memory flashes, she knew that it wasn't true.

She had bonded the Obiex.

The new forbandt clustered within her mind next to Azrin's, brightening as she focused inwardly on it.

Fatigue flowed through her so suddenly, she swayed on her feet. Numbed by the intense exhaustion she dragged herself the few feet to her bed and curled on top of her covers.

She opened her eyes, finding herself in a hall packed full of bodies.

'I volunteer.' A clear voice rang out into the packed hall. A man's timbre – but her own – she realised.

'No.' A woman's voice hissed to his right. He looked over, and saw a flawlessly beautiful lady whose rose petal pink eyes matched the long shimmering gown she wore. Desperation filled those soft eyes, making them appear wider and larger than they usually were.

'Ambriel.' The name found its way to his lips. 'This is important.'

'You don't need to sacrifice yourself, Irin.' Tears filled her eyes and his hand rose to wipe them away, brushing back a strand of platinum hair which had feathered across her face.

'A sacrifice creates powerful energies, particularly when the focus volunteers. We left Heaven for a reason, to help protect mankind. This is how I can do that.' He shook away her hand which had gripped his arm and moved forward, refusing to look back at her for fear he would lose his nerve. 'I volunteer,' his voice rang out into the room filled with the buzz of conversation.

The crowd fell silent, parting around Irin as he walked to the front podium.

Elim looked down, sorrow and joy warring within him. 'Thank you, brother.'

'I volunteer.' A second voice rose from within the crowd, and his skin pebbled at the voice that was as familiar as his own.

'I am not staying here without you,' Ambriel said defiantly, as she stepped up beside him on the dais. 'If you believe the cause is just, then I trust you and will follow you, even to the depth of hell if I must,' she muttered the last bit almost to herself.

As much as he wanted to deny her, tell her to go back to her place within the crowd, his lips didn't move. Instead they stood shoulder to shoulder, unspeaking, taking comfort in each other's proximity.

Within the murmured voices of the collective group, several other voices spoke out and soon eleven brothers and sisters stood before Elim.

'We have our volunteers. I need some time to brief them.' Elim, their elected leader addressed the rest of the crowd, dismissing them from the room.

Most filed out immediately but some stalled, congregating in small groups as they slowly inched their way out, clearly trying to hear what was said.

Their placid natured leader waited patiently for the room to clear completely.

Irin took this time to inspect the rest of the volunteers, whom he knew to varying degrees.

Kasdeja, aloof as always, stood a few paces away from the rest, staring at something only he could see;

Raman and Rata, as inseparable as Ambriel and himself, stood close together. Raman met Irin's gaze and inclined his head, in greeting and acknowledgement.

The large and golden skinned Polial was no surprise to find here with his views on the sacredness of life.

Daena and Erethe spoke quietly together. Both personified honesty and truth, yet as similar as they were in roles, they were as disparate in looks as it was possible to be.

Daena dark and exotic, fixed him with a level stare as if challenging him, whilst the willowy and pale Erethe gave him a small shy smile.

Yet it was Ophiel who stood beside them that was a surprise. Known for his views on mankind which bordered on hostile at times, Irin didn't know what he could gain by being one of the eleven.

Mithra and Godiel were the last two onto the dais though he didn't know them well enough to presume their motivations.

Elim cleared his throat, fixing eleven sets of eyes to him. 'As you know some of our brethren have waged war on the Chronicler populations. A way has been found to protect them, though at no small cost. Shall we commence?'

'Now?' Mithra asked worriedly.

'Every moment we delay more lives are lost,' Elim said. 'If you wish to revoke, I understand. It is a monumental thing you do. One that cannot be reversed. And it cannot be entered into lightly.'

No one moved away.

Irin's feet moved forward almost of their own accord. 'I will go first.'

Ambriel gripped him in a tight hug before releasing her hold, almost pushing him away.

'Will it hurt?' Curiosity filled him, rather than worry.

'No,' Confidence and truth rang in their leader's words.

'Will I still be me?' This time Elim hesitated. 'How much of your personality will be transferred I do not know. You will always be aware of the mission. But any more than that–' he cut off, looking deeply into Irin's eyes. Sorrow filled them.

'Mourn not brother, it is a just thing we do,' Irin said. With a deep breath, he looked into Elim's eyes and then the world disappeared into a haze of white.

CHAPTER 36

Irin

Kess flung awake, sitting bolt upright as she struggled to understand her dream. Instead of being able to focus however, her mind was filled with emotions, thought and feelings. They whirled about, clashing and jangling every nerve fibre in her head, making it hard to breathe, and impossible to coordinate movement or speech.

She rolled her eyes around, the one faculty she still had control of, and would have cried out in frustration if she could. The one time she needed help, and she was alone in her room. Not a Guardian in sight.

Kess slid from the bed, movements spasmodic, trying to reach the door to get help. Yet her legs collapsed in twitching heaps beneath her, planting her on the ground, back against the bed. Her own panic momentarily overshadowed the emotions flooding from her forbandt bonds.

Incapable of moving any further she curled her legs up tight against her chest.

The flow of voices and emotions didn't stop, and as much as she tried to shield her bonds, they resisted somehow, and the babble continued. She pressed her hands against her ears and pushed tight.

Something tried to pull her hands away so she gripped them tighter to her head. Her eyes were scrunched tightly shut, the blackness giving her some relief.

Something grabbed her shoulders, shaking her lightly. Then again more insistently when she ignored the movement.

Tears leaked down her cheeks, as the constant stream of noise and emotion which battered down every wall she tried to erect to shield herself, shifted from being overwhelming, to excruciating.

'Kess.' There was panic in the voice. A voice she knew; rousing her, forcing action.

She peered through slitted eyes at the unfocused face before her. She blinked trying to clear her vision. The blurred figure became Thrain who looked as close to panic as she had ever seen.

As she opened her eyes, he cupped his hands against her cheeks, his palms warm against her skin. 'Are you hurt?' he demanded.

Leaning her head against his hands, she concentrated on the sound of his voice, trying to subdue the cacophony in her head. 'Bonds. Can't shut them off,' she whispered. Her hands twitched, half raising to her ears again before she lowered them.

'I thought you had them under control.'

'I did but–' she shut her eyes, her mind too overloaded to deal with sight.

'But–' he pushed.

'I bonded the Obiex.'

A shocked stillness met her statement. When the silence continued she opened her eyes a fraction and saw his grey eyes, widened in astonishment.

'How?' He kept his words to a minimum, seeing how hard it was for her to concentrate.

'It – he – was an Angel.' She paused, scrunching her eyes shut tightly, trying to focus. The clamour in her head was so loud, barraging her senses with endless images, thoughts, feelings and emotions from every one of her eight forbandt. 'It's going to kill me.'

'It's alright. Tell me later.'

She nodded and winced as the movement jarred within her head, searing like a lightning bolt right through the middle of her mind. She suppressed the whimper trying to rise out of her throat, and hunched in on herself, trying to keep herself together. It was hard enough to breathe, let alone try to think, or talk.

'Kai, you fallen bastard, where are you?' Thrain yelled into the room, which was empty save for the two of them.

He crouched down in front of Kess again, who had curled herself up as tight as she could, and was once again covering her ears with her hands.

~

Thrain struggled to control himself.

The muscle in his jaw clenched and unclenched in time with his fists as he sought the calm he had always lived within. Yet it was as if the fear he had denied his entire life, now sought to tear him apart from within. Kess's forbandt bondings were overwhelming her, and there was nothing he could do to help.

'I'm here, Kess,' he whispered. 'Just hold on.' As gently as he could he lifted her into his arms, cradling her head against his chest and looping his other arm under her knees. She flopped against him, as lifeless as a rag doll. His hands shook as he juggled her, trying to open the door.

He raced through the halls, as fast as he could without jostling the near unconscious girl in his arms unnecessarily. As he passed the training rooms, a set of footsteps followed behind him racing to catch up.

'What's going on?' Miah demanded as she matched his pace. 'Is she hurt?'

'She bonded the Obiex. It's overwhelming her.' Thrain's voice was controlled, yet fear underlined each word. He didn't slow his pace, even though he realised that the Commander of the Guardians racing through the halls would cause no end of worry and speculation. He found he didn't care.

'She–' Miah's voice halted shocked. 'How?'

'Apparently the stone used to be an Angel, which explains how she was able to form a forbandt with it.'

Miah nodded, then raced ahead pulling the large front doors open allowing Thrain to race through barely slowing.

'Where are you taking her?' she asked, taking the stairs two at a time to keep up with his long strides.

'To the stone. It caused this. Maybe it can help her.' Miah nodded and kept pace with him, shooting worried glances at the Chronicler who had become so important to them all.

'Hold on, Kess,' he whispered in her ear.

~

Kess knew she was being moved, the rocking motion of Thrain's steps was soothing, amidst the cacophony in her mind.

Then, as if from a distance, she heard her name yelled, then the sounds of a scuffle.

She opened her eyes a fraction and saw Abram struggling in Miah's grasp.

'Kess?' he yelled again frantically.

'Chronicler!' Miah barked in a tone which had him immediately stilling. 'We are doing what we can. The best thing you can do is calm–' The rest of her words were lost as Thrain strode quickly away.

Kess tried to move her lips but couldn't seem to remember how. Crushed under the weight of too many thoughts, images and emotions; her mind was too overwhelmed to form any type of coherency, or coordination for movement.

Tears leaked through her closed eyelids as she sunk into Thrain's chest, unable to even raise one of the hands, folded across her middle, to block out the surrounding noise.

Just when she thought she could take it no more – that one more moment would tear her apart – there was peace.

The maelstrom within her mind calmed so suddenly, the silence seemed deafening.

Within the darkness a single spark began to glow.

Kess. A voice whispered.

She pushed it away. Wanting nothing more than the solitude, the glorious silence of the blackness.

The voice pulsed again. *Kess.*

This time she recognised it, from a bubble in her mind; her newest forbandt. *Obiex?*

The voice chuckled and if a voice could smile, this one would be.

Or would you prefer Irin?

Irin. His lilting voice caressed the word. *I have not heard that name in a long time.*

But that is your name, she pressed.

That name once belonged to an Angel, though I am not sure I am still that being. It has been so long.

You must still be you, or we wouldn't have been able to become forbandt. But I don't understand, this didn't happen when I bonded the other Angels.

Muted surprise filtered to her. *You have bonded others?*

Six Angels. And one demon, she added hesitantly, knowing the confusion that admission always caused.

A dæmon? That should not be possible. The ability to bond has never been common, but when it was less rare, even then, forming a bond with a denizen of hell was impossible.

Improbable maybe, but obviously not impossible.

She had the sense again of a mental head shake. *Dæmons do not possess souls, rending them incapable of forming a forbandt bond.*

She changed tact, tired of being told that what she did was impossible. She had bonded a demon. As far as she was concerned that was incontrovertible proof. *Do you know what went haywire with the bonding?*

I– Irin hesitated. *I am afraid that may be my fault. I have been without any contact for so long. I think I was almost lost within the stone. Your touch revived me, and–*

And almost broke my mind. She finished without ire.

It would seem so.

So why am I okay now?

An image floated through her mind. A man – Thrain – cradling her in his arms, placing her hand against the stone.

Kess realised this was what Irin had seen. Thrain, saving her.

When you touched the stone again, our bond was completed. The forbandt brought back enough of my consciousness that I could sense the damage I was doing to you.

Will that happen again if I bond another Angel? Or another Obiex?

Your previous bonds were fine, and if by chance you did bond another Obiex then my presence should protect you from the same thing happening again.

Irin, can I ask you something? Kess's dream was coming back to her and now that she could concentrate again, questions filled her.

The bond gave her an almost physical nod.

I dreamt that you volunteered to become what you are, to protect us. You, Ambriel, and nine other Angels.

Ambriel. The name sighed through her mind and a sense of pink eyes and soft platinum hair floated before her vision. Sadness filtered through her, not her own.

I've made you sad.

No. Yes. But it is good to remember. It is time for you to wake now. There is someone in the room, whose worry for you grows.

Wearily Kess opened her eyes.

~

Thrain held Kess, who had lain unmoving in his arms for hours.

He had no idea how long he had stood, holding her hand against the Obiex. Yet as soon as he had placed Kess's hand on the stone, it had come to life, colours flaring so brightly he'd had to look away.

She murmured against his chest, and he saw with relief that colour had returned to her face, which was no longer pinched in pain.

At first Miah had stood with him in his vigil, but his attention had only been for the Chronicler, who against all odds had endeared herself, not only to him, but all the Guardians who now protected her. A few hours ago, after the fifth head had poked into the room, his sub–commander left to guard the main door, turning away the growing number of Chroniclers and Guardians alike who had heard that something was wrong with Kess.

Reluctantly, an hour or more ago, he had removed her contact with the stone so he could relieve the strain on his muscles which, much to his chagrin, trembled and ached, refusing to hold her aloft any longer.

Yet he didn't let her go.

He sat with his back against the wall, and cradled Kess in his arms.

He opened his eyes instantly alert, realising he had dozed, and what had awakened him. Kess was starting to move.

He saw her head tilt up, focusing on his face. A look of wonder made her emerald green eyes look larger and her face seem younger than her twenty–one years.

'Thrain,' she said it softly, neither as a statement nor question. The word caressed his ears.

She shifted in his arms, not pulling away, just moving so she could see him better. 'You helped me.'

He shook his head. 'I didn't do anything.' The words emerged tinged with bitterness. 'I tried, but I couldn't even summon your Angel.'

Her eyes glazed as she turned her head looking blankly at the wall.

For a moment, he feared that she had been overwhelmed again, but then she spoke. 'They are in the forest, outside the walls. Irin – the Obiex's barrier stopped them.'

'All of them?'

She focused again, then nodded. 'Don't worry they won't be seen,' she reassured the Commander.

Thrain cursed himself for a fool. He should have thought of that. 'Some Guardian I am,' he muttered.

'You brought me here.' She continued to look at him in that wide–eyed way of hers.

He didn't release his hold of her, and she did not ask for it. She searched his face, and found something he had tried to keep hidden deep within.

Working one of her arms free she hesitantly touched the side of his face, her fingertips smooth and soft against the roughness of his skin.

He froze under her touch, barely daring to breathe.

She traced the hard contours of his cheekbones, and followed the definition of his jawline, stopping at the cleft in his chin. Her face inched closer to his.

He couldn't stop his gaze from dropping to her lips, then back again to her soft green eyes.

Pressed up against him, he could feel the racing of her heart inches from where his own had started to thump. 'Bond me.' The words were out of his mouth, before he realised what he had said.

Her hand froze against his cheek. 'What?'

'I want you to bond me.'

She shifted away from him, coldness flooded between them where warmth had been. 'Is that even possible?'

'You are forbandt with a demon. And a stone. Why not a Guardian?' The more he thought about it, the more he realised this was what he wanted.

Uncertainty filled her eyes. 'I'm not even sure how to.'

'Try,' he replied calmly.

~

Kess stared at Thrain apprehensively.

He was looking at her like she could accomplish anything. Yet after the craziness of what had just happened with her last unintentional bond she was reluctant to try again.

But she had to admit that her hesitancy didn't just stem from that. This was Thrain, who she realised she had some sort of feelings for, though she had tried to deny it.

He hadn't moved away from her touch, had held her in his arms, yet maybe that was just his Guardian concern again. If it was only that and she bonded him, what if he could sense her growing affections?

Kess took a deep breath, then shifted herself so she was sitting on his legs. Resting her elbows on her knees, she reached out touching the sides of his neck with the palms of her hands, and looked deep into the storm grey of his eyes.

She waited for the whirlwind sensation to flow through her again, like it had started to a few nights earlier, yet there was nothing.

Lines of frustration crinkled the edges of her eyes and she sighed, trying not to feel relieved. 'Nothing's happening.'

For once, Thrain's emotions were painted starkly on his face; crushing disappointment.

Something crumpled within Kess's chest.

She flinched, as he drew back from her, withdrawing himself not only physically, but emotionally as well. She watched as any softness he had let escape disappeared, replaced with icy hardness. The withdrawal went all the way to his eyes, making them appear like flint.

'Miah and Kisho are outside.'

Her eyebrows furrowed in confusion.

'You didn't think I could leave Aldoak carrying you limply in my arms, and not be noticed? Miah has sent Zuri and Bannen and several of your Chroniclers away already.'

Thrain gripped the tops of her arms and shifted her off his legs, then stood brusquely, brushing his hands along his pants. Walking to a section of the wall, he pressed his hand against the stone, releasing the sliding door and strode through.

She watched him go, knowing he needed a moment, and so did she.

~

Thrain burst out of the narrow corridor into the fresh air, and the first rays of the rising sun.

He wiped a hand over his face, wearied by his night long vigil, and his worry over the Chronicler.

He saw her face again, looking up at him in wonder, and felt something deep within him warm and try to break free of the wall he'd shielded himself with. He stamped down on that kernel of emotion with the ferocity of a stallion pounding a snake to death, trying to deny its existence.

'Thank the gods,' he whispered.

~

Kess rested her hand on Irin–Obiex, and felt his bond bloom within her mind. Sensing her turmoil, he radiated calmness towards her. She leant forward resting her head against the stone until she heard the soft tread of boots behind her.

Miah stood within the room, a few feet away, a look of concern plastered on her face. 'You had us worried. How are you now?'

'Apart from annoying Thrain again, I'm alright.'

Miah raised an eyebrow

'I'm tired,' Kess admitted, 'and I could use a few aspirin but apart from that–'

A warm light pulsed around her hand.

'So, it's true,' Miah said, nodding her head. 'You actually bonded the Obiex.'

'Irin.'

The dark–haired warrior looked at her questioningly.

'His name was Irin, and he sacrificed himself so that we would be safe.' Finally aware how the stones were made, she wanted it known how much some Angels had sacrificed in order to protect their ancestors.

'Huh.' She looked at Kess thoughtfully but didn't ask any of the questions that had to be running through her analytical mind. Instead, putting the welfare of her charge first, Miah said, 'We should go. You need to rest. You look like crap.' Her voice was light, taking the sting from her words, but if Kess looked half as wrung out as she felt, then she could understand her Guardians worry.

Goodbye, Irin.

Fare you well, Kess. Seek your rest. She couldn't help the small smile which quirked her lips. She'd acquired yet another guardian.

Kisho was pacing when they entered the small antechamber. Though his back to them, he stiffened as he heard the whisper of their boots, then spun closing the gap between them in a few steps and wrapped her in his arms.

She appreciated his uncomplicated affection, like that of a concerned older brother worried for his younger sibling. 'You certainly know how to keep your Guardians on their toes. It's good to see you on your feet again instead of swooned in Thrain's arms.' His tone was light; joking, yet she saw his worry creased in deep lines along his forehead. With one more squeeze he let her go, and turned to leave when a familiar dark–haired Chronicler blocked their path.

'You are welcome here any time,' he told Kess, then with a hasty look at her companions added, 'and your Guardians, of course. I don't know what you did, but the Obiex has been stronger since your last visit. We even detected a resonance, like the stone was trying to reach out, perhaps to one of the other Havens' Obiex.'

Miah said nothing, merely raised an eyebrow causing the Obiex Chronicler to stammer. 'That is pure conjecture of course, my own unproven suppositions.'

Though obviously cowed by a mere upturn of her Guardians brow, his eyes still lingered on Kess, full of curiosity and speculation.

She fought the urge to sigh. Instead of blending in like she had been supposed to do upon arriving back to the Haven, she had somehow found herself the focus of more and more attention.

'Thanks, ah–' Kess paused, not knowing his name.

'Chronicler Pipkin, umm, Isac,' he added, cheeks reddening as he found himself under three sets of eyes. As a Watcher of the Stone, and primarily alone, he was clearly unused to being the focus of attention, particularly by Guardians.

'Isac,' she repeated. 'I may come to visit Iri – ah – the Obiex again.'

A light entered Isac's almost black eyes and she knew she'd slipped up; that his curiosity was now well and truly piqued.

Miah hustled her from the room before she could open her mouth again.

~

Thrain paced the few steps of his room, unable to calm himself down.

He was ten times a fool for letting her soften the wall he had built around himself.

The door flung back, rebounding against the wall so forcefully he heard the timber groan in protest.

'What happened?' Miah demanded storming into the room, a dangerous light gleaming in her eyes.

'What happened where?' he answered coolly, not at all fazed by her stormy countenance.

'What happened with Kess?' she replied flintily.

'Nothing.'

'Nothing doesn't have you storming off by yourself without a word to anyone after what just happened.'

His shoulders hunched. 'I asked her to bond me.' The words stuck in his throat.

The anger drained from Miah's face, like water leaving a bathtub. 'Oh. And.'

'And nothing. She couldn't,' he said shortly, feeling the same stab of disappointment cut through him. 'Or wouldn't.'

'So you got angry at her,' Miah surmised, nodding as his face became blank. 'Damn it all,' she cursed. As he met her gaze, her eyes softened. 'I know, Thrain,' she said in exasperation.

He shot her a look hard enough to make even her recoil. 'You know nothing,' he spat.

'What happened with Elaria–'

Thrain snarled and whipped around, eyes filled with such anger and pain, that Miah had to gather herself before she continued. 'What happened with Elaria wasn't your fault.'

'Get out,' his voice trembled with emotion.

Thrain turned away but not before he caught the look of pity on her face. He braced his hands on the window sill, and didn't turn around even after he heard the soft pad of footsteps and the door close.

He brushed his hands through his hair roughly, exhaling loudly.

He was a fool.

~

'What is it?' Kisho asked, catching Kess's glance.

She smiled fondly, realising that as she came to know her Guardians, they too were becoming familiarised with her. 'Can you take me to the gate? Kai and the others are out there. They would have felt what was happening.' She didn't continue, knowing that he would understand.

Without argument Kisho changed direction leading them not to Aldoak, but through the gate, and into the forest beyond.

As soon as they were out of view of Athenaeum, Kess's seven forbandt materialised, flocking around her in their concern.

'Kess! Thank the Light you're alright!' Kai exclaimed, pulling her into a hug so tight she had trouble breathing.

'What happened?' Azrin asked, at the same time.

Kai released her, and reluctantly stepped back a pace, knowing that like himself, the other bonded Angels would want to touch her, to reassure themselves of her health.

'Thrain took me to visit the Obiex. I heard it humming and when I touched the stone, I bonded it.'

'You bonded an Obiex,' Nakir, ever quiet, said disbelievingly.

'He – Irin, was an Angel who sacrificed himself to protect Chroniclers.' She looked around the group, feeling their shock at her announcement. They hadn't known the source of the Haven's protection came from one of their brethren. 'You didn't know.'

'No,' Azrin confirmed. 'After the atrocities done to your forebears, the making of the Havens was a closely guarded secret.'

You came close to dying. Lumiel told her through the bond, eyeing Kisho carefully.

'Thrain took me back to Irin, and when he placed my hand on the stone, the bond was sealed and Irin regained enough sentience, to realise what he was doing to me.'

Treil hung at the back of the group, behind the midnight Kasbeel and golden Caliel, watching her carefully.

Kess approached her, reaching out to touch the two Angels as she passed them by. Without a word, she put her arms around the kîngkã, laying her face against the rough skin of her chest. The demon put her arms around her forbandt without hesitation, neither saying anything.

Eyes closed, Kess realised how weary she felt, yet before she could even move, Treil said, 'You need rest bond–mate.'

Azrin pulled her into a one–armed embrace before she left, whispering into her ear, 'Take care of yourself, little Chronicler, you are too important for us to lose.'

~

After being unconscious all of the previous night Kess knew she should feel rested, yet weariness seemed to have settled into her bones.

She stood at the window looking out across the training field, where Guardians fought mock night battles, yet couldn't banish the bitter disappointment which Thrain had tried, and failed to keep from his eyes. The thought of it made her stomach clench.

Hours later, the sleep she craved still eluded her as she stared at the roof, listening to Kisho's soft deep breaths, haunted by a pair of grey eyes.

CHAPTER 37

A Haven No Longer

Kess emerged from the bathroom refreshed after her shower, and halted as she realising she wasn't alone.

Leora lounged on her bed, back resting against the wall, booted feet on her quilt, whilst Abram looked out the window, a look of discomfort on his face.

Her eyes widened slightly, but after so much time with the Guardians, she was learning to control her facial movements, and schooled her face carefully blank. She glanced at the young Chronicler reclined on her bed. 'You made yourself comfortable I see?'

Abram's cheeks reddened at her comment as he gave her an apologetic glance.

'Kisho said we could come to see you any time.'

'And you can, but a little courtesy wouldn't go astray.' She chided, then sighed, she wasn't cut out for mentoring. 'What's up?'

'How do we go about getting an escort to and from classes?'

The low seriousness of her voice made Kess instantly forget her irritation. 'What happened?'

'Kadence had an accident on her way to classes today.'

Kess felt her heart speed up, as she thought of the petite brunette. 'How accidental was it?' she asked, fearing she knew the answer already.

The look on Leora's face confirmed her suspicions.

What was going on in the Haven? It used to be the one place in the world where you could be guaranteed to be safe.

'Get a timetable for everyone.'

The caramel–skinned girl held up a few sheets of paper in her hands. 'Already done.'

Kess nodded, unsurprised by the Chronicler's forethought. Leora was proving herself smart, practical and determined and most importantly, she looked out for those around her. She would have made a fine Guardian.

'It's probably best if I only take one of you when I see Miah.' She gave Abram an apologetic smile.

'I'm good here,' he said holding both hands out in front of him like he was fending off the suggestion.

Turning to Leora, she said grimly, 'Come with me.'

Though precluded from training for a few days, at her Guardians insistence, they didn't deny her request to wander around within Aldoak itself, which was where she had bumped into Miah heading into the training room earlier.

She heard the clash of weapons before they reached the room so wasn't surprised to see Miah and Zuri pitched in mock combat. To an unknowing bystander it might have looked like they were out for each other's blood, such was the ferocity of their strokes.

Beside her she heard a gasp, and found Leora mouth agape with a look; not of worry, but envy, glowing in her eyes. Kess knew exactly how she felt.

Some may have found it frightening or intimidating to watch, but for her, it was mesmerising. The warriors made it a dance of grace and precision, one she longed to be able to achieve, and she could see in Leora's face, that she felt the same. She shook her head at the irony of her newfound friendship. Who'd have thought she'd have found a kindred spirit amongst the reclusive Chroniclers.

They watched them flow to and fro for several minutes before Miah called a halt. 'I assume you two have a good reason for being here, other than to gaze at my stunningly shaped calves.'

Leora blushed at the comment, but Kess, used to the Guardians sense of humour now, made a point of looking at the warrior's legs. 'Well they are lovely, but no. Kadence Worsley had an accident,' she bent the two forefingers on each hand to show how accidental the mishap was, 'on her way to classes. Can we arrange a Guardian escort for each of the twelve Chroniclers?'

With each word Miah's face had become tighter, losing any semblance of jest. She turned to Zuri, who sheathed her haladie.

'On it.' As she strode past them she grabbed Leora's arm. 'Come with me.'

Thinking this was as good a time as any, Kess asked, 'Considering the circumstances, would you consent to defence training for Leora, and any other Chronicler who wants to learn?'

Miah's dark brown eyes stared at her unblinking.

'You saw something in me,' she reminded the warrior.

'You were different.'

Kess tried to ignore the inflection in her words, the same words she seemed to be hearing too often lately. 'If you saw something in me, surely you see the same in some of them, Leora for example.' She met the warrior's unblinking stare, fighting the urge to writhe under Miah's fierce stare.

The echo of footsteps behind her stopped and knew that Leora in particular, was paying close attention to the outcome.

'Very well,' Miah conceded grudgingly. 'But only those who request it mind. Some of that lot couldn't wield a butter knife without doing themselves harm, let alone a sword.'

With a short nod, Kess turned on her heel saving her victorious smile until she faced away from the warrior. Leora returned her smile, then followed after Zuri who was already several paces ahead, but not before she saw the look of determination blazing in the Chronicler's eyes. Angels help the Guardian assigned to train or guard her.

She returned to her room and found Abram seated on the ground, leaning against the wall near her door.

'Abram?'

He opened his eyes, smiling as he focused on her.

'Are you alright?'

'I would only have been waiting in my room by myself, pacing nervously,' he explained with a rueful grin.

Kess extended her hand which Abram gripped, helping him to his feet. His hands were soft beneath hers, so different from the calloused grips of the Guardians.

As he stood fully, coming face to face with her, colour singed its way across the defined lines of his cheekbones. The hand holding hers dropped away hastily and he took a step back, distancing himself.

Ignoring the staining to his cheeks Kess opened her door, which she didn't bother to lock – if she couldn't trust the Guardians who could she trust – and strolled through plonking down on the edge of the bed, glad for the chance to rest, if only for a moment.

'Leora?' the dark–haired boy asked.

She thought of him as a boy, yet he could only have been a year or two younger than her at most. 'Organising Guardian escorts for each of you.'

'They agreed?' His eyebrows rose in unfeigned surprise.

'Of course.' She huffed, offended at the insinuation that the Guardians wouldn't care. 'I know Chronicler education is somewhat lacking but do not ever doubt the warriors' dedication for the safety of everyone within Athenaeum.'

Remorse flickered across his features at her remark. 'Sorry. I didn't mean it like that. I'm just surprised they agreed so quickly,' he amended.

'Don't assume everything is black and white as we were taught, there are many shades of grey,' she explained, easing her testy tone.

'That's why we're here instead of being with the other Chroniclers,' Abram said softly. 'So we each get a Guardian?' he asked, leading the conversation in a different direction.

'Yes. Are the rest of the Chroniclers here?'

He tilted his head thinking for a second then nodded.

'Could you gather them?'

'Now?'

When she nodded, he strode from the room, seemingly determined to make up for his earlier comment. Within a few minutes her room was full of curious Chroniclers, talking quietly amongst themselves as they waited for the last straggler to join them.

Kess saw Kadence sitting on the spare bed, between two other girls. A dark bruise marred her cheekbone, and she had a bandage wrapped around her head, covering a noticeable lump on the temple. She nodded at the girl, heartened when Kadence returned a small smile, glad that she hadn't lost her spirit because of the attack. Despite the obvious injuries she still found it hard to believe that someone could hurt the cheerful girl.

The last to arrive, a gangly youth yet to grow into his tall frame, stumbled into the room stammering an apology as he realised they waiting for him.

'Right, that's everyone?' Kess stood addressing them.

Abram looked around and nodded.

'Leora's missing.' Edee Damrosch, a delicate–featured ginger–haired girl, spoke up.

'She will be along shortly.' Kess looked around the group of curious faces. 'Right, to jump right into it, because of the incident with Kadence you will each be assigned a Guardian.'

Excited murmurs had just broken out amongst the group when Zuri popped her head in the door, and with a tilt of her head disappeared out of view again.

'I'll be back in a moment,' she told them as she followed the Guardian out into the corridor.

'They're ready, in the meeting hall.'

'Right, let's go,' she told the gathering, then matching her pace to the dark–skinned Guardian, led them deeper into the Aldoak complex. The group quietened as they walked behind them, content with looking around the unfamiliar surroundings.

'I'm sorry about what happened at training,' she murmured, pitching her voice so it wouldn't be overheard.

Zuri glanced over. 'We have no problem Kess.' She flashed a white toothed smile. 'It wasn't about us anyway.'

Kess's eyebrows furrowed in confusion. 'What do you mean? Who was it about then?'

Hesitancy entered her pale blue eyes, then she shrugged. 'The Commander is a complicated man.'

'You're telling me this like I don't already know.'

Zuri gave her a tight–lipped smile as they stepped into the meeting hall where a row of leather–clad Guardians awaited.

Leora looked up from a conversation with a young female warrior – presumably her paired Guardian – then broke away from her, coming to stand beside Kess.

Miah stood off to the side and waited until the last Chronicler was through the door before speaking. 'As a matter of precaution each Chronicler has been assigned a Potential – a Guardian in training. Do not under any circumstance leave the complex without them. Think of them as your new shadow,' she set her piercing gaze on each of the young scholars, making sure she had their attention. 'Each Potential will have different methods to ensure your protection, so I will leave the details up to them.'

She turned back to the warriors. 'Before you go to speak with your new charges collect their timetables from Zuri.'

'Right,' she looked down at her list. 'Deserai and Leora. Lucian and Abram. Gillen and Kadence. Casper and Edee. Micah and Sorabella.' The names droned on, and with Kess knowing less than a third of them, they started to blend together. 'That leaves, Rory and Chronicler Dex.' As Miah finished calling out the names she folded the sheet of paper she'd been reading from, clenching it at her side.

Seeing everything was under control, Kess seized her chance and started to make her way to the door. 'Before you go,' Miah called out halting her, 'I've had a request from Bannen to become your Guardian.'

'What?' She didn't bother to hide her shock. 'Why would I need anyone else when I already have you four?'

'As flattering as that is,' Miah said dryly, 'I have granted his request. Another set of eyes never goes astray.'

Kess pursed her lips together but didn't argue, why bother when there was no point. Whether she liked it or not, she'd just acquired another Guardian. 'Fine, but he doesn't have to take nights, does he?'

Zuri snorted with laughter. 'That was the part he was looking forward to the most.'

'Whatever, I'm going to train.' Kess left before they could see the flush on her cheeks.

'Want some company?' Zuri, never one to miss a training session, asked hopefully.

'Sure.'

'Go easy with her,' Miah reminded Zuri, surprising Kess when she didn't argue. 'She is supposed to be on bed rest.'

CHAPTER 38

Deus

Kess emerged from her room into a flurry of activity.

Chroniclers and their Guardians – the Potentials – filled the hall, carrying bags or arm loads of belongings.

They were going in and out of rooms, in a type of organised chaos that Kess couldn't make heads nor tails of.

Kess saw the sprightly Kadence, and grabbed her arm as she zoomed into her room. 'What's going on?'

'We're shifting rooms,' she stated as if that should be obvious.

'Didn't you just move in?'

Kadence gave her a bright smile. 'Our Guardians are going to share our rooms with us, so half of us are moving to create enough space.'

Kess shook her head in wonder, at the changes. Not long ago, the dozen Aldoak–Chroniclers – as they were now calling themselves – wouldn't have dared to speak with the young Guardians, let alone share a room with them.

The Chronicler continued her explanation, 'Because our Guardians still have to train, and as we have the same classes, half of the warriors will guard us to and from classes, while the others train, then at lunch they're going to swap over.'

Kess shrugged. 'Whatever you have worked out is fine as long as everybody has a Guardian with them at all times.'

The girl's face took on a haunted look, and not for the first time Kess wondered what had actually happened to her. 'No one goes anywhere alone,' she said seriously. Then as if gloomy thoughts couldn't hold her cheerfulness for long, a smile brightened her face again, and she took off again finishing her move.

~

Kess ignored the ache in her shoulders and neck as she studied yet another book.

Bannen, her Guardian for the day, didn't bother trying to cover his bored yawn. Unlike Miah, he didn't offer to help.

'Glad you asked to become my Guardian?' she asked sweetly.

'Definitely,' he grinned, looking her up and down.

Shaking her head, she resumed reading, trying to ignore his eyes which lingered on her.

After four hours though, he didn't try to hide his relief when Miah came to relieve him.

'Don't think he will be so keen to volunteer for duty next time,' Miah said with a fiendish grin.

'You organised that he would have a Vault shift deliberately?' Kess laughed.

Miah peered at the pile of books which never seemed to go down. 'Have you done anything today or did you just sit and stare at young Bannen?'

Kess raised her eyebrows, not bothering to rise to the brunette's taunt. 'He's not my type.'

Instead of laughing, Miah looked at her closely. 'No, I don't suppose he is,' she said cryptically as she reached for a book and settled back in the chair Bannen had just vacated.

She was just about to return to her book, when she saw a fine–featured woman in the medium green robes of a Captol, heading towards their table.

‘Greetings, Chronicler Grayson. My name is Sunisa. Tomas and Seren sent me to talk to you. They said you may be interested in my field of study.’

This close up Kess saw the dark lilted eyes and light brown skin tone which placed Sunisa as a native of Malaysia or one of the surrounding islands.

She caught the subtle shift as Sunisa pulled at her collar which revealed a familiar crescent–shaped brand, though unlike Kess’s own, hers was pale, healed with time. She nodded carefully acknowledging the Captols allegiance.

‘Seren?’ Kess queried, lowering her tone. ‘The Custodian? Seren Pendry? She’s a member?’

‘She is,’ Sunisa replied carefully.

‘What did they think we would be interested in?’ Kess extended her hand, indicating the chair opposite hers.

Glancing at Miah, clearly hesitant, she sat in the chair Kess had indicated, settling herself comfortably before beginning to talk. ‘The libraries within the Havens are some of the greatest in the world, yet so much has been lost; so many books destroyed throughout history during wars, natural disasters, and the decimation of the other Havens.’

‘Other Havens?’ Kess had some idea of this, from her bonding with Irin–Obiex, which had shown eleven volunteer Angels.

‘Though not widely known, there were once seven other Havens confirmed to have existed within the countries now known as Africa, America, Spain, Mongolia, India, Cambodia, and Brazil.’

‘What happened to them?’

‘That I cannot tell you other than all of their inhabitants were slain and every part of the Havens razed to the ground,’ Sunisa shrugged.

‘Why aren’t we taught any of this?’

‘Havens are believed to be safe, impregnable. If it was widely known that other Havens have been breached, it would cause unease amongst the remaining areas inhabitants.’

Kess looked at the woman unhappily. 'But it's alright to have people falsely believe they are safe when they're not.'

'I didn't make the rules, and I did not say I agree with them.' The woman countered, unfazed by Kess's anger.

'How is it that you know so much about all of this?' Miah asked, watching the Captol closely.

'It is the work of a lifetime of research.'

'So, you belong to the Historicals.'

'Yes.'

'What else do you know?' Kess asked, believing that if Wessler sent this woman to her, then she must have information of value.

'I have a volume here you may find interesting,' Sunisa said sliding a thin book across the table. 'If you want to speak with me again, tell Tomas, and he will arrange it. Good luck in your hunting,' she said, clearly believing Kess's research had to do with locating the *Scuro* in their midst.

Kess bid the woman goodbye then turned her attention to the book she'd been given. 'You don't want to check it for hidden weapons?' She grinned at Miah's sour face, before she opened it and began reading.

Kess had only read a few pages when she straightened so suddenly Miah's hands flew to her sabre.

'Sorry,' she smiled sheepishly. 'I found something!'

Miah pushed her book aside with such gusto it careened into a pile of their discarded texts almost toppling it over. She ignored the wobbling stack focusing on Kess, who began reading in a hushed voice so as not to be overheard.

"There has been rumoured to be a secret guild, not associated with Chroniclers or the Havens. The members of the sect are said to have great stores of information at their fingertips."

The excited smile on her face faltered as she saw Miah's scepticism. 'That's not a lot to go on. It sounds like that the author wasn't even sure about the existence of this secret group. When was it written?'

Kess placed her finger marking the page she was reading then opened the front cover. '1568,' she said, unperturbed.

Something about this felt right.

'It's not like there are not secret groups within the Haven. Why couldn't there be a secret group elsewhere?'

Miah still looked doubtful. 'Just don't get your hopes up. Does it even mention where this group is supposed to be?'

Kess scanned further down, then shook her head. 'It says they dwell with those closest to Deus,' she slumped back in her seat. 'What's a Deus?'

'It's Latin for God,' Miah informed her. At Kess's surprised look she said, 'I've been around long enough to pick up a few things.'

'Those closest to God,' she whispered, thinking.

'Jerusalem?' Miah supplied.

But Kess shook her head, that didn't feel right.

An idea started to form in Kess's head and she let herself talk to give her thought coherence. 'The voice of God on Earth is the Pope. When was Vatican City built?'

'I think there have been Basilica's built on the site for over fifteen–hundred years.' She didn't sound sure at all, but excitement rose in Kess's chest.

This was it! The secret group, if it still existed, was in Vatican City!

But how was she going to get there, and what was she to look for when she arrived. It wasn't like there would be a great big sign indicating, Vatican Tours on the left; meet a Member of the Secret Ancient Guild on the right.

She kept reading, hoping to find out more.

The next page was an excerpt from a different author, making it seem to Kess that the book was a collection of works from various writers, all about the same topic.

I have heard whispers, of the secret sect, from several sources, though not one of any credible origin.

The ramblings of an old senile Chronicler, a story passed down through a family the last survivor of which is a resident of a Narrentürme, and the latest an unintended slip from a Fryar, well known for his partiality to whisky.

But three random hearings from completely independent sources cannot be mere happenstance.

I discovered a name, Augur, who may be one of the secret sect who will provide answers to the questions of those with the will to find him.

Whilst I could locate nothing other information about this Augur I found a symbol which could be of relevance. ⧗

‘What’s a Narrentürme?’ Kess asked, not at all sure she got the pronunciation right.

‘A what?’

Instead of attempting the word again, Kess handed the book over to Miah, pointing it out on the page.

Miah’s eyes narrowed. ‘It sounds German, but I don’t know enough to be able to tell you what it means.’

Kess walked to the front of the Vault where she knew the dictionaries, language books and a variety of thesaurus were shelved. Scanning through the titles she found a German dictionary and returned to their table, flipping through the pages to find the letter ‘N’.

‘It’s a medieval term for an asylum,’ Kess said, surprised.

‘You really believe because a crazy person ranted about a secret order that it actually existed, and still does, somewhere within Vatican City?’ Miah groaned. ‘Let me guess, you want to go there to find this Augur.’ Miah groaned. She cut off as a stern, homely faced Chronicler strode past.

‘Excuse me,’ Kess said halting the woman’s progress. ‘Is there any way I can loan out this book?’ she said, indicating the thin tome.

‘Loan?’ The Chroniclers eyebrows rose in high arches on her forehead, and a scandalous look crossed her face, almost like Kess had asked if she could draw on the pages. 'We do not *loan* out any of the historical volumes contained within the Vault.'

She sniffed, affronted at being asked such a question.

Miah raised an eyebrow at the woman, sending her scurrying away.

Kess watched, trying to keep a straight face, as her Guardian slipped the small book inside the front of her leather jerkin the moment the woman's back was turned.

'Shall we?' Miah asked, as she pushed her chair neatly back into the table.

As they left the Vault, they passed by the stern Chronicler again, who sniffed at them, still outraged by her question.

Miah bared her teeth in a snarl as she stalked past, leaving Kess trying to stifle her laughter as the woman had a near apoplexy.

Kess wasn't put off by her Guardians obvious reticence, the information she'd found in the book – currently stuffed down the front of Miah's shirt – was what she'd been looking for.

The book had said the Augur answered the questions of those with the will to find him. She had the will, but would that be enough to locate him hundreds of years later? And would he be able to tell her what she was or what the markings covering her body meant?

First things first, getting permission to leave the Haven.

CHAPTER 39

The Battle Lines are Drawn

Kess woke to a hand on her shoulder. 'Kess wake up.' There was urgency to the voice which dragged her awake.

'What's going on?' she groaned, mumbling in her pillow.

Bleary eyed, Kess blinked a few times trying to clear the stinging sensation from her eyes. She glanced at the clock. Three minutes past two.

After a somewhat extended training session with Zuri last night, she'd fallen into bed only a few hours earlier.

No wonder her eyes stung painfully.

Kisho – who had no doubt awakened the moment the brunette warrior laid her hand upon the door – sat on the edge of his bed, raking his hands through his hair, looking as glassy eyed as she felt. The tiredness of sleep fled as Kess saw the stress on Miah's face. 'What's going on?'

'Thrain's gone.'

'What?' She and Kisho yelled at the same time. With a quick glance at each other, Kisho asked, 'When?'

'They just took him.' Miah started pacing, leathers creaking softly with her agitated movements.

'Who did?' Kess didn't think anyone could take Thrain anywhere he didn't want to go.

'We have been asking a few discrete questions about some of the oddities going on around here.'

‘What do you class as discrete?’ Kess was sure their definition of caution and tact were worlds apart from her own.

Miah sidestepped the question, confirming her suspicions. ‘It seems that Samael openly refused Drazen’s orders about letting the delegation in, saying that no one would be allowed entry to Athenaeum on his watch, without being properly searched. Later the next afternoon he disappeared.’

Kess’s qualms about their rashness was forgotten. ‘Well that’s no coincidence.’

‘Thrain has been questioning the Guardians that have been on gate duty since Drazen’s order was given. A few hours ago, he went to speak with Castaldi–’ Miah paused at her frown. ‘Zeke Castaldi.’

She had never understood the hierarchy amongst the Guardians, where the lower ranked warriors were always referred to by their surnames, whilst the leaders and higher–ranking members were addressed by their first names.

She shrugged, never having heard of that Guardian, though that wasn’t surprising considering they numbered nearly six thousand. ‘And what did he find out?’

‘I don’t know, they got him on the way back.’

‘Whose they?’ Kisho asked, looking as close to violence as she had ever seen him.

‘Drazen and several of his lackeys.’ Miah paced the room, hands repeatedly returning to her weapons before removing them, only to have them drift back moments later.

‘How would they make Thrain go anywhere he didn’t want to go?’ Kess voiced her earlier thought dubiously. The commander was the deadliest person she knew; armed or unarmed. There was no way anyone, particularly a Custodian, would be a match for him.

‘Drazen had him arrested! For failing in his duties to protect the denizens of Athenaeum!’

‘How did you find all this out?’

‘Castaldi.’

‘He just stood there and let them take Thrain?’ Kisho who had been listening quietly, asked incredulously.

Kess’s opinion of the gate Guardian diminished drastically.

‘He said that he tried to intervene, but Thrain told him to stand down.’ Her eyebrows furrowed revealing her uncertainty, yet Kess had no doubt that was exactly what the Commander would have done.

‘Where’d they take him? There are no prisons here.’

‘Oh Kess.’ Exasperation filled Miah’s voice, at her naivety. ‘Of course there is.’

Questions flashed through her mind faster than she could ask. But she settled for the most important one. ‘What are they going to do to him?’

‘I don’t know. They said something about a trial, but–’ she cut off and shrugged, even that movement was agitated. She resumed pacing, like that was the only thing stopping her from racing from the room and attacking the Custodian.

‘Why would they arrest him when he hasn’t done anything wrong?’

‘Well of course he hasn’t,’ Miah said indignantly. ‘It seems–’ She cut off looking at Kess, as if judging how much to say.

‘Seems like what,’ she prompted, knowing this was important.

‘–like Drazen wanted him out of the way.’

‘The question is, out the way of what,’ Kess muttered more to herself than the warrior. She didn’t refute Miah’s allegation.

‘You aren’t going to tell me I’m crazy?’ the dark–haired warrior asked disbelievingly.

‘No. Something’s off with him.’ She looked to Kisho, poised on the edge of the bed, and Miah pacing the room. ‘What are we going to do?’

‘What can we do? Thrain could only have been imprisoned if all of the Consilium agreed. Nothing like this has ever happened before. There are no protocols for it.’ For the first time Miah looked unbalanced.

‘Break him out. You can’t leave him in there to face a trial by Kangaroo Court.’ Kess used the term she’d read about and remembered because of its quirkiness.

A scandalised look crossed Miah's face, for a split second. 'Break him out,' she repeated slowly. 'Excellent!' A huge grin broke out on her face. 'Kisho, go get Zuri. I'll meet you at the base of the tower.'

Kess heard the thudding of his footsteps as Kisho ran down the hall.

Miah strode towards the door, and was halfway out before she realised Kess was following her. 'What are you doing?'

'I'm coming too,' she said, as if that wasn't already obvious.

'No.' Miah shook her head and blocked the doorway with her frame. While that would be enough to physically stop her, Kess wasn't deterred.

'Lucifer's twisted horns I'm not.'

'Has anyone ever told you that you have a very extensive range of curses for a Chronicler?' the dark–haired Guardian said shaking her head. 'Where under the Heavens did you hear that one?'

'Read it in a book,' Kess said with a grin.

Miah shook her head but didn't argue further as Kess shadowed her out of the room.

~

Miah led them to an area of the Haven Kess had never seen before. As Zuri scouted the area, the warrior pointed out the building where the cells were located. When Zuri gave the all clear Kisho opened the door and drew both of his tantou swords, as he cautiously entered.

'I don't like this,' Miah said, scanning around them. 'It's too easy.'

'Trap or not, it doesn't change anything. We need to get him out,' Kess uttered quietly, wishing Kisho would hurry. They were too exposed, and would be visible from hundreds of feet away, congregating as they were outside the door.

'Well of course we do,' Miah huffed indignantly, attention turning to Kisho as he returned.

'All clear. There are twelve steps immediately when you enter. They are steep so watch your footing.' With that he disappeared back into the darkness.

'Zuri, can you hold the door?'

'With my life,' the Amazonian replied seriously.

Miah nodded, then looked at her. 'Down you go.'

~

The rectangle of light from the doorway receded, fading completely as the staircase circled to the left. Kess pulled out her sai, finding the weight of the weapons in her hands calming, and followed the sound of Kisho's footsteps until she gradually saw a faint glow ahead.

The sliver of light was narrow, rectangular and near the ground, and seemed to be coming from behind a closed door. She locked her eyes on it hungrily and kept shuffling her feet forwards carefully, halting only as she met Kisho's outstretched hand.

As her eyes adjusted to the dim light, the darkness became a murky gloom allowing her to see Kisho as he crouched down, peering under the door. As he stood, he unsheathed one of his swords, then threw back the door leaping through.

Kess surged through after him, weapons extended, eyes blinking furiously in the dull light which seemed as bright as a summers day after the blackness of the tunnel. The small stone brick room was completely empty of anything save a doorway leading further in.

'Kisho guard this door,' Miah directed, taking the lead.

The warrior nodded, but didn't look happy at being left behind. With a consoling look to him, Kess followed the soft scrape of Miah's boots and caught up with her several paces from the door which Kisho had shut behind them.

The corridor was lit by torches mounted sporadically along the walls length. Oily smoke rose from them in black tendrils which made Kess's eyes sting and water. She blinked furiously but with both hands occupied didn't stop to wipe them.

Miah paused, peering to either side of the confiningly narrow hall, then stepped closer to an open doorway, before moving quickly on.

She couldn't help but look in, even knowing that if her Guardian passed by, it was empty.

The room beyond was tiny barely the length and width of a single bed and completely stone, with no windows, no bedding – nothing. The floor, walls and ceiling were all carved from the same grey stone making the cell appear even more lifeless and wretched.

The cold pervaded the walls, permeating deep into her skin, making her shiver. She couldn't imagine what it would be like to spend a night in the cell.

Kess turned her back on the room and kept walking, determination thrumming through her.

They had to get Thrain out.

She saw Miah halt in front of a door, four cells down and forced the latch back with a mighty shove.

Kess winced at the screech of metal on metal, which echoed along the empty corridor, then followed as the warrior strode through into the cell.

Thrain sat on a stone bench lining the wall, like he was relaxing at home instead of a prison cell. Bruises dotted his jaw and cheek and although he favoured his recently injured side he looked alright; apart from the chain anchoring him to the wall by his ankle.

'Miah, what are you doing here?'

'Breaking you out.'

'No,' he said firmly.

'The hell we aren't. You're our commander. We aren't leaving you here.'

His eyes flickered behind the brunette, settling on Kess. 'What is she doing here?'

‘Have you tried stopping her?’ Miah quipped. ‘Look we’ve got more important things to worry about now than our rogue Chronicler.’ The smirk on Miah’s face faltered as she looked over her shoulder. In one movement, she pulled her spatha and faced the door, angling herself between Kess, and the mysterious light that was growing brighter.

A voice emerged from the darkness of the corridor. ‘Well you certainly saved me some trouble coming down here, Sub–Commander. I have been racking my brain how to come upon you alone, but you provided the perfect opportunity yourself with this pitiful rescue attempt. But, you being in the company of this troublesome Chronicler, well that’s just an added bonus.’

While she’d recognised his voice, Kess still couldn’t quite believe it when Custodian Drazen stepped out from the shadows. She took an involuntary step forward, around her Guardian’s outstretched arm, as if somehow in that one pace she would realise her mistake, and find a stranger threatening them; not one of their highest–standing members who was supposed to protect the Haven’s inhabitants. Yet his iron–grey hair, carefully manicured moustache, and hard blue eyes remained, distinguishing him.

That he would openly move against the two highest ranking Guardians, within the walls of a Haven, was more than troubling. *But why now? And what did he want?*

He came to a halt in the doorway, at the edge of the lantern’s illumination. Standing partially in the light, the left side of his face became a contrast of shadows. The dramatic pose looked so pre–planned, she couldn’t help the scornful ‘hrrmppf’ of breath which escaped her throat.

The sound focused the Custodian’s attention on her, and his eyes narrowed as a leering smile crossed his face. Then apparently having no fear of what Miah would do, he walked up to Kess and ran his hand up her arm, squeezing the flesh above her biceps.

Unable to repress a shudder she wrenched her arm back retreating so close to Miah that the sides of their bodies touched from shoulder to hip. Together they took another step backwards, distancing themselves from Drazen.

Behind them Kess heard the rattle of the chain securing Thrain to the wall, but she kept her gaze forwards, firmly trained on the Custodian.

'What's this about, Drazen?' Thrain asked, making a point of emphasising the lack of the Custodian's title.

'You are a nuisance, Commander. Too honest and rigid to let the matter of a stray demon attack drop. You had to keep digging, snooping where you didn't belong.' A look of distaste crossed his features before he looked over at Kess. 'And *you* are just as bad. Consorting with Guardians. Inciting your fellow Chroniclers to associate with them.'

'Where is Samael?' Kess knew she should stay quiet, but couldn't help herself.

'Who?' Drazen drawled, eyeing the three of them distastefully.

'The gate Guardian who went missing.' Kess's voice rose with anger.

A viscous smile lit the former–Custodian's face. 'He also proved a nuisance.'

'What did you do to him?' She refused to acknowledge him, even in her own mind, as their leader.

'Let's just say you don't have to worry about him anymore. I'd be more concerned about myself if I was you.'

Sorrow stabbed through her at his insinuation of Samael's fate, yet she saw his eyes flit back towards the door, just for a second.

Hope flared in her chest.

Was he lying? Did he also have Samael locked up somewhere down here?

'What do you think you're going to do?' The brunette warrior's voice was hard, barely controlling the thunderous menace seething within her.

'I plan to have you locked in a dungeon,' Drazen said matter–of–factly.

'And who is going to accomplish that? You?' Scorn filled her words as her body tensed preparing to fight.

'Me? Heavens no!' Drazen looked at them with such aversion, like he might a cockroach which had crawled onto the floor in front of him, yet his obvious revulsion disappeared replaced by a malicious smile. 'No, but my – associates are more than happy to subdue you.'

As he spoke the flames of the torch bracketed to their right wavered and dimmed, like the light was being sucked from the air. The shadows lurking in the corners of the room lengthened, and grew around them, until the gloom seemed oppressive and tangible.

Kess watched, unable to believe her eyes, as the darkness surrounding them began to writhe and flex, and with a final heave, birthed demons.

She immediately moved, placing herself in front of Thrain, much to his exasperation, as several demons materialised, only paces away.

'You work with hells spawn,' the commander said flatly.

'Better them than Guardians,' Drazen spat.

Her hand moved slowly towards her concealed short sword.

Miah saw the movement and gave a slight shake of her head.

Kess's eyebrows furrowed asking the unspoken question – *Why?* – yet the dark–haired warrior repeated the small motion. Unsure about the wisdom of it, she lowered her hands to her sides, and settled for glaring at Drazen instead.

As a triumphant grin settled on Drazen's smug face, she realised belatedly that Miah was protecting her. A fight within the confines of this small room, outnumbered as they were, and with Thrain restrained, would inevitably result in them all sustaining injuries, perhaps serious ones. Miah was protecting Kess, by giving herself over without a fight.

'I will come with you,' Miah said confirming her suspicions.

Kess turned, unable to believe that the warrior would give herself up so easily.

'But Kess goes free, unharmed.'

'No!' she said, aghast.

'You are in no position to bargain with me, Guardian,' Drazen's cold eyes found hers as his smirked, buoyed by his own perceived power. 'She goes nowhere.'

Kess glanced at Thrain, seeking permission to attack, and saw his stance firm; then, hand already moving towards her weapon she looked to Miah, but got her answer as the warrior's sword rasped from its sheath.

Yet even as they moved, a demon stepped forward from the others. The demon – a crazy tarantula spider–snake hybrid – tilted its head back, lowering a snake–like jaw wider than should have been possible. Mist began to form, condensing into a ball, deep within the cavern of its mouth.

'Thor's beard!' Thrain cursed, launching forwards, at the same time as Miah, trying to reach their charge.

Thrain grabbed her, holding her tight against him and turned her away, shielding her with his body. The creature released a spray of liquid into the air.

With her face pressed against the commander's chest, she felt the thrum of his heart against her cheek, felt the heat of his body warm her, and felt him stiffen as the hells spawns venom struck him.

As the mist surrounded them, it stuck to her face, burning her like a thousand little pin pricks. Her eyes stung with such fierceness, it reminded her of the time she had gotten shampoo straight in her eye, but a million times worse. The pain was excruciating, and in her panic it took her a moment to realise that her vision was fading. 'Thrain!' she called desperately.

'Kess–' he croaked before falling to his knees beside her.

Miah was already slumped on the ground having been closer to the demon as it released its spray of mist.

As her eyesight became a pale blur, she heard a thump beside her.

Then as her own knees collapsed, she had one final moment of blind panic, before the world went dark.

CHAPTER 40

Thrain

Thrain woke to find himself hanging by his wrists, in a room as dark as a night during the new moon.

The pain from the metal cutting into his skin was what roused him, but he didn't move. Keeping his breathing even, as if he still slumbered, he assessed his surroundings.

The stillness of the air suggested he was alone.

Cautiously, he lifted his head and waited for his eyes to adjust to the blackness, though even after several minutes he could barely make out any features of the room.

The absence of even a small window slit, combined with the coldness, which permeated the air from the damp stones against his back, chilled his skin, and could only mean that he was deep underground; below the cell where he'd been kept previously.

Confident now of his solitude, he pushed himself to his feet grimacing as the wound across his ribs pulled, stretching the recently healed skin. Ignoring the ache in his manacled wrists he followed the chain back to its source – two heavy bolts driven deep into the stone wall.

Grabbing one of the lengths, he braced his feet against the ground, and tried to loosen the shoulder height fixture using the strength of his leg and arm muscles. He strained, until his side ached and his hands bled, but apart from a small crack, the bolt remained firmly embedded in the wall.

'Kess,' his voice croaked, throat dry and sore. He swallowed a few times, lubricating his throat.

'Kess!' He yelled, and was rewarded this time as his voice echoed clear and strong around the room.

A loud scrape from outside the room gave him warning of someone approaching. Positioning himself with his back to the wall, he pulled himself erect and waited.

The door opened with a protesting squeal, and Drazen walked into the room holding a torch which he mounted in a bracket on the wall, adjusting it just so before turning to face him.

'Awake at last.'

'You son of a goat horned demon!' Dots danced in front of Thrain's visions as his eyes adjusted to the brightness of the torch.

'Temper temper, Guardian. Is that any way to speak in the presence of the gentler sex?' Drazen gloated as Kess was dragged into the room between two demons.

~

Kess hung limply in the grip of the two demons that held her as Drazen approached, eyes still stinging from whatever had been in that demon's venom.

A viscous light entered his eyes as he forced a scrap of material between her teeth like a bit, catching strings of her hair as he tied it tightly at the back of her head.

She glared at him, not wanting to give him the pleasure of trying to talk through the restraint.

Unimpressed by her defiance he turned and walked towards a door a few feet away. He slid back a heavy bolt and with a squeal of metal strode through, signalling the demons to wait outside with her.

As Drazen's form disappeared through the doorway she rotated her jaw trying to loosen the binding which held her mouth open uncomfortably, pulling at the tender skin at the corners of her mouth.

Kess shifted her arms against the grips of the demons who held her, knowing it was futile but felt driven to some kind of resistance, pathetic as it was.

She stilled as she heard Drazen's voice from inside the room, and strained to hear what he was saying, but then his voice rose in malicious delight. 'Not so high and mighty now, Commander. I hope you are finding your lodgings comfortable. I would hate to think you unhappy.'

Kess's heart sunk. They had Thrain. She knew they would, but some small part of her had been hoping he had escaped somehow.

After a pause, she heard Drazen speak again obviously not eliciting a response from the stony countenanced warrior. 'I know our young Chronicler had some complaints, but you know women, so picky.'

She heard a rattling sound and realised with horror that Thrain must be chained again. Kess let her knees buckle, hoping the demons grip would shift as her weight fell unexpectedly, yet their hold remained so tightly about her arms they were starting to cut off her circulation.

She wrinkled her nose against the feculence surrounding her – the dank, unpleasant hallway, smelling of malodorous growths that spawned in patches along the walls and ground, and the stench of the two demons that held her, who reeked of sulfuric brimstone and somehow – pain.

Then she heard Thrain shout.

This time she did yell, or try to through the gag which muffled her cry.

At some unheard signal, she was dragged into the room.

The first thing she saw was Drazen's back then as she was pulled further into the room, Thrain came into view. He was chained to a wall by both wrists which were about a metre in length and didn't allow him much range, not even to sit or crouch down without putting weight on his manacled wrists.

~

The hells spawn wrenched their grips upwards, bringing Kess up onto her toes to avoid having her shoulders dislocated.

Thrain pulled at the bindings holding him, trying to get closer to her.

She glanced at him, and though she had tight control of her emotions, he could read the fear in her eyes. Yet the look of bored disdain she levelled at Drazen, heartened him. She had a Guardians courage.

Drazen looked slyly from Thrain to Kess, delighting in their captivity. 'I thought you might like to see your charge,' his smile turned malicious, 'one last time that is.'

Kess's two demon captors wrenched her arms again with enough force that her back arched with pain. She gritted her teeth together, but remained silent.

'Treacherous Gargan!' Thrain snarled.

Drazen tisked at him, shaking his head. 'Now now, Guardian. A snake, am I? We haven't even begun. I thought you might like to see the extent of your failure to protect even one citizen of Athenaeum. Not to mention your fellow Guardians.' The blade he slid free from his belt glowed orange in the flickering light of the torch.

Kess raised her chin, meeting Drazen's eye, defiance shining from her like a beacon.

As the moustached former–Custodian took a step forward, she spat at him. The glob of phlegm hit him on his right cheek, spraying into his eye.

His face turned an ugly shade of puce as he wiped the saliva from his face with the sleeve of his robe. A muscle twitched under his left eye, and the veins across his temple and down his throat, distorted grotesquely, in response to his outrage. 'You shall regret that.'

She answered him with a mocking grin that Thrain recognised from her bonded Angel – Azrin.

Drazen's face twisted in an ugly sneer, making the tufts at the end of his moustache ride up like a little animal shifting on his face. The sound of the slap as he backhanded Kess, echoed through the room. His eyes gleamed with delight as his knuckles tore the soft skin around her mouth, drawing blood.

An involuntary grunt escaped her lips.

Thrain jerked the chains. 'Don't!'

Drazen raised his knife closer to Kess's face, twisting the blade back and forward, catching the metal in the light, making it gleam.

Thrain twisted, putting his back to her. Pulling the chains taut he wrapped them around his hands and he put his feet on the wall. Using the leverage of his bent legs he pushed out with all his strength, pulling at the same time with his arms trying to rip the fastening from the wall.

With his head tilted back he saw the perverted pleasure in Drazen's smile as he slid the blade down her neck. 'Don't you touch her!' he yelled, incensed by his inability to protect her.

The metal bracket on the wall shifted sending a small trickle of dust to the ground, but remained firmly within the stone. His feet slid down touching the ground, he turned, facing Kess again.

'Why not? She is here because of you. She is here because you never could learn your place.' Madness glinted in the former–Custodian's eyes.

The blade came closer to Kess's face, almost caressing her skin, then travelled down her jawline, to her throat. She pulled her head back, trying to put distance between the sharp metal and her skin, yet the movement only gave Drazen a better target, as his knife grazed over the point in her neck, where her pulse pumped strongly. The blade drew a shallow line across the soft skin, bringing bright red blood bubbling to the surface.

Thrain's eyes never left Kess's who locked gazes with him, refusing to acknowledge the presence of the hells spawn holding her arm, or Drazen in front of her. To his amazement she gave him a small smile, and when he saw it something inside him snapped.

'Drazen!' Thrain bellowed madly, yanking and jerking on his chain, uncaring of the damage it was doing to his wrists.

He strained against the shackles anchoring him to the wall. Muscles and veins bulged in his arms as he fought against the bonds which held him, the skin on his wrists tore and blood streamed down his arms, yet he remained tethered.

The former–Custodian looked maliciously at the blonde warrior before he cut a deeper line down her neck. A steady trickle of blood flowed down Kess's throat, pooling in the hollow of her collarbone. He flicked the knife to the other side of her neck and made an identical cut on the left side.

Kess's red gold hair shook around her as she tensed against the demon's grip on her arms, yet she remained still.

With an annoyed glance at her lack of response, the former–Custodian turned to Thrain. 'Where shall I cut next?' Drazen asked as he laid the width of the blade along her skin, tracing it down to the hollow of Kess's neck and across the covered expanse of her chest.

Grabbing a chunk of olive green material, he cut downwards through the neckline of her tailored shirt, then stared, frozen in shock.

He looked up at her, eyes narrowing as he realised what he was seeing was not a tattoo, but something else. 'This cannot be!'

'Cannot and should not seem to be liberal words these days,' Kess said, pointedly not looking at the two demons clutching her arms. Demons that were clearly obeying the orders of a Custodian.

Pride swelled in Thrain's chest. Like Miah he had spotted the potential dormant within Kess, yet unlike his next in charge, hadn't at first, been willing to give her a chance because she was a Chronicler. Now like a flower bud, that potential unfurled before him as a spectacular bloom.

Defiance blazed in her eyes, making them glow brilliant green like flawlessly cut emeralds and though tousled, she had never looked more amazing.

She was magnificent.

He let himself savour it, just for a moment, before clamping it down again.

~

Drazen hacked his knife down the front of Kess's shirt, uncaring as the tip of the blade nicked into her skin, with each movement. She held her breath, not daring to breathe for fear of the knife penetrating deeper.

The former–Custodian's breath caught visibly, as her body; which had become lean and toned from training, was exposed.

Kess's skin crawled as his eyes roved all over her.

But it was not the sight of her flesh that captivated him, but the cuneiform which covered her. The usually pale and ethereal writing flared in the flickering torchlight, appearing golden and luminescent. 'What is this?'

Kess heard the speculative calculation in his voice, and for the first time since their capture, felt panic rising within her. Belying the feelings raging inside her, she raised her head high and looked at him evenly, refusing to answer.

'No matter,' he tapped the knife against his chin thoughtfully. 'I know someone who will pay well for whatever it is that you are.' A fervent light entered his eyes, as avarice claimed what was left of his soul.

He turned to Thrain. 'Seems like you get your wish. She will be spared, for now,' his greedy eyes found hers. 'Though you may come to wish before too long, that I had killed you.'

She looked to Thrain, knowing the fear rising within her shone in her eyes, but was unable to contain it, until she saw the abject horror reflected within his grey gaze.

Steeling herself she clamped down on her emotions, determined to emulate a Guardians steadfastness. 'Karma's a bitch,' she told Drazen coldly. 'I will watch you die, for all that you have betrayed.'

The ice–cold certainty in her voice drained some of the bravado from the former–Custodian's face before he forced a grim smile. 'Brave words considering the circumstances.'

The smile that Kess returned, all teeth and full of cold promise, made Drazen step back.

At that moment, she looked deadlier than the demons restraining her.

~

With *Thrain*'s attention fully on his charge, it took a moment to register a flicker of movement on the stone wall behind Kess.

He focused on the area and saw the dark stone shift; something was moving behind her.

Thrain thrashed against the chains that held him as another demon appeared, materialising out of thin air.

Their chances of escaping vanished. Two demons they had a chance however remote; unarmed and contained as they were, but three made it all but impossible.

He opened his mouth, to yell a warning to Kess, yet she caught his eye, shaking her head slightly.

He blinked in amazement as the lizard demon grabbed the throat of the hells spawn holding Kess and twisted, snapping its neck with a violent crack.

Thrain watched in amazement unable to believe a demon had saved his charge, no matter what Kess had tried to convince him of.

~

Taking advantage of their distraction, Kess pulled her Angel blade, and slammed it under the jaw of the hairless demon pushing with all her strength so that the tip rammed through the top of its grotesque grey–skinned head. The protruding tusks clacked together as its mouth opened and closed, convulsively. 'Should have checked me for weapons,' she told the demon as it slid to the ground and flamed into non–existence.

Drazen looked horrified that she now faced him with a weapon of her own. 'But – you're a Chronicler, you shouldn't have any weapons!'

She laughed in his face. 'You want to talk to me about what Chroniclers should or shouldn't do.' She lunged forward aiming a killing stroke at Drazen's torso, but was blocked by a demon who lurched out of the darkness of the hallway. Its armoured turtle shell–like body would have turned any weapon aside, but Kess wasn't wielding an ordinary weapon towards it. This was an Angel blade, created to kill the spawn of Satan.

The blade carved through the rock hard plated bone like a knife through jelly, creating a deep slash from one side to the other. The creature lurched around to face her, opening its armoured beak revealing a black worm–like tongue. It hissed angrily at her as it fell, exploding in flames.

She stepped back, trying to avoid the inferno but as her hand brushed the flames, she felt a vacuum sensation pulling her down.

Drazen gaped as the three demons fell in a blaze of flames and fled from the room, knife clattering from his hand in his haste to leave.

~

Thrain watched horrified, as Kess's hand plunged into the hells fire.

He knew first–hand the agony those flames could bring, yet her face showed none of the pain he expected.

Her eyes became distant, like she was seeing more than the stone walls surrounding them. Her eyebrows rose in surprise, then a more thoughtful look crossed her face, before the descent flames died, leaving the room in near darkness.

He kept his eyes open, not wanting to lose sight of Kess, even for a moment. When they adjusted he saw she was still standing hand outstretched, pondering something. Knowing her, it would be rash and reckless.

The chains on his arms rattled, bringing back her attention. She whipped around, looking first for Drazen, then turned to him with an annoyed look, which slid from her face when she saw the blood running down his arms.

'Thrain.' Her obvious concern, her worry, sent a fire through him.

'Are you alright?' his voice was rough.

'Me?' She looked surprised for a moment at his concern. 'I'm fine. Look what you've done to yourself.' She looked at the chain, then ran to the door disappearing for a moment before returning empty handed. 'They always keep the key on a hook beside the door in the movies,' she said with a sheepish grin.

He shook his head, returning her smile, unable to help himself. One day he would have to watch some of these movies she kept referring to.

She lifted his wrist, twisting it gently around to see the lock, a determined look in her eyes. 'Do you trust me?'

‘With my life,’ he said without hesitation.

She nodded, expecting his response. ‘Hold your wrist against the wall and turn your head away.’

He ran his arm along the wall, extending it as far as he could, then angled his wrist so the lock rested against the stone. He pulled his hand back, as far away from the manacle as he could, then holding his arm in place, looked back at her with a nod.

She looked like an angelic warrior, red gold hair glowing, illuminated in a halo of light from the torch behind her. He turned his head away, enough to satisfy her but not enough that he couldn’t see her.

Watching her out of the corner of his eye he saw her grip the weapon backwards, so that her thumb rested against the base of the hilt, with her pinkie nearest the blade. Angling herself so that she stood in front of Thrain she pulled back her hand then brought her arm forwards in a quick movement, stabbing the lock. Any normal blade would have stopped as it hit the forged steel, yet the blade slid through the metal easily.

With a flick of his wrist, the damaged manacle clattered to the ground.

He extended his other arm, fighting the urge to rub the damaged skin which ached from the tight confinement. With a quick motion, she freed his other hand.

‘Let’s get out of here,’ she turned looking towards the doorway. ‘Treil.’

The lizard demon appeared from the dark hall, obviously having been standing guard. Never having been this close to a demon without attacking it, Thrain took a moment to study Kess’s forbandt.

It was tall, standing well over six feet in height, and looked similar to the Chameleon lizard for which it was named. The kîngkã’s skin colour shifted returning to a neutral shade, after mimicking the dull grey of the stones.

His gaze fell to the whip long tail, held aloft, which had a viscous point, sharp enough to skewer anything unfortunate enough to be in the way.

All in all, a totally ferocious, fearsome demon, yet Kess showed nothing but fondness for the creature.

Knowing their predicament would have ended a completely different way were it not for the kîngkã, and to appease Kess whose worry was evident as she glanced between the two of them, he spoke. 'Thank you kîn– ah Treil–' he amended using the name that Kess had called it, 'for helping us.'

With a quick glance to Kess, it nodded at some unspoken word between them. 'You are welcome, Guardian.'

'How did you get within the Haven?'

'The barrier which protects this place had been distorted allowing entry for my kind.' At Thrain's concerned look, Treil added. 'Fear not, Guardian. That distortion was rectified days ago.'

~

Kess saw Thrain glance at her, knew that he had to be thinking the same thing as her, that the barrier had been mended when she had bonded Irin–Obiex.

For the first time, she looked around the room. 'Miah?' she questioned.

Thrain shook his head. 'I haven't seen her since we were knocked out.'

Reversing her grip, she offered her Angel sword to the Commander whose weapons had been removed. When he started to shake his head, she huffed. 'You need to be armed. I have these.' She drew her sai, then strode from the room with Treil only a step behind, leaving Thrain to bring up the rear.

She stopped a few feet up the corridor, and peered through an open viewing slot in one of the doors. Finding nothing Kess continued along stopping at each door she passed.

The fifth slot she peered through brought a smile to her face. She slid back the bolt and charged through before Thrain could utter any cautions.

Moments later she returned with Miah in tow, looking relieved at finding her charge yet chagrined at having to be rescued by her.

‘Thank the Angels. Are you alright?’ Miah asked, as she exited the cell, indicating the blood on her neck.

With everything else going on, Kess had completely forgotten about the cuts that Drazen had made. She touched them, feeling the dried blood crusted to her skin. ‘What – oh yeah I’m fine.’

Miah’s eyes scanned her over, taking in her shredded, gaping top and the blood covering the other side of her neck. She raised an eyebrow but didn’t comment further, turning to Thrain instead. ‘Glad you got her out of there,’ she said, assuming his actions resulted in their escape.

‘Actually, that was Treil,’ he grimaced. ‘I too had to be rescued by Kess and her forbandt.’

Miah grinned. ‘Well at least I don’t feel so bad now,’ her levity faltered. ‘Drazen?’

‘Escaped. When they took out the demons.’ He nodded towards Kess and her kîngkã.

‘Damn it,’ Miah cursed. ‘Where are you going? The exit is that way,’ she said pointing in the opposite direction of where Kess was continuing along the hallway.

‘We can’t leave yet,’ Kess said calmly.

‘Why the hell not?’

‘Samael,’ she started.

‘–is probably dead, Miah finished. ‘No one has heard anything of him in weeks.’

‘Drazen said–’ Thrain tried to caution Kess, worried about her reaction should she find something unpleasant in one of the cells, instead of a live Guardian.

‘Drazen’s a liar!’ Kess shook her head stubbornly and set off down the hall. ‘Samael’s down here somewhere. I know it.’

‘Bollocks,’ Thrain swore before running after her.

The torch Kess had grabbed from the cell wall spluttered in her hand as she moved it from side to side searching. They were probably right, she should turn back, but something niggled at her, urging her forwards. It was the way the former–Custodian's eyes had shifted towards the door when he mentioned the warrior.

She had peered through the bars on several cells before she breathed a sigh of relief. She slid back the lock and flung the door open.

At the movement, the bulky Guardian within rose to his feet holding a hand out from his eyes, protecting them from the torch, blinding bright, after a week of confinement within the pitch–black cell.

'Kess?' he asked incredulously.

'Are you alright?'

'How did you get in here? Is anyone with you?' Only when he came to within a step of the door did she see his face.

'By the Angels, Samael!'

Though not a pretty man to begin with, his nose now hung crookedly on his face, swollen to twice its normal size. The whole left side of his face was a mass of livid purple bruising apart from his right eye and cheekbone which were swollen, red and angry. Some of the contusions were fresh, though some were mottled from days of healing.

Kess had no medical knowledge or training, but thought from the swelling that his cheekbone could be fractured. She couldn't imagine the pain he must be in, but he was a Guardian and took it in his stride.

'Kess, what are you doing here?' he asked again.

Before she could answer, Samael's attention shifted to the warrior who had moved up behind her at her exclamation. 'Sub–Commander.'

Miah gave the man mountain a quick scan checking his wounds.

'Just stiff,' he said, watching her assessing him. 'What's going on?' He peered past her, eyes catching sight of Thrain, who stood a few paces down the corridor watching for signs of attack.

'Commander.' Samael's words were both a statement and a question as to what was going on.

'We'll explain later. Right now, it's time to leave,' Miah said, glancing up and down the hall anxiously.

'You know there are demons within the Haven? They're working for–'

'Drazen, yeah we know,' Kess finished. She glanced around and saw that Treil had vanished, which was probably for the best, they needed to escape quickly, not stand around having the good–demon versus bad–demon conversation with Samael. She concentrated on her forbandt and found her bonded demon not far away.

Thrain led the way with Kess in the middle despite her protests. They walked quickly following the corridor to a closed door. Thrain put his head to the door holding a finger to his lips for silence.

He gave a hand signal to Samael – a fist with two fingers extended.

Understanding the command, the man mountain grabbed Kess's shoulder pulling her back behind him as Thrain threw open the door and ran into Kisho.

'Thrain!' The samurai warrior exhaled in relief. 'Is Kess with you?' he asked trying to peer past his shoulder.

'Back here,' she responded working her way around the mountainous Guardian.

'Samael!' Kisho exclaimed. 'What the bloody hell happened to you?'

'Kept trying to escape,' Samael shrugged.

'Who else is with you?' Thrain asked, business as usual, cutting over their chatter.

'Zuri's patrolling. Here, I think these belong to you,' he said, handing over Thrain's sword and axe. 'I found them while I was waiting for you lot to return,' he said with a grin.

The commander took his weapons, clearly glad to have them back. He handed Kess back her Angel blade with a nod of thanks.

'Ready?' Kisho questioned.

At Thrain's nod, Miah led the way out.

CHAPTER 41

The Battle for Athenaeum

Miah, first in line, held out her hand halting everyone's ascent of the stone stairs. Signalling to Kisho, the warrior flipped open the doorway, and they leapt forwards.

Behind Thrain, she was close enough to hear Miah's call of all clear.

As Kess emerged back into the very early hours of morning, she saw Zuri jog into view from around the corner of the building.

'About time you showed,' the Amazonian warrior drawled, but underlying her sarcasm, Kess heard relief. 'Nice to see you topside again, Commander.'

'Report.' Thrain, as always, had no time for pleasantries.

Zuri's brow furrowed. 'It's madness. I was with Wessler – who was frantic about Kess's disappearance – when a force of Guardians, about a hundred strong came past armed to the teeth.' She gave the commander a grim look. 'They had demons with them.' She shook her head as if despite witnessing it, she still couldn't believe it. 'Wessler and I were far enough back that they didn't spot us. After they passed I sent him to find Cadder, and rouse the Guardians still with us. I didn't want you walking out into all this unprepared so I waited here.'

'I see you haven't missed out on all the fun,' Miah said dryly, inclining her head towards several scorch marks burnt into the grass.

'A few demons came sniffing around.' Kess heard the delight in Zuri's voice.

‘Kess, come here.’ Miah searched her pockets pulling out a small roll of white medical tape. She gestured for Kess to hold the pieces of her ruined shirt together and wrapped tape over her ribs and around her back creating a four–inch wide binding that covered her exposed torso, whilst still allowing her freedom of movement.

A sharp whistle drew everyone’s attention.

Kisho stood at the corner of the building closest to them, standing lookout. ‘You’re not going to believe this,’ he said moments before a small group came into view led by Bannen.

Hands flying to weapons the warriors watched the band approach. They were obviously not a threat otherwise Bannen wouldn’t have led them over, but even so her Guardians never took chances.

Kess’s eyes widened as she saw the familiar faces of Abram, Leora and Kadence, who though holding herself a bit stiffly kept pace with the other Aldoak–Chroniclers and their appointed young Guardians.

‘What are you all doing here?’ Kess stepped forward, determined to intervene before her zealous companions.

‘We overheard the Guardians – they said demons are in the grounds,’ Leora said, in a voice that sounded like she wanted Kess to deny it.

Kess saw a short sword sheathed at her side, and wondered where she had gotten it from, until she saw a Potential shadowing her – Deserai – she thought her name was, and knew that somehow Leora had talked the warrior into arming her.

‘Which is why you should be somewhere else, somewhere safe,’ Kess said, taking a step towards Leora.

Suddenly Kess was surrounded by a ring of Guardian bodies, weapons drawn. ‘Oh, for Angels’ sake, they won’t hurt me.’

‘No,’ Zuri said calmly. ‘But they might.’ She was looking at the tree line where shadowy figures had started to emerge.

‘What–’ Leora started.

‘Two rings. Six on the outer,’ Thrain barked indicating the older, more experienced Guardians. ‘The rest will form the inner ring, with Kess and the Chroniclers at the centre.’

‘Inside the ring,’ Kess yelled at the dozen bewildered faces.

‘Kess, in,’ Thrain yelled.

‘Not a chance, Commander,’ she said seriously. ‘There’s only six of you.’

‘We are Guardians.’

Kess sighed. ‘But–’

‘No,’ he said stubbornly. ‘You are our charge.’

‘Even the best can be overcome by numbers.’

Thrain started to speak again but Samael overrode him. ‘She’s right, Commander. We need to hold until we can find the others. Besides,’ he said looking at her, ‘she holds them like she knows how to use them, and I’m sure this lot haven’t wasted any time training her.’ He indicated Kisho, Zuri and Miah.

Thrain scowled, but surprisingly didn’t argue further.

Kisho ushered the last of the now frightened Chroniclers into a ring formed by their partnered Guardians, ignoring their protests that they could help. She saw several awkwardly holding short swords, which they obviously had no idea how to use, and which she had no time to even show them the basics.

‘Protect them,’ Kisho told his young brethren, as he joined the outer ring.

The darkness of the early morning was lit only with sporadic building lights, interspersed with ground lights marking the paths. Yet it was enough to identify the approaching figures as clearly not human, with too many arms or legs, and strangely shaped heads and bodies.

‘Here we go,’ Bannen muttered, his excitement obvious as he whirled his sword around in a flashy display.

Miah to her right grinned a fierce tight–lipped smile, clearly looking forward to the fight.

She watched the distance close. Tightening her grips on the sai’s handles.

30 feet.

20.

10.

A fully formed demon, looking like a grotesque goldfish, with huge rounded eyes bulging from the side of its head, attacked her with the wickedly pointed end of its fin–like appendage. Its grey skin was coated with globules of slime which slid continuously over its strange body in a never–ending stream.

Repulsed Kess thrust out her sai blocking the flipper with her right while her left pierced deep into the soft skin of its belly, right up to the prongs. Instead of roaring or grunting, the hells spawn opened its mouth in a silent scream. She pulled her sai back and kicked the creature forcefully enough that it fell, and didn't get up again.

A few seconds later, silhouetting the outline of the next demon it died in an inferno of flame.

Demons pressed in all around them.

Her own weapons flashed again meeting the next attack. As Kess parried a particularly vicious strike from a tick–like creature, she flinched as the hells spawn exploded in flame, with one of Miah's throwing knives in its eye.

Glancing over, she gave a nod of thanks to the warrior.

They kept moving, pushing forward, trying to find the bulk of the Guardian numbers. But all they found were demons.

There must be thousands of them in the Haven, Kess thought grimly. She hoped the Chroniclers had sense enough to stay out of the way and hide somewhere safe.

Though they started with an outer and an inner ring to protect the young Chroniclers, with the barrage of demons attacking them, the Potentials had merged with their circle, helping to keep the line from breaking.

Never far from her side, Thrain and Zuri guarded her right, with Miah and Kisho on her left. Samael and Bannen were scattered through the line of younger warriors, helping them maintain their edge.

'Leora!' Kess shouted, when she found her path momentarily free of demons. As the Chronicler rushed to her side she said, 'Keep an eye out.

If you see any demons approaching, or see the rest of the Guardians yell out.'

The caramel–skinned girl nodded, and set up three others within their group, each watching a direction.

Kess felt a flaring in her bonds seconds before six figures materialised in front of them.

She heard a scream behind her and turned, knowing from the bulge in the seventh blaere who she would find.

The bunched Chroniclers fought against each other, panicked by a demon who had materialised from thin air, in their midst – even though that demon was standing immobile looking at Kess.

'It's alright. She's a friend,' she exclaimed, looking behind the tall chameleon demon towards the Chroniclers.

'A demon is your friend?' a freckled red–haired young girl said incredulously.

'Are they with you too?' Abram pointed out her forbandt Angels cleaving and hacking paths through the hellions.

'Yes.' She shrugged, turning back towards the battle, not having time for lengthy explanations.

Bannen cursed, swinging his sword around when he saw the kîngkã near the defenceless Chroniclers.

'No!' Kess screamed, bringing her sai up catching the strike in the guard. The force of the blow numbed her hands, yet she held on. 'She's with me.'

She saw the strain on Bannen's face as he struggled to understand, then heard Miah exclaim laughing, 'Treil's with Kess. She takes in any stray that comes her way, doesn't she Kai?'

'I'm a bloody Angel, not a stray!' Kai yelled indignantly coming to stand in front of Kess, as a bewildered Bannen rejoined the line.

She ignored the shocked gasps from behind her.

Are you okay? he asked through their blaere.

Yes. Aloud she asked, 'How did you get in?'

'The Obiex is down.'

Panic flooded through Kess, as she sought her last bond. *Irin, are you alright?*

Kess, did your Angels get through?

You let them in? Thank you.

'Irin let you in.' She grinned up at the Angel she had first bonded, who now guarded her right.

'Well give him our thanks,' he added nonchalantly as if he weren't in the middle of a battle.

'If your Obiex let them in, can he expel the demons?' Thrain called, as he dispatched a mottled brown skinned creature with a mouth full of hundreds of sharp spindly teeth, that continued to snap at him even with his sword through its chest. Then without slowing, he launched into a complicated series of manoeuvres which left a disgusting cockroach demon in several pieces before it flamed out.

Irin, can you expel the demons?

Their bond was quiet for a moment. *There are too many. I am sorry. I will do what I can.*

Thank you.

'He said there are too many for him to remove. But he will do what he can.' Kess yelled, as she spun back around catching a flash of movement right near her. A hellion charged, neatly dodging the weapons flashing around her, then lunged straight at her, mouth wide open.

Something tugged at Kess's side, yet she couldn't spare a glance, struggling as she was against a demon whose fangs she could barely keep from her face.

The viscous mouthful of teeth inched closer, sending a wave of foul breath, like rotted meat, in her face. It pushed forward again, so close now, the drips of its saliva struck her cheek and chest, burning her skin.

Then the demon roared, pulling back in pain.

It took Kess a moment to comprehend the respite, until she saw her knife protruding from its chest. Not a fatal wound, but enough to distract it.

She glanced around, and saw Leora at her side, a triumphant look on her face, until the demon lashed out knocking her to the ground.

The Chroniclers who had huddled together in fear only moments before, surged forwards hacking and slashing wildly at the demon who had hurt their friend. The creature collapsed to its knees under the attack, bleeding from stabs all over its body before erupting in a geyser of flame.

Stunned, Kess watched, thinking the warrior blood of ages past still flowed strongly in some of the current day Chroniclers.

Kess glanced over her shoulder seeking her Guardians, needing to know they were alright, and saw Kisho leap forwards, in a move that was as graceful as any dance. Using his momentum, he struck the creature in the face with his fist, then impaled it with the sword in his other hand. The creature crumpled, fire exploding from it before it even hit the ground.

Miah fought at his side, and while being every bit as deadly as the commander, she was more graceful, and tended to flourish her strikes, using twists and turns to gain momentum, like a ballerina with swords pirouetting her way across the stage.

Then silence, as the last demon fell.

Path cleared again, they were about to move on when a group of Guardians appeared in a clearing nearly a hundred feet ahead, led by a pale–haired warrior.

Thrain leant to his left and murmured something to Bannen who nodded, and ran towards a group, the leader of which he obviously knew and trusted.

After a few brief words, the pale–haired warrior and his group of thirty sprinted over, not slowing until they were several feet away.

'Commander!' There was obvious relief in the leader's voice.

'Cadder,' Thrain nodded a greeting.

Kess recognised the name, remembered Conall blanching at the prospect of being punished by the fearsome warrior. Seeing him now, she didn't blame her fallen Guardian; his face was even sterner than Thrain's.

Cadder's gaze flitted around the group assessing, halting as he saw Samael. 'You look like hell,' he said gruffly. This close up she saw his hair was so light, it was almost white.

Samael smirked. 'You have no idea. I was rescued by a Chronicler.'

The pale–haired warrior raised an eyebrow, his sharp gaze seeking her out amongst the group. He gave Kess a short nod, acknowledging her actions, before he turned and looked at Thrain grimly. 'Any idea how they got in?'

'Drazen,' Thrain spat.

Cadder didn't blink at the revelation of the Custodian's betrayal. 'The Guardians have mobilised,' he advised. 'All Chroniclers have been evacuated to the Vault, though I have a team sweeping for stragglers. Three battalions are sweeping the woods dispatching any hellions they find.'

Kess thought he had done well under the circumstances, but Thrain only nodded, as if he expected no less. 'Set another team to guard outside the Vault, and two teams at the gate to make sure no more hells spawn get in.'

Cadder gave a nod, and sprinted with his warriors towards the gate.

At Thrain's command their group continued on, searching for more hells spawn to kill. They rounded a corner and found themselves on the edge of the green, a large open expanse amidst the buildings, and saw battle everywhere.

Guardians fighting demons.

Demons fighting other demons, she saw with some bewilderment.

She gasped in horror, as she saw a Guardian strike down another Guardian from behind, hacking at the fallen warrior several times before stalking away. 'Lucifer's horns,' she cursed. 'Did you see that?'

'Yes,' Lumiel said sadly. 'Evil corrupts everywhere, even amongst those most honourable.'

'They are *Verità Scuro*?' Even though she had been told they existed Kess couldn't understand what would drive someone to betray their brethren.

The Haven–loyal Guardians, hard pressed already, were soon fighting on all fronts, having to watch for their own as well as the demons.

Sadness ripped through her.

‘This isn’t right,’ she sought out Thrain, and found his face twisted in anguish as he watched his kinsfolk slay each other; in viscous attack, or regretful self–defence.

‘Move!’ he shouted, wiping his face clear of emotion as he caught her eye, but she saw her own horror reflected in his eyes still.

Clearly he had no wish to join this battle, and she couldn’t blame him.

They moved around Athenaeum’s grounds, assisting the Haven–loyal where they could; now easily identifiable having tied bits of coloured cloth to their upper arms.

Their circle, stretched and distorted at times as individuals shifted about in their skirmishes, remained unbroken. Though Kess saw, to her sorrow, that it was smaller than when they had started out, with several of the Potentials having fallen under the unrelenting press of demons. A quick headcount of the Aldoak–Chroniclers, showed they too were missing some of their number, with only ten remaining.

At times, the path in front was clear, and they covered ground quickly; at others, they were surrounded, fighting not only demon but the Guardians and Chroniclers who sided with them.

Kess took another step forward and stumbled, almost landing on the body of a young man, no older than herself, a traitor, by the knife in his hand. She looked at his face, eyes glazed in death, and wondered how he could look so ordinary.

‘Kess?’ Thrain yelled.

Kess, Kai thought.

Both voices, aloud, and in her head, were enough to snap Kess out of the daze she realised she had been in.

She glanced up, and saw her Guardians dispatching the last of this batch of demons.

By unspoken agreement, the group didn’t move on immediately, catching their breaths, binding bleeding wounds, and giving their tired arms a moment’s respite.

Samael, another cut streaming blood down the side of his face giving him a grizzly macabre appearance, stood still as Kisho tied a tourniquet around his muscled upper thigh, trying to stop the bleeding from a gash above his knee.

Miah too was injured, sporting a bandage around her upper arm, already stained with blood.

Bannen, had a number of shallow cuts, though like the others he was rubbing the Guardian–issued cream into them, to prevent demon toxins from spreading through their bodies.

Her Angels, not needing rest like they did, had spread out, keeping a watchful eye on their surrounds.

'Time to move,' Thrain told their group after several minutes had passed.

She saw, to her relief, that he was unmarked by wounds. His eyes met hers, just for a moment, and she knew he was scanning her for injuries, just as she had done with him.

The Chroniclers in their midst had taken the opportunity to sit, though she saw that a few of them too were stained with blood.

Leora, ever watchful, saw her worried glance. 'Blood from those they tried to help,' she confirmed.

'The others?' Kess asked, unable to help the responsibility she felt for the missing Chroniclers.

'Tried to help their Guardians when they fell,' Abram said sadly.

Kess laid a hand upon the pair's shoulders, then turned before they could see the moisture gathering in her eyes, joining the Guardians as they formed their ring configuration again.

The path before them, clear only moments ago, now swarmed with demons, and in their midst was Custodian Drazen.

Standing grimly at his side were several Chroniclers and Head Captols, who although looking at the demons surrounding them with aversion, didn't move away. She recognised a blonde amongst them; Lisbeth.

'You were imprisoned for crimes against the Haven,' the former–Custodian screamed wildly, spying their group.

A gap of only twenty feet separated the two groups, yet incensed by Drazen's complete and utter betrayal, Kess stepped forward, flanked by a pair of Angels and a pair of Guardians.

'You would speak to me of crimes against a Haven?' Kess's voice rang out. 'It was you, wasn't it? Who sabotaged the Obiex. Who let the hells spawn enter our Haven? Who let in the demon that killed my mother.'

'Ah, Anna. She was lovely you know.' There was something in Drazen's eyes when he mentioned her mother's name, something feral and vindictive.

'*You* betrayed her,' Kess realised. 'You sold her to the demons who broke her.' The malicious smile which lit his face confirmed her hunch. 'Why?'

'I heard she fought like a banshee when she was captured. She took weeks to break, you know. I arrived later, but oh the things we did to her; mind, spirit,' he cast a wicked glance at her, 'body. She endured it for weeks, but she talked – eventually,' he smiled at Kess leaving her to imagine the worst. 'She told us all sorts of delightful things but never a word about you.' Drazen looked at her speculatively. 'No matter what they did to her. The others thought this normal parental protection, but the look in her eyes when your name was mentioned, that brief flash of,' he paused trying to find the right word, '–fear before she clamped down, well that piqued my interest. So, when you arrived I kept an eye on you, and my suspicions about you have proven correct, haven't they?'

Kess's gaze flitted to Lisbeth, who catching her attention smirked.

Drazen saw the exchange. 'Yes, your *friend* has been a wealth of information,' he chortled.

Kess's view to the former–Custodian was blocked as a wall of Angels suddenly separated them. Anger tightened their faces into tight masks of barely controlled fury.

Her fury.

Realising the danger that several wrathful Celestials could cause, she clamped down on her emotions, sealing them away from her bonds.

Kai's eyes flicked to hers quickly, but he didn't lower his weapons, his gaze returning to the demon horde in front of them.

She looked to the other five furious Angels; Azrin with a sword in each hand looked ready to combust with fury, even Lumiel splattered in demon ichor seemed ready to tear Drazen limb from limb.

Peace, forbandt.

Drazen's eyes gazed over them, assuming them Guardians, buoyed in his confidence of being surrounded by demons.

Turning her attention back to Drazen, she saw, perhaps for the first time, his true self – the arrogance, cruelty and madness which almost oozed from him.

She focused on the Chroniclers flanking him, addressing them instead, 'It is not too late to turn from the path Drazen has taken. Look at what he has brought upon the Haven,' she spread her arms wide, indicating the demons surrounding them.

One or two shifted their feet anxiously, but all remained where they were.

'So be it,' Kess intoned, with a finality that seemed to echo against the buildings. 'I renounce you as a Custodian of Athenaeum. I renounce you as Head Captols, Captols and Chroniclers of Athenaeum. May the Angels have mercy upon you, for we surely will not.'

Unfazed, Drazen spoke to an ape–like demon, taller than the others, standing beside him. 'Kill the commander, and the rest,' he pointed to Kess. 'But I want her alive.'

The giant ape let out a mad holler and as one the demons surged forwards; howling, yipping and hissing their excitement, their need to kill.

The Guardians shared a glance and surged past Kess, raining death amongst the demons. Her Angels formed two lines of defence, protecting the Chroniclers.

Kai looked about to protest as Kess joined him in the second line, however took one look at her face and said only, 'Stay beside me.'

She wiped away the sweat that trickled down her forehead absently with the back of her hand, waiting for the demons to break through.

Kess anxiously watched the warriors, yet her eyes drifted most often to Thrain, who was swinging his axe against the demons in a maelstrom of fury, dancing death amongst any hells spawn foolish enough to enter his range. Every movement was fluid, yet infinitely powerful. He was beautiful to watch. Kess smirked to herself, she'd never tell him that though.

In the first row; Lumiel, Kasbeel, Nakir and Caliel, were soon pressed as more and more hellions appeared.

Kess, flanked by Azrin and Kai made up the last line of defence, in front of the young Chroniclers she felt responsible for.

Alone, Treil guarded their rear.

Kess's heart stammered as she saw Samael lurch forwards, almost pulled from his feet. He hadn't seen the demon approaching, as his right eye was swollen shut.

Azrin and Kai shared a look, Kai nodded and Azrin vanished, appearing amidst the Guardians and helped the man mountain regain his footing. His swords became a blur of shining metal, and the air in front of him glowed with the hells fire of the demons he slew.

The front line of Guardians buckled as the demons pressed forward driven mad in their lust for violence.

'Miah!' Kess cried as she saw a demon clamp down on her shoulder. She started to move but was stopped by Kai. 'I will go,' *Stay here,* he waited for her nod before vanishing, appearing at the warriors injured side, cutting and slashing any hellion that approached.

Kess attention was drawn to the left flank as she spied a gigantic snake demon slither past the occupied warriors, tongue flicking as it scented the air, eyes fixated on the Aldoak–Chroniclers.

Kess sheathed her sai, and pulled a knife from her boot, throwing it within seconds of palming it.

The snake moved at the last second, narrowly avoiding a killing shot as the blade glanced off the side of its neck. It hissed at her angrily, opening its mouth wide revealing two fangs, nearly the size of the blade she'd just thrown.

She pulled her axe next, and like she had practised with Thrain, threw it, sending it caterwauling head over end nicking the skin of the snake's neck, sending a chunk of its flesh flying, enraging the demon–snake further.

She drew the Angel blade.

With a flick of its tail, the creature sped towards her as fast as a loosed arrow. She waited until the last moment before swinging the blade in an arc, knowing that if she missed, she wouldn't have the chance to strike again.

Kess froze, blade aloft, panting, as she looked down.

A river of black demonic blood gushed from the neck of the decapitated creature.

Kess, felt a movement near her, rather than heard it, and spun, finding herself face to face with a Chronicler, not part of her group.

The sword she'd started to swing froze.

He was the enemy, but she couldn't bring herself to strike. His eyes were wide, breaths coming in gasps as he back peddled, stammering, 'Pp–please.'

Her blade fell to her side. 'Go.'

Not waiting for her to change her mind, the Chronicler ran away, looking over his shoulder only once, to make sure she wasn't following.

She turned and found Thrain's eyes upon her. 'I – he–'

'I understand,' he said, eyes softening. 'Just because he has betrayed his values, doesn't mean that you should also.'

Side by side they took on the next demon, working together when Thrain saw her strength beginning to ebb.

Kai who had stayed with Miah assisting her dispatch a particularly nasty Rask, returned, guarding her other side.

And then, just when she thought she couldn't raise her arms one more time, couldn't counter one more strike, the space in front of her was clear.

Kess looked around, barely comprehending the emptiness.

She let herself drop to the ground, sitting heavily on the grass. Her eyes, like her arms, were leaden, and she fought the urge to lay down and give in to the sleep her body craved.

The sun shone high in the sky overhead, surprising her, it must be mid–morning. She hadn't even noticed the dawn. No wonder she was exhausted.

Then she heard a voice which had her on her feet in a second, weariness forgotten.

Drazen.

Somehow, amidst all the violence and death, he had managed to survive.

CHAPTER 42

The Cost of Victory

Kess saw him standing thirty feet away, scowling distastefully at the Guardians who had surrounded him.

Everything fell away. Except him.

She walked closer.

And saw the exact moment that he noticed her, when his lips curled in a mocking smile.

She clenched her fists at her sides, nails breaking through the skin of her palms, as she tried to remain calm.

That's when he moved.

Drazen pulled a dagger from the hidden folds of his robe.

She heard a yell pierce the air.

Saw the glint of silver as he hurled it straight at her, and twisted trying to deflect its path, which was aimed at her heart.

She heard the thunk of knife hitting flesh, its sound unmistakable, and waited for the inevitable pain to come.

Yet it didn't.

She turned and looked around, eyes widening in horror as she saw a prone figure on the ground.

She walked around the body, feeling as though she waded through a bog, movements sluggish and slowed. She knew who lay before her from the mop of thick brown hair.

Soft brown eyes looked up at her, and although filled with pain, determination shone in them.

'Oh, Abram, what have you done?' Kess asked as she knelt down beside him, blinking back the tears blurring her vision.

'Did I get there in time?' His voice was as soft as a whisper as a thin trickle of blood ran from the corner of his mouth.

Having nothing else, she wiped it away with her hand.

Kess felt someone kneel beside her, saw the shaved sides of his hair out of the corner of her eye.

'You acted like a Guardian and saved someone you cared about,' Thrain said softly, answering for her, because she couldn't.

A smile lit Abram's lips briefly before they tightened in a grimace of pain.

'Why?' she whispered. 'I'm not worth it.'

'You are our hope.' The whisper of words died as his eyes glazed over, and his breaths stopped. One last trickle of blood ran from his mouth and then that stopped too.

Forgetting everything around her, Kess lowered her head, letting her tears fall unashamedly.

'Why?' she repeated softly.

'Because he cared about you,' Thrain said gently.

'And because of that he is dead,' she said harshly. 'Just like my mother. Just like Conall,' she shrugged away Thrain's hand which had come to rest on her shoulder. 'I bring nothing but death to those around me. You would be better off, safer, as far away from me as you can get.'

Thrain stiffened beside her visibly. 'Don't dishonour their sacrifice. The boy was right, you are worth their sacrifice, any sacrifice. We believe you will play an important role in what's to come.'

What's to come. Her mind refused to process that.

Kess stood so suddenly Thrain was left on his knees.

Her grief solidifying into molten rage, fiery hot and acidic, burning a path through her where her grief had been only moment ago.

She whipped her short sword from the sheath at the small of her back and advanced to where Drazen struggled, vainly trying to escape the vice grips of Samael and Bannen.

Seeing the wrath in her eyes they pushed the former–Custodian to his knees, and held him there awaiting her judgement.

'Go on. Do it!' Drazen hissed, looking up to where she towered over him like an angry avenging Goddess. Madness raged in his eyes, urging her on.

She shook with rage, with the need to remove this foul creature from this sacred place.

'Kess. Don't,' Thrain spoke softly, laying a warm hand on her shoulder. She tried to shrug it off determined not to let him talk her out of killing Drazen. But he firmed his grip and spun her around, looking at her with grey eyes softened with concern.

'Don't do it,' he repeated. 'He deserves death but do not burden your conscience. He is not worth it. Taking a human life is different from a demon's, it will haunt you. That's why you couldn't kill that Chronicler.' Something in his voice cracked the battle rage which had consumed her, clearing her head, allowing her to think.

The former–Custodian smiled, clearly thinking he had won.

'As Commander of the Guardians, Last Defender of Athenaeum, I charge you, Drazen von Braun with treason against the Haven. With the murder of all the Guardians and Chroniclers who have died today and in the days preceding due to direct actions taken by you,' he glanced at the battered group behind him. 'Of consorting with demons. Of desecrating the Obiex. Of bringing death and destruction to a Haven. For the direct murder of Chronicler Abram Hadlee.'

'I second this charge as Sub–Commander of Athenaeum,' Miah stated, stepping forwards beside Thrain.

'And I, as a Chronicler of Athenaeum,' Leora stated, taking a step towards them, tears flowing freely down her face.

Almost as one the whole assemblage added their voices of assent, condemning the man who had brought chaos upon them.

The smile slid sickeningly from his face as he looked around and saw only hostile faces. 'The Highest shall rise again and you shall wish for your deaths on that day. You are all lost.' He spat contemptuously towards Thrain.

'By majority of vote you have been found guilty of the charges. Because of the seriousness of the crimes, you are sentenced to death,' Thrain uttered, clearly taking no joy in what he was about to do.

He drew out his sword, looked to the heavens as if asking forgiveness, and with a mighty swing sent Drazen's head bouncing to the ground.

Silence reigned around them.

In honour of their fallen.

At the death of their enemy.

CHAPTER 43

Honouring the Fallen

Kess was not the only one who had tears streaming down her cheeks as Custodian Pendry inserted her torch into the wooden platform.

The massive pyre had taken all day to construct and Kess's arms still ached with fatigue yet she and her forbandt, Guardians and the Aldoak–Chroniclers had helped until the last log had been laid.

As Pendry stepped back a dozen Guardians and Chroniclers moved forward thrusting their own torches into the timber. The fuel soaked wood combusted with several loud 'woompfs'.

Within seconds the flames rose high, mercifully concealing the muslin wrapped bodies. The bodies of the dead traitors were also in the pyre, laid away from their own fallen for whom they mourned.

The heat was intense and Kess shuffled back a few steps to distance herself from the searing heat.

She glanced at Thrain who stood to her right.

Anyone else would just see his anger; the flinty hardness of his stony grey eyes, the corded muscle in his cheek where he clenched his jaw tightly. Yet she saw his pain and sorrow as well.

Miah stood to Thrain's right watching the burning pyre through watery eyes. Surprisingly Wessler stood with her, rather than with the other higher–ranking Chroniclers.

Kess watched the flames dance high, consuming everything around them. All of Athenaeum's surviving loyal inhabitants surrounded the inferno.

When the tide of the battle had turned the traitorous Chroniclers and Guardians fled the Haven, before they could be hunted down. The demons though had fought until the last one died, growling with a sword through its chest.

Kess watched the shifting tongues of orange flame until she realised she was searching for Abram, lying somewhere amongst the dead.

Kai put his arm around her, drawing her close to his chest.

Concealing her emotions took concentration, something she wasn't capable of today, her mind and body were drained to the point of exhaustion, and so her bonded Angels felt her every emotion like it was their own.

Lumiel wept openly, her beautiful face contorted in grief at the loss of so many lives.

Though many had seen Treil fighting at Kess's side, it was too soon to have a demon openly in their midst, after fighting against her kind. The kîngkã waited in the woods close enough to see without being seen.

Surprisingly, Kess felt Azrin standing with her in her vigil and felt a surge of pride at the Angel who once hadn't hesitated in trying to kill her.

Thrain broke away from her, taking one step forward; then another, then a third until Kess feared his clothes would start to singe. He knelt, settling one knee on the ground. The Guardians all around the circle stepped forward creating their own inner ring closer to the pyre.

'I am the sword and shield,' Thrain said solemnly.

The warriors joined their commander completing the Guardian oath honouring their dead. 'I am the dagger and the bow. I stand till the last. And to the last I fight. My final breath given freely. To protect the light and the light's flesh.' A hushed silence fell, as their final words rang out into the night.

Kess tried to swallow away the lump which rose in her throat making it hard to breathe.

Forty–three Guardians and seventeen Chroniclers had died and she knew Thrain felt every loss keenly.

As the fire started to burn down most left seeking their beds.

Yet she remained with the Guardians, keeping vigil over their dead.

Kess watched the pyre, until nothing but smouldering embers remained. She felt numb, like she was no longer connected to her body, and blinked firmly trying to force herself to stay awake, but the fuzzy light–headed feeling didn't go away.

Her vision blurred and she swayed.

Kai's face entered her vision, full of concern, lips moving.

She knew he was saying something, yet her head felt like it had been stuffed with cotton wool making everyone sound like they were talking from a distance.

~

Kess's thoughts sluggishly returned and with it the ache in every part of her body.

She ached in muscles she didn't even know she had before now. Her mind shied away, preferring the blissful nothingness she'd had only moments before, but the murmur of voices caught her attention.

'Are you sure, Angel? It's been more than twelve hours. She hasn't even moved.' Thrain's voice filled with worry.

'Peace, Guardian. She is awake,' Kai responded calmly.

You'd better open your eyes before he has an apoplexy, he suggested through their blære.

Reluctantly Kess did as her Angel suggested and opened her eyes blinking a few times to clear the exhaustive sting from them.

Much to her embarrassment, her room contained not only Thrain and Kai, but Miah who sat on the edge of the bed; Leora, curled up asleep on the corner of the mattress, and Zuri who looked like she had stopped mid–pace.

'Is this all you could muster for my waking?' Kess asked wryly, wondering how long they'd all been there watching, while she slept.

She had a vague recollection of arms carrying her but nothing else. 'Is everyone else alright?' She worried about the faces not present. 'Kisho?'

'Is getting food. We had to make him leave. His stomach was gurgling so loud we thought it would wake you,' Zuri said, a relieved smile on her face as she looked at her charge.

Kess reached out to her forbandt bonds and breathed a sigh of relief as she found them all safe, and mostly still within the Haven. 'Treil, you can come out now.' She looked past everyone to the wall behind where Zuri had been pacing.

The Amazonian warrior's hand twitched towards her weapon as Treil materialised, and Leora who had woken from the sound of their voices gasped.

Treil made her way over to the bed where Kess struggled to push herself up and laid a taloned hand gently against her arm. 'Are you well?'

'Tired,' she admitted. 'And I ache in more places than I care to admit, but I'm okay. What happened?'

'You swooned as the ashes were being gathered,' Kisho said, as he entered the room, speaking around a mouthful of the foot long roll he held in his hand. He seemed unsurprised to see the kîngkã. 'Here, I brought you this.'

Kess caught the double decker bar he threw at her grimacing at the ache in her arms. Her cheeks reddened at his comment. 'I didn't swoon,' she retorted.

'Well you did a fair impression of it then,' he said with a smile, as he placed a hand to his forehead and threw his head back. 'Though at least you managed to make it through a demon attack without putting your arm into one of their mouths.'

'You know that you aren't literally meant to push yourself until you collapse,' Miah interrupted, voice tight with worry.

Guilt nestled in Kess's breast. They had more than enough to deal with without worrying about her as well.

She saw that they had all showered and changed, and fresh bandages were visible on them including Thrain, whose wrists had a thin wrap of white around them, from the damage he'd done to them when he'd been manacled in the dungeon by Drazen.

The growth of stubble shadowing Thrain's face indicated he hadn't left her side. Though surely he had more pressing Guardian things to do than watch her sleep. 'How long was I out?'

'Nearly fourteen hours,' Thrain said, voice tight with suppressed emotion.

'What?! What's been going on? Have you found where all the Scuro Chroniclers and Guardians went? Have new Custodians been elected? Are there many wounded?' The questions poured out of her.

Apart from the traitor Drazen, Kess had heard that another Custodian had died during the attack. Wilmoth's body had been found outside the Archive, dragged into one of the bushes, obviously by his demonic attacker who'd torn out his throat.

'Where are Azrin and the others?' While she didn't ask anyone in particular, her gaze flitted between Thrain and Kai.

'They are sweeping the Haven, making sure no demons remain,' Thrain said.

'Nothing that you need to worry about for the moment,' Miah said. 'Wessler can tell you the Haven goings on when you are better rested.'

Not willing to concede without a fight, she countered, 'Only if you lot will stop watching me sleep.'

With a laugh, Miah agreed, and began ushering everyone out of the room.

CHAPTER 44

The Truth is Revealed

Alone at last, Kess pulled off her shirt to change and caught sight of a flash of silver in the mirror.

Throwing her shirt onto the bed she stepped closer looking at her skin. She had taken to avoiding looking in the mirror, not wanting to see what marked her out as a freak.

But looking at it now, in the dim light of her shuttered room, her body almost seemed to shine of its own accord. The indecipherable script looked strange and exotic, hinting at the unknown, but refusing to reveal any of its secrets.

The writing seemed more settled on her skin, if that were possible, a part of her now.

Kess's eyes rose, at the inhalation of breath behind her, and stared into the reflected surface, meeting a pair of grey eyes. Unlike their usual metallic hardness, they seemed to be made of molten silver, writhing with the emotion he never revealed.

Thrain walked forward slowly, almost like he didn't realise he was moving, until he stood behind her, so close she could feel the material of his uniform rub against her exposed skin.

She held his gaze in the mirror, unwilling to look away.

She saw his hand rise from where he had clenched it at his side, fingers lightly tracing the flow of the symbols across the bone and muscle of her shoulder blade.

Kess shivered, and started to turn when the thumping of feet, quickly approaching, echoed up the hall.

His hand dropped from her instantly and Thrain stepped away putting distance between them again. He picked up her shirt from the bed and handed it to her. 'I think you'll be needing this,' he said with a soft smile.

Kess flushed, realising she'd been standing half naked in front of Thrain, and hadn't even cared. She slid her arms quickly into the sleeves, and as she poked her head through she saw that Thrain's gaze hadn't left her, and that the silver in his eyes still flowed molten hot.

~

Kess leant her elbows against the table, ignoring the ache in her tender muscles. 'I need to leave the Haven "officially".'

Wessler's brows furrowed, 'Why?'

'I need to travel to Rome.'

If the newly promoted Head Captol felt any surprise at her announcement, he didn't show it. 'Most Chroniclers are avoiding travelling at all these days because of the attacks. And as you are aware, newly appointed Chroniclers rarely leave the Haven in their first year.'

'I'm not worried about attacks,' Kess brushed off his concern.

'You should be,' he said gravely. 'The only common factor between the attacks is that all of the Chroniclers were members of *L'Ultima Luce*.'

'What?' Miah's voice was deadly soft. 'And this is the group you talked my charge into joining?'

Wessler shrugged, squirming under Miah's fierce stare. 'We only just connected them.'

'How many attacks needed to happen before you figured that out?'

His cheeks flushed. 'We are not warriors, nor are we versed in the science of investigation. Custodian Wilmoth was looking into it,' he said, naming the Custodian killed during the attacks. 'I requested that Seren assign the investigation to me. It took a few days to see the pattern. Every attack was different. There seemed to be no correlation between the cities, age, race, sex of the Chronicler, or Chapter they belonged to. No discernible pattern until I looked at the names. No one else made the connection, because none of them were Luce and none had access to the names of all the *Luce* members.'

'And you do?' Kess queried.

'Yes.'

'Why?' Miah asked sceptically.

'I am the leader of Athenaeum's branch of *L'Ultima Luce*,' he admitted somewhat reluctantly.

'Their leader?' Kess asked sharply, though she realised she shouldn't be surprised he was the leader of the secret faction. He had cultivated his "weasel" persona, maintaining the facades for years to gain information, and misdirect suspicion about his activities. He was obviously well educated and had good reasoning and deduction skills, which allowed him to piece together events from observations and snippets of gossip; like her involvement in slaying the demon all those weeks ago.

'What about the man who conducted my Initiation?'

'A decoy,' he said, shrugging.

'Why are your members being targeted?' Miah crossed her arms about her chest, clearly not happy with this revelation.

He brushed his hands though his dark hair in frustration. 'I don't know.'

'What were they researching?' Kess asked, as dread started to worm through her insides.

Wessler's face went blank for a moment then he looked at her uncomfortably. 'I don't know.' He sounded chagrined, obviously thinking he should have thought of that connection. 'I will look into it.'

'Will you let me know?'

A sideways shift of his eyes. 'If I can,' he said evasively. 'I will also speak to Seren, but on one condition. If I'm going to be sticking my neck out for you don't I deserve to know why?'

Kess looked at him. 'You told Custodian Pendry about the demon attack didn't you. That's why she went storming into Drazen's office that night. How she knew so much about the attack.'

Wessler smiled. 'The *Luce* will always fight the darkness,' he leant against the table. 'But what about you? You have sworn by our tenants, fight against the darkness, but will you work with us? Will you trust me?'

Kess eyed him back, unwilling to reveal anything.

Wessler folded his arms about his chest, a stubborn look settling on his face. 'You obviously have secrets, Kess. I am not asking for you to reveal them all, just what you think I should know.'

She opened her mouth ready to deny him, when Miah surprised her speaking out. 'Maybe he deserves to know, Kess. If he's going to get involved, he deserves to know the danger.'

Kess looked into Miah's dark–brown eyes, thrown off guard. The Guardians had always advised silence and caution.

'Alright,' she huffed, shrugging her shoulders. 'But once you know, there's no turning back. Just knowing about – me, well – we don't know how dangerous it will be for you.' After a glance to Miah, she added. 'You must swear on an oath I know you can't break that you will not reveal any of this.'

Wessler looked astonished by her request for an oath of that magnitude, but instead of arguing he held out his hand.

Kess stared at his outstretched palm blankly not understanding, until Miah withdrew one of the knives hidden within her sleeve, offering it to him hilt first.

With a quick motion, he slashed a line across his palm, clenching his hand a few times to make the blood flow. 'By the Light of the Angels, I swear never to divulge any secrets revealed to me by you, Kess Grayson, or your Guardians; Miah Cordova, Thrain Storgaard, Kisho Akiyama and Zuri Brzoza, upon damnation of my eternal soul within the fires of Ereshkigal.'

That he knew so much about her Guardians, even their last names, shocked her. Clearly, he had kept a closer watch on them than even the warriors had thought.

'You are sure? We haven't overestimated the risks. If anything, I don't think we have impressed their enormity upon you.'

Wessler nodded his understanding and acceptance of the risk then leant forward eagerly.

Taking a deep breath Kess began, 'You have seen Kai and Azrin?'

Wessler looked at her, deliberating. 'I saw them. And the other four that kept you under close watch,' he admitted.

Deciding not to mince words, she jumped right in. 'They're Angels,' she expected shock or disbelief, but Wessler just nodded calmly like he met members of the Celestial host every day.

'I see.' When she remained silent, he added, 'That is not the big secret, that required such an oath is it?'

Miah snorted. 'Show him.'

'Show me what?'

With a deep breath, and a confirming look to Miah, she pulled up her sleeve to her elbow revealing the silver shimmering marks which ran up her arm.

Wessler's breath whooshed out of him in a long rush. Leaning forward in his chair, he had a closer look at her arm. 'May I?' he inquired, fingers poised above her skin.

Waiting for her consent, he rubbed his thumb over the markings, 'They are not raised like a brand would be. It seems to be embedded in your skin, like a tattoo,' he twisted her arm, watching the light shimmering off the writing, 'but different. What is it?'

'We don't know. It is the reason, well one of them, why we returned.'

'Now this, this is worth the oath,' his shrewd eyes narrowed. 'This was your research?'

As Kess nodded, he asked, 'What did you find out?'

'Not a lot,' she admitted, rolling her sleeve back down. 'I must thank you for sending Sunisa to speak with us. The book she gave me is the reason I have to go to Rome.'

Wessler held up his hand forestalling her. 'I think, the less I know of your plans the better. Suffice to say that you found out something that leads you to believe you need to travel to Rome for further fact finding,' he reached out and patted her hand. 'Thank you for trusting me with this. I will speak with Seren, and impress upon her your need to leave, without revealing anything of course.' A small smile found its way to his lips, 'Your mother was right, all those years ago. You are a very special person, Kess. Look after her Guardian.'

'With our lives,' Miah replied, deadly serious.

Nodding, Wessler stood, and letting Miah lead the way, left to speak with Custodian Pendry, the new leader of the Haven, following Drazen's betrayal.

~

'Kess, visitor!'

Kess finished the sword blocking manoeuvre Miah was teaching her, then sheathed her blade.

Wessler waited just inside the training room door, with Kisho who must have escorted him in. 'Custodian Pendry has requested a meeting.'

'Thank you.'

'For what?' he asked, innocently, reminding her of his oath to keep shtum.

With Miah and Kisho as her guard, Kess followed Wessler as he led her to the new Haven leader who stood surrounded by a group of Chroniclers.

With a quick word to them she excused herself, and approached where they waited.

'Congratulations Custodian Pendry on your promotion,' Kess said respectfully. She recognised Pendry from the night of the demon attack when she had stormed into Drazen's office berating him.

The Custodian's brow furrowed. 'I only agreed to take this position because the rest of them are like a herd of bleating sheep, unable to accomplish anything. I hear,' she said glancing at Wessler, 'that you have requested to travel to Rome?' She spoke with an inflection that reminded Kess of someone from Cambridge; or the Queen.

Kess nodded.

'I take it this has to do with the research Tomas said you were conducting?' Her eyes were sharp and assessing, revealing the calculating mind which lay within.

Kess opened her mouth but Pendry forestalled her. 'It's best if I don't know and I prefer you not to lie. Officially you will be researching within the Vatican Library. There will be no date of return listed. As a fellow *Luce* member, I am trusting you to conduct yourself accordingly, and above all with secrecy. You will have clearance to leave immediately.'

CHAPTER 45

Loose Ends

Kess stood in Aldoak's training room watching Thrain as he spoke with the pale haired Cadder.

'What's he doing?' She asked Miah, who these days was never far from her side.

'He's giving command of the Guardian to Cadder.'

Kess's head whipped around. 'What?'

'There are more important things now, Kess.'

Kess watched as Thrain clasped forearms with the newly appointed Commander, then strode into the room heading straight for them.

She didn't know what to say, he was clearly giving up something important to him. Because of her.

With his appearance, the others in the room – Angels, Azrin and Caliel; and Guardians, Kisho and Zuri came closer.

'Ready?' She asked them, eyeing the packs on the back of each warrior and the array of weapons on their bodies.

Kess took Kai's arm and with a final glance around them, watched as the Haven disappeared before her eyes.

Then she was standing on a roughly–bitumened street, in front of arched wooden doorway framed with green vines. She stared at the brown semi–circular sign, 'La Sacrestia Ristorante'.

'Welcome to Rome,' Kai told her.

THE WAR OF DARKNESS

Follow Kess's search for the Augur…

AN EXCERPT FROM BOOK TWO

'Have you decided to see reason yet and admit that your mythical Augur doesn't actually exist?' Kai asked as Kess threw herself down into a chair resting her head in her arms against the tabletop after another day of fruitless searching.

Two days.

That was all the time she had left. She knew without asking that requesting more time from Thrain would be a waste of breath.

'No.'

'Kess!' Kai hissed. 'We have been searching for nearly a week. There is a reason why you can't find any trace of the Augur, because even if he once lived there, he doesn't now. We will have to find the information you seek elsewhere.'

The hopeful look on Kai's face died as Kess shook her head. 'No. The Augur is there. I'm just missing something.'

The Angel gave her a growl so reminiscent of Thrain that she laughed.

I am not stubborn, she said catching the glimmer of thought coming from him.

'We have scoured the halls, museums, library, catacombs, chapel and basilica. We even searched the rooftops, and courtyard colonnade including all one hundred and forty saint statues and found nothing. No sign of him or his mysterious mark. Short of turning up to dinner with the Pope and asking him, I don't know where else you think you can search. I haven't even sensed a glimmer of someone as powerful as the Augur must be.'

'Why are demons there then?' Kess challenged.

'There are a million reasons why a demon would be in the Vatican, not the least because of the State's religious significance to humans.'

Kess tried to hide her smile as she felt Kai's mental huff of frustration.

'They would no doubt find it ironically amusing that they, soulless abominations could freely walk the halls of the most religious grounds in this world without bursting into flames like most humans would no doubt expect.'

'Two more days,' the commander said not looking up from sharpening the head of his axe.

Kai threw his hands up in frustration, clearly expecting back up from the warrior. 'Come on then.'

To be continued...

Printed in Australia
AUOW01n2359090818
R6756400001BA/R67564PG301146AUX27BA/1

9 781786 938756